MURDER AT BLACKWATER BEND

MURDER AT BLACKWATER BEND

CLARA McKENNA

WHEELER PUBLISHING
A part of Gale, a Cengage Company

Wheeler Publishing Large Print Cozy Mystery.
The text of this Large Print edition is unabridged.
Other aspects of the book may vary from the original edition.
Set in 16 pt. Plantin.

LIBRARY OF CONGRESS CIP DATA ON FILE.
CATALOGUING IN PUBLICATION FOR THIS BOOK
IS AVAILABLE FROM THE LIBRARY OF CONGRESS.

ISBN-13: 978-1-4328-8481-9 (softcover alk. paper)

Published in 2021 by arrangement with Kensington Books, an imprin
of Kensington Publishing Corp.

Printed in the United States of America
1 2 3 4 5   24 23 22 21 20

To the people who call
the New Forest home.

CHAPTER 1

ust 1905
npshire, England

ly Atherly didn't dare look at her hus-
nd. She couldn't trust herself not to over-
ct. And then what would everyone think?
She'd once thought William exceedingly
ndsome. But she'd lived with him too
any years, endured that self-satisfied glint
his eyes too many times. Instead, she
ared straight ahead at the swirling as-
embly of colorfully dressed dancers, the
rilliant light of the chandelier reflecting off
he ladies' jewels, their dresses' sparkling
embellishments, the highly polished floor.
The musicians, as good as any you'd find
up in London, had begun the Lehár piece,
"Gold and Silver." Lady Atherly was partial
to Johann Strauss II, remembering a time
when she'd whirled about on the arm of a
well-turned-out beau to Strauss's "Viennese
Blood," but she loved all waltzes, even this

7

new one. Lady Atherly's jaw ached i[...]
attempt to keep a scowl from her face.
"You'd think you'd be pleased, Franc[...]
Pleased? William would say something
that. She knew why he was happy. He'd
ten everything he'd wanted. Besides, [...]
did happiness have to do with it? This
about tradition, decorum, survival. [...]
everything rested precariously on the sh[...]
ders of a young, ill-bred American girl. H[...]
could that possibly make her happy?

The girl in question whirled by, cl[...]
enough the women's eyes would've met h[...]
Lady Atherly not avoided Miss Kendric[...]
gaze. The hem of Miss Kendrick's ivory la[...]
and rose satin gown swished along the flo[...]
as she yet again took a misstep. Even in t[...]
arms of a highly capable partner (Hadn[...]
she warned her son not to dance too ofte[...]
with the American?), the girl lacked grace.

"Isn't she lovely?" William said. Lad[...]
Atherly rolled her eyes and held her tongue
Fool.

Of course, all the men admired her. How
could they not? Miss Kendrick was beautiful and offered smiles and compliments to
everyone like they were sweets. Her persistent questions made them think she was
interested in what they had to say. But the
women knew better. Just look at the way

8

Cowperthwaite and Mrs. Edsall whis-
about Miss Kendrick behind their
as the girl passed. No well-bred lady
interested in horse breeding or fossil
ing or fishing or who was elected to
ament or any other such masculine pur-

d then Lady Philippa Fairbrother
zed past. Lady Philippa was graceful.
was witty. She was stunningly beautiful.
d she didn't show her teeth like a horse.
her emerald and ivory satin gown, she
the quintessence of good English breed-
. And hadn't she adored Lyndy? As the
ughter of a marquess, she was everything
nother-in-law could want.

f only Lady Philippa had married Lyndy and
t Lord Fairbrother. Morrington could've
een saved from ruin without Lady Atherly
uffering the humiliation that was the
mericans. If only Lady Philippa had inher-
ed more.

"You insisted Miss Kendrick attend,
Frances. So why are you scowling when
your future daughter-in-law is the belle of
the ball?"

Because no well-bred lady laughed while
she danced either, nor would she ignore the
disapproving stares of the society matrons.
What did Miss Kendrick even have to laugh

about? It certainly wasn't something I
had said. Her son was not that amusir
From the beginning, Lady Atherly se
to put a stop to Miss Kendrick's outla
behavior. No more stepping out with L
unchaperoned or driving herself in
motorcar. No public displays of affec
no unauthorized visits to the stables,
no more shirking her social obligations.
despite Lady Atherly's best efforts, M
Kendrick still acted on impulse, let her
be swept away by emotion, and worst of
persisted in asking inappropriate questio
Lady Atherly had made the mistake
insisting Miss Kendrick and her insuffe
able family move out of Morrington Ha
With Miss Kendrick living at Pilley Mano
though, Lady Atherly lost control over th
girl. Whom she fraternized with was
constant concern. Lady Atherly had alread
nipped the inappropriate friendship witl
that silversmith's daughter in the bud. Bu
just tonight, Lady Atherly heard an unten-
able rumor that Miss Kendrick was well
acquainted with the old village hermit, a
snakecatcher of all things.

*Will the girl stop at nothing to embarrass
this family?*

"Lovely evening, isn't it?" the rotund wife
of a minor landowner said, sidling up beside

10

ler crimson silk dress clashed garishly
the woman's ginger hair, her scent a
r overuse of rosewater. Lady Atherly
nvited her to one garden party years
and the woman presumed to speak to
on familiar terms at every social gather-
since. Lady Atherly acknowledged her
the barest of nods. The woman col-
ed her fan and pointed it across the
m. "Oh, dear. Whatever is your child up

ady Atherly, knowing her daughter, Al-
had gone in to dinner, sought Lyndy on
ballroom floor. A cluster of dancers had
opped and gathered on the far end. Lyndy
d Miss Kendrick were among them. A
otman, his expression uncharacteristically
nowing concern, spoke to the group and
estured toward the door. Before the foot-
nan had finished talking, Miss Kendrick
itched up the train of her skirt and dashed
past him, disappearing from the room.
Lyndy chased after her.

Lady Atherly let out a long, silent sigh.
What now?

With all the self-control Lady Atherly
could muster, she pinched her lips together,
lightly pressed her fingertips against the
cold diamonds in her tiara, and said, "If
you'll excuse me."

What she wanted to do was scream
husband, "See what you've done tc
family, William? See what I must pu
with?" But she didn't. She deliber
maneuvered her way across the crov
ballroom as she made her mind up. '
was going to stop.

Tom Heppenstall flicked back the tap h
dle too late. The frothy head bubbled
over the rim and foam slid down the side
the glass. He shook his head in disgust
he reached for the towel draped across ,
shoulder. After wiping the glass dry, he s
the pint down on the bar and collected t
tuppence, all without glancing at who ha
ordered the stout. Instead, he stared acro
the sea of ruddy faces toward the door as
opened.

Ah, bloody hell.

Standing in the doorway, with an olc
potato sack flung across his shoulder, Harvey Milkham scowled beneath the dusty,
worn hat that flopped down on both sides
of his head. Had Tom ever seen him take it
off? The snakecatcher's hair was greasy
white, Tom knew, in part because everyone
knew Harvey was as old as the New Forest.
Some joked Harvey once met King Rufus
himself before that royal's unfortunate

12

premature demise. But also, Tom knew because of the thick, curly gray eyebrows that protruded wildly out from under the hat. It was a wonder the old man could see. But he had eyes as sharp as a tawny owl, and those eyes scanned the crowded pub.

On any given day, Tom would pour Harvey his usual, before the old bloke reached the bar. The regulars didn't have a problem with the hermit; he kept himself to himself. On slow, rainy nights, Tom even enjoyed prodding the snakecatcher with questions. Had Harvey found a new barrow? Had he visited Lord Duddleton to feed His Lordship's talking bird with snakes he'd caught that day? Had Harvey met with the gentlemen from the London Zoo? Or had he been to Pilley Manor yet again, to visit with the Americans? What an odd pair, those two, Miss Kendrick and the snakecatcher, but their friendship made a bit of sense; they were both a bit daft.

But (God help him), on a night like tonight, Harvey's arrival could spell disaster. Not all of the locals were as welcoming. And Harvey didn't help his case much. On more than one occasion, the snakecatcher had decided the crowd at the Knightwood Oak was too thick to traverse and had emptied the contents of his potato sack on the floor.

The local greengrocer, and who knows who else, hadn't set foot across the threshold since.

Tom had to get to Harvey before the old snakecatcher decided to do it again.

Ignoring someone's call for a pint of bitter, Tom hobbled from behind the bar as fast as his swollen ankle would allow him and pushed into the lively crowd. If Harvey Milkham weren't standing in the doorway with that blasted sack on his shoulder, Tom would've been pleased with the uptick in business lately. Ever since the previous vicar's murder and rumors spread that the killer had spent his time pondering his crime in the Knightwood Oak, Tom has seen an influx of new customers. Mostly folk from the nearby villages, some traveled from as far away as Ringwood and Minstead to drink a pint in the same pub as a murderer. Luckily the rumors hadn't reached beyond the boundaries of the Forest. The moment grockles started pouring in, for all the trouble they were worth, Tom might have to put a stop to all the idle gossip. Until then, who was Tom to argue?

"How's the ankle, Tom?" a well-wisher asked, as the publican tried to push past. Tom answered with a grunt and a shake of his head, as he spied that good for nothing boy who was the bane of his existence and the cause of his swollen ankle. The boy held a tray piled with dirty pint glasses before him. As he tried to navigate by a cluster of men, the boy lifted it. The glassware, teetering dangerously above his head, clanked but didn't fall.

"Oi!" Tom yelled. "Watch what you're doing there, lad."

Yesterday, unbeknownst to Tom, the boy had spilled a glass of half-finished cider on the floor, purportedly after hearing the ghost of Old Bertie, the original proprietor of the pub. Tom knew it was just the wind blowing, not the moaning of an apparition of a man who'd died languishing in prison for smuggling more than a hundred years ago, but the boy believed the legend. The boy also failed to clean the spilled cider up. This morning, after checking on the stores in the cellar, Tom slipped on the sticky liquid and twisted his ankle. Tom, not one to fuss, simply choked down a syrupy teaspoon of laudanum before demanding the boy mop the entire floor. But even he knew standing behind the bar all day wasn't doing himself any favors. Tom, his ankle throbbing, limped by the well-wisher toward the door.

"Harvey! Harvey!"

The shout — which rose above the din in the room as field hands, clerks, merchant's assistants, and farmers unburdened themselves of the day with alcohol-loosened tongues — didn't come from inside the pub. Men looked up from their beer as Tom neared the open doorway. A groom from Morrington Hall leaped from a dogcart and pulled the horse into the gravel yard of the pub.

"Oi! Move your horse," Tom yelled. Nothing good came from mingling the scent of a fine bitter with that of sweating horseflesh. But the groom, his face flush, obviously anxious, ignored him and unwisely grabbed Harvey's arm with the hand not holding on to the reins of his horse.

"You have to come with me. Now."

Harvey, startled, swirled around to push the groom away. The burlap sack slipped from his shoulder to the threshold of the pub. Several men nearby jumped back. With spikes of pain shooting up his leg, Tom lumbered forward as fast as he could.

"Harvey, Miss Kendrick needs you," the groom added. At the mention of the American lady, Harvey rubbed his bristly chin and followed the groom to the dogcart.

"But isn't the lassie at a party?" the grizzled old voice asked.

"She is, but Tully's been bitten by an adder. You have to come quick."

The two men leaped into the cart, the old snakecatcher being nimbler than Tom would've credited him for, and were driving past the green before Tom reached the threshold. He carefully reached down toward the abandoned potato sack as something wriggled inside. Tom snatched up the burlap bag, twisting the open end tightly closed in his fist. He limped slowly out the door, across the gravel yard of the pub — past the wooden tables that had been there so long they looked rooted — across the lane, and onto the village green. After approaching a dense flowerbed on the edge of the green, Tom set down the sack on its side and backed away. A long, thin tongue flicked out as a sleek brown head protruded from the bag. The rest of the body, marked with a dark brown zigzag on its back, followed, slithering out and disappearing under the brush.

"Bloody hell." Tom hated snakes. Who didn't, but Harvey Milkham? But it wasn't only the snake he cursed. Tom was profiting, yes, but why must it always be off the misfortunes of those up at Morrington Hall?

Stella leaped out of the automobile and

jerked to a stop. She twisted around to see what was holding her back. Her ball gown had snagged on the corner of the door.

"Augh. Let go."

She yanked on it with both hands, ignoring the tearing sound as a rent a foot long sliced up the side of her rose-colored satin skirt. Free of the door, she dashed toward the stables.

I told them something like this would happen.

Inside, darkness pervaded. The long orange rays of the setting sun, seeping through the half-open windows, barely lit the way. Why hadn't the lanterns been lit yet? She rushed down the aisle that she'd treaded a hundred times in the past two months, dodging the anxious, downcast eyes of stable boys lining her way like the suits of armor up at Morrington Hall. She passed the stalls of the other horses. Most of the horses were calm, but curiously sticking their heads out the stall doors. Orson, their thoroughbred stallion, barely pulled his head away from his hay. But Tupper, their promising filly, whinnied as Stella passed, sensing something was wrong.

When Stella finally reached her horse's stall, she could barely make out the familiar shape of the prone figure on the strawcovered floor.

"Tully!"

She flung herself to her knees beside the horse, ignoring the prickly straw sticking into her silk stockings. Tully didn't respond; no welcoming nicker, no raised head, not even an acknowledging glance. The horse's eyes were closed and stayed that way, as Stella leaned down, snuggling her head against the thoroughbred's sleek neck.

Please, God, let her just be sleeping.

A clean, white bandage was wrapped around Tully's swollen left front knee. With her hand shaking, Stella reached toward the inside back of Tully's uninjured right front knee. She nearly wept when she found a clear and consistent pulse. But it was faster than it should be.

Harvey had warned her that he'd seen a high number of snakes in the area lately. And with the adder-breeding season in full swing, even she knew a pregnant adder was a dangerous snake. Stella had told Lyndy, but he'd explained that it wasn't his place to alert the estate manager. She'd warned Lord Atherly, but he'd been too preoccupied with the upcoming visit of Professor Gridley to care. Finally, she herself had approached the estate manager. But without word from Lord Atherly, the estate manager merely shrugged at his inability to act. These hierarchical rules were maddening.

And they say Americans do stupid things.

A movement in the straw drew Stella's attention. Until now she'd ignored everyone but Tully. She lifted her head and recognized the old man kneeling nearby, his floppy, old hat nearly covering his eyes. She grabbed his rough hand in relief and hopeful desperation.

"Harvey, tell me she's going to be all right."

"Oh, aye, lass. She'll be lancing over the heath in no time." Harvey gently patted Tully on her rounded barrel. "She's sleeping soundly now." His voice was heavily accented and gravelly, but Stella didn't need to understand every word he said. His reassuring tone was enough. Stella flung her arms around him, clamped her eyes shut, and hugged the old snakecatcher. He smelled of damp soil and sweet pipe tobacco, like Grandpa Luckett. Stella had loved Grandpa Luckett.

When the footman had told her about Tully at the ball, Stella's heart had stopped. She'd thought only about getting to her beloved horse's side. Who cared if Daddy didn't have a way home? Who cared if Lady Atherly would disapprove of her abrupt departure? But now, in the grim silence of the stables, relief easing its way through her tense body, she missed the glittering ballroom, the music, dancing in Lyndy's arms. She'd been enjoying herself.

In the past few weeks, Stella had attended, and dreaded, countless dances, teas, dinner, card, and garden parties, smiling, making witty banter, and learning to play whist. All in all, everyone, even Daddy and Lady Atherly, seemed surprised how charming she, the "American," could be. But Stella had enjoyed little of it. Until tonight. Tonight, despite Lady Atherly's objection, Stella had decided to dance only with Lyndy (and what a dancer he turned out to be!). It had made all the difference. In the past couple of months, she'd become quite fond of the viscount.

"Eh-hem," someone coughed behind her.

Stella opened her eyes and glanced over her shoulder. Lyndy, as handsome as she'd ever seen him in top hat and coattails, stood in the door of the stall, his arms folded tightly against his chest. He'd ridden beside her in Daddy's Daimler. But so too in the door were Mr. Gates, the head coachman, and several stable hands clustered behind Lyndy. Someone had lit the lanterns, and they could see everything. Stella, self-

21

conscious, pulled away from Harvey. She sat back on her heels, pushing a loose strand of hair behind her ear. She wasn't wearing her hat. In her haste, she must've left it at the ball.

"Is Tully going to be all right, sir?" one of the stable hands stammered, his eyes wide as he cranked his neck to look around Leonard, the taller groom. It was Charlie, the boy who mucked out Tully's stall and fed her every day. "I saw her trembling and sweating not long before."

"Oh, aye," Harvey said slowly. "She'll be right as rain. Adders can't kill a horse, but they sure can make it uncomfortable. What you saw, laddie, was the poison working its way."

"But you've given her the antidote ointment, right?" Stella asked.

Could it have only been a few weeks ago, when Stella, sneaking away, just her and Tully, without even a groom knowing, had come across this odd, grisly old man in a floppy hat, kneehigh boots, and wooden cleft stick? She'd led Tully to a narrow stream running through Whitley Wood. Mr. Harvey Milkham, or the snakecatcher as she would later learn the locals called him, had been on the other side, poking his stick under a pile of mossy rocks. Stella had watched to see what he was doing. He must've known she was there; Tully never drank very quietly, but he never acknowledged her presence. After a moment or two, Harvey had pulled a long, wriggling snake up with his stick and had draped it around his neck. He'd done the same again until three snakes dangled about his shoulders. Looking over at Stella and Tully on the other bank of the creek, he'd unwrapped the snakes from his neck, picked up a burlap sack, and dropped them in.

"You be the American lassie staying at Pilley Manor, I presume?" he'd said.

"Yes, I'm Stella Kendrick."

"Lovely to meet you, lass." He'd promptly launched himself across the creek, swiped his palm against his dusty coat, and jutted out his hand. "Welcome to the New Forest."

Without hesitation, Stella had shaken it, grateful for the hearty, honest introduction. His hand had been rough and gnarled like a tree trunk, but like everything about the old man kneeling beside her, unexpectedly strong and reassuring.

"Aye, lassie," Harvey said. "Always carry a bit of antidote about with us."

He stood and brushed the straw from his well-worn clothes. Stella did the same, only now realizing she'd ruined her gown and her leg to the knee was showing. Mr. Gates quickly turned his head as he vainly tried to shoo the gawking stable hands away. No one budged.

After that first meeting, Stella had continued to seek out Harvey, even visiting him once at his home. They'd drank tea with a splash of scotch ("What the doctor had ordered," he'd said) from tin cups. She'd relished lounging in his abandoned coal-burner's hut made of tree branches and covered with sod, listening, not to yet another conversation about the weather but of the sprains, bruises, and adder bites Harvey had healed with his antivenom ointment. Instead of a future English viscountess on display, she'd been a character in *Robinson Crusoe.* What a refreshing change.

For that memory alone, she wanted to hug him again. Instead, she looked down at Tully, resting comfortably in the thick straw, and pulled the torn pieces of her skirt back together.

"How much do we owe you?" Lyndy said, stepping into the stall, carefully avoiding Stella's gaze. Was he angry or trying desperately not to laugh? Stella still couldn't read Lyndy's expressions right.

"Tuppence for a pint wouldn't be turned

down, Your Lordship."

"My father will pay far more than tuppence, Harvey," Stella said. "You've saved a precious horse today. How can we possibly repay you?"

"No need for that, lass. This fine, strong mare did most of the work." Harvey smiled as he took off his hat and swatted at a fly buzzing around Tully's head. His two front teeth were missing.

"You won't get off that easily," Stella said. "Mark my words, Harvey Milkham, I will find a way to pay you back for your kindness, whether you like it or not."

"I've no doubt, lass, no doubt at all that you'll do whatever you set your mind to." He nodded slightly to Stella and then to Lyndy before plopping his hat back on his head. "Congratulations, milord, on your upcoming nuptials." As he made his way through the stable hands crowding the door, he indicated Stella with his thumb. "And good luck with that one."

Lyndy chuckled as he plucked a piece of straw from Stella's hair. "Thank you, my good fellow," Lyndy said congenially. "I'm going to need it."

CHAPTER 2

"Damn you, Fairbrother."

Lord Fairbrother chuckled as he raised the cigarette to his lips. The commoner didn't think he was going to get away without paying, did he? The fellow was a dolt if he thought so.

"What do you expect? I'm taking a risk in doing you this favor." Not to mention having to leave the ball early, and his wife unattended, for this rendezvous. Fairbrother wasn't leaving empty-handed. "Or have you changed your mind?"

"No," the commoner grumbled as he produced a packet of folded ten-pound notes. He looked about him as if anyone would be out this time of night, before slowly handing the money over. Fairbrother flipped through the notes with his thumb, counting.

One, two, three, four, five. The commoner frowned. Fairbrother didn't care. He didn't trust the man. Who would? *Six, seven, eight.*

"You'll do as we agreed?' The commoner licked his lips.

Fairbrother slipped the packet into his breast pocket. "We're done here."

The commoner hesitated and grumbled something incoherent beneath his breath before retreating from the river's edge.

Fairbrother inhaled deeply as he watched the fellow's figure cast a longer and longer shadow as he moved stealthily across the open heath beyond. The fragrant smoke billowed across Fairbrother's vision as he slowly exhaled through his nose. The taste of Turkish tobacco recalled the tediousness of the war. But these recent illicit riverside meetings were quite amusing.

Splash.

Fairbrother jerked his head toward the sound. His eyes searched the shadows. What was that? A brown trout feeding, perhaps? Or a fallen branch? Or could his chosen spot have been discovered? In all the nights Fairbrother had stood here, he'd seen no one. No one, except the men he'd arranged to meet. Fairbrother was still amazed at how many unscrupulous characters the New Forest held. And of course, he'd seen the snakecatcher, on the odd occasion, catching trout for his supper. But the old man was notoriously disinterested in the comings and goings of other men.

Fairbrother held his breath and listened. All was still again but for the breeze ruffling the leaves above and the distant tinkle of cattle bells. He looked back across the heath. The cagey fellow he'd met tonight was but a shadow on the horizon. There was no one else about. He was safe.

He removed his top hat and leaned against the furrowed bark of the towering oak tree beside him, its thick roots stretching over the bank and into the rippling water. The sustained trill of a nightjar rang out through the night. He would wait a bit longer. With his long stride, and at the fast clip he preferred, he could easily catch up to the commoner. That would never do. He lifted his watch from the pocket of his single-braided trousers, the dappled light from the bright moon striking its gold, embossed surface. He flipped it open. He had a bit longer before anyone would notice his absence. *If Philippa noticed at all.* The abrupt departure of Lord Lyndhurst and that American fiancée of his had been enough of a distraction for him to slip away. He clicked the watch shut, shoved it back into his pocket, and took another long puff on his cigarette. He always did enjoy a little fresh air after dark.

Especially on a night as profitable as this one.

He patted his tailcoat pocket. The bulk beneath wasn't as thick as he would've liked. Perhaps he'd ask for more next time. The snort of a pony echoed across the heath as Fairbrother exhaled again. As he well knew, there was always a next time.

Harvey edged around the mire, careful not to get wet, and then stopped, swaying a bit on his feet. He raised the thick glass bottle, despite its heaviness in his hand, and took another long swig, liquid dribbling down the side of his mouth. Clutching the neck of the bottle in his fist, he wiped his chin with the sleeve of his shirt and started off again.

He was exhausted. The worry alone had sapped his strength. How could he have faced the lass if real harm had come to her horse? But all in all, a good day's work. And what thanks! The woody scent of the lass's perfume still clung to his clothes. Could he even remember the last time a lassie had hugged him? Not to mention the gratitude of the lass's father, giving Harvey as many bottles as he could carry, of what the American breeder called "the finest bourbon in the world." Harvey had never had bourbon before, but it tasted an awful lot like scotch, and he loved scotch. Harvey took another drink. Yes, he approved. But he'd drank too much. During that last nip, Harvey had thought he'd seen the bottle glowing a blurry bright red. Bourbon was brown, not red. A smoky aftertaste he'd never noticed before lingered long after the liquor slid down his throat. Harvey dropped the almost empty bottle and rubbed his eyes with his fists. His eyes were bleary, but the red glow he'd seen through the bottle didn't go away. He squinted toward the reddish light, his muddled mind trying to make sense of it all.

The still, silent night sky was aglow. It looked like Bonfire Night had come a few months early this year. But there were no cottages, no estates, no travelers' encampments in the area, only his . . . Harvey stumbled over his own feet as he ran toward the blaze. Flames leaped fifteen, twenty feet in the sky. He rushed forward, but the searing heat was like an invisible wall keeping him from getting too close.

"NO!" he roared, his yells instantly swallowed by the crackle and whoosh of the fire engulfing his home. "NO!"

Who would do this? Who? Why?

Harvey swiveled around, hoping to catch

a glimpse of the perpetrators. With the fire still raging, a ring of light stretched out for several yards in all directions. They couldn't have gotten far. But as he stumbled about, Harvey tripped on the stones that once paved the way to his hut, and he fell. An unopened bottle, tucked into the pocket of his overcoat, shattered beneath him. Covered in bourbon and shards of broken glass, Harvey crawled as close to the blaze as he could, sat back on to his heels and watched all he had in this world — but the sack on his shoulder and the clothes on his back — burn.

He'd get whoever did this.

A snort behind him roused him from his thoughts of revenge. Harvey looked over his shoulder beyond the shadows cast by the flames. The wide eyes of a pony, reflecting the fire, looked at him warily from the safety of the dark. And then he knew.

"Fairbrother," Harvey whispered, the name a curse on his tongue.

CHAPTER 3

Stella gazed out the tall, French window at the lush, formal gardens that encompassed Pilley Manor — tightly clipped borders of boxwood lining linear gravel paths, triangular flower beds of pink roses, and the long rectangular pool edged in gray limestone reflecting the bright morning sun — and took another nibble of her pancake. Why couldn't they have breakfast outside for a change?

"Someone to see you, Mr. Kendrick," Tims, the butler, said.

"I don't care if it's the czar of Russia," Daddy said, his mouth full of poached eggs. The morning broadsheet was spread out on the table before him. No one interrupted her father when he was eating breakfast and reading the news. "Tell them to come back."

Without waiting, a woman with a boyish figure, a gray traveling suit, and hair the color of the red foxes that raided the henhouse back home strode into the breakfast room. The woman, ignoring Stella, thrust out her hand to Stella's father, who squinted at her and scowled.

"What do you want?"

"Miss Jane Cosslett, at your service, Mr. Kendrick. I'm from the *Daily Mail.* I've come down from London, and I am here to cover your daughter's wedding."

"The wedding isn't for weeks yet," he said.

"That's why I'm here now. I wouldn't want anyone else to get the exclusive."

"Well, slap me silly," Stella's great-aunt said, from across the table. "Why would a London reporter come all the way here to write about our little Stella's wedding?"

Why indeed? Stella, spearing the last few bites of her pancake with her fork, waited with anticipation for the answer.

The reporter dismissed Aunt Rachel after a glance. Her gaze lingered longer on Stella but, after crinkling her nose, she returned to face Stella's father.

"I'll be honest. Being here could be the making of my career."

"How's that?" Daddy mumbled as he shoveled a whole broiled tomato into his mouth, the juice from it dripping down his chin. Stella had to look down at her almost empty plate. She couldn't stand to watch her father eat. But the reporter was un-daunted by the tomato seeds clinging to the tip of his mustache.

"I'm not exaggerating, Mr. Kendrick, when I say your daughter's wedding to the Earl of Atherly's son and heir will be the talk of London. What am I saying? It will be the talk of Kentucky, of . . ." The reporter raised her arms and looked around the room. One of Pissarro's paintings of the Boulevard Montmartre in Paris hung on the wall above the buffet table. The reporter pointed to it. "Of every place civilized people dwell."

"Will people read about it in New York?" Daddy asked.

The reporter nodded.

"And Newport, it still being the Season and all," she added. Daddy's eyes lit up as he set down his fork and folded his news-paper.

"Why would they?" Stella asked. She could understand if she were Consuelo Vanderbilt or Cora Colgate, but no one had ever cared about anything she'd done be-fore. Why would they now?

"Why wouldn't they?" her father said through clenched teeth.

"Exactly," Miss Cosslett said. "It's not every day that the beautiful daughter of the world-renowned Elijah Kendrick marries a peer of the realm." She indicated Stella with outstretched hands, as if revealing a prize, but without taking her eyes off Daddy. "And with your help, I could bring every detail of that celebrated event to the eager readers of the world."

"Lordy, Lordy," Aunt Rachel said. "You sure do have a flair for the dramatic, missy." Stella quickly raised her napkin to her mouth, stifling a laugh. "Perhaps Miss Cosslett should write for the theater instead of the newspapers."

Daddy glared at Aunt Rachel and then at Stella, who'd let her giggle escape. Then he turned to the reporter. "What do you need from me, young lady?" he said, with a broadening smile. Stella's stomach flipped. Nothing good came from her father's smiles.

"All I want from you, Mr. Kendrick," Miss Cosslett said, staring into his eyes, "is a promise to give me exclusive access to anything and everything pertaining to the wedding."

"Like what?" Stella had already agreed to let Aunt Rachel follow her around like a stray puppy. She'd already had the entire population of Hampshire gawking at her wherever she went. Stella certainly didn't want to open her life up to a reporter.

"I'll need to see your wedding gown and veil."

"Done," her father said before Stella could object.

"I'll need to see the invitation list."

"Done." The reporter stepped closer with each request until she and Daddy were almost touching.

"I'll need a preview of the wedding gifts, the flowers, the cake. I'll need a tour of your lovely home, the groom's estate, the church."

"Don't I have a —" Stella began.

"Done, done, and done." The reporter stepped back and smiled. Stella dug her fingernails into her fist and said nothing. What good would it do? "And of course, you'll attend Stella's engagement party."

Stella silently groaned. Her father had begun insisting Stella host an engagement party the day they moved from Morrington Hall to Pilley Manor, the Earl of Atherly's dowager house. Stella wanted nothing to do with hosting a party, but Daddy had already had bourbon sent from his preferred distillery in Kentucky, just for the occasion, as if the world's finest bourbon could guarantee the event's success. But now he'd gone and invited the reporter? Wasn't it enough that Stella had but a few days to finalize every detail for a dinner that included the Bishop of Winchester and Lord Montagu among the guests? She was already dreading the evening. Now she'd have a reporter recording her every move.

"That is most kind of you, Mr. Kendrick, but I have nothing appropriate to wear," Miss Cosslett said.

"Not to worry. I'm sure the girl has something that will fit you." Daddy glared at Stella, challenging her to contradict him.

"But circulating among the likes of Lord and Lady Atherly. I am only a commoner, after all." She batted her eyelids. Was this the same brash woman who had forced her way in?

"No one will be more common at the party than me," Daddy said, laughing. Stella shook her head before taking a sip of her coffee. Did he realize what he'd just said?

"You've convinced me, Mr. Kendrick. You are most persuasive." Daddy beamed. "Am I too late for breakfast?" The reporter snatched a slice of bacon from the buffet and snipped off the end with her teeth. "After that long train ride, I'm quite peckish."

With her pancakes suddenly dry as sawdust in her mouth, Stella dropped her fork on her plate, her appetite gone.

"Breakfast, nothing. Help yourself," Daddy said, indicating the buffet laid out with poached eggs, bacon, several types of cereal, hot porridge, broiled tomatoes, cold ham, a variety of fresh berries, buttered toast, sweet buns, pancakes (or drop scones as Mrs. Downie, their cook, called them), and Daddy's favorite cornmeal muffins, "and then you'll come with us to the fair."

"But I thought . . . ?" Stella began.

Daddy shot her a cold glance. He wanted no reminding that he'd denounced today's fair — and its Cecil New Forest Pony Challenge, where the breeder who produced the finest New Forest pony was presented with a silver cup — as beneath him when Lord and Lady Atherly turned down his offer to be a judge. The event was the highlight on the New Forest social calendar. Before now, he'd had no intention of going. It was one of the reasons why Stella was looking forward to it.

"I wouldn't want to impose on anyone," Miss Cosslett said, as coy as a kitten.

"It's no bother. No bother at all," Daddy said. "I insist. There is the pony breed competition, of course, but there will also be games, food, music. Everyone will be there."

"Will the famous plant hunter Cecil

Barlow attend? Someone did an article on him for my newspaper and said he was positively divine. Supposedly he faced down a snarling tiger to collect a new type of jungle orchid. I thought I heard rumors in London he was presiding over a local horse breed competition."

"Pony," Stella said.

"I beg your pardon?" The reporter looked Stella in the eyes for the first time and blinked several times.

"It's a pony breed judging competition. Not a horse breed competition."

"If you say so," the reporter said, before turning her attention back to Stella's father.

"Of course Barlow will be there. The guy's named Cecil, isn't he?" Daddy laughed at his joke. The reporter pinched her eyebrows in confusion.

"The competition is called the Cecil New Forest Pony Challenge," Stella explained. It wasn't the first time he'd made the horrible pun.

"Then, thank you, Mr. Kendrick, I would be happy to," Miss Cosslett said, her face brightening.

Daddy patted the place at the table beside him, and the reporter slipped into the seat. The pair grinned at each other as if they'd pulled off a long-planned coup. Stella pushed back from the table, threw down her napkin, and stood. She had had enough of these two; she needed some air. She headed to the buffet and plucked a fresh apple from the fruit bowl.

"Good, good." Daddy pointed to the buffet. "What would you like, Miss Cosslett? The girl can dish it up for you."

When broodmares run the Derby, I will. Stella headed toward the door, tossing the apple in the air as she went.

"Where are you going?" he demanded. As if he cared.

"To check on Tully, of course," Stella said over her shoulder, waving Tully's apple in the air. She ignored her father's grumbling and Miss Cosslett's call of "Are you going to Morrington Hall?" and gladly strode briskly from the room.

Lord Fairbrother stood between the taut ropes holding down the competitors' tent. The white canvas flapped in the steady breeze. It was going to rain. He clenched his fists until they ached, willing himself not to lash out at the infuriating woman in front of him. He'd hailed her over to him when she'd arrived, had ducked to this outer side of the tent and had confronted her. Again.

Who did she think he was? A pathetic little

man she could toy with? Did she think a simper and bat of the eye would make him forget? What was she playing at? She reached up and traced the lines of his chin, stoking his anger with each brush of her soft fingertips. If she were a man and committed such duplicity, he'd have her flogged. No one made a fool of him.

She tugged playfully at his tie. He brushed her hand aside and straightened his tie. "I said I was sorry," she said, pouting. She fiddled with the buttons of his tweed coat and unbuttoned it.

"Sorry isn't good enough." This time there had to be consequences. "I know what happened in London. And now you're thinking about doing it again here."

She slipped her hands beneath his coat and encircled him. "I don't know what you're talking about." Her breath smelled of bacon.

Today was to be his day of triumph, the day of the Cecil New Forest Pony Challenge. He was to add to his collection of silver cups with his name etched in them. Everyone knew he had the best pony on the Forest and had for several years running. He'd be blasted if he let her ruin it with her antics. She nuzzled her head under his chin, her silky hair tickling his neck.

"Forgive me?" she purred. But Fairbrother knew this trick. It wasn't going to work this time.

"I've a mind to contact a solicitor. Perhaps Sir George Lewis would take the case?"

All pretense gone, she yanked her hands away and stepped back. Fairbrother braced himself for the strike that never came. Instead, she smoothed the hair at her temples and plucked an invisible thread from her sleeve.

"You wouldn't dare," she said dismissively.

"Wouldn't I?" She snapped her attention to his face, searching for his level of resolve. "I've been to war. I've faced death countless times. I'll not hesitate to expose you."

"But —"

He preempted her argument. "Regardless of what it will cost me."

Her lovely face paled when she read the truth in his gaze; he was more than willing to set everything in motion, and in fact, already had. "I've already apologized," she said, more defiantly than she should have. She laced her arms across her chest, daring Fairbrother to demand more. He'd once admired her confidence, but he'd seen how treacherous it could be. "What more do you want?"

If she were a man, he'd demand money,

as he did with all those punters who begged favors of him. But she was different. She wasn't begging, though he wouldn't mind if it came to that.

"Do as I say, and there won't be a need for any further fuss." He brushed a stray hair from her face and thrilled at the shudder his touch produced. "Do we have an understanding?"

She glared at him. "To a point," she said.

"Of course." He held out his arm, indicating for her to precede him away from the tent. "Now then, shall we go and enjoy the competition?" He rubbed his hands together in gratification when she did as he said. "I have a suspicious feeling that I'm going to win."

CHAPTER 4

Stella fought her growing restlessness by pressing her fingers into the palms of her hands. If she hadn't been wearing gloves, her skin would be crosshatched with fingernail marks.

"From what Lady Atherly has told me, this will be the first dinner you've ever hosted," Lady Philippa Fairbrother said, glancing again at the tiny gold and diamond pendant watch pinned to her shoulder.

Stella, her future mother-in-law, her future sister-in-law, and her Aunt Rachel clustered around Lady Philippa, as servants hustled back and forth with trays of refreshments for the fair. It felt close and stifling after spending the morning in the stables with Tully, who much to Stella's relief was on the mend and heartily ate the apple. With her back nearly touching the flapping canvas side of the tea tent, Stella could feel the breeze stirring up outside.

She should be out there, by the paddocks, sizing up the competition; she'd recommended Lyndy's entry in the Cecil New Forest Pony Challenge, after all. But Lady Atherly had insisted; her close friend wanted to show off her houseguest. As the houseguest had yet to arrive, the conversation had drifted to Stella's engagement dinner. They were attending one social event talking about another.

Who does that?

"She's right. I've never hosted anything before," Stella said, ducking down to peer out of the tent. The nearest paddock was several yards away, far enough to keep the scent of horses from mingling with that of brewing tea. A stunning roan mare was bobbing her head and prancing around. The pony knew she was a beauty. But could she beat Moorington, Lyndy's pony? Stella would have to get closer to see.

"Pity," Lady Philippa said. "Not having much occasion to mix with the right sort in your own country, it will be a challenge now that you're forced to do so here." Stella, bristling at the comment, returned her attention to those inside the tent. Lady Philippa's mouth was turned up in a smile, but her eyes reflected the condescension in her tone. "I do hope you realize it is not like playing house. This party isn't to gather your nearest and dearest together, like a Christmas dinner."

"Or to placate the minor landowners in the area," Lady Atherly added.

"This is a night of strategy," Lady Philippa said, resting her hand on Stella's arm as if she were doing her a kindness. Stella steeled herself against shaking it off. "You've invited the most important and influential people in the county, and you must treat them as such if you are to ever get on as Lady Lyndhurst."

"To think, Lady Philippa, she wanted to invite Miss Snellgrove," Lady Atherly said.

What was so wrong with Miss Snellgrove? The young woman was interested in horses and talked about topics beyond the Season and the weather. She'd even sent a Battenberg cake to Pilley Manor after Stella mentioned how much she enjoyed it at a tea last week. What if she were the daughter of the local silversmith? The young woman had been kind to Stella. Unlike Lady Philippa, who had feigned friendship with Stella only to use every social occasion to comment on Stella's inferiority.

"Perish the thought!" Lady Philippa snapped her fingers at one of the maids bustling by with a tray and demanded tea be brought. Never looking at the girl, she didn't see the maid roll her eyes. "I would never have accepted the invitation to Miss Kendrick's dinner if I had thought I'd be obliged to suffer the likes of Miss Snellgrove."

Like we're all obliged to suffer the likes of you, Stella thought but kept to herself.

"Hello. Am I late?" a pleasant voice called.

The ladies all turned to see a man, barely past his fortieth birthday, leaning heavily on a cane, limp into the far side of the tent. He wore a brown Stetson hat. He slowly navigated the army of servants setting up the tables and chairs, laying out the dishes, teacups, saucers, silverware, and napkins and carrying trays of cakes, scones, and finger sandwiches. His arrival was a welcomed diversion.

"Mr. Barlow." Lady Philippa's face lit up as she reached out her arms to greet him. Stella had never seen the woman beam at her husband like that.

Mr. Barlow was quite handsome, with tanned, unblemished skin, thick, walnut brown hair and mustache, and deep-set, dark brown eyes. His suit was tailored to highlight the taut muscles in his arms. In his lapel, he wore an exotic orchid with silky, fan-like ivory petals streaked with rose-colored veins. His wide grin stretched the length of his face. His teeth were large and white. But the smile didn't reach his eyes.

"My dear, Lady Philippa, now don't you look ravishing." And she did. Even in a simple, high-collared, white lace tea gown, Lady Philippa's beauty rivaled that of Lillian Russell or Evelyn Nesbit, with large green eyes, silky black hair, and an hourglass figure Stella could only envy. "And what company you keep. Who are these charming ladies?"

"Mr. Cecil Barlow, may I introduce the Countess of Atherly, her daughter Lady Alice Searlwyn, Miss Kendrick, and Miss Luckett. Lady Atherly, Mr. Cecil Barlow."

Mr. Cecil Barlow bent at the waist, took Lady Atherly's offered hand, and kissed her on the back of her hand. "But surely this must be Lady Alice? Where could the countess be?"

Stella grimaced at his unctuous compliment and was astonished to see Lady Atherly blush and reward Mr. Barlow with a smile.

"Of course, this is my daughter," Lady Atherly corrected, indicating Lady Alice, standing beside her. As she offered her hand to be kissed, Lady Alice didn't take her eyes

48

off him. "We're quite pleased to make your acquaintance, Mr. Barlow," Lady Atherly continued. "It was kind of you to accept our invitation on such short notice. I'm certain your presence will be a highlight of the day."

"You are most gracious, Lady Atherly. I was honored to accept. But who knew I would meet such handsome women as you and your daughter? You could be twins." Lady Alice giggled.

"Don't be ridiculous, Mr. Barlow," Lady Atherly scoffed, waving away the absurd suggestion with her hand while a slight upturn of a smile lingered. Lady Alice gawked at the newcomer as Lady Philippa chuckled to herself. They were acting like schoolgirls. Even the maid, returning with a teapot and five cups and saucers, gaped at Mr. Barlow as she set down the tray. Was Stella the only one unaffected by the man's charms?

"Then you must be Miss Kendrick?" he said, shining his bright, empty grin on Stella.

"Yes, I am. Pleased to meet you, Mr. Barlow."

"And I, Miss Kendrick, am forever your servant," he said, removing his Stetson and bowing with a flourish. With his shirt unbuttoned at the top, Stella could see the hollow of his neck shadowed by hints of curly black hair. He wasn't wearing a tie. Stella self-consciously covered her neck with her hand as he straightened and faced Aunt Rachel. "Why, Miss Kendrick, I didn't know you had a sister." He reached down and took Aunt Rachel's hand. Blood rushed into Aunt Rachel cheeks.

"Well, I'll be a bison's backside," Aunt Rachel declared. "From the stories I've heard, you're a crazy young bronco, ain't ya, Mr. Barlow?" Instead of dropping her hand, he laughed and raised it to his lips.

"You know I am, Miss Luckett," he said, and winked. Aunt Rachel cackled in delight. *Her too?*

"Is it true you are a plant hunter, Mr. Barlow?" Stella asked, hoping to learn more about him beyond his ability to flatter.

Stella loved reading about adventurers, fictionalized and real: explorers, mountain climbers, fossil hunters, plant hunters, deep-sea ships' captains. She'd never met one. She'd been so looking forward to meeting Professor Gridley, the world-famous paleontologist and fossil hunter, but so far this man, supposedly one of those daring adventurers who sought fame and fortune through the discovery of new plants wherever they may be, was a disappointment.

"Do you not know, Miss Kendrick?" Lady Alice whispered behind her hand. "Mr. Barlow is . . . is . . ." Her voice trailed to silence as she gazed in awe at the man.

"Is perhaps the most famous plant hunter since Baron von Humboldt," Lady Philippa supplied as she handed Lyndy's mother the first cup of tea. She then skipped Stella and Lady Alice, offering the next teacup to Mr. Barlow. As he took it, his fingers brushed against hers.

"I wouldn't compare myself to the incomparable Humboldt, but yes, I have done a bit of plant collecting of my own."

"Come now," Lady Atherly chided as her daughter, flushed and gaping like a fish, floundered trying to find her own words of reassurance.

"How you underestimate yourself, Mr. Barlow," Lady Philippa added.

Mr. Barlow smirked as he took a sip of his tea, his eyes noting the flustered reactions of the women over the rim of his teacup. Stella inwardly sighed. False humility was unbecoming in a man, something she could never accuse Lyndy of. Humility, false or sincere, wasn't in Lyndy's nature. But Mr. Barlow, on the other hand . . .

"I did discover this little beauty." He

stroked the petals of the orchid on his jacket. The other women cooed in admiration. *How could the others not see it?* "And all it took was scaling the side of a mountain seething with snakes and a variety of predatory cats."

"I was just reading a most harrowing account of your expedition through the Amazon jungle," Lady Alice, finding her tongue, said, revealing the copy of the *Ladies' Home Journal* she'd held clasped to her chest all morning. The cover illustration was of Mr. Barlow holding a ruggedly carved pole two feet taller than himself. An improvised cane he'd made himself, no doubt. "Did you truly find a jaguar sleeping beneath your hammock?" Mr. Barlow nodded, his eyes closed in false modesty. Lady Alice turned to Stella, her cheeks flush, her eyes wide and bright. "And yet he returned with no less than thirty new plant species, many of them orchids."

"And nearly died doing it," Lady Philippa said, reaching her hands out to the plant hunter again, who immediately took both hers in his. "Until recently, he was thought to have perished in that dark place."

A look of sympathy and understanding passed between the pair that had Stella and Aunt Rachel exchanging glances and casting their gaze around the tent. Had anyone else noticed? While Mr. Barlow enthralled Lady Philippa, her husband was most likely preoccupied with settling his pony in the holding pen. *Thank goodness.* What would Lord Fairbrother think?

"I had no idea that was you," Stella said, hoping to bring Mr. Barlow's attention back to botanical exploration.

Stella remembered hearing of a plant hunter killed in South America several years ago but had never heard that he'd re-appeared alive and well in England. After catching her sneaking them to her room at night, her father hadn't allowed her to read newspapers in over a year. She'd only begun stealing them again since moving to Pilley Manor. Mr. Barlow's survival and subsequent return to civilization must be some story. Perhaps he could redeem himself with the tale.

"I'd love to hear your story, Mr. Barlow."

His eyes brightened, and he leaned toward her conspiratorially. "It all started with a nerve poison, or black curare, of the Ticuna tribe. Quite deadly when used on arrow tips."

"But first tell where you got the Stetson," Aunt Rachel interrupted. Stella too had been surprised to see him wearing a hat more appropriate to a cattle drive than a pony breed show.

"Do you like it?" He smiled and touched its brim. "It was a gift from a new investor, a rancher from Texas in America."

"You're planning another plant-collecting expedition?" Stella asked.

Considering his limp, she was surprised. Stella wanted to question him about it: Where was he planning to go and when? What would be the goal, to discover and collect new species of orchids like before, or something more useful? But his only response was another false smile. Mr. Barlow was clearly not prepared to divulge any more information.

"As I was saying, my last expedition began in the town of Esmeralda, on the Orinoco River, where I'd stopped to discover the secrets of the most infamous botanical products in the Amazon, the nerve poison used by the Ticuna tribe to hunt game. I learned, to my dismay, that if enough of the concoction enters the bloodstream, it's fatal to men as well."

"The natives poisoned you?" Lady Alice gasped.

Mr. Barlow shook his head. "No, dear lady, they presented me some of the stuff, and the plants they derived it from as a gift.

But not long after, a strong wind took our canoe and spilled the jar of poison. It seeped into my clothes, which I discovered only after putting on an affected pair of socks. The bleeding sores from insect bites on my feet exposed me to the black curare's torturous effects. I had to be left behind at a remote village. It was months before I'd recovered. But on my trek back to Esmeralda, I discovered a dozen new orchid species. Not bad for a dead man, don't you think?"

"That's incredible," Stella said.

"Beg your pardon, my lady," a footman interrupted, addressing Lady Atherly, "but the judges are ready for Mr. Barlow."

"Of course," she said. "Shall we?"

As Lady Philippa laced her arm through the plant hunter's, Stella said, "We're to meet Daddy here." Aunt Rachel hobbled over to grab herself a cup of tea before it cooled completely.

"Suit yourself," Lady Atherly said, turning on her heels and leading the way out of the tent. Lady Alice quickly stepped in behind her while Lady Philippa and Mr. Barlow, with his lumbering gait, trailed several paces behind.

As the pair passed Stella, heads bent together and oblivious to anyone but themselves, Lady Philippa quietly chided her companion, "What kept you, Cecil?"

"Your husband, my dear lady. Lord Fairbrother was showing me his champion pony."

Lady Philippa scoffed, her lip curling into an ugly sneer. "The blighter hasn't won anything yet."

Stella dropped her gaze to hide her surprise. Lady Philippa's crude retort wasn't about the pony — Lord Fairbrother's entry into the competition was a filly.

"Have you met Barlow yet?"

"The plant-collecting fellow?" Lyndy asked, deftly sidestepping a pile of horse manure.

Lord Fairbrother nodded. With a swagger to his step as they made their way from the temporary holding paddocks, Lyndy's neighbor strode alongside Fairweather, a black filly with a small white patch on her forehead. She was a magnificent example of the New Forest breed, but Lyndy wasn't about to tell the pompous ass that. Of course, Fairbrother, ever so confident, never asked Lyndy his opinion about the pony. He never asked anyone's opinion about anything.

"Not yet. Why?"

Lyndy accompanied Moorington, his entry in this year's Cecil New Forest Pony Challenge. Stella, with her keen eye, had found the splendid bay mare among his family stock. Lyndy patted the pony on its muscular thigh as his groom led her toward the show ring. A cheer from the gathering crowd rose at their first glimpse of the newest entries. Fairbrother waved to the spectators jockeying for space closest to the white fence. His groom trotted Fairbrother's pony forward, ensuring it entered the ring first.

And so, the competition begins. Lyndy snickered to himself.

The ring, a fenced off area already devoid of turf from the day's earlier competitions, smelled of fresh soil and horse dung and teemed with other exceptional ponies. Barnard Smith, William Fancy, and John Bowman had all entered chestnut mares with excellent pedigrees. George Parley's ponies consistently eclipsed everyone else's, and his entry this year, a beautiful roan mare, was no exception.

Would this be the year someone defeated Fairbrother? Lyndy doubted it. He'd won every Cecil Challenge Cup since the chalice was donated by Lord Arthur Cecil several years ago. Granted Fairbrother's entries had always been good, well-built animals, but everyone knew his success had more to do with his status as chairman of the Verderers' Court, a position of power and influence unique to the New Forest, than with the quality of his ponies.

"He's staying with us at Outwick House," Fairbrother said. "Came down a few days ago, to preside over this year's pony challenge. The chap's name is Cecil, after all." Fairbrother chuckled at the jest while smiling at the appreciative crowd. Lyndy didn't see the humor in it. Mr. Kendrick's constant use of the pun had seen to that.

"Philippa met him in London at the Duchess of Charford's last Season," Fairbrother continued, "and devised this outrageous scheme to invite him down for the competition. I don't have to tell you how hesitant I was, allowing a stranger in the house, one who has lived half his adult life picking flowers and slashing his way through jungles, nonetheless. Would the fellow be more savage than gentleman, I wondered? But Philippa insisted, and Philippa gets what she wants." Fairbrother flattened his lips. "If you know what I mean."

Lyndy knew precisely what he meant. Thank God it wasn't always true.

"But," Fairbrother said, brightening, "I admit, the chap has been most amusing."

Fairbrother didn't elaborate but pointed toward the raised podium, decorated with swags of red and white bunting, next to the show ring.

Lyndy shielded his eyes from the glare of the sun. A string of seated dignitaries lined the platform: local politicians, the judges, and Lyndy's family. Two seats in the middle remained empty. With Alice staring into her lap and Papa squinting without his lorgnette, Mother, by the high tilt of her hat, generously embellished with towering feathers, was the only one comfortable with looking down upon the multitude. Typically, Mother would've presented the Cecil New Forest Pony Challenge Cup. But this year she'd graciously granted Philippa her desire by allowing the plant-collecting fellow to step in. That was before Philippa had married Fairbrother, before Papa had arranged Lyndy's engagement to Stella, dashing Mother's hopes for Philippa as a daughter-in-law. Would Mother have been so accommodating had she known Philippa could never be Lady Lyndhurst? Perhaps. Mother adored Philippa. Why, Lyndy could never understand.

"There's the chap now," Fairbrother said.

A well-built man wearing an unusual wide-brimmed hat and leaning on a cane was mounting the steps of the platform one at a time. Philippa clung to his arm, pacing herself to his slow gait. Was Philippa's aid necessary or was she a hindrance Mr. Barlow was too much of a gentleman to admit? Knowing Philippa, it was the latter.

Lyndy looked about for Stella. The competition grounds, set on the site of one of the more extensive grazing lawns in this part of the Forest, consisted of the judging ring, temporary paddocks filled with animals to be judged — ponies, cattle, and repulsively loud, snorting pigs — along with several bright red and white canvas tents flapping in the breeze. The tents were filled with people taking tea. Musicians settled into the bandstand. Shouting, laughing children clustered around games such as coconut shy and ball in a bucket set between the tents and the paddocks. With the fete spread out over at least two acres, Stella could be anywhere.

Lyndy spied Mr. Kendrick first. No, it had been the young woman with ginger hair with Mr. Kendrick who had caught Lyndy's eye. He'd never seen her before. She was holding the oaf's arm, even when that meant stepping on her skirt, as Mr. Kendrick plodded toward the ring. A few steps behind them the old aunt hobbled along on her cane beside Stella, who was as bright and refreshing as Philippa was dark and deceiving, radiant in her rose-colored dress and gracious smile.

How Lyndy loved that smile. He'd basked in it for the past two months, getting to know the woman who wore it. He'd never done anything as frustrating, challenging, or thrilling; much like the woman herself. To dance with her last night had been torture, holding her in his arms without so much as a kiss. And then to have seen her throw herself into the arms of that filthy old man in the stables afterward infuriated him. One might've thought he'd been jealous. Now he had to watch her trail in the wake of that brute.

With his family in tow, Mr. Kendrick, more rotund than any of the villagers, farmers, or forest folk who'd come to enjoy the festivities, parted the crowd like a whale in a minnow pond. Having arrived but two months ago, the Americans were still an oddity, a spectacle to behold, and for many locals, this was their first glimpse. Lyndy felt sorry for Stella, a feeling that surprised him. Before Stella, empathy wasn't something he'd made a habit of, but she didn't deserve the public's scrutiny, and having gotten to know her more, he understood how unwelcome it truly was. But how could Lyndy fault the gawkers? Who couldn't take their eyes off the bumbling millionaire horse breeder and his beautiful daughter destined to become their mistress one day?

Fairbrother for one.

When Lyndy pulled his attention away from his future bride, Fairbrother was still staring at Philippa and Mr. Barlow on the podium. With Philippa standing behind him, Cecil Barlow stepped unaided in front of the megaphone and waved to the crowd. The band played a snippet of a jaunty tune. Several hundred people, from all over the fete grounds, cheered and clapped. When the din died down, Mr. Barlow began.

"To the lovely people of the glorious New Forest, may I welcome you to the annual Cecil New Forest Pony Challenge." Cheers rose. "Thank you to Lord and Lady Atherly and to Lord Fairbrother and Lady Philippa Fairbrother for permitting their humble servant to be here with you today." Mr. Barlow looked at each in turn as he said their name, even finding Fairbrother in the crowd near the ring and bowing his head slightly. When he acknowledged Philippa, her face lit up, a flush of red on her cheeks, apparent even at this distance. Cecil Barlow winked at her before again addressing the crowd.

"I am honored by your welcome and hospitality. I can't imagine a better way to spend this lovely summer day than here in the New Forest." And then Mr. Barlow leaned into the megaphone and put his hand to the side of his mouth as if whispering something in confidence into someone's ear. "It certainly exceeds where I was this time last year." Laughter arose.

"Where was he last year?" Lyndy said, his hands tapping the top of the fence as the grooms led the ponies to the center of the ring.

Fairbrother looked at Lyndy for the first time and frowned.

"The South American jungle, of course. Where have you been for the past year, Lyndhurst?"

"If he doesn't train, own, or ride a racehorse, I don't keep up."

"Without further ado, let the competition begin," the plant-collecting fellow bellowed.

While the others on the podium clapped politely, Alice nearly bounced out of her seat, adding her enthusiastic applause and obvious admiration to that of the rest of the crowd. Lyndy wasn't used to his sister not having her nose buried in her magazines.

But then again, wasn't Mr. Barlow one of her magazine personalities come to life? Alice had felt that way about Stella initially too. Now Stella was like everyone else, someone to be ignored.

"May the best pony win," Cecil Barlow shouted.

"Bloody chance of that happening!" a shout rang out above the applause. Abruptly murmurs and gasps replaced the applause and cheers. "Seems more likely me pony will sprout a horn than win as it should."

Lyndy craned his neck to see who the bloke who shouted was. A nearly bald man with broad shoulders, thick forearms, and a long, pencil-thin mustache pushed his way around the outside of the ring. It was George Parley, the minor landholder with the excellent ponies. His hat crushed in his fist, Parley jabbed a tan, leathery finger up at the dignitaries when he reached the platform.

"This here better not be fixed this year. There'll be hell to pay if it ain't fair. And I don't mean Fairbrother." A tittering of nervous laughs broke out at the fellow's play on words. The judges, three members of the local breeding society, muttered among themselves.

"Fixed? That's outrageous," one of the

judges protested.

"Of course, it will be fair, my good man," Cecil Barlow said, loud enough to be heard over the murmuring crowd. Philippa took hold of the plant collector's arm. Why couldn't she leave the poor fellow alone? He didn't need Philippa's help to stand. He had his cane for that. But Barlow didn't seem to notice. His attention was on Parley. "Why wouldn't it be? From what I understand, these fine judges run the institution that defines the breed."

"Obviously you stayed in the jungles longer than what was good for you," Parley scoffed, folding his arms and planting his feet like stakes holding down the tents.

"I say, Lyndhurst, shall we proceed?" Fairbrother, nonplussed by George Parley's accusation, pushed open the gate in the fence and entered the ring. "I have no doubt the judges know a good pony when they see one."

Lyndy didn't doubt it either. Pity they probably weren't going to let the best one win.

Lord Fairbrother motioned toward the judges to join him in the ring. They jumped to their feet and scrambled toward the steps. Lyndy tugged at the cuffs of his coat as the entries were lined up. There were twelve in all — twelve varying examples of the New Forest pony breed. From his vantage point, George Parley had every reason to expect to win. Lyndy's Moorington was a lovely animal, but George Parley's was a stunner. Lord Fairbrother's entry, while excellent, clearly wasn't up to Parley's perfection.

With the crowd hushed in anticipation, Lyndy caught snippets of the judges' comments as they moved down the line, examining one pony after another and jotting notes on their marking sheets: "good bright brown eyes, weak step, hocks too wide apart, plenty of flat bone, mutton withers, blood spavin."

The ponies were then trotted around the ring, their heads bobbing, ears twitching, their eyes watching everything. A few breathless minutes passed as the grooms led the ponies from the ring and the judges convened. George Parley, his nose flaring like a horse, glared on and off at Fairbrother, who laughed and watched the proceedings with a smug, confident air.

"And the winner of this year's Cecil New Forest Pony Challenge Cup is . . ." Mr. Barlow bellowed from the stage, "Lord Fairbrother!"

The crowd released a pent-up roar of applause and cheers as Fairbrother approached the podium and skipped up the stairs. Mother handed Fairbrother a bouquet of roses as the plant hunter fellow passed him the large two-handled silver cup, about a foot and a half tall, embossed with swags of ribbons and engraved with 1905 THE CECIL NEW FOREST PONY CHALLENGE CUP.

"I bloody knew it! The bastard. He's a cheat." The disgruntled George Parley, shaking his fist, hurled insults and accusations. But soon his complaints were drowned out by the happy cries of the crowd. Everyone loves a winner. As Fairbrother uttered some words of feigned surprise and appreciation from the podium, Parley shoved his way through the crowd, his lips moving. He was still muttering to himself as his shoulder brushed past Lyndy. "There'll be bloody hell to pay," he said. "Bloody hell."

CHAPTER 5

With a drizzle developing, the tea tent was crowded and Lord Fairbrother, standing next to one of the many tables, cradled his silver cup and received well-wishers like a king on his throne.

"Can't believe his pony won," Stella's father grumbled under his breath as they entered the tent and saw him holding court, undaunted by his competitor's accusations.

As he was tall in stature with silver threads running through his well-trimmed blond mustache and pleasing blue eyes, Stella would've considered Lord Fairbrother handsome if it weren't for his too thick lips and a swagger to his every step. Those plump lips rose in a crooked smile as he greeted an elderly couple wanting to congratulate their lord. At his side, Lady Philippa did little to mask her boredom, covering her mouth with her fingers and yawning.

"What's done is done, Daddy."

Stella, rubbing her hands up and down her arms to ward off the chill, headed for the nearest food table. Having skipped the luncheon to spend more time with Tully in the stables, she was famished. The scent of wet grass, pungent at the edge of the tent, was replaced by that of freshly baked scones, strawberry jam, and warm tea. Stella helped herself to a plate of sliced lemon drizzle cake. Miss Cosslett and Daddy followed.

"Maybe there's something to that bull of a guy's rantings," he continued. "Maybe this competition is rigged in Fairbrother's favor. You, there." He stopped a plump kitchen maid carrying a tray of dirty plates. Hadn't Stella seen her serving at a garden party at Baron Branson-Hill's estate? "Where can a guy get a cup of coffee around here?"

The maid scampered off as Stella's father reached for a slice of sponge cake without bothering to pick up the plate. Miss Cosslett handed him the cake's plate, followed by a napkin. Daddy took it, without comment. Who was this woman who forced manners on him without so much as a grumble for her pains? Stella should be glad about it, but she wasn't. She'd lived with him too long not to worry what it all meant.

"There's Cecil Barlow," Miss Cosslett said, spotting him chatting nearby.

Daddy waddled over and shoved out his hand, to the dismay of the giggling granny who'd been the sole object of the plant hunter's attention. The older woman's shoulders drooped like the faded flowers on her hat as Stella's father forced her aside.

"Elijah Kendrick, at your service, Barlow." Mr. Barlow shook his hand heartily. "Didn't get a chance to catch you before the competition."

"Well met, Mr. Kendrick. I've heard a great deal about you."

"I'm sure you have. I'm as famous for breeding racehorses as you are for planning disastrous expeditions."

"Daddy," Stella chided.

"If you call single-handedly rescuing the rubber tree industry from ruin by smuggling seventy thousand seeds past Brazilian customs officials and having over a dozen exotic flowers named after you disastrous, I'm your man." Daddy sputtered an ineffectual reply. Mr. Barlow bared his teeth in a Cheshire cat-like grin before turning his attention to Miss Cosslett. "I've already met your daughter. So who is this fine woman?" Miss Cosslett's eyes rounded like saucers.

"That is what I was about to ask," Lord Atherly said, entering the tent with his wife and daughter gliding across the well-trodden grass beside him. Lyndy, scowling, arrived several paces behind them, his eyes immediately fixating on Lord Fairbrother. Raindrops glistened on the shoulders of his coat. Stella caught his eye and smiled. His face brightened a bit.

"Jealous, are you, Atherly?" Daddy said, smirking at Lord Atherly's admiring expression while Lady Atherly stared down her nose at the reporter. "This is Jane Cosslett."

"Are you a New Forest pony enthusiast, Miss Cosslett?" Mr. Barlow asked, noticing how the reporter openly gaped at him, ignoring everyone else.

"No, Barlow. She's a reporter, down from London. Come to cover the wedding, not the pony competition," Daddy said. "Supposedly there are folks all over the globe who will pay good money to know how many pearls are stitched into my daughter's wedding gown. So, I've taken this charming creature under my wing. Who am I to stifle the press? Especially if it means the Astors in New York get wind of it." Daddy laughed, his protruding belly jiggling. "You couldn't ask for better publicity."

"One could strive for no publicity at all," Lady Atherly said, breaking her silence. "If you'll excuse me." Without waiting, she sauntered over to the other side of the tent.

Stella took the opportunity to step closer to Lyndy, her closest ally in the tent. She hadn't talked to him all day.

"You must be disappointed," she whispered. "I know I am. Moorington was definitely the better pony."

Lyndy chuckled softly. "Will I ever grow accustomed to your forwardness?"

"If you are to be believed, Lord Lyndhurst, it is one of my charms," Stella teased.

"Yes, and no."

"What do you mean by that?" She made a face at him.

"I mean . . ." Lyndy reached up and lightly brushed the back of two fingers across her cheek. He'd never done that before. Or anything like it, in public. His touch was surprisingly soft and gentle. Stella decided she liked it. "Yes, it is one of your charms, but no, I'm not disappointed." He let his hand drop. "I knew, going in, that Fairbrother's pony would probably win."

Then why had he stared at Lord Fairbrother like George Parley had, like a man who'd been cheated? Before she could ask, a gentleman in his fifties wearing spectacles and mopping drops of rain from his high, shiny forehead strolled into the tent.

"Lord Atherly, I was just talking with a man outside, and I wondered if . . ." The

72

newcomer, stuffing his handkerchief in his jacket pocket, was now intent on getting his pipe to light in the damp.

"Well, I'll be damned. Amos Gridley." Daddy pulled away from Miss Cosslett and slapped the newcomer on the back. "Aren't you a sight for sore eyes. It's about time we had more Americans around here. How long has it been?"

Stella had only heard of Professor Gridley. He was the famous paleontologist from the Smithsonian Institution's National Museum. He and her father had met through racing, but Stella knew the professor's passion wasn't for living horses but ancient, fossilized ones. Hence his connection with Lord Atherly. Professor Gridley was, however indirectly, partly responsible for Stella and Lyndy's recent engagement. Lord Atherly had funded the professor's most recent fossil-hunting expeditions to Wyoming, the expenditure nearly bankrupting the family. Not everyone welcomed the professor's presence, but Stella couldn't wait to meet him.

"Two years this past May, at the Preakness."

"Yes, that was it," Daddy said. "St. Florian's filly won it. I made lots of money off that stud."

"And I lost a five-spot by betting against her." The two men shared a laugh.

"You two must have a lot to hash out after that big dig, eh, Atherly?" Daddy said, adding another slice of cake to his plate. "How did it pan out?"

"It was an extraordinary expedition, Mr. Kendrick, absolutely extraordinary."

"I'm so glad to hear it was such a success, Lord Atherly," Stella said. For some odd reason, Stella was the only woman Lord Atherly allowed into his private sanctuary to examine his fossils or use his hand lenses whenever she wished. With all her many social obligations, she'd barely stepped foot in his study, but she'd eagerly followed the expedition's progress, questioning Lord Atherly about it as much as she could.

"I couldn't be more delighted." Lord Atherly puffed out his chest a bit, his eyes bright with enthusiasm. "Perhaps, Miss Kendrick, you'd like to join us tomorrow and hear more about it? Gridley is going to show me some of what he found."

The words, "I'd love to," faded on Stella's lips as Jane Cosslett pushed herself forward, stepping on the hem of Stella's dress.

"You're Dr. Amos Gridley?" Professor Gridley nodded. "Really?" She sounded disappointed.

"This must be your daughter, then, eh, Kendrick?" Professor Gridley said, smiling at the reporter. "You seem familiar. Have we met before?"

Miss Cosslett shook her head as Stella pulled on her skirt, forcing the reporter to lift her foot.

"No, no," Daddy scoffed. "Of course not. No, this exquisite creature is Miss Jane Cosslett."

Professor Gridley nodded, then shifted his broad smile to include Stella. "Then, this must be the bride to be."

"Indeed, it is, Professor," Lyndy said, capturing Stella's gaze and holding it. For a moment, everyone else faded into the background. What was Lyndy thinking? His face, stoic and unreadable as always, gave nothing away. But was that pride she heard seep into his voice? Was that glint in his eyes a sign of approval? Then suddenly, his focus jerked away, and his expression hardened. Stella followed his gaze toward Lady Philippa, chatting with Lyndy's mother.

What had his mother said this time? Stella would have to ask Lyndy later. After two months of being on her best behavior, Stella knew she hadn't won Lady Atherly's approval. Would she ever? Did she care?

"How nice to finally meet you, Miss

Stella," Professor Gridley said pleasantly. "I can't believe we haven't met before. Your father's a scoundrel for not telling me more about you."

"Well done, Fairbrother," Lord Atherly said as the competition's winner and his wife joined the group. "I believe that makes several wins in a row."

"It does."

"I do apologize for all that silly business with Mr. Parley beforehand."

"Not to worry yourself, old chap. The best pony won in the end." Lord Atherly nodded congenially, glad to have that out of the way. But Stella's father wouldn't let it rest. Lyndy started rocking on his heels.

"Did it?" Daddy said. "If I were judging, Parley's pony would've won hands down."

"But no one asked you to judge, now did they?" Lord Fairbrother said, running his finger across his name etched in the silver trophy still cradled in the crook of his arm.

"Lord Fairbrother, I don't believe you've met the leader of Lord Atherly's latest fossil expedition," Stella said, hoping to diffuse the rising tension. "Professor Amos Gridley is the world-famous fossil hunter from the States. Professor, this is Lord Fairbrother, his wife, Lady Philippa Fairbrother, and their guest, Mr. Cecil Barlow."

"*The* Cecil Barlow?" Professor Gridley said, breaking with etiquette and ignoring the Fairbrothers. "The plant-hunting explorer?"

"In the flesh," Barlow said, sweeping his Stetson hat off his head in a florid bow. Lady Philippa, who would've cringed if Stella had done such a thing, chuckled. Lord Fairbrother frowned. Lyndy fidgeted with the cuffs on his sleeve. Professor Gridley was unfazed.

"What luck," the professor said. "I was telling Lord Atherly this morning that my colleagues have largely ignored South America. I know you specialize in exotic botanicals, Mr. Barlow, but if you have time, I would love to get your opinion on —"

"I've seen you before, you know, Professor," Lord Fairbrother said, interrupting.

"You have?"

"At the opening of the dinosaur exhibit at the Natural History Museum in London. Since His Majesty was a sponsor, all the best set attended."

"The one for the *Diplodocus carnegii*?" Lord Fairbrother nodded.

"I saw you there too, Miss Cosslett. Covering the event for your newspaper, were you?" The reporter blanched — what a strange reaction. Stella would have to ask later what that was all about.

"But that's unbelievable. I can't remember what I had for breakfast, let alone a face that I'd seen in a crowd." Professor Gridley laughed. "There were so many there that day, thousands perhaps. How could you possibly remember seeing us there?"

"I never forget a face."

"Or a single indiscretion," Lady Philippa muttered under her breath.

Had anyone else but Stella heard her? Lord Fairbrother, congenially chatting with the professor and Lord Atherly about the merits of the exhibit, at least didn't appear to. But Lyndy must have; he was frowning, as was Cecil Barlow. Miss Cosslett was biting her lip.

"Fairbrother!"

The pleasant conversation ceased as Harvey Milkham stormed into the tent, water dripping off the rim of his old, floppy hat. He hadn't changed out of the clothes he'd worn last night, but unlike last night, the heavy scent of burnt wood and smoke permeated everything about him. Those not seated, many with teacups or dessert plates in hand, backed away as the snakecatcher aimed straight toward their group, dragging a burlap sack along behind him. With tea over, everyone was preparing to leave. Stella moved to meet him. The additional stench of bourbon reached Stella before he did.

"Harvey? What is it? What's wrong?" she said.

"I say, hold on there, old fellow." Cecil Barlow grabbed hold of Harvey's arm. "What's this all about?" Harvey struggled in the plant hunter's firm grip but was no match. Stella approached her friend, reaching out to comfort him, but Cecil Barlow, shaking his head, blocked her hand and then stepped in her way. "You better step back, Miss Kendrick. This fellow's more animal than man."

"How dare you!" Stella said. "He's my friend. Leave him alone." But Mr. Barlow wouldn't budge.

"What's it this time, Harvey?" Lord Fairbrother scoffed. "Not like the fine I imposed in court? You know you don't have any right to the common of pasture. You can't just turn your pony out. I was only upholding the law."

"You burned down me house, Fairbrother!" Harvey jerked about, still trying to shake off the plant hunter's hold.

"What?" Stella whirled around to face Lord Fairbrother; his arms still cradled his new silver chalice.

"Don't be ridiculous," Lady Philippa said,

leaning back as if to distance herself without giving ground. "Why would my husband want to do such a thing?"

"For the land, milady. The land. Ask him." Harvey shook a long, gnarled finger at Lord Fairbrother, who rolled his eyes. "He's been trying to get us off the land for years, and now he's gone and burned down me house."

"Fairbrother?" Lyndy said. "Is this true?"

"He's drunk. What would I want with that land? It's not even near Outwick House."

It was the second time today someone had accused Lord Fairbrother of behavior unbecoming of a gentleman. First George Parley insinuated the judges curried Lord Fairbrother's favor by letting him win. At the time, Stella thought Mr. Parley's complaint a case of sour grapes. But her father had been right; Lord Fairbrother's pony had flaws. It shouldn't have won. And now Harvey blamed Lord Fairbrother for burning down his hut. Harvey wouldn't lie about a thing like that, and Lord Fairbrother didn't outright deny it. Who could be so despicable?

"You're a liar, Fairbrother," Harvey shouted. "You can't fool us. I'm not like those barmy commoners you bamboozle out of their hard-earned money." Harvey wrenched his free arm around. "You've got to make this right, or else."

"Lyndy, the bag," Stella warned, as Harvey lifted the burlap sack and hurled it like Stella had seen a baseball pitcher do with a ball once when she was little.

The sack flew like an elongated clump of mucky horse hay, scattering the occupants of the tea tent like flies. Cries and gasps mixed with the sounds of wooden folding chairs tipping, teacups, saucers, and plates clattering as the bag smacked Lord Fairbrother full in the face.

"Aaahh!" Lady Philippa screamed through her fingers, splayed across her mouth and eyes.

Lord Fairbrother swatted frantically at the bag, leaping back as it tumbled down the front of his waistcoat and onto the ground. A bright red splotch marked where the bag had connected with his cheek. As Lyndy and Professor Gridley scrambled to grab the sack, Harvey shook off Cecil Barlow's hold.

"Catch him!" Lord Fairbrother yelled.

No one moved to stop Harvey as he stumbled his way out of the tent. All eyes were riveted on the bag, now wriggling on the tamped down grass. Lord and Lady Atherly had pulled their daughter several feet back, expressions of curiosity and repulsion clear on their faces. Stella ignored Lady Alice's pleas to move away. Lady Philippa, too, seemed rooted to the ground.

Lyndy snatched up the bag and peered inside. With an unbecoming sneer on his face, he upturned the bag and dumped the contents at Lady Philippa's feet.

"Aaahh!" Screaming again, Lady Philippa jumped back, caught the edge of a chair with her hip and tumbled back, bumping against her husband's chest. Wrestling herself out of his steadying arms, Lady Philippa saw that not snakes but live trout lay flopping about at her feet. She glared at Lyndy, her lips pinched, her cheeks burning red. Lord Fairbrother rested a hand on her shoulder, attempting to comfort her. She shrugged it off. Was she more embarrassed than angry? Stella couldn't tell.

"Lyndy!" Lady Atherly scolded. "Apologize at once."

"I say, that was uncalled for, Lyndhurst," Lord Fairbrother added. Stella agreed.

"Was it?" was all Lyndy said, his jaw clenched.

Stella hadn't seen Lyndy act like that before. He was often smug, haughty, and pretentious, but malicious? Never. So why had he done it? Before she could ask, he turned up his coat collar, threw back the red and white canvas, and braving the rain, now coming down in torrents, marched out of the tent.

CHAPTER 6

Hodgson stood still and listened. Ah, blissful silence.

This was the Outwick House butler's favorite task of the day. Especially after one as turbulent as this turned out to be.

Despite having won the Cecil Challenge Cup again, Lord Fairbrother had returned from the competition in a foul mood. And despite their guest's presence at dinner, His Lordship and Her Ladyship had argued throughout the meal. Poor Mr. Barlow had tried to lighten the mood with a jest or a diverting tale of his adventures. The one about the giant rodents, capybaras he'd called them, swimming alongside his canoe, was most amusing. But His Lordship rebuked Mr. Barlow for his attempts, calling his tales fantastical, raising the ire of Her Ladyship even more. Like any good servant, Hodgson hadn't heard a word of it.

Not so the talk in the servants' hall later.

What Hodgson gleaned from Mrs. White, the housekeeper, who brought him a cup of tea and stayed for a chat, was that the snakecatcher's hut had burned down last night and the snakecatcher was blaming Lord Fairbrother for it. Was it only yesterday that the old man had visited Outwick House because the gardeners found snakes in the rockery? To think Hodgson had thought kindly of the fellow. But how could he now? According to the housekeeper's sister, who had helped serve tea in the tent, the snakecatcher threw a sack full of snakes at Lord Fairbrother, or was it trout? Mrs. White's sister wasn't sure. And then there was Mr. Parley. As a landowner in this part of the Forest, he was a frequent visitor to Outwick House, discussing business with His Lordship. One of the grooms told the housekeeper that Mr. Parley publicly accused His Lordship of cheating. His Lordship had denied everything, as of course, he would. But Her Ladyship's maid confided that Lady Philippa was still furious, finding the public humiliation intolerable. And rightly so. Hodgson felt the blood rise in his face just thinking about the gall of some people, airing their frustrations at their betters in full view of everyone. What were they thinking?

Hodgson put that all behind him now. With Lord Fairbrother out taking his nightly constitutional and Lady Philippa and their guest retiring to bed, Hodgson could make his nightly rounds. Strolling from one room to another, he made certain all the lights were extinguished, all the clocks were wound, all the fires were banked, all the doors were locked. Having a key, Lord Fairbrother would let himself in. Hodgson turned off the hall light and paused again, relishing the dark stillness, disrupted only by the high-pitched *ding* of the nearest clock as it struck half past eleven.

Slam!

What in heaven's name was that?

Hodgson flicked the light back on and strode purposefully across the black and white checked marble tile of the hall toward the origin of the sound. He entered the conservatory, where moonlight, streaming through the glass-paned walls, cast frond-shaped shadows of the palms fluttering in the chilly night breeze, and saw the outside door was swung wide open. The orange and lemon trees permeated the air with their citrus scent.

Meow.

For goodness sake, what was that doing in here?

From the safety of the shadows beneath the white wicker lounge chair, a tabby cat, its green eyes shining in the dark, peered up at him and hissed. Hodgson had noticed the cat before. Nelly, a chambermaid, was known to put out milk for the stray. Hodgson did not approve — cats made Lord Fairbrother itch — but the housekeeper had a soft spot for the animals and was turning a blind eye to the maid's indiscretion. But here now, Hodgson had a good reason to banish the feral thing from the grounds — the cat had found its way into the house.

"Shoo, shoo." He flapped his hands, trying to scare the cat from under the chair. When it refused to move, Hodgson retreated to the kitchens for a dish of milk. When he returned, he carried the dish outside and set it down several yards away. The cat dashed past him and happily lapped up the treat. Hodgson quickly closed the conservatory door and locked it. Satisfied, he turned to leave, but stopped and glanced back.

How had the cat entered the conservatory in the first place?

Hodgson jiggled the doorknob, satisfied it was securely locked. The butler snorted his displeasure. For the wind to have blown it open or for the cat to have pushed it, someone must've left the door ajar. But who? The gardener? Highly unlikely. The gardener was conscientious and meticulous. He'd never have left the conservatory in a state that would threaten the health of the plants. Nelly? More likely. Banishing the cat would only serve the maid right. She'd be lucky if that's all he did.

Why hadn't she ever done this before?

The water swirled and rippled around Stella's knees, pushing and pulling, forcing her to plant her feet solidly in the gravel streambed and bend her knees to keep from falling. She gripped the long willowy rod, as Lyndy stepped behind her and pressed against her back, steadying her. With the warmth of his breath tickling her ear, he guided her arm in a methodical wave of the rod, sending the line into the air, flowing back and forth above her head. Water droplets, clinging to the translucent line, reflected the purple and pink and orange of the rising sun. The intimacy of it was almost her undoing.

"Now," he said.

She flicked her wrist, as he'd shown her, and aimed for a dark pool beneath the feathery branches of an overhanging willow. A silent splash marked where her line entered the water.

"Brilliant," Lyndy said, his words low and muffled by the rushing water. "You're a natural." He leaned in and nibbled her ear but stepped back as soon as she began to giggle. "Keep doing that, and we'll be eating trout for breakfast."

Stella grinned at him as he waded a few yards away. His usually immaculate hair, unkempt and damp, stuck to the side of his face. His hat lay on the bank, and his tie dangled loosed around his neck. She hadn't seen him this relaxed since the Derby. Who knew dressing in rubber wading pants and forging into the middle of the Blackwater was all it took to be near him when he was like this? Why hadn't she done this sooner?

Because he'd never asked. Until yesterday.

When he'd left the tea tent after the Cecil Pony Challenge, Stella had run after him, ignoring Lady Atherly's demand to let Lyndy be. Without discussion or agreement, they'd shared Stella's umbrella and crossed the heath back to Morrington Hall in silence. Stella had so many questions. Did Lyndy think Lord Fairbrother had anything to do with burning down Harvey's hut? Did he believe Mr. Parley's accusation of cheating had any truth in it? What did Harvey mean about Lord Fairbrother taking men's money? Why had Lyndy so rudely dumped the sack at Lady Philippa's feet? But his brooding expression had stilled her tongue and she'd said nothing. When they'd arrived, and Stella turned toward the stables to check on Tully, Lyndy had caught her by the hand, pulling her to him and kissing her with a ferocity that left her breathless. Where did that come from?

"You seemed to have recovered your good humor," she'd teased as a sly smirk crept across his face.

"Come fishing with me tomorrow," he'd whispered, his lips flushed and his eyes shining. "I'd like to teach you." Of course, she'd agreed, the strength of his arms still wrapped around her. She never imagined she'd enjoy it so much.

As her fly, a clever combination of tiny feathers and thread coiled around the flat end of the hook, bobbed on the current toward her, a heron leaped into flight from atop the nearby fir tree. Stella swept the riverbank with her gaze, past the slumbering figure of Aunt Rachel, toward the open heath, unbroken for miles by nothing but swaths of purple, flowering heather, clumps of gorse bushes that looked like stunted fir trees, and a scattering of ponies grazing on the lush green grass. She breathed deeply of the earthy scent of the streamside vegetation mingling with the pungent odor of her rubber pants. She thrilled at the strange combination, associating it with the sudden freedom she felt. Here there were no expectations, no constraints, no rules of etiquette to follow. Just the rhythmic peace of swish, cast, and reel. Swish, cast, reel.

No wonder Lyndy looked so relaxed.

Stella reeled in her line, swished it above her head, and cast again, this time without Lyndy's help. Almost immediately, she felt the pull of something. But this couldn't be a fish. There was no tug or play, as the fish tried to swim away. This was a heavy, static pull.

"My line is caught on something," Stella said as she slowly waded against the current toward the overhanging tree. "Don't worry. I can get it," she added when Lyndy began wading toward her.

Her line had disappeared into the branches of the willow on the bank. Stella tugged on it as she approached. The branches bobbed, rustling the leaves, but her fly was stuck. Stella pulled again. It was no use. She ducked beneath the overhanging branches, the fronds tickling her face, hoping to spot her snagged fly and pry it loose by hand. But the sun hadn't reached this dark hollow, and she tripped. She let go of her rod, frantically snatching at the nearby branches to keep from falling, but her clumsy, heavy boot became wedged under something beneath the water.

"Ohhh!"

Stella buckled forward and splashed to her knees, expecting to connect with the sharp gravel bottom. But her knees jabbed into something softer and squishy. It wasn't a large clump of fallen leaves, accumulated by the current, or a moss-covered log covered over recently by the seasonal rains. It was a man's body, caught in the roots of the tree.

"Oh, no!"

"Girlie, are you okay?" Aunt Rachel shouted from the stream bank.

"Stella?" Lyndy's call was muffled and far away.

Stella clambered frantically backward, water splashing in her eyes, branches tangling her hair. She twisted around, but the rubber pants were filled with water, weighing her down. She could barely drag herself away. She crawled as she went until Lyndy reached her and hauled her to her feet.

"What is it?" he demanded, his face creased with worry. "Are you hurt?"

"No, it's not me," she said, pointing

toward the willow. "It's Lord Fairbrother. And, Lyndy, he's dead."

CHAPTER 7

Stella stared into the rushing water. A thin, brown branch floated downstream, momentarily catching between two large algae-covered rocks jutting up through the surface. How could the water be so clear, so clean with a dead body in it? She rubbed her hands up and down her arms. Despite Lyndy draping the picnic blanket around her shoulders, she was still shivering.

How could this have happened again?

Constable Waterman, as burly as he was, squeezed into Lyndy's borrowed rubber pants and boots and waded toward the spot beneath the willow. With one forceful jerk, he pulled the dead body from the tangle of roots and heaved it up onto the bank. Water rushed from the body back into the stream as if frantic to escape its grim touch. Bile rose in Stella's throat.

"Perhaps you'd like to wait in the carriage?" Inspector Brown said gently. Furrows formed on his high forehead.

Stella looked back at the carriage, parked behind the police wagon and its calmly grazing horse. Leonard, the groom from Morrington Hall who had accompanied them on their fishing trip, stood beside it. With his face buried in her neck, the groom stroked Sugar, Lord Atherly's Hanoverian, over and over as the horse snorted and neighed nervously. Aunt Rachel huddled on the seat under a thick woolen blanket the police had provided and stared into her lap. Stella shook her head.

What good would that do? No matter where she was, in the carriage, on the bank, with her eyes open or closed, she'd still see Lord Fairbrother's face, the minnow darting out of his open mouth, his eyes staring unblinking up at her as if he was as surprised as she was. She shivered again.

The policeman nodded his understanding before stepping over to where the constable had laid out the body and squatting down to inspect it.

Lyndy, who had been pacing the bank like a tiger in a menagerie, stopped to wrap his arm around her. "You do need to get into drier clothes."

"Not yet," was all she could say, staring at Lord Fairbrother's feet. One boot had fallen off, and a small tear in his black silk hose revealed a patch of bluish-tinted skin.

What happened? Was it an accident? Or something more sinister? And when? Only yesterday the lord was basking in the glow of his Cecil Challenge Cup win. Then Harvey threatened him. When she'd found the body, her first thought was of the snake-catcher. She couldn't fathom why. Was it the way Lord Fairbrother's hair had waved among the roots that made her think of snakes? Or was it finding Harvey's empty burlap sack laying on top of a bush when they'd first arrived at the river this morning? With Harvey nowhere around, she'd tucked it under the seat in the carriage. No, she couldn't leave yet. Not until she knew if Lord Fairbrother had been murdered and if Harvey had something to do with it.

"Are you up to answering some questions then, Miss Kendrick?" Inspector Brown asked, his gruff voice almost at a whisper when he approached them again. Lyndy opened his mouth to protest.

"Yes, Inspector, you know I'll help any way I can," she said.

"Lord Lyndhurst?" Inspector Brown asked.

Lyndy hesitated, searching her face for his answer. She struggled to smile, but her efforts were feeble and exhausting. He acquiesced and nodded. "But let's get this over as quickly as possible, shall we?"

Inspector Brown waved his fingers to his constable when Waterman had finished stripping off the rubber pants. The constable, still in stocking feet, pulled a notebook and pencil from his uniform jacket pocket.

"Which of you found the body?" Inspector Brown asked.

"I did," Stella said. "It's horrible, I know, that we left him there. But we thought . . . just in case it wasn't an accident." She rested her hand at the base of her throat, struggling to swallow. "Like last time."

Inspector Brown nodded appreciatively. "No, you did right. Now, what time did this happen?"

Stella looked out at the horizon and took a deep breath. "A little after sunrise." It had been so beautiful, so peaceful. She shuddered knowing Lord Fairbrother had been trapped under the water all along.

"We sent the groom to alert you the moment we found the poor chap," Lyndy added.

Stella could barely remember the interval between Leonard's departure and his return with the police. How long had it been, ten minutes, twenty minutes, an hour? She had no idea. She'd sat on the bank, hugging her knees and staring into the water. Lyndy had alternatively sat beside her and paced. They'd barely spoken.

"We just saw Fairbrother yesterday at the fete." Disbelief clouded Lyndy's voice, echoing Stella's thoughts.

"I wasn't there myself, but Waterman here was," Brown said, glancing at his constable sitting on the ground putting on his shoes. "The lord won the Cecil Challenge Cup again, apparently."

"Didn't do him much good, did it?" Lyndy said, without a trace of sarcasm.

"No, I'm afraid not. Did you see Lord Fairbrother out on the heath this morning? Or anyone else, for that matter?"

Stella shook her head and said nothing about Harvey. Why should she? Just because his sack was there didn't mean he'd been here this morning. It could've laid there for days. At least that's what she told herself.

"No, it was still a bit dark when we donned our wading gear," Lyndy said.

"We? I'd assumed . . ." The policeman stammered.

"That I'd found the body from the bank?" Stella saw in the inspector's eyes that that's precisely what he'd assumed. "No, I was in the river. Lord Lyndhurst is teaching me to

98

fly-fish."

"Good for you, Miss Kendrick," Inspector Brown said as if a woman learning to fly-fish wasn't any more unusual than rain on a summer's day. He tipped his hat. "Thank you, Miss Kendrick, Lord Lyndhurst. You've been most helpful. Of course, I may have to speak to you again."

"Of course, Inspector," Lyndy said, ushering Stella gently toward the carriage. "We understand."

"But —" Stella sputtered.

"We need to get you warm and dry. You need to get a cup of tea in you." Lyndy meant well, but she hadn't asked any of her questions yet. She twisted in his embrace to face the policeman again.

"But what happened to him, Inspector?" She'd avoided asking but couldn't stand it any longer. She had to know. "Did he drown, or was he murdered?"

Lyndy halted midstride, impatience etched across his brow. Was he overly anxious to get her safe and dry, or was he too eager to learn what the policeman had to say? Perhaps a bit of both.

"Heavens to Betsy, girlie," Aunt Rachel called from the carriage. "Murder? Why are you crying cyclone just because the wash on the line is flapping? The man fell in and drowned, is all."

Aunt Rachel had been at the fair. Didn't she remember the threats? First, Mr. Parley, and then Harvey. Killing someone over the results of a breed competition did seem far-fetched, but Harvey had accused Lord Fair-brother of burning his house down. The inspector hadn't been there, but his constable must've told him.

Inspector Brown hesitated as if he loathed having to say it out loud. "It's too soon to be certain, but . . ."

"But you suspect foul play," Lyndy said. It wasn't a question.

Brown nodded. "Yes, I'm afraid, I do."

With Constable Waterman taking notes over the body, Brown surveyed the scene. Finally.

Miss Kendrick had refused to leave, wanting, for her own unspoken reasons, to accompany him to Outwick House. Not that Brown minded; he wasn't relishing the task. Having Miss Kendrick there might soften the blow when he informed Lady Philippa of her husband's death. Besides, Brown had thrown away any semblance of standard protocol when these two aided him with his last murder case. They'd caught the killer, hadn't they? What was the harm in involving them again?

But the American lady stood there shivering, cold river water dripping from her hair and clothes. So, Brown struck a deal: Miss Kendrick would go home, change into dry clothes, have a spot of tea and a bit of toast, and when he finished up here, Brown would meet her and Lord Lyndhurst outside Outwick House. They would inform the widow of her husband's death together. Miss Kendrick had readily agreed — she was a quick lass — leaving Brown to examine the banks and nearby area without distraction.

He started next to the overhanging willow, where Miss Kendrick had found the body. Its lowest leaves floated on the water. There was no obvious point of entry, no treads in the bank where the man was dragged in, no broken branches as his body fell. Waterman, when he'd entered the water and retrieved the body, had been careful to preserve this stretch of bank. But to no avail. Nothing here indicated this is where the man went in.

Brown ambled upstream along the bank. He found nothing, no tracks, no traces of anything until he came to the site where the fishing party had laid out their blanket and gear. Had they disturbed something pertinent to the case? He couldn't tell. He continued walking. The splash of unseen frogs, leaping into the water, marked his advance as he followed the distinctive curve in the bank known as Blackwater Bend. Eventually Brown came to a towering oak tree, the grass around and near the base trampled and worn. Could this be a favorite watering spot for the ponies? Perhaps, but it was also the preferred spot for someone to rest and smoke. Brown knelt and picked up the nub of a cigarette. It still smelled strongly of Turkish tobacco. As Brown widened his inspection, he found two spent matches and several more cigarette nubs, two flicked out onto the heath and four crushed into the riverbank soil. Brown preferred cigars himself. Some men puffed a pipe. The only cigarette smokers he knew were men who had brought back the habit from the Boer War.

Had Lord Fairbrother fought in South Africa? Had he taken up with cigarettes? Or could this be evidence of something more nefarious? Someone had stood here smoking for quite a bit. Had it been Lord Fairbrother or had someone been waiting for him?

Brown pocketed the cigarette nubs and marked the oak by tying his white handkerchief on the upper part of a root arching out over the bank. He continued with his search up the bank but found nothing more. He returned to the willow, where Constable Waterman stood guard over the body, and walked downstream, his eyes on the ground searching for drag marks, deep cuts in the bank, broken limbs, or anything that indicated where Lord Fairbrother entered the water. All he found was a tweed cap caught in the current beneath an undercut in the bank. Presuming it belonged to the deceased, Brown retrieved it, picked off bits of clinging algae, wrung it out, and shoved it in his jacket pocket.

Lord Fairbrother must've gone in near the oak.

When Brown returned, his constable was kneeling beside the body. The lord had dressed for walking: Wellingtons, tweed jacket, and pants. Brown had also found signs of a walking stick poking into the exposed soil near the oak but never found one. If Lord Fairbrother had used a walking stick, it was far downstream by now. Twigs and leaves intertwined with the lord's hair, his skin was bluish, and his fingers were puckered and wrinkled like dried fruit. But Brown, not being an expert on the effects of water on a dead body, couldn't guess how long the lord had been in the water. Brown would trace the lord's last steps and leave the rest to the medical examiner.

With no apparent injuries to the dead man's head or neck, all evidence pointed to accidental drowning. But Brown knew better. Bodies that drown don't float, at least not for several days, and this body had floated up in the constable's grasp. Lord Fairbrother was dead before he entered the water. Brown knelt opposite his constable as Waterman began turning out the man's pockets. A distasteful job but needs must. They found no cigarettes or means to light one, only a key in a trouser pocket. The lord's watch, an elaborately engraved silver piece, dangled at his side, still intact and attached to his pocket by the fob. Brown flipped it open. It was stuck at 11:03. He tapped on the watch crystal; the hands didn't move. Had it wound down on its own or stopped when it entered the water? Brown wished he knew. He set down the watch and reached into the man's waistcoat. Lodged in the inside pocket was a thick wad of paper. Limp and drenched as the envelope was, its contents were unmistakable. What wasn't obvious was why it was there in the first place.

"There must be over four hundred pounds there," his constable exclaimed, staring at the soggy stack of fifty-pound notes, almost four months' worth of the constable's wages.

"Right!" Brown leaned back on his heels. Now they were getting somewhere.

CHAPTER 8

"I don't understand why you want to be there."

Lyndy could certainly think of better ways to spend the rest of his day. Hadn't they had enough of murder? And this time, the death had nothing to do with them. They had no cause to be involved. It was strictly Philippa's concern. Besides, he didn't relish spending a moment more in that woman's company. But Stella was adamant about going, and he'd be damned if he let her do this alone.

"How can I explain it?" Stella said, sitting next to him behind the wheel of the Daimler, her pink driving veil fluttering about her face.

Lyndy had directed Leonard to drive them to Pilley Manor before returning the carriage to Morrington Hall, insisting the distressed groom take the rest of the morning off. Stella had dried off, changed, and had a bite to eat while he waited. Luckily Mr. Kendrick had been out. When they'd clamored into the motorcar, Lyndy could barely see Stella's shape, form, or face, bundled up in her duster coat, gloves, and veil, but her exquisite blue eyes had a glint to them again.

"Perhaps it's because I found him," she said, pressing down on the gas.

The motorcar bumped and tilted as they drove through ruts in the lane that cut across the open heath, the wind rushing in his ears, threatening to lift his cap from his head. Swaths of pink and purple heather interlaced with patches of feathery bracken and wide stretches of lush green grazing lawns spread out for miles on either side of them. And they were alone; Miss Luckett, the old chaperone, had retired to her room, too shaken by the morning's events to care what they did. If they weren't heading to Outwick House, Lyndy would be quite enjoying the ride.

"That doesn't make you responsible," Lyndy said.

Back at the Blackwater, Stella's comportment had troubled him. With her wet hair clinging to her pale face, she'd seemed numb, oblivious to him. While they'd waited for Leonard to fetch the police, she'd sat clutching her knees. He'd tried to chat with her, even recruiting the aid of Stella's Aunt Rachel. But Stella sat, unresponsive. Lyndy hated her silences. He'd rather she railed against him for dragging her to the river this morning or rattled on with a hundred questions than blankly staring at the stream. He'd turned to pacing. But luckily, she seemed herself again — insisting they do something unprecedented.

"To me, it does. Besides . . ." She hesitated. She frowned and looked around her, on the seat and then at the floor.

"Stella," Lyndy warned as she veered off toward a wooden mileage post at the crossroad. With multiple pointed signs jutting this way and that — to Burley, Sway, Boldre, Minstead, Beaulieu, Lyndhurst — the tall, thick post was a formidable obstacle. Quite likely if they hit it, they'd be walking the two miles it indicated toward Rosehurst.

"Eyes on the road, please." The Daimler swished its back end, like a fish in the water, as she righted them on the lane.

Stella bit her lip. "Sorry, I was just looking for something." She glanced down quickly again. "Oh, I forgot we brought the carriage to the river and not the car." She sounded relieved, but Lyndy frowned. How could she possibly forget that? He'd thought she'd recovered from her shock of finding Fairbrother. Was he wrong? Should she be driving at all?

Suddenly she jerked the wheel. The motorcar swerved hard, sending Lyndy crashing against the metal door. As they entered a side lane, the wheels kicked up a cloud of dust. Lyndy closed his mouth and adjusted his goggles. This was not the way to Outwick House.

"Whoa," he shouted, but he needn't have asked where they were heading. The chimneys of Morrington Hall were in sight. Had she changed her mind? "I think I need to learn to drive this contraption." He'd said it as an admonishment, but it wasn't a bad idea.

"Don't you appreciate my driving, Lord Lyndhurst?" she said mockingly. Her smirk was the closest to a smile he'd seen on her face since . . . far too long.

"It's much like breaking in a feral horse, Miss Kendrick," he said. "Dangerous yet necessary." She laughed. Music to his ears. "Why are we going to Morrington?"

"I need to get something." Her smile faded, all levity gone. They raced up the gravel drive, but she surprised him yet again. Would she ever stop doing that? He hoped not. She turned toward the stable, instead of circling up to the house. "I'll be back in a minute." With that, she opened the motorcar door, clamored out, and rushed into the stable.

Did she expect him to sit there and wait?

True to her word, she was racing back toward him before Lyndy could decide whether to follow or not. She held a small bundle against her chest. She tossed it into his lap, started up the car, and they were off again.

Lyndy unfurled the burlap cloth that smelled like an animal had died in it. It was a sack, like the one the snakecatcher threw at Lord Fairbrother. A smile tugged at Lyndy's lips as he relished the look on Philippa's face when she thought snakes were in the bag. But then he remembered where they were going.

"Why ever did you come back for this rancid thing?"

Taking a hand off the wheel, Stella snatched the sack from him and shoved it into the little drawer under the seat. A glance inside it revealed a clean pair of gloves, a hand mirror, a handkerchief, and a tin of chocolates.

"I don't want to lose it. I didn't tell you about it sooner because I didn't think it important at the time. But now . . ." What was she prattling on about? "That's another reason I want to be at Outwick House."

"But how does a potato sack have anything to do with Fairbrother's death?"

"It's Harvey Milkham's. I'm sure of it."

"And?"

"I found it at Blackwater Bend," she said slowly. "Near where we were fishing this morning."

No wonder she'd behaved so curiously, so distant. Is this what she'd been fretting about? Lyndy attempted to catch her eye, craning his neck to see around her veil and goggles, but to no avail. She was for once doing what she should — facing straight ahead watching the road.

"You suspect the snakecatcher killed Fair-brother?" he said, as they whisked past a scruffy old donkey grazing at the edge of the lane.

"No," she said, her hands tightening on the wheel. "I don't know."

As the motorcar careened down the lane, Lyndy and Stella sat in silence, the rumble of the speeding motor loud in Lyndy's ears. They passed a field dotted with grazing cattle, men in shirtsleeves working scythes, and bales of hay. On this day that promised to be unseasonably hot, the long winter the field hands were preparing for seemed far away. And then Outwick House came into view. Lyndy's lip curled at the sight. He'd almost rather be out in the fields with the men.

The rectangular, three-story, limestone building with two symmetrical chimneys and a marble-pillared portico was more reminiscent of a prison than a home. Tucked into a clearing in one of the ancient stands of trees, it felt isolated, cut off from the rest of the New Forest. Lyndy doubted the house's occupants could ever see the sun rise or set here. Once the country estate of the Marquess of Outershaw, it was a wedding present to Lady Philippa, the marquess's daughter, for her exclusive use.

How many times had Lyndy danced, dined, and suffered there? And yet here he was racing toward it. Why? Not due to any sense of loyalty to Philippa, or Fairbrother, for that matter. It wasn't proper to speak ill of the dead, but Lyndy never did take to the pompous ass. Then why? Lyndy pushed his goggles onto his forehead and studied Stella's exquisite face: the soft curve of her chin, the turned-up tip of her nose, the bow-shape of her lips he longed to kiss, the bright, inquisitive sparkle in her deep blue eyes.

Because I'd do almost anything for this amazing creature. Why Stella affected him like no other woman he'd ever met, he may never know.

Lyndy leaned in to kiss those lips he'd been admiring the moment the motorcar came to a halt. But he hesitated at the sound of footsteps crunching the gravel drive.

"Shall we?" Inspector Brown called, as the policeman approached Outwick House's front door.

Damn. Without hesitation, Stella swung open her door and clambered out, leaving Lyndy little choice but to follow. She slipped out of the duster coat, driving hat, and veil, and tossed them into the backseat. Lyndy offered his arm and was rewarded with a smile as she slipped her arm through his. Her fragrance, that heady mix of floral and woody tones, scented the little space between them. His heart pounded as they joined the policeman on the portico, frustrated by the policeman's interruption. He wasn't looking forward to being under Philippa's roof again either.

"My dear, Lyndy, this is a pleasant surprise," Philippa cooed after Hodgson announced them.

Philippa made them wait while she dressed. She'd donned the lacy, green day dress. Mother once commented on how it matched Philippa's eyes. As if Lyndy should care. The woman's cold, sly smile as she rose to welcome him hadn't changed in all the years he'd known her. Philippa wasn't fooling him. She wasn't happy to see him; she was happy he'd wanted to see her. This time she'd be wrong. Her cold, enchanting beauty, which had once derailed him, no longer had any effect.

Philippa indicated for him to sit on the plush, ivory sofa, the vines of the floral-patterned cushions threatening to entwine him. He stood his ground. The ever-present scent of gardenias, from the vase on the end table, permeated the room. Lyndy hated the smell of gardenias. Staring up at the geometric pattern of plasterwork on the vaulted ceiling, Lyndy pulled on his lapels. *How soon will this be over?*

"Ah, Miss Kendrick," Philippa said, with less enthusiasm, when her eyes settled on Stella. "I should've known you were behind this little visit. Men don't know such things." Philippa playfully swatted Lyndy's arm. "But you, Miss Kendrick, should know by now the proper time to call." Philippa smiled, but Stella's fingers tightened on his arm.

"Inspector Brown of the Hampshire Constabulary, my lady," Hodgson announced as the policeman stepped into the room. He slipped off his hat.

"What is going on? Lyndy?"

The confusion, the consternation on Philippa's face, was unsettling. Self-assuredness was Philippa's trademark. Lyndy should rejoice in her uneasiness. Instead, he felt nothing but pity: Stella's influence, no doubt. And as if reading his mind, his compassionate fiancée stepped away from him and took Philippa's hands in hers. But Philippa only stared at Lyndy, demanding an explanation with her eyes.

"I'm so sorry, Lady Philippa," Stella said gently. "We were fishing and . . . I found your husband —"

"Well, where is he?" Philippa said, yanking her hands free from Stella's. "Must you all look at me like that?" She brushed past Stella, knocking her in the shoulder as she passed, and glared up at Lyndy. "Lyndy. I demand you tell me what's happened."

His pity for Philippa vanished as he looked over her head at Stella. Hurt and tears welled in Stella's eyes. How dare Philippa demand anything from him.

"Fairbrother's dead," he said bluntly.

"What are you talking about?" Philippa demanded. She grabbed hold of his arms.

Lyndy stiffened but took no steps to remove her grip. She pinned him with her imploring eyes. "I know you can be cruel, Lyndy, but this lie is too much even for you."

Lyndy saw the alarm Philippa's accusation caused in Stella's wide eyes. He could only imagine what she was thinking. He wanted to rush to her and explain everything, but Philippa's nails were digging into his arms through his coat.

"I'm afraid, Lady Philippa," Inspector Brown said, "what Lord Lyndhurst says is true. Miss Kendrick and he discovered your husband's body in the Blackwater this morning."

Philippa opened her mouth to protest. Then her grip relaxed on Lyndy's arm, her body swayed haltingly, and her eyes fluttered. He'd forgotten how long her lashes were.

"What are you playing at?" Lyndy demanded, certain she wasn't undone by the message they'd brought; she hadn't loved Fairbrother in the least. Her theatrics were unbecoming.

Philippa squeaked in reply, staggered back on one foot, and collapsed. Only Lyndy's reflexes saved her from crumpling to the floor.

■ ■ ■ ■

Professor Gridley highly approved. Lord Atherly's study, a small enclave in the back of his large manor house, was a private haven with everything necessary close at hand: maps, notebooks, microscope, hand lenses, a bottle of cleaning vinegar, with only a hint of it in the air, and a clever desk lamp that they could raise or lower depending on the need. Lord Atherly had cleared the large desk, which dominated the room, of everything but a sheet of clean, heavy, white cotton canvas on which to lay the bones.

Click.

"Now, my good fellow, we are certain not to be disturbed," Lord Atherly said, with childish glee. "I've locked the door." Wasn't being the lord of the manor enough to guarantee a lack of interruption? Perhaps Lady Atherly was more intrusive than she appeared.

With three strides (it was a tight space), Lord Atherly was leaning over the desk, adjusting the lamp lower in anticipation. Gridley, taking his cue, bent down, flipped up the lid of his steamer trunk, and lifted out the first bone. To his satisfaction, the fragile metacarpal was perfectly intact. Gridley had had the good fortune of crossing paths with the brilliant Mr. Hatcher when both men were at Yale. Having revolutionized the method of collecting fossils, Professor Hatcher had instructed Gridley in his way of preserving the integrity of each field site and each find. No more tedious reconstruction of broken fragments in the laboratory, no more unexplained chips after a long, arduous journey. Lord Atherly's eyes widened as Gridley set the smooth leg bone on the desk. Hand lens at the ready, Lord Atherly immediately began inspecting the fossil.

"A *Miohippus,* you say?"

"I have no doubt," Gridley said, unwrapping the tiny phalanx bones and arranging them so Lord Atherly could see the skeleton's three-toed structure.

"But *Mesohippus* are three-toed as well," Lord Atherly said, gingerly lifting a phalanx to his hand lens.

"Yes. But wait." Lord Atherly's anticipation was palpable. Gridley continued unwrapping bone after bone until a partial skeleton of the extinct horse spread out across the entire surface of the desk. Lord Atherly inspected each bone in turn.

"No teeth?" he said, with a hint of irritation. "How can you say it is . . ." Lord Atherly stroked his chin as Gridley placed the decisive bone on the desk — the jaw. The extinct animal's entire array of molars and premolars was intact.

"You found an intact lower jawbone?" Lord Atherly stammered.

Gridley pushed up his spectacles and beamed. "I thought you'd be pleased."

Lord Atherly gingerly reached out to touch the bone. When he looked up from gazing at the fossil, Gridley couldn't read the thoughtful expression on the lord's face.

"Pleased? Gridley, you've uncovered more than I could've hoped for. Well done, Professor. This is one of the most significant finds to date."

Gridley nodded. He couldn't agree more. "As you no doubt noticed from the teeth, it is not only a *Miohippus* but an undescribed species of the genus. With your permission, I would very much like to present this to the Royal Geology Society next week when I present my paper on the Paleocene mammal fossils of the Fort Union Formation in Montana."

Presenting his paper to the RGS in London had been the primary purpose of Gridley's trip. His side visit to Morrington Hall was to be but a courtesy call. That changed the week before he was to leave New York. The telegrams reiterating his colleagues' concerns over the site he'd decided to excavate would've been enough to unnerve him. But then the letter came from Elijah Kendrick about Lord Atherly's inability to produce the funds he'd promised, throwing the future of the entire expedition in doubt. Gridley had booked an earlier passage and packed a second steam trunk, risking possible damage or, God forbid, loss of his most significant find. He'd hoped seeing fossils would impress upon the lord how necessary, and worthwhile, his continued patronage meant.

"I thought I'd name it *Miohippus atherli.*" From the look of astonishment on Lord Atherly's face, Gridley's gamble had worked.

"You would be doing me a great honor, Professor." Lord Atherly cradled the jawbone of the species to be named after him in his palms. He gently put it back on the desk.

"Should we discuss plans for another expedition, then?" Gridley said, eager to put to rest his concerns about Lord Atherly's financial commitment.

"Not quite yet, for there is something I would like to show you, Professor."

"My lord?"

Lord Atherly slid open a drawer in the desk, pulled out a small, blue, oval-shaped, velvet box, and opened it. Instead of a ring, a horse premolar protruded from the crease in the velvet. "A cheek tooth of what I believe belongs to *Equus spelaeus.*"

Gridley had come to Morrington Hall prepared to impress Lord Atherly. Suddenly, the boot was on the other foot. Gridley snatched up a hand lens and held the tooth beneath the light of the lamp.

"It would be the first example of its kind ever found in Britain. Have you told anyone?" If Clive Hale found out about this discovery, Gridley's rival would stop at nothing to get his hands on it. "Where did you uncover it?"

"In one of the barrows, not far from here." Gridley was skeptical. Could the ancient horses discovered near Bruniquel, France, have found their way onto the British Isles?

"When was this?"

"Years ago, when I lent a hand at excavating one of many Bronze Age burial grounds found throughout the Forest. I've been waiting to show someone who could verify my find. What do you think?"

"Based on one tooth, it's hard to tell. Is there any way we can go back and see what more we can find?" Gridley felt the familiar flutter of excitement in his stomach. Even if the tooth proved to be from a recently deceased pony, to excavate a Bronze Age barrow would be a unique experience.

"Of course. I shall arrange for us to go —"

Squeak, click, squeak, rattle, click. Someone was turning the doorknob and trying to get in.

"What in the world . . ." Professor Gridley muttered under his breath.

Lord Atherly held up a hand to silence him. The rattling continued as the intruder persisted in trying to get past the locked door. Eventually, they abandoned their attempt to get in. After several seconds of continued silence, Lord Atherly lowered his hand.

"You certainly employ persistent maids," Gridley said.

Lord Atherly, still wearing a concerned frown on his face, shook his head. "The maids know better." Gridley had wondered about the dirty teacup and overflowing wastebasket. "No one is permitted in here without express permission."

"Your wife, then?"

"She would've complained to me through the door."

"Miss Stella? You did invite her to join us."

"No, she and my son went fishing instead."

"Then, who?"

Lord Atherly stroked his chin. "I haven't the faintest idea."

"When we leave, you can lock this room from the outside, can't you?" he said. Lord Atherly shook his head. Gridley's stomach churned; his excitement had transformed into fear.

"I shall ring Fulton immediately," Lord Atherly said. "The fossils will be safe with the silver downstairs."

Will they? Gridley stared down at the precious jawbone on the desk. He'd thought his concerns for his fossils were over. Who would've thought they wouldn't be safe at Morrington Hall? But then again, hadn't someone been killed in this house a couple of months ago?

CHAPTER 9

"Must you do this now, Inspector?" Mr. Barlow demanded.

Stella cringed at his high-handed tone.

The plant hunter had arrived moments after Lyndy unceremoniously plopped Lady Philippa on the couch — Lyndy's second act of ungentlemanly behavior toward the lady in so many days. She'd revived from her stupor with miraculous speed. Now, the lady sat glaring at Lyndy, with the plant hunter's arm protectively around her shoulders, nearly crushing the fresh orchid in his lapel. She had yet to shed a tear.

"Can't you see Lady Philippa has had a shock?" Mr. Barlow insisted.

Was Lady Philippa in shock or had she allowed her understandable anger at Lyndy's rough treatment and Mr. Barlow's presumptuousness to supplant her grief? Stella couldn't tell. Nor could Stella fathom what had gotten into the two men.

Inspector Brown nodded. "Yes, needs must, I'm afraid."

"Then do it quickly and leave the poor lady in peace." Inspector Brown bristled at the command but said nothing.

"He is only doing his job, Mr. Barlow," Stella said. "He knows only too well how necessary it is to get all of the facts as soon as possible."

Stella glanced over at Lyndy. He leaned against the wall, his arms folded across his chest, and stared out the French windows at their automobile parked in the gravel drive. She didn't have to guess what he was thinking. She couldn't wait to jump in the car and get out of here either, since the atmosphere in the room was stifling. But she couldn't go, not yet. Not until she learned if the police suspected Harvey was involved. Happily, he'd cracked open the window to let some fresh air in.

"I agree with Cecil," Lady Philippa said, patting the plant hunter's hand. "Be quick about it so I can get on with things. I do have a funeral to arrange."

Stella was stunned by Lady Philippa's callousness. But she held back judgment. She'd learned long ago that everyone reacted to the news of a loved one's death differently.

"Of course, my lady," Inspector Brown

said, nodding to the constable standing unobtrusively near the door. The constable pulled out his notebook, flipped it open, and poised his pencil at the ready. "Would you mind telling me —"

"You say my husband drowned?" Lady Philippa interrupted. She'd taken a moment to smell the bouquet of gardenias on the table nearby. Stella couldn't understand why. Their scent pervaded the room.

"I said we found him in the Blackwater," the inspector corrected.

"How could that be? My husband was an excellent swimmer. We have a yacht moored near Lymington that he sailed quite often, and the pony show wasn't the only competition he won. He also placed first in the swimming race across the Solent three years running."

"That may be, Lady Philippa, but I suspect Lord Fairbrother died before he entered the water. The medical examiner will determine if I'm correct."

"Are you saying my husband was murdered?"

"No, my dear," Mr. Barlow said, squeezing her shoulder. "He could've had an accident, bumped his head or had his heart give out before he fell in."

If only Stella could believe it was an accident. From the expression on his face, Lyndy didn't believe it either. Neither did Lady Philippa. She was shaking her head.

"What Mr. Barlow says may be true," the inspector said, surprising Stella by giving credence to Mr. Barlow's speculation. "Why do you think someone killed him, Lady Philippa?"

"Do you know nothing?" Lady Philippa snapped. "Just yesterday, that vile snake-catching man threatened my husband at the fete. Threw a sack full of slimy fish at him."

There it was. The accusation Stella had been waiting to hear. She held her breath, wondering what the inspector would make of it.

"And why would he have occasion to do that, Lady Philippa?"

Lady Philippa, fuming, said nothing.

"The odd, old fellow blamed Lord Fairbrother for the destruction of his house, Inspector," Mr. Barlow offered.

"Thank you, Mr. Barlow," Inspector Brown said, with a hint of annoyance. He'd wanted Lady Philippa to answer the question. "I've read the report about the fire. The cause was blatant arson. Harvey Milkham was right. Someone did purposely burn down his hut and cared little who knew it."

"You think my poor dead husband had something to do with it?"

Lady Philippa dabbed her dry eyes with a handkerchief. It had an *L* embroidered on it in navy blue. How did Lady Philippa get one of Lyndy's handkerchiefs? Stella hadn't seen him offer the grieving widow one. Stella looked to Lyndy for an explanation, but he'd left his post at the window. He'd pulled out his watch and was now comparing the time on it to that of the clock on the mantel. Stella's heart started pounding. The tips of her ears burned as she remembered the way Lady Philippa had greeted Lyndy, the way she'd clung to him, demanded of him, called him cruel as if she knew him well, stared at him, even now, as if he were something to her, or had been once.

Had he been?

In all the time they'd spent together, Lyndy had never once mentioned Lady Philippa. Was Stella imagining things? With her father's recent betrayal so fresh in her mind, could she be letting her father's deception cloud her judgment? No. Stella hadn't imagined Lyndy's unusually rude behavior toward Lady Philippa, and the handkerchief was real enough. Something wasn't right. Stella had believed Lyndy was different from the others. She'd come to trust him.

She relied on him to help her tackle this strange predicament they'd found themselves in. Could she have been wrong? Were all men like her father, after all? Stella tried to brush aside her questions, and her fears, concentrating on Lord Fairbrother's death and Harvey's possible involvement, but seeing the handkerchief in Lady Philippa's hand made it impossible.

Lady Atherly had made no pretense of approving Stella and Lyndy's engagement. Lyndy's mother liked Lady Philippa. Perhaps she had preferred her to be Lyndy's future bride. Maybe Lady Philippa had wanted that too. There seemed no love lost between her and Lord Fairbrother. But what of Lyndy? Had he been courting Lady Philippa before circumstances forced him into a match with Stella? Had the relationship turned sour and hence the need to find another bride? Or had money been the only obstacle? Either way, why keep her ignorant of it? He'd told her about women in his past, mostly silly girls at balls his mother insisted he dance with. Why not Lady Philippa? Did he think so little of Stella's constitution? Did he think he was sparing her pain? Or was she a case of wishful thinking and he didn't tell her because he was still in love with Lady Philippa?

She had to ask him. She had to know. But with him standing across the room with his back to her, she couldn't even get his attention.

"Why else would Harvey accuse Lord Fairbrother of burning down his house, if he didn't think he did it?" Stella blurted, in response to Lady Philippa's question, her frustration, her fears seeping into her voice. *Harvey doesn't lie or hide behind false civility,* is what she wanted to say.

Lyndy snapped his watch closed and looked over at her. Stella avoided his gaze and watched in anticipation of Lady Philippa's reaction. Everyone else's gaze followed. Indignation flashed in Lady Philippa's eyes.

"How should I know?" Lady Philippa retorted.

Thump! Stella shuddered, and Lady Philippa twitched around in her seat as a bird smashed into the glass of the French window. Relief washed over Stella as she saw the blackbird soar away.

"Perhaps you know, Mr. Barlow?" the inspector said, drawing everyone's attention back from the window by not hiding his sarcasm.

"Me? Why would I know anything?" Mr. Barlow said.

"Quite," Inspector Brown said, seemingly satisfied, before shoving his hands in his jacket pockets and turning his gaze on Lyndy. "Lord Lyndhurst?" Lyndy shrugged before tugging on the collar of his shirt. He wasn't going to endure this much longer. And neither was Stella. She had to get out of here. "Miss Kendrick? Do you have anything more to tell me?"

Now was not the time to tell the inspector what she knew: about the burlap sack hidden in her glove compartment, George Parley's accusations of cheating, Harvey's hints of bribery. She would wait and speak to the policeman in private, away from Lady Philippa, away from this house.

"What would she know?" Lady Philippa mocked. "She's only been here a few months. What does she know about anything?" Stella bristled at the insult but held her tongue. For now.

"Do you recognize this, Lady Philippa?" Inspector Brown pulled out a tweed cap from his pocket. "Could this have belonged to your husband?"

Lady Philippa shrugged. "I can't be sure, but it looks like the one my husband was wearing last night."

The policeman nodded. "I confirmed it with your husband's valet. And what about this?" From his inside pocket, the inspector produced a thick, wet envelope. He peeled back the top flap. A stack of matted pound notes filled the inside. Stella hadn't seen that much money in one place since the Derby.

And see all the good that did.

"I say, it looks like money," Barlow offered. "A great deal of it."

Inspector Brown clamped his lips together. "My question is for Lady Philippa, if you don't mind, Mr. Barlow."

"But why? Why would you expect me to recognize it? I never carry the filthy stuff around with me. My husband dealt with all that."

"We found this on your husband when we pulled him from the river. Can you explain why he would be carrying such a large amount of money on him?"

"I have no idea," Lady Philippa said, without her usual rancor. "He'd only gone out for his nightly walk." Despite herself, Stella believed her. Lady Philippa seemed as puzzled as the rest of them were.

"Do you think the money has something to do with his murder?" Stella asked. As usual, the inspector refused to answer. Frustrated, Stella blurted, "But Harvey couldn't have gotten his hands on that kind of money."

"Who says that he did?" Inspector Brown asked. Stella pressed her hand to her forehead. Had she just made things worse for Harvey? Had she made things worse for herself? From Lyndy's frown and Lady Philippa's expectant glare, the answer was yes. "Is there something you want to tell me, Miss Kendrick?"

So much for waiting for a private word.

"Lady Atherly to see you, my lady," Hodgson announced. Lady Philippa's attention turned immediately toward her visitor. Stella sighed in relief. She'd never been so happy to see Lady Atherly. Then she caught the frown on Inspector Brown's face. He wasn't as pleased with the interruption.

"Oh, my dear Lady Philippa," Lady Atherly said as she swept into the room. "I know this is unexpected, but I just had to —" She stopped midsentence, noticing the somber faces in the crowded room. "Whatever is going on? What are you doing here, Lyndy?"

Lady Philippa let out a soft sob. Cecil Barlow tightened his grip around her shoulders.

"Mother, you may want to sit down."

Lady Philippa, dabbing her eyes with Lyndy's handkerchief again, nodded. Stella dug

133

her nails into the palms of her hands as Lady Atherly settled on the edge of the nearest chair.

"I'm sorry to inform you, Lady Atherly," Inspector Brown said, "but Lord Fairbrother is dead."

"Murdered by that snake man," Lady Philippa hissed.

"We have no evidence of that, Lady Philippa," Inspector Brown said.

"But you are here, are you not, Inspector?" Lady Atherly said. "Is that not reason enough, to suspect something untoward has happened?"

"We do believe he was murdered, yes, Lady Atherly, but as to who —"

Lady Atherly cut him off. "Lyndy, you didn't answer my question. What are you doing here? And, Miss Kendrick, where is your chaperone?"

A man was dead, Lyndy might be hiding a past relationship with his widow, and all Lady Atherly could think of was the whereabouts of Aunt Rachel? Would Stella ever understand this woman?

"Lord Fairbrother was found this morning in the Blackwater," Inspector Brown said. "Your son and Miss Kendrick found him."

Lady Atherly didn't gasp or clutch a fist

in her mouth or faint. Instead, she turned slowly to face Stella. "You found him?" she said, her words clipped and seething with accusation, as if Stella had killed Lord Fairbrother herself. "How is this even possible? What could you possibly have been doing there?"

"Lyndy is teaching me how to fish."

Lady Atherly blinked twice before raising her nose and turning away, dismissing Stella from her mind. "Don't fret, Philippa," Lady Atherly said tenderly. "You'll see. Everything will be right as rain." Stella had never heard the countess speak to anyone like that, not even her children. "Everything will be as it should be, especially if I have anything to do with it."

What did Lady Atherly mean by that? A man was dead. Nothing would ever be "as it should be" again. Would she soon say the same for her relationship with Lyndy too?

Lady Atherly rose from her chair and, without asking, strolled over and rang for the butler. "Until you have news that will soothe this poor, suffering soul, Inspector, I would leave Lady Philippa to her grief."

Inspector Brown hesitated before nodding. "I may have further questions, my lady," he said to Lady Philippa as Hodgson appeared in the door, "but they can wait."

"You may all go," Lady Atherly said, staring at Stella.

"With pleasure," Lyndy muttered as he bolted toward the door.

"I will stay and comfort my lady," Cecil Barlow said. Lady Philippa looked up into his eyes and gave him a weak smile.

"That's lovely of you, Mr. Barlow," Lady Philippa said. From Lady Atherly's expression, she didn't find anything lovely about it.

"Is there anything I can do, Lady Philippa?" Stella said, hoping to make up for the ill-will she felt toward this woman. Whoever she may or may not have been to Lyndy, she had just lost a husband.

Lady Philippa, lowering Lyndy's handkerchief, turned to face her and sneered. "Haven't you done enough?"

Before she said or did something she'd regret, Stella dug her nails into her palms, swiveled on her heels, and strode from the room, head held high.

CHAPTER 10

Lyndy took a deep breath of fresh air and struck out toward the motorcar. More than talk of the dead had been oppressive inside. He couldn't wait to see Outwick House disappear into the distance.

"Lyndy?" Stella caught up with him in the middle of the gravel drive. Creases of worry marred her porcelain brow. She reached out to touch him but thought better of it. He snatched her hand in his, irritated by her hesitation, or the cause of it. Her hand was icy cold.

"What is it?"

Why had he asked? He knew what Stella was going to say. How could he not? Only a blind man would've missed that handkerchief. Why had Philippa kept it? He couldn't even remember when he'd given it to her. Or could he be mistaken? Was it Philippa's cruel treatment that troubled Stella, and not the handkerchief? Or lingering sorrow for Fairbrother and the shock of finding him dead? He could only hope. He suddenly felt wretched.

"Are you still shaken by finding Fairbrother?" he said.

"No. Lyndy, I have to ask —"

"It is not what you think," Lyndy blurted. Why did he sound defensive? When had Lyndy ever felt the need to justify himself to anyone? Besides, he'd done nothing wrong. It was Philippa's fault. No, it was all Mother's fault for putting the idea in Philippa's head. "Let me explain."

"Please do," Stella said, a tremble in her voice.

Damn Philippa and that blasted handkerchief. They had done what finding a dead body had not — crushed this gentle spirit.

He pulled her to him, the lace on her dress collar tickling his neck. In their rush to escape Outwick House, Stella had forgotten, yet again, to don her hat. It dangled in one hand at her side. To avoid the questions and concern in her eyes, he gazed then, into her hair, spun around her head like a billowy brown turban, gleaming in the sunlight. He resisted the urge to pull out a strand and wrap its silkiness around his finger.

"You were saying?" she urged. But the

scent of coconut oil in her hair, mingled with her perfume, intoxicated him. Lyndy was suddenly in no hurry to talk about another woman, let alone Philippa.

"I was young and —"

"Eh-em. Hullo," a gruff voice called from behind them. They both started. Lyndy's head snapped up; Stella dropped her hat into the dust of the drive.

Inspector Brown strolled toward them from the direction of the lane. Hadn't he left a while ago? Stella quickly wiggled out of Lyndy's embrace, snatched her hat from the ground, and stepped a few feet back. She pinched her lips in frustration.

"Inspector," Lyndy said, "are you still here? Hadn't you left before us?"

"Quite. But we broke down in the lane a bit of a ways out." He pointed behind him, down the wooded lane that led from the Fairbrothers' estate. He swatted his hat against the dust on his trouser leg. "A crack in one of the spokes. My constable can ride old Matilda back, but I didn't fancy having her carry us both."

"I bet you didn't," Lyndy said, imagining the scene. Poor old Matilda, indeed.

"Speaking of horses, how is your Tully, Miss Kendrick?" Inspector Brown knew of the thoroughbred's misfortune? The policeman was more informed than Lyndy assumed. He'd be wise to remember that.

"Thank you for asking, Inspector." Stella's face brightened at the mention of her beloved horse. "Tully is doing much better. She should be up and ready to ride in a day or two."

"All thanks to Harvey Milkham, I hear," the inspector said. Stella's shoulders slumped again. Her enthusiasm for her horse's recovery was instantly replaced by her apprehension regarding the snakecatcher.

"Yes, Harvey was a godsend."

Stella hesitated as if she was going to say more, perhaps about Harvey's sack that she'd found? The inspector, with brows raised, waited in anticipation. Had he mentioned the incident with Tully, hoping to spur a discussion about the snakecatcher? Because he suspected Harvey in Fairbrother's death, as Stella predicted he might? If so, the inspector was shrewder than Lyndy assumed as well.

"Right!" Inspector Brown said when Stella refrained from saying more. "I wondered, Miss Kendrick, if you'd be willing to let me ride back with you to Morrington Hall. I can telephone the station for someone to fetch me from there. That is where you're headed, isn't it?"

"Of course, Inspector," Stella said, with feigned enthusiasm. "Anything to help."

She shrugged at Lyndy, a troubled half smile on her lips, before turning toward the motorcar. He appreciated her disappointment. Their conversation about Philippa would have to wait. So why was he so relieved?

When they arrived at Morrington Hall, the family dogcart, laden with tarps, folding chairs, a large picnic basket, and several tin pails, was parked in the drive. Stella peeked inside. Stuffed into the tin pails were all sorts of odd tools: wooden picks, shovels, brushes, trowels, pencils, string, metal files, a tape measure, nails, and a frame of metal mesh. They clanked and clattered as the footman pushed in more pails. Clucking like old hens, Professor Gridley and Lord Atherly anxiously directed the footman's progress in packing it all. Stella couldn't help but smile.

"What's all this, then, Papa?" Lyndy asked after Inspector Brown stepped inside to use the telephone.

"We're off to Furzy Barrow," Lord Atherly said excitedly. "Care to join us?"

"It would be an excellent distraction,

Stella," Lyndy was quick to say.

"I don't think I'm up to it," she said, casting him a meaningful look. "It's already been an eventful morning." Besides, they hadn't finished their conversation. Lyndy had all but admitted she'd been right; Lady Philippa had meant something to him. She had to know the whole truth.

"Yes, we've only just heard." Lord Atherly frowned. "Pity." Then his face brightened, his somber tone gone. "But I think Lyndy's right. It's best to get on with things."

Professor Gridley nodded eagerly in agreement. "Lord Atherly explained your keen interest in our work, Miss Stella," the professor said. Dropping his voice to a conspiratorial whisper, he added, "You'll be excited to know that His Lordship has possibly found the first evidence of *Equus spelaeus* in all of the British Isles."

Stella had no idea what *Equus spelaeus* was but, given the contents of the dogcart, she couldn't deny her curiosity to find out. Nor could she deny that Lord Atherly and Professor Gridley's enthusiasm was infectious. She found the older gentlemen refreshing compared to Lady Philippa and Lady Atherly. And Lyndy was right. After *all* the morning's deeply unsettling events, not just finding Lord Fairbrother, Stella definitely needed a more pleasant diversion.

Perhaps Lyndy could explain some things on the way.

"Will you be back for dinner?" Lyndy asked as she alighted from the larger family carriage. The dogcart would follow.

"I expect so," Lord Atherly said, "but tell your mother not to wait if we're not back by the gong."

"You're not coming with us?" she asked him, hurt that he'd contrived to distract her and avoid his long-overdue explanation.

Lyndy raised an eyebrow in surprise. "Me? No. I've seen enough barrows to last a lifetime."

"It's true the Forest is full of them," Lord Atherly said, as he climbed into the carriage, "ancient, Bronze Age burial sites is what they are, but only a few have been properly excavated. One never knows what one will find."

"Hopefully more *Equus spelaeus* fossils, Lord Atherly, more evidence of *Equus spelaeus,*" Professor Gridley said, rubbing his hands together. He sprang in beside Stella, his energy belying his age, rocking the carriage as he did.

"But, Lyndy —" Stella started to protest, her displeasure blatantly apparent. Lyndy reached up, laying his hand on her knee.

"We'll talk when you get back. I'll answer all your questions, tell you everything you want to know." With his expression unreadable, Stella studied his eyes. She liked what she saw. It was enough for now. She nodded. He patted her knee before stepping back. "Enjoy yourself," he called as the horses pulled forward and clomped down the drive.

"I've never been to an archaeological excavation before," Stella admitted to the professor, feeling her excitement rise the moment the carriage turned off the lane and rumbled out into the open heath. Stella had seen stunning stereoviews of the ruins of the Cliff Dwellers of Mesa Verde, in Colorado. But she'd never been exposed to anything so ancient as the Bronze Age.

"Don't you worry, Miss Stella," the paleontologist said, "once you get your hands dirty, you'll forget all about your morning's upsets."

"Quite right, Professor," Lord Atherly concurred. Stella looked over her shoulder to see the spires of Morrington Hall disappear behind the trees.

She certainly hoped so.

But when they arrived, Stella was disappointed. What had she expected? Furzy Barrow was nothing like the dramatic cliff dwellings of Colorado or even like the humble pioneer graveyards in Kentucky. There wasn't a single carving or engraved stone in sight. No, their destination was a grassy mound, much like an upside-down punch bowl, almost indistinguishable from the open heathland surrounding it. Only the sunken ditch and parallel earthen bank that surrounded the barrow marked it as peculiar. Then they rounded to the other side of the site. There Stella could see where the earth had been carefully scooped away from a large section of the mound. Rectangular areas of more deeply dug earth dotted the inside. Stella rose to her feet.

Maybe this was going to be fun, after all.

Stella didn't know who alighted from the carriage more quickly, her or the professor. Lord Atherly chuckled, pleased to have such enthusiastic company.

"Mind yourselves now," Lord Atherly said, as he led them in. They traversed a long wooden plank, laid across the "ring ditch," as Stella learned the sunken earth around the barrow was called, so not to trample it. But inside, animal tracks of pony, cattle, and deer crisscrossed the barrow's earthen floor.

So much for being careful.

"What happened here?" Professor Gridley

145

said, pointing to the tracks. "Wasn't this site protected from being run over by animals?"

"I'm not one to speak ill of the dead," Lord Atherly said, "but several of us petitioned the Verderers' Court to erect a fence, on multiple occasions. Lord Fairbrother always voted against us."

"Why would he do such a thing?" Professor Gridley said, smoothing away several tracks with his boot.

"The landowner was always against it," Lord Atherly said.

"Whose land is this?" Stella asked.

"It belongs to a fellow called Parley."

"George Parley?" Stella said. "The man who accused Lord Fairbrother of cheating at the Cecil Pony Challenge yesterday?"

"One and the same," Lord Atherly said.

But why would Lord Fairbrother do any favors for George Parley? From their interaction yesterday, the two men weren't on friendly terms.

"Shall we proceed?" Lord Atherly said. Professor Gridley and Stella readily agreed. "Over here, Professor. This is where I found the *Equus* fossil." Lord Atherly crouched down, studying a patch of the barrow's earthen wall. Professor Gridley bounded to his side.

Stella, a small wooden shovel in hand,

146

picked a spot on the other side of the barrow and started digging. The smell of the newly disturbed soil surrounded her. The hard impact of each jab of the trowel soothed her frustrations. Within minutes, she had forgotten all about Lord Fairbrother and George Parley and Lyndy and was kneeling on her skirt in the dirt, bent over what looked like the rim of an ancient clay bowl buried in the ground.

"I think I've found something."

"You're a natural, Miss Stella," Professor Gridley said, as the two men joined her. He leaned over the place where she'd been digging. He handed her a trowel. Stella stabbed into the ground and began scooping away the dirt until she'd revealed the full depth of the bowl. With Stella on one side and the professor on the other, they slowly lifted the rough bowl out of its hole. But it wasn't a bowl after all; it was conical and two feet deep, like a large clay flowerpot with a spotted pattern decorating the upper third.

"It's amazing," Stella said, studying the ancient artifact up close.

Professor Gridley laughed at Stella's wide-eyed wonder. "Ah, who doesn't remember their first find, eh, Lord Atherly?" Stella had only known the Earl of Atherly a couple of months but was already well acquainted with the story surrounding his first fossil find and how it propelled him toward an obsession that almost bankrupted his family. "Maybe Miss Stella will be the next Gertrude Bell or Harriet Boyd Hawes."

Lord Atherly scoffed. "I pray not, Professor. What would Lady Atherly say?"

Lady Atherly, indeed. She already disapproved of Stella for being an American. Stella couldn't imagine what the countess would do if Stella took up archaeology.

"But I must admit, Miss Kendrick, you've certainly found an impressive example of a Bronze Age cinerary urn your first time out," Lord Atherly said. "Well done, I say."

"What is a cinerary urn?"

"It is the vessel in which the ancient people buried the ashes of their dead." Stella gasped and let go of her side of the urn.

"Whoa," Professor Gridley said, the clay pot suddenly slipping from his grip. Lord Atherly lunged forward and caught the urn before it smashed to the ground.

"I'm so sorry." Stella's hands were shaking.

That urn had remained intact for thousands of years. The ashes inside had rested in peace for thousands of years. And she'd almost scattered it. Stella sat back on her heels and tossed the trowel into the dirt.

"Now, now. Chin up," Lord Atherly said as he moved the urn to the other side of the barrow.

"Perhaps I'm not a natural, after all."

Professor Gridley kindly patted her on the back. "Or maybe you've just had enough of dead bodies for one day."

Self-consciously she laughed as she brushed away a tear with the back of her soiled hand. "Yes, Professor. I think that might be it."

Brown hated this room. But not for the obvious reasons. Yes, the smell of formaldehyde was an acquired odor, the whitewashed walls and ceiling illuminated by a row of lamps hanging low and bright were stark, and the dead body on the table in the middle of it all was not the company Brown preferred to keep. And he could've done without stepping into a spilled puddle of carbolic; now he'd need a new pair of shoes. But no, Brown hated being in this room because a citizen under his jurisdiction, under his "so-called" protection, had met a violent, heinous end. Could he have prevented it? If it was the result of a crime, would he solve it? Would Brown bring closure to the victim's loved ones? Or would this be the case that made him want to walk away from it all? Brown shivered. He should've brought his overcoat. He'd forgotten how cold this room was.

"Ready?" the medical examiner asked.

Dr. Lipscombe stood opposite Brown as they conferred over Lord Fairbrother's prone body on the examination table. Brown nodded. He'd worked with Dr. Lipscombe since the good doctor arrived in Lyndhurst eight years ago. And from his conciliatory tone, Brown knew he was about to convey bad news. With white hair and mustache and wearing a white coat, the doctor hovered over the body like a ghost.

"I have done a thorough external examination and have aspirated water from the victim's stomach and lungs."

"I was wrong, then? He drowned?"

"I didn't say that."

"So, he was dead before he went into the water?"

"I didn't say that, either."

Brown was right; it was troubling news. "Then what are you saying, Doctor?"

In response, Dr. Lipscombe gently lifted the white sheet that covered Fairbrother's head and pulled it just below the lord's ribs. A slit-like wound, to the right of his sternum, stood out against his otherwise unblemished chest.

"I'm saying, Inspector, that our victim was stabbed, and was quite possibly unconscious before he went into the water. Hence the presence of some fluid in his lungs and stomach."

"But the cause of death wasn't drowning?"

"No. There wasn't enough fluid in the victim's lungs to have killed him."

"Then he died of a stab wound?"

Dr. Lipscombe peered up at Brown, silently weighing his answer, before returning his focus to the body on the table. Brown wanted to thump the bald spot on the back of the doctor's head. Typically, Dr. Lipscombe was a congenial man. Why wouldn't he tell Brown what he needed to know so he could get out of this blasted room?

"In the absence of any evidence of antemortem injury or trauma, I should say so, yes."

"So, he could've been stabbed by a branch or a sharp stone while in the river?" Even as he asked, Brown knew the answer. But he had to be sure.

"No, absolutely not."

"Could he have otherwise survived the wound?"

Dr. Lipscombe shook his head. "No. The

weapon penetrated his lung and nicked the hepatic vein."

Brown closed his eyes to the white all around him — his eyes were starting to sting — and pinched the bridge of his nose. Why couldn't the doctor have told him this from the start?

"But, Dr. Lipscombe, we examined the riverbanks. We found cigarette butts but no sign of blood."

"We may find evidence of blood when I analyze the victim's clothes, despite their being submerged for hours. But I suspect most of it washed away when the victim fell or was pushed into the river."

It made sense. Hide the blood and the body in one swift push. It might even look like an accident, to the amateur eye, when or if the body resurfaced downstream. But luckily, Brown was no amateur. Just in case, he would go back to the river and look for traces of blood.

"And the suspected weapon?"

"I believe the wound was caused by a smooth, thin, doublesided blade such as a dagger or small, narrow sword."

Brown opened his eyes. The glaring starkness of the room made him regret it. "Is it your opinion, as the medical examiner, that the victim was stabbed deliberately?"

Dr. Lipscombe slowly pulled the sheet back over the dead lord's head. Brown's throat burned as he tried to swallow.

"That is what I'll be reporting to the coroner, yes."

"Right!" It was time to get out of this bloody room and catch himself a killer.

CHAPTER 11

A strong cup of coffee and something to eat.

That's what Professor Gridley recommended Stella retrieve from the picnic basket in the dogcart. Whether it was his concern for her welfare or for that of the barrow's ancient treasures, Stella didn't care. She was grateful for the suggestion; she needed a break.

Stella stood up too quickly. She started toward the dogcart, but she was still a bit dizzy when she reached the plank that bridged the ditch around the barrow. Misjudging the width of the board, Stella stepped off the edge and fell straight down into the sunken ring ditch.

"Ow!" Her hands met with soft, grassy earth as she caught herself, but a sharp rock jutted into her knee. She sat back, rubbed her knee, silently apologizing to Ethel, her maid, for the grass and dirt stains on her skirt, and waited for the world to settle.

"Miss Stella? Are you okay?"

"I'm fine, Professor," she called, thankful the men hadn't seen her clumsiness. *That's what you get for not eating anything but a piece of toast all day,* she chided herself.

She stood, slower this time, and brushed herself off. Not wanting to clamber back up onto the plank, she followed the circular path of the ring ditch around the barrow, loosening her sore knee. Almost halfway around, she spotted something hidden in the grass. She crouched down and picked it up. It was a dagger. The blade, plain but smooth and highly polished, sparkled as the late morning sun broke through the clouds. The copper-colored grip and pommel were intricately decorated with winged female figures and braided wire. Light to hold, it fit perfectly in her hand. It was stunning.

How could any of the excavators have missed this?

"Oi!"

Stella looked up at the shout. George Parley, with his horse cantering toward her, stood up in the stirrups, his legs as thick as tree trunks.

"What are you doing here?" He leaped off his chestnut Hanoverian, leaving the reins to fall to the ground, and stomped toward her. She stood to meet him. "Bloody hell," he cursed, holding up his hands and retreating.

Stella looked down. She was inadvertently pointing the dagger, clutched tightly in her fist, out before her. Directly at the oncoming George Parley. When had she done that? And why? She hastily dropped her hand, and the dagger, to her side.

"What are you doing, woman?"

"You will address my future daughter-in-law as Miss Kendrick if you don't mind, Mr. Parley," Lord Atherly said, appearing from inside the barrow. Professor Gridley's head poked up beside him. He was squinting in the sun.

"My apologies, Lord Atherly," George Parley said, bowing his head slightly. "I didn't see you there."

"So it would seem."

"I thought you were finished here, milord."

"As did I, Mr. Parley."

"But I wanted a crack at it before it was filled in again," Professor Gridley said.

"Find anything of interest?" Mr. Parley said, shifting his gaze from the men to Stella.

"Miss Stella found a fine urn earlier," Professor Gridley offered.

"I also found this." Stella held up the dagger, point down, for the professor and Lord Atherly to see. Immediately the two older men scrambled down to her side. "Did this, too, belong to the Bronze Age people?"

"It's marvelous," Professor Gridley said, as Stella placed it in his outstretched hands. He turned it over and over. "But I wouldn't have said Bronze Age. What do you say, Lord Atherly?" Professor Gridley handed the dagger to Lord Atherly.

"Medieval, I should think."

"Look at the gleam on that blade," Professor Gridley said. "I can't imagine how it hasn't tarnished. How on earth it got here must be some story." He handed it back to Stella.

"How it got on me land, you mean," George Parley said, wiping the back of his neck with a handkerchief. "I'll take that now, miss." He held out his hand. He scowled when Stella hesitated. "Miss." He shoved his outstretched palm closer, insistent. Stella gripped the hilt of the dagger tighter.

This man had threatened Lord Fairbrother in front of hundreds of people. Now Lord Fairbrother was dead. She wasn't giving him anything.

"No need for that, Miss Kendrick," Lord Atherly said. "You found it. You shall keep it. Good day to you, Mr. Parley." Stella loosened her grip; her knuckles ached.

"As you say, milord," George Parley said, his lip curling. He spun on his heels and stalked toward his grazing horse. "But mind that she's careful," he called over his shoulder. "I fear your daughter-in-law is bound to get hurt."

"If I didn't know better, that man just threatened us," Professor Gridley whispered, his astonishment plain on his face.

Stella shuddered as George Parley swung up into the saddle and rode off. She looked down at the dagger, clutched tightly again in her fist. She released her grip and switched hands.

"And look what happened to the last person he did that to," she said, rubbing the braided wire design of the dagger etched across her palm.

Creeaak.

Lyndy set down his cup of tea, put his feet up, and snapped the pink newspaper in place. *Let's see who's running in the Yorkshire Oaks next week.*

Creeaak.

Lyndy read down the names of the horses: Costly Lady, Queen of the Earth, Lord Derby's Verdiana, Lord Ellesmere's Koorhann, and Sotto Voce. All excellent horses. But Lyndy, having seen Cherry Lass win at Epsom, would have to put a hundred down on Colonel Walker's filly. *Now to the Gimcrack Stakes.*

Creeaak.

Lyndy sighed at the persistent creaking of the floorboards. Now, who could that be?

Mother, still consoling Philippa, had rung not long ago, asking Alice to join her at Outwick House. They weren't expected back until after tea. Stella, Papa, and Professor Gridley would be gone until dinner. Lyndy was glad for that. Better to have Stella's mind occupied by something besides the events of the morning. She would enjoy the barrow and Papa would adore her all the more for it. Her visit also gave Lyndy time to consider how to tell her about Philippa. He had Morrington to himself. Only the servants went about their business. *You would think they'd be quieter about it.* Lyndy snapped the pink racing sheet again.

Now, where was I?

Creeaak. Lyndy tossed the paper down in frustration and rang for Fulton.

"Fulton, the house is creaking," Lyndy explained to the butler when he arrived moments later. "Is there yet another new maid, one who feels the need to tiptoe about?"

"My lord?"

"How often am I alone in the house? I've been trying to enjoy this rare peace. But every time I try to concentrate on my racing paper, someone starts creeping about, causing the floorboards to creak."

Fulton, as stoic as a garden statue, tilted his head slightly. "I beg your pardon, my lord, but the staff have all been downstairs taking their morning tea."

"But someone has been about the house."

"Everyone is accounted for, my lord. Perhaps it's simply the natural sounds of the house?"

"I know what I heard, Fulton. I've lived my entire life in this drafty old manor, and I can assure you I've never heard such incessant creaking before."

"I'm sorry, my lord. Would you like me to —"

"Never mind, Fulton. You may go back to your tea."

"Thank you, my lord." The butler nodded, dismissed as he was, but not before Lyndy caught a slight wrinkle in the butler's brow.

He thinks I'm hearing things.

The moment the butler closed the door, Lyndy swung it open and strode into the grand saloon. He crossed the large hall to the staircase and stomped up the stairs. Not a single floorboard creaked until he deliberately ascended them slowly. Then, on the middle of the sixth step — *creeaak.*

Someone had been tiptoeing up the stairs. Lyndy didn't make the same mistake and dashed up the remaining steps, taking two at a time. From one end of the upstairs corridor to the other, Lyndy flung open doors — Mother's bedroom, her bathing room, Papa's bedroom, his dressing room, Lyndy's room, the east guest bedroom, the west guest bedroom. In this room, Stella's bedroom, or so he still called it, he hesitated. She'd stayed here when the Americans first arrived. Lyndy took a deep breath. Though faint, it still smelled like the Forest in the springtime. No manner of airing, dusting, or carpet sweeping could rid the room of Stella's heady perfume.

Would she choose this room again after they wed or select another? Or would Lyndy be able to convince her to share his bed? It was rare but not unheard of. Then he could wake to that scent every day. He'd first have to tell her about Philippa. He reluctantly closed the door.

Creeaak.

Lyndy whirled around to catch a glimpse of uncovered ginger hair bobbing down the

161

stairs. As far as he knew, Morrington didn't have any redheaded servants. But would he have noticed, if it did? Perhaps not. Whoever it was, they needed to be taught to step properly on that stair. Lyndy peered over the balustrade to the grand saloon below as the culprit crossed the expansive hall on tiptoe.

Miss Cosslett? What was she doing here?

Lyndy had yet to warm to the London journalist. She was like so many women he'd met in London, wanting something, be it platitudes, compliments, gifts, or in her case, information, without any intention of returning the favor. Besides, anyone who voluntarily kept company with the American buffoon, Mr. Kendrick, was questionable. And here she was lurking about Morrington without a "by-your-leave."

Lyndy stealthily descended the stairs, avoiding the creaking sixth, and watched as Miss Cosslett tiptoed from door to door, peering inside. His ire rose with every step. Why was she sneaking about his house like a thief? Why was he? When she disappeared out of sight down the hall, Lyndy sprinted lightly across the grand saloon, avoiding the creaking board outside the library, and followed her to Papa's study. He ducked into an unused sitting room and peered around the doorjamb.

What was she doing?

Papa's study was off-limits to women. Not even the housemaids were allowed in. The maintenance of the fires and any necessary cleaning were done by Papa's valet or Fulton. Only Stella — he often wondered how she managed it — was allowed in. But even Stella, "the American," as many still called her, knew to wait to be invited.

But the journalist wasn't letting concerns for the rules of common decency stop her. Instead, throwing furtive glances about her, she reached out for the doorknob. She twisted it and pushed. The door didn't open. She jiggled the knob and pulled. The door still wouldn't open. She yanked on the knob harder, back and forth, rattling the door, the wall, and the floor around it. The door still wouldn't give.

Now, why would that be? Papa restricted who could enter his study, but Lyndy had never heard of Papa locking it before.

The journalist crouched down and peered through the door. She slapped the door with her palm in frustration. She turned to look about her. An expression of consternation, of determination and anger marred her youthful face. From his hidden vantage point, he saw an ugliness that repelled him,

163

more than her disregard for his father's privacy. Much like Philippa.

Damn. Thoughts of Philippa reminded him again of his conversation with Stella. If only he'd been able to explain before the inspector interrupted them. If only Philippa hadn't kept his handkerchief. If only he hadn't assumed Stella would never find out.

But Lyndy knew better. He could've told Stella about Philippa long before a square embroidered piece of linen forced the issue. Why hadn't he? Did he presume Stella wouldn't care? Did he imagine he didn't owe her the truth? No, he merely assumed his relationship with Philippa, as with every other woman who had come before Stella, didn't matter. But would he be able to convince Stella of the truth? He must. Their future together depended on it. First, he had to deal with this.

"Miss Cosslett?" he said, his voice stern and unyielding. He stepped out into the hall.

"Oh!" Miss Cosslett declared, jolting upright and putting her hand to her chest. "My, Lord Lyndhurst, you startled me."

"What are you doing here?"

"I'm here to record the wedding gifts. You'd be surprised how moonstruck my readers become over descriptions of other people's wedding gifts."

"I am sure I would have no idea what your readers enjoy. Now, if you please." Lyndy held out his arm to indicate she head back down the hall.

"But the door is locked. I thought Lady Atherly would be here to meet me. I feel so embarrassed to admit that I may have come at the wrong time."

"Mother isn't here. She was called away . . . unexpectedly. Besides, the morning room, where Mother keeps the presents, is back that way."

"Oh, how silly of me. I must've gotten lost. This is such a grand home you have here. What is this room then, the earl's study?"

She wasn't fooling Lyndy. She'd peered through the keyhole. She knew very well it was. Why lie about it?

"After you," Lyndy said, still waiting for her to precede him back down the hall.

"Would you show me the way, my lord?" Miss Cosslett said, her voice syrupy, her eyes batting. "I wouldn't want to get lost again."

"I will do better than that," Lyndy said. "I'll escort you to the very door." Mistaking his intentions, she wrapped her hands around his arm.

"As I said, I was expecting to find Lady

Atherly at home, but I have to admit, I'm quite pleasantly surprised to find you instead."

"Lady Atherly knew you were coming?" Lyndy asked, escorting her down the hall, through the grand saloon, and unbeknownst to Miss Cosslett, past the morning room door.

"Of course. I wouldn't have presumed to come otherwise," the journalist said, smiling.

"Who let you in?"

The smile never left her face, but her eyes darted for a moment. She was thinking of what next to say. She batted her eyes and shrugged.

"You will think me presumptuous, my lord, but when I knocked, and no one answered, I let myself in."

At least she hadn't lied about that. Unfortunately, Lyndy wasn't surprised to hear no one was manning the door. Lyndy knew too well that the family's financial constraints had left Morrington understaffed for months. With the first footman off with Papa, and Lyndy alone in the house, why wouldn't Fulton and Harry, Lyndy's valet currently serving as second footman, take tea at the same time? Lyndy certainly wouldn't complain. The family's finances,

166

or lack thereof, had saved him from Philippa and brought him his American heiress. He'd trade a footman at the door for Stella in his arms any day.

"And here you are, Miss Cosslett," Lyndy said as they approached the front door. "The door."

"But I thought you were going to take me to the morning room." She flashed him a weak smile. "The wedding gifts, remember?"

Lyndy reached down and opened the heavy oak door, the ornately carved brass knob cold against his skin. Sunshine streaked across the parquet floor.

"But, my lord," Miss Cosslett said, as Lyndy shoved the journalist over the threshold.

"Good day, Miss Cosslett," Lyndy said cheerfully, before slamming the door in her face. The crash reverberated through the hall. Lyndy had never opened or closed the front door before. Quite satisfied with the result, he fancied he might do it again.

CHAPTER 12

Stella stared down at the dagger in her lap, as James, the footman, cleared away the remnants of their late afternoon picnic. She loved eating outdoors, and this picnic, with its welcomed informality and the extraordinary feast of ham, minced chicken or veal-loaf finger sandwiches, cold miniature pork pies, stewed fruit, cucumber slices, chunks of cheese, fruit turnovers, slices of pound cake, tea, and coffee, had been no exception. She'd enjoyed every moment. But now, with her hunger satisfied and her body relaxed, the events of the morning weighed on her mind.

"Back to it, I think," Professor Gridley said, rubbing his hands together. He stood, and the footman picked up his chair, folded it, and packed it back into the dogcart.

"I think I'll head home if you don't mind, Lord Atherly," Stella said.

"Of course, Miss Kendrick. The ruminations of two old men must be a bother to you."

"I'm surprised you lasted this long," Professor Gridley added, an approving grin on his face.

"Oh, it's just the opposite. You both are so interesting. I've learned so much today. And to think you may have found another part of an *Equus spelaeus* skeleton . . ." Stella had marveled at Professor Gridley dancing a jig when they'd found a tiny toe bone earlier. But then he'd explained the significance, and she'd danced with him. Lord Atherly had smiled indulgently at the two boisterous Americans but kept his feet still. "No, I hate to leave, but I was up early this morning and . . ."

She didn't have to say more. The men nodded understandingly.

"I am most sorry for what you had to endure back there," Lord Atherly said kindly, waving vaguely in the direction of the Blackwater. "I do hope my son was a comfort to you."

"Yes, Lord Atherly, he was."

Did it matter what Lyndy had to tell her about Philippa? Would it change the way she felt? When she closed her eyes and concentrated, she could still feel the strength of Lyndy's arm around her shoulders as they waited for Inspector Brown. They'd sat in silence, but his embrace said more than words ever could. She could've stayed in the warmth of his arms forever. Unless it had all been a lie. Stella shuddered.

"James can take you back in the carriage," Lord Atherly said. "Miss Kendrick?"

Stella's eyes popped open. "I think it best I walk. The brisk exercise will help clear my head." Stella stood and brushed herself off. She rummaged through the dogcart for a piece of the linen brought to protect the day's finds and wrapped up the dagger.

"Good day to you then, Miss Kendrick," Lord Atherly said. He'd been one of the first to accept Stella's independent ways. Unlike his wife, who didn't abide anything about Stella, yet.

"Here, take this." Professor Gridley handed her a canvas bag to put the dagger in. She looped it around her wrist. "And this." He retrieved an unusual walking stick from the carriage. Hand-carved, but highly polished, its handle was the head of a deer. "Made for me by a local tribesman in Oklahoma, it has helped keep me steady on countless treks across the plains."

"Thank you, Professor." Before she'd walked ten yards, the two men had returned to the barrow, their heads bent together in discussion.

Stella laughed. What a contrast between these two men and Daddy. In fact, most of the Englishmen Stella had met since arriving had been kinder to her, more respectful of her than her father. Even Lord Fairbrother had sought her opinion on his pony's chances of winning the Cecil Challenge Cup. This morning, Daddy hadn't asked how she was, where she was going, or why she was missing breakfast. All he wanted to know, as she left to go fishing, was whether she had something Miss Cosslett could wear to the engagement party.

She lifted the walking stick in her hand to study swirls in the wood, a knothole perhaps. Professor Gridley was kind to lend it to her. Why couldn't her father be more like that? An errant thought popped into her mind.

Please don't let Lyndy betray me as Daddy did.

Stella brushed away the terrible notion and struck out across the heath toward Pilley Manor. Within minutes, she was relishing the trek and her freedom. No Aunt Rachel, no Daddy, no Lady Atherly, no Lady Philippa, not even Lyndy was there to tell her what to do or where to go. She walked where her feet took her, the walking stick coming in handy for the unexpected dips and bogs in the terrain. She stopped when she wanted, to sample the sweet fragrance wafting up from the purple flowering heather or to admire the sudden appearance of a brightly colored green woodpecker. Only the absence of Tully threatened to dampen her spirits. As always, she'd rather be riding her horse.

In Tully's stead, Stella had the New Forest ponies to enjoy. Along her hike, Stella frequently came upon the free-ranging animals. When she did, she approached them only close enough to see if and how their tails had been cut. Tail markings, Stella had learned, were distinctive for each of the four corners of the Forest. Most of the ponies Stella encountered hadn't traveled far from home, but once she'd happened upon a mare and her foal that belonged to a commoner from far up north. She marveled at how the commoners could let their precious ponies graze as they may, in hopes they could find them again.

Standing alone on the vast heath, with billowy white clouds floating across the blue sky above, and strands of loose hairs tickling her face in the breeze, Stella felt like a New Forest pony. She relished the feeling.

Spying a donkey Lady Alice had named

Headley, Stella walked toward it until she caught the scent of smoke. Leaving the animal to graze in peace, she scuttled between clusters of gorse, careful to avoid snagging her skirt on the prickly spines, over a ridge thick with feathery green ferns, and through a line of trees, their leaves singed black. She stepped into a spongy moss-covered clearing beside a heaping mound of white ash and charred pieces of roughly hewn clapboards. All that was left of Harvey Milkham's home.

"Oh, Harvey," she said, spying metal bed springs that stuck up through the ash. After kicking away a pile of the partially burned pieces of wood with her boot, Stella knelt to retrieve a tin cup hiding beneath the ruins. It was covered in soot.

"Lassie?"

Stella, having thought she was alone, dropped the cup and jumped to her feet. "Who's there?"

Harvey's head poked out from behind an ancient oak, wide enough to hide him from passersby.

"What are you doing, Harvey?" Stella asked, wiping the soot from her hands on her skirt. "Why are you hiding?" Had he already heard about Lady Philippa's accusations against him? Stella pictured the sack she'd found. Did he have reason to hide?

"Are you alone, lass?" Stella nodded that she was, and Harvey slipped from behind the tree and approached what was once his home. His eyes were bloodshot, and he reeked of sweat and bourbon. Her father's Kentucky bourbon. "I'm sorry you have to see us like this."

"I'm sorry about your home, Harvey."

" 'Tisn't so much the hut. Me, I can build another. It's the loss of me rights, lass. Now, I've no rights to graze me old horse, to dig up peat for the winter, to collect wood from the Forest. That's what bothers me so. Now, I'll be having to grovel before that Lord Fairbrother every time to do a thing. Worse, he'll have someone else on this land before I can petition to build again."

"Harvey, haven't you heard?" Stella couldn't believe he didn't know.

"Heard what, lass?"

"Lord Fairbrother is dead."

The old snakecatcher squinted at her, the bushy hair on his eyebrows almost touching. "Say again?"

"He was found in the River Blackwater." Stella hesitated to say more, to acknowledge her part in the discovery. "At Blackwater Bend."

"Drowned?"

"The police don't think so. . . ." Again, she hesitated. How did she tell him that the police suspected murder and Lady Philippa thought Harvey did it?

"Then, how?"

"Harvey, I don't know how to say this. You've been so good to Tully and me, but . . ." But better it came from her than from anyone else. "But Lady Philippa thinks you killed him. She's told the police."

"Us?" Harvey staggered a little as he pointed his finger to his chest. "Kill that snake in the grass? Never."

"But you threatened him, Harvey. In front of lots of people. If the police determine Lord Fairbrother's death was murder, as they suspect, they're going to think you had something to do with it."

"Let them think what they want."

"But you were there, weren't you? I found one of your burlap sacks nearby. But don't worry, I hid it before anyone else saw it."

His eyes wide, Harvey pushed his hat up from his forehead and right off the back of his head. It fell to the ground. His hair, where his hat had been, lay matted against his scalp.

"You don't think . . . ?"

"No, I know you wouldn't flick off a spider crawling across your dinner plate,

175

but Lady Philippa . . . You should go talk to the police."

"And tell them what? That I left me bag behind because the trout weren't biting?" He bent to snatch up his hat but after three failed attempts to grab it, dismissed it with a wave of his hand.

"Is that what you were doing there, fishing for your dinner?"

"As I do every night."

"Did you see Lord Fairbrother? Did you see anyone else near the river last night?"

"The verderer sometimes, aye. But not last night." Maybe Lord Fairbrother was already dead. Or maybe Harvey left before Lord Fairbrother got there. Stella bent down, retrieved Harvey's hat, and handed it to him. It still smelled of wood smoke. "Nor anyone else."

"Have you been back there this morning?"

Harvey shook his head, lifting a small metal flask from his jacket pocket. "Had this for me dinner instead, and me breakfast." It broke her heart. If only she'd brought some of the picnic leftovers along. Harvey needed something that would stick to his ribs.

"You need to go to the police," Stella repeated. "Before they come looking for you."

"Let them look," he said, plopping his hat

back on. What did that mean?

Stella looked down at the burnt remains of his hut. "Where are you living now? Do you need someplace to stay?"

"Don't you be worrying about us. I found me a grand place to kip." He chuckled as if he'd told himself a joke. Before Stella could press him, he added, "How's that handsome mare of yours?"

"Tully is almost fully recovered, thanks to you."

"Then why are you out here on foot?"

"I was helping Lord Atherly and Professor Gridley excavate one of the barrows. It was so interesting, Harvey. Have you ever been?"

"Oh, aye. Even dug up me own urn once." Of course he had. He was a life-long resident of the New Forest, and his snake catching took him to every nook and cranny of it. "And now the vessel and its contents are the same," he said sadly, swaying unsteadily, staring into the remains of his home. "And Lord Atherly made you walk, from where?"

"Furzy Barrow." Stella turned and pointed back the way she'd come, appreciating the distance she'd traveled. "And you know me, Harvey. Lord Atherly didn't make me do anything. I wanted to walk. I thought it might clear my head after . . ."

Stella turned back to face Harvey again. But in the few moments her back was to him, the old man, drunk as he was, without a word of good-bye, had quietly snuck away.

CHAPTER 13

"And what time was this?"

Constable Waterman wobbled at the makeshift desk, an old, musty chopping block hauled in from the woodshed, as he sat across from the butler at Outwick House. Brown shifted his feet again as he leaned against the wall.

The dark, stifling cupboard, which was the only way to describe the tiny room off the boiler room, had been set aside for Brown's use during the investigation into Lord Fairbrother's murder. It had room enough for the chopping block and two small, rickety, wooden ladderback chairs, also hauled in from goodness knows where, and that was all. At least if he ever felt claustrophobic, it would take but three steps and Brown would be in the corridor. And it was as quiet as a tomb.

"That would be at ten o'clock," Hodgson said, sitting ramrod straight, as if he'd shoved the back of the chair inside his waist-coat.

Butlers were interchangeable to Brown: all full of selfimportance and righteousness, all determined to protect the image of the house and the family that lived therein. In Brown's experience, as keepers of their institutional secrets, butlers weren't much help in uncovering the truth. "Lord Fair-brother always took his nightly constitutional at ten o'clock."

"And who would know of this routine?" Constable Waterman said.

Hodgson thought a moment. "Anyone in the house. Anyone who knew Lord Fair-brother more than just in passing. Perhaps the farmers along the routes His Lordship favored?"

"And what routes did His Lordship favor?"

"That I wouldn't know," Hodgson said.

"I see. Did Lady Philippa ever accompany him on these walks?"

"No one accompanied him." Hodgson pinched his lips as if daring them to make him say anything else. Was he trying to protect Lady Philippa or telling the truth? Brown couldn't tell.

"Where was Lady Philippa last night?"

"Her Ladyship dined here, with Lord

Fairbrother and Mr. Barlow, and then retired to her room."

"And she stayed in her room?"

"I couldn't say, Constable," Hodgson said, the very idea of questioning Lady Philippa evident in his tone. "But I can tell you she gave strict instructions not to be disturbed until breakfast."

That wasn't the same as staying in her room, was it? Quite the opposite. Brown had hoped to tick Lady Philippa off his suspect's list. But now?

"She was quite devastated to learn of Lord Fairbrother's absence when her maid brought up her breakfast tray," the butler added.

Devastated? By a mere absence at breakfast? Irritated or concerned, perhaps, but devastated? Brown thought it unlikely. These "betters" of his were never devastated by anything short of a scandal. But then again, who could tell with this widow.

Brown had gone straight from Dr. Lipscombe's surgery to Outwick House. He'd found Lady Philippa draped in black, yes, but sipping tea and eating slices of sponge cake with Cecil Barlow, Lady Atherly, and the countess's daughter, Lady Alice. Hardly the devastated widow. Before Brown had a chance to tell her his news, that someone had stabbed her husband, she demanded the arrest of Harvey Milkham. Brown assured her, and the others who were keen to add their voices to that of the widow, that he would investigate all possible lines of inquiry, that he would find her husband's killer. But she was determined to throw the blame on the snakecatcher and would hear nothing of other possibilities.

Brown should've known better, to be asking Her Ladyship questions with her posh friends about. After seventeen years in the Hampshire Constabulary, he knew he was lucky to be in her drawing room at all. Still, he'd been taken aback, when, after he'd asked Lady Philippa for an account of her whereabouts last night, she'd snatched the thing closest to her, a crystal vase full of gardenias, and had thrown it at him.

Hence the dismal accommodations to conduct his interviews. But he wasn't to be deterred, not by a cramped cupboard, not by a petulant widow, not by a tight-lipped butler. Brown had a killer to catch.

"His Lordship had never before been absent in the morning?" Brown asked, loosening his collar a bit. God, it was hot in here.

"Never," Hodgson declared.

Then why hadn't Lady Philippa mentioned she knew her husband hadn't returned this morning? Another question to pose to the grieving widow. When she'd calmed down, of course.

"You mentioned Mr. Barlow. Where was he after dinner?" Constable Waterman asked.

"I saw Mr. Barlow in the smoking room. He'd rung and requested a glass of port before retiring himself."

"Does the name Harvey Milkham mean anything to you?" Brown asked.

"Of course. Mr. Milkham is the local snakecatcher." Brown studied Hodgson as he answered. The butler showed no sign of dissembling, no indication that he suspected why they'd mentioned Milkham's name. "The gardeners have hired him on numerous occasions when they found snakes on the estate."

"Has Harvey Milkham ever come into the house?" Constable Waterman asked.

"Why would he do that?"

Good question.

"Would he know of Lord Fairbrother's nightly walking ritual?" Brown asked.

"I don't see how he would," Hodgson answered slowly, wrinkling his brows together. The butler's suspicions were rising, but Brown had learned enough.

"Thank you, Mr. Hodgson. May we speak to the housekeeper, um . . ." Constable Waterman consulted the list Hodgson had provided of all the servants. It was considerably longer than what they'd encountered at Morrington Hall. Perhaps the rumors of the earl's financial troubles were true. "Mrs. White."

"Of course."

Hour after hour, Brown and Waterman, squeezed into that suffocating room, asked the same questions of servant after servant. With only slight deviations, all accounts pointed to the same as the one the butler told: Lord Fairbrother left the house for his nightly constitutional at ten o'clock, Lady Philippa retired directly after dinner, and Mr. Barlow enjoyed some solitude in the library until he too retired to bed. It all seemed straightforward. And it was getting them nowhere.

Mary, the scullery maid, flopped down on the chair across from Constable Waterman. Frizzy wisps of her curly brown hair stuck out from around her cap like a thin mane about her face. She rubbed her bulbous nose with her sleeve, leaving behind a smudge of ash on the tip. She'd begun talking the moment she'd stepped into the room. She couldn't have been more than fifteen years old.

"I know I'm not supposed to speak ill of me betters, let alone thems that is dead, but I dinna like milord, and I thinks you need to know about it."

Constable Waterman looked down at his notes, his face twitching as he struggled to stifle a laugh. Brown found nothing humorous in this pathetic creature. He'd wager, if he were a betting man, she was the first honest person to sit in that chair all day.

"And why didn't you like Lord Fairbrother, Mary?" Brown asked.

"One" — she held up a finger, wrinkled and red-raw — "he was cruel to milady." Waterman's head shot up as both policemen took note. This was the first Brown had heard of any such behavior. "And two —"

"How was he cruel to your mistress?" Brown asked before the maid could continue.

"Well, I'm not supposed to see or hear anything, am I? But I've got two working ears and eyes, don't I?"

"And those decent, hardworking eyes and ears saw and heard what?" Brown asked.

"My ears work harder than me eyes, seeing as I'm almost always bent over the fire grates, aren't I?"

"And those ears heard?" Brown knew when patience was the order of the day. He was instantly rewarded.

"They heard arguments, didn't they? And shouting and crying. Always me mistress crying. One time something smashed against the wall. When I came to clean it up, broken glass was everywhere." Brown could believe it. But who had done the throwing, he couldn't say. "I cut me finger, something awful. Got blood on me apron. Mrs. White took the cost of a new one out of me wages."

"What would they argue about?" Brown asked, steering the conversation back.

Mary shrugged, wiping her nose on her sleeve again. "What do I know of such things? I'm a good girl." What did she mean by that? Brown waited, but she seemed satisfied with her answer and said nothing more.

"You'll have to give us more than that, Mary," Constable Waterman said.

For the first time, the maid hesitated. "I've heard other names mentioned, but it's mostly Cecil they argue about."

"Cecil Barlow?" Brown demanded. He could imagine the presence of the charismatic plant hunter could strain any marriage.

"And something about being first," Mary added, ignoring Brown's question. "And milord mentioned his fancy pony, a lot."

Brown sighed. The maid overheard them quarreling about the Cecil Pony Challenge, not Cecil Barlow, then. But why would they be arguing about the pony breed competition? Brown wiped his forehead with a handkerchief. He'd have to get out of this room soon, or he'd melt.

"And they did this with you in the room?" Constable Waterman asked, incredulous.

To his credit, Brown's constable was an honest, fair-minded lad. He couldn't imagine how some of his betters treated the lowest in their households. Unfortunately, Brown knew all too well.

"I'm not really there, though, am I? Not to them. Most times, I'm in the next room or the hall. But I still can hear them, all right."

"I find it hard to believe you were the only witness to this, Mary," the constable said.

"Me, the only . . . Ha! No, if I knows about it, everyone knows about it." Her logic made sense, but not a single other servant had mentioned it. Why? Most likely, Mary was the only one brave enough, or more likely foolish enough, to reveal the family's secrets to the police. Brown vowed to protect the maid from retribution if possible.

"You mentioned a second reason for not liking Lord Fairbrother," Brown reminded the girl.

"That's right." She held up two fingers. "Two. I know I'm not supposed to repeat what I hear . . ." Brown didn't remind her she had done just that a moment ago. ". . . but milord burned down the poor snake-catcher's hut."

So, Harvey Milkham's accusations against Lord Fairbrother had reached the attentive ears of Outwick House's scullery maid, had they? Then the whole of the New Forest probably knew about the snakecatcher's threats.

"Why do you say that, Mary?" Brown asked. "Because you heard that Mr. Milkham accused your lord of doing so? Or because someone told you Lord Fairbrother did it?"

Mary shook her head vigorously, sending the frizz about her face waving. She swept the hair from her face with the back of her hand. "Because I heard them talking about it, didn't I?"

Brown was starting to lose his patience. Hearsay, from a scullery maid no less, only took his investigation so far. And it wouldn't help Harvey's case either, what with Lady Philippa calling for his head. He shifted his weight against the wall again; his shoulder blade was starting to ache.

"Who did you hear talking? One of the other servants?"

"No," she said, as if speaking to a child. She waved the two fingers she held up as a reminder of her number of grievances. "Lord Fairbrother. He was on the telephone, wasn't he? And he was the one doing all the talking."

In the rush of jubilation, Brown could've kissed the pitiful creature, but instead handed her a fresh handkerchief to wipe the ash off her nose. "Keep it, and thank you, Mary. You've been most helpful. Most helpful, indeed."

CHAPTER 14

"Lady Philippa is coping surprisingly well, Lyndy; you'll be pleased to know."

Mother smoothed her skirt across her lap. As usual, she'd chosen a drab-colored tea gown. This one happened to be the color of dried mud and as cheerless as Lyndy's mood. Mother and Alice had returned from Outwick House far sooner than Lyndy had expected, and after changing from their traveling clothes, had settled, not in the drawing room as was usual before tea, but into the library with him. Mother perched awkwardly on the edge of the leather club chair nearest to Lyndy, sitting snug in the corner of the Chesterfield sofa. Alice nestled into the opposite end. So much for peace and quiet.

"I don't care, and I didn't ask, Mother."

"I have to say, if something like that were to happen to me, I wouldn't be able to eat a bite. But not Lady Philippa. She has such courage, such strength, to continue on as she has."

"Jolly good for her."

Mother continued as if she didn't hear the sarcasm lacing his every word. "It may be inappropriate of me, but don't you think Lady Philippa looks quite becoming in black?"

Alice, flipping through her magazines, looked up. Lyndy craned his neck to see what she was reading about this time. A photograph of Cecil Barlow wearing a wide-brimmed, floppy hat and holding a tall, wooden stick, surrounded by towering trees lay open on her lap.

"No widow is becoming in black, Mummy," Alice said, frowning.

Lyndy picked up his racing paper. He hadn't finished reading it yet, thanks to Miss Cosslett's intrusion. Perhaps with no one paying her attention, Mother would stop singing Philippa's praises, or better yet, leave the room.

"Well, I think Lady Philippa could wear window drapery and look more appealing than most women look in silk evening gowns," Mother said.

"As Mr. Barlow looks dashing without a tie," Alice said. Mother grimaced. She obviously didn't agree. "Speaking of Mr. Barlow, have you seen my copy of *McClure's Magazine,* Mummy?" Alice began sorting through the stack of magazines on her lap. She didn't see Mother lift her eyes, appealing for strength from above. "I know it's got to be here somewhere." When she didn't find it, she plopped the magazines one by one on the floor.

"You should go to Lady Philippa and pay your respects, Lyndy," Mother continued, ignoring Alice's question. Lyndy turned the page on his paper and snapped it straight. "Lyndy, are you listening to me?"

"You seemed to have forgotten that Stella and I were there this morning."

"How could I forget? I don't know how Lady Philippa bore such a visit, Miss Kendrick bragging how she pulled Lord Fairbrother out of the river with her fishing line."

Lyndy slapped his paper down against his lap. "Stella wasn't bragging, Mother. She was trying to explain what happened."

"Well, I don't think I'd admit to doing such a heinous thing, especially not to the grieving widow." Mother raised her nose and puckered her lips, as if even talking about it was distasteful.

"Do you think Stella enjoyed her ghastly discovery?" he asked indignantly.

Mother shrugged. How dare Mother insinuate such a thing? Lyndy couldn't escape the feeling of Stella shivering, like a hare cornered by a hound, despite being wrapped in the carriage blanket, despite being enfolded in his embrace. "She was devastated by it."

"What was Miss Kendrick doing there in the first place?"

"Does it matter?" Lyndy tossed aside his racing paper, leaped from his seat, and strode to the nearest bookshelf. He pulled out the first title his hand touched, *A Popular Guide to the Geology of the Isle of Wight,* and opened it. He flipped through the pages, unseeing. It smelled of dried paper and dust.

He'd hoped that as she got to know Stella, Mother would come to, not love perhaps, but accept Stella. Approve of her for who she was, not just as "the American heiress" and all that implied. And for a time, Mother seemed to, at least, tolerate Stella.

Until today.

"I know I had it right here, with these others," Alice said, sifting through her pile of magazines again, oblivious to the tension in the room.

"Aren't the ones you have enough?" Lyndy asked.

His sister shook her head. "All of these have been published since Mr. Barlow's reappearance. The one that's missing is rare. It features the tale of Mr. Barlow's first plant-hunting expedition years ago. It only just arrived the other day from the bookseller in London."

"Oh, Alice," Mother sighed, shaking her head. "How can you concern yourself over a missing magazine when the fate of this family is at stake?"

"I haven't gotten an opportunity to read it yet," Alice insisted. "How can I be witty and interesting the next time we meet? How am I to impress him with my knowledge of his adventures? What if I were to win his heart? Wouldn't that, too, affect the fate of the family?"

"Alice, don't be absurd," Mother said. Alice, her cheeks burning from the sting of their mother's dismissal, hugged the magazines to her chest. Mother could be so cruel.

Lyndy snapped his book shut. "Do you know, Mother? That London reporter, Miss Cosslett, was here earlier."

"She was? Why?"

"She said she had your permission to view the wedding presents, to write about them for her newspaper."

"I said no such thing." Just as Lyndy

suspected, the journalist had lied and was snooping about. What was Miss Cosslett playing at? "You didn't answer my question, Lyndy," Mother said.

"What question?"

Alice again buried her head in her magazines. Lyndy shoved the book into its place on the shelf and strode over to the mantel. He picked up one of a pair of Chinese cloisonné vases decoratively bursting with large flowers of violet, blue, and red. Someone had given them to Papa as a gift. It was lighter than it looked.

"Why was Miss Kendrick in the river fishing? What kind of behavior is that? Next, she'll be lassoing ponies, like some heathen cowboy." Lyndy had to stifle a chuckle at the thought. Knowing Stella, she just might. "And I suppose the two of you were out there alone? I've warned you before about causing a scandal."

"Miss Luckett was with us the entire time, Mother, as was a groom."

"Well, still. I can't imagine a proper English lady, like Lady Philippa, for instance, would willingly traipse into water up to her knees."

"I'm teaching Stella to fish."

"My point exactly. Only a common woman would want you to teach her to fish."

"It was my idea."

"And a proper English lady would have scoffed at your ridiculous idea." Lyndy knew too well how proper English ladies acted. Hence his attraction to Stella. "Where is Miss Kendrick now, by the way?" If she didn't like the idea of Stella fishing, Lyndy couldn't imagine Mother's reaction to Stella joining Papa in digging in the barrow. "I should like to have a word or two with her about —"

"What is this about?" Lyndy set the vase down and faced his mother. "I thought we were past this."

"I've been having second thoughts."

"What?"

Mother stiffened her back, but her words rushed out, showing her exasperation. "In my estimation, Miss Kendrick has fallen far short of all expectations. She is simply not up to the task of being Lady Lyndhurst."

"How can you say that? Stella has done everything you've asked of her."

"As she should."

"Including dragging that poor old aunt of hers everywhere, be it a picnic on the Forest or an early morning fishing lesson." Much to Lyndy's chagrin, it was true. He relished the few moments they'd stolen to be alone.

"As I said, we don't want the slightest hint of scandal." Mother retrieved her book from the oak inlay side table: *The Life of Nelson.* From the position of the gold-plated bookmark, she was halfway through. She left it unopened in her lap.

"Scandal? At your insistence, Mother, Stella has accepted every invitation you thought worthy. She's planning an engagement dinner she's loath to attend. She has read every English history book you've handed her. She even sat through those ridiculous etiquette and elocution classes. And you know what happened? She knows more about this country than I do. She's charmed all of New Forest society. She's befriended everyone from the governess whom you hired to teach her to the local silversmith's daughter to the insufferable Branson-Hills."

"I can't help the girl's unfortunate habit of being familiar with servants and merchants' daughters. I had to insist she not invite Miss Snellgrove to the engagement party."

"My point, Mother, is that everyone from Bournemouth to Southampton thinks highly of her. Everyone but you, and Philippa."

"Lyndy's right, Mummy," Alice said, closing her magazine. An illustration of Cecil

Barlow's smiling face stared back at him. "Miss Kendrick has been trying very hard to live up to your expectations."

"As she should. If she's ever to deserve a place in this family."

"I would argue she has succeeded, Mummy," Alice said. Mother scoffed.

"Why do you criticize her at every turn?" Lyndy asked, sitting down again on the sofa and facing his Mother square on. "When her horse nearly died, you sent her a kind, sympathetic note. When she finds the body of a dead man, a man she knew, you have nothing but disdain to offer her. I want to know, Mother. What has changed?"

Mother stared across the room toward the mahogany display case, which housed Papa's bird collection. Which glasseyed, stuffed bird held her attention, Lyndy could only guess. Or was she avoiding looking Lyndy in the eye? "Lord Fairbrother is dead."

"Yes, we have established that fact."

"And after the requisite period of mourning, Lady Philippa will be free to marry again."

"As there are many fools about, I'm sure she will."

Mother finally met his stare. "Free to marry you, Lyndy."

Lyndy leaped to his feet. *"What?"* How

could his mother entertain such a notion?

"Whatever do you mean, Mummy?" Alice said, her face as pale as the linen and lace dress she wore.

"Don't you see, Alice, dear. With Lady Philippa free, he can marry her, instead of that brash American girl. After a respectable mourning period, of course," she added as if she were canceling a picnic on account of rain. Regrettable but necessary.

"I am to marry Stella, Mother."

"Only because you had to. But don't you see, Outwick House was a gift to Lady Philippa from her father, His Grace. And with no children to lay claims, Lady Philippa will now inherit enough from Lord Fairbrother's estate that we won't have to grovel to those American peasants anymore."

"Is this why you ambushed me in the library?"

"I certainly wouldn't call it that, Lyndy, but yes, I thought we might discuss —"

"There's nothing to discuss."

"But what about the contract with the Kendricks?" Alice asked. Lyndy glanced at his sister in surprise. How did Alice know of such things? But then again, his sister was almost marrying age herself. With his upcoming wedding over, she would be next. Lyndy pitied her, knowing Mother would make the match.

"Your father will find a way to break the engagement," Mother said. Lyndy doubted that. "And when he does, Lyndy will be able to marry Lady Philippa. Isn't that splendid?"

"I wouldn't marry Philippa, Mother, if she were the last woman in England."

Mother slapped her unopened book back onto the side table, rattling the empty teacup Lyndy had set there earlier. "Lyndy, you ungrateful child. You should be pleased."

"I already have a bride, Mother. One with plenty of money to satisfy even you."

Mother scoffed. "But not one with a pedigree like Lady Philippa. No, I've made up my mind. Your father had his way and look how that turned out. Now you will do as I tell you."

"Doesn't Lady Philippa have a say?" Alice asked, not knowing Philippa as Lyndy did. Philippa didn't do anything she didn't want to do.

"Of course, she does. We've already discussed it."

Lyndy, who had been pacing the length of the sofa, locked his knees and stopped. "You . . . what?" he stammered, imagining the two women, one in black crape, the other in drab brown, both wearing smug smiles as they hatched this devilish plan over the tinkling sound of porcelain teacups.

"I don't like to speak ill of the dead," Mother continued, "but Lord Fairbrother was not the best of husbands. When I suggested the arrangement, Lady Philippa was most amenable. She always did have an eye for you, Lyndy."

An eye? Philippa was a viper, willing to do anything to get her teeth into him. But this abominable plan was all Mother's doing. He hadn't thought her capable.

"It's unseemly, Mummy, and you of all people should realize that. Widowed for mere hours and already, Philippa is discussing future marriage plans?" Lyndy nodded vigorously in agreement.

"But don't you see," Mother sputtered indignantly, surprised to have both her children against her, "this is best for all of us."

"Listen to me carefully, Mother," Lyndy said, tensing every muscle in his body from his jaw to his fists to his knees. "No matter what you say, no matter what you do, no matter what plans you make, I'm going to marry Stella. Do you hear me? Not Philippa, Stella."

"But, Lyndy —" With his mother renewing her argument, he threw up his hand to stop her.

"Not another word." Then, releasing his pent-up frustration, he swiveled on his heels and rushed out of the room as fast as his dignity would allow.

CHAPTER 15

"Girl, is that you?" Daddy called.

Stella handed Tims, the butler at Pilley Manor, her walking stick as she stepped into the hall. "Yes, Daddy. I'm back."

"Come in here." Small clumps of mud flaked off Stella's boots as she followed the sound of her father's voice across the marble floor to the library.

Her father, in the oversized leather chair, his black and red smoking jacket tied around his considerable girth with a velvet belt, had a newspaper draped across his bulging middle. Miss Cosslett, seated primly across from him on the edge of a gilded armchair, held a notepad and pencil. She was wearing a very familiar blue tea gown with pink satin ribbon threaded through the Battenberg lace on the collar and down the sleeves. She smoothed the silk fabric across her lap and smiled sheepishly.

Is that my dress?

A dozen other newspapers were strewn about the carpet. Despite it being August, a small fire crackled in the grate. Like Stella, her father wasn't used to the damp. After her long walk across the heath, the warmth that caressed her wind-burnt cheeks almost made up for the coldness in his tone. Aunt Rachel, with a delicate white shawl of ice wool and silk wrapped around her shoulders and her chin drooping toward her chest, blissfully slept in a rocker by the fire.

"Where have you been?" Daddy said through teeth clutching a cigar.

"With Lord Atherly and Professor Gridley at one of the ancient barrows," Stella said, slipping the pin from her hat. Her white-lace-inlaid shirtwaist was clean, but her tan and pink skirt was creased and smudged with soil. What did she care? A benefit of living at Pilley Manor — no Lady Atherly there to judge her. Besides, Ethel was a wonder with stains.

Stella flung her hat onto the curving walnut molding on the back of the couch. She knew she should hang it on the hall tree or better yet, should've given it to Tims, but she didn't bother with formalities here. Unlike at Morrington Hall.

Pilley Manor almost felt like home.

In that, she and Daddy agreed. He liked

Pilley Manor so much that he jokingly, at least Stella hoped he was joking, offered to buy the mansion. Lord Atherly politely refused. The manor house was much smaller than Morrington Hall, with only four bedrooms, as many servants (Tims, a housekeeper, a cook, and Ethel), and a compact garden on the edge of the village of Rosehurst. But it had a spacious, airy dining room, this cozy library with its glass-faced book cabinets and expansive collection, and a drawing room happily absent of any daunting family portraits. With plenty of windows to let the sun in, light-colored walls, furniture, and drapery, and a large fireplace in every room, it was brighter, warmer, and more reminiscent of their home in Kentucky than Morrington Hall. Only the carriage house, too small for anything more than a buggy and a carriage horse, was lacking; Tully couldn't be stabled here.

If only she and Lyndy could live here and not at Morrington Hall after they were married. Without her father in residence, that is. They could always build a proper stable.

"Why were Lord Atherly and Professor Gridley at the barrows?' Miss Cosslett asked.

"Looking for fossils, what else?" Stella

plopped down on the couch. She hadn't realized how tiring the walk had been. "But I found some wonderful things."

"It's all over that Lord Fairbrother's dead," he grumbled, "and that you're the one who found him."

"Is it true?" Miss Cosslett asked. The pair regarded her expectantly.

"Yes, it's true."

"Jeepers, girl, what's wrong with you? Here we are, having already started on the engagement announcement set to run in New York and Newport for you, and what do you do? Something that might threaten your chances that this wedding will ever happen."

Typical Daddy. A man was dead, and all he could think about was the potential inconvenience and a way to blame Stella for it.

"We looked at lots of society announcements today, from London, Europe, New York." He motioned toward the newspapers on the carpet. "Hopefully our efforts aren't in vain. Read what we've got so far, Jane."

Miss Cosslett held up her notepad and read, " 'Daughter of world-renowned horse breeder to wed son of the Earl of Atherly. Engagement is announced. The Kendricks of Kentucky will now be connected with the principal noble families of England. The engagement —' "

"Those will be the headlines," Daddy said, interrupting. "Now read her the text."

Miss Cosslett continued. " 'The engagement between the young Viscount Lyndhurst, son of the Earl of Atherly, to Miss Stella Kendrick, daughter of Mr. Elijah Kendrick, was formally announced tonight at a party held in their honor at Pilley Manor, Hampshire, England.' "

The party. Stella was already dreading it.

" 'The wedding is to take place later this year,' " Miss Cosslett concluded.

"But, I thought the wedding date had been moved up. So that the bishop could officiate."

When Stella had finally agreed to it, they'd set the wedding for October with Reverend Paine, the local pastor, presiding. But then, due to her father's persistent requests and, in no small part, the promise of a foal sired by Orson, his champion thoroughbred stud, the bishop had finally capitulated, offering to officiate in mid-September. Stella didn't care who presided over the wedding, but the sooner she and Lyndy got married, the sooner her social obligations would end, and the sooner Daddy would go back to Kentucky.

"We're still negotiating. That's why we've left it vague."

"What do you think, Miss Kendrick?" Miss Cosslett smiled, but the glint in her eye was unnerving. Or maybe it was seeing her wearing Stella's dress.

"It doesn't matter what she thinks," Daddy said, crushing the stub of his cigar in a silver tray, flecks of tobacco fluttering onto the table beneath. "It's what the likes of Mrs. Astor think."

Stella couldn't care less about what the likes of Mrs. Astor thought.

"And regarding the engagement dinner," Daddy added, "Jane came up with some good ideas I want you to implement."

"The dinner's only three days away," Stella said, hoping he'd think that meant her plans were fixed. And they were, sort of, almost. She'd planned to do a final check with the housekeeper and Cook tomorrow and had no intention of bringing up "Jane Cosslett's ideas."

"Look what I found," Stella said, changing the subject. She pulled the dagger from the canvas bag Professor Gridley had given her and unwrapped it. Inside this cozy room, with the yellow glow of the fireplace glinting on the blade, the dagger seemed sinister somehow.

"What is that?"

The reporter reached over and, without permission, snatched the dagger from Stella's hand. Miss Cosslett held it up to the light, admiring the superior craftsmanship.

"It's remarkable," Daddy said, admiring it from afar. "Look at those figurines, that wire braiding on the handle. Could be made of bronze, perhaps, or even gold." If nothing else, he had a keen appreciation for priceless treasures.

"You have had a busy morning, haven't you, Miss Kendrick?" Miss Cosslett said, not too kindly.

"Yes, I have. So, if you don't mind." Stella held out her hand.

"Give it here," Daddy said. Without taking her eyes off Stella, Miss Cosslett placed the pommel and grip into his outstretched hand. He weighed the dagger in his palm. "My guess is bronze. Not heavy enough for gold. Where did you find it?"

"At the barrow."

"Did you or the others find anything else at the barrow?" Miss Cosslett asked.

But before Stella could answer, Daddy ran his thumb along the blade. "Damn it, girl," he cursed, sucking the blood from the cut on his thumb. "If you found this at the barrow, why's the blade so sharp?"

"I have no idea." Stella couldn't believe it. Lord Atherly said it was medieval. A blade, hundreds of years old, would've dulled over time. Could it have been recently sharpened?

"What an odd fish you are, Miss Kendrick. First, you find a dead body and then a dangerous knife."

"It's a dagger," Stella corrected.

"Either way, it's an astonishing coincidence, don't you think?" The reporter smirked.

"What do you mean?"

"Didn't you also find the body of the vicar who was supposed to marry you and Lord Lyndhurst? And wasn't he stabbed with a knife?"

"I did find the vicar," Stella said, more somber than annoyed. "But no, Reverend Bullmore wasn't stabbed."

Stella thought of Reverend Bullmore often. She hoped the pain, the guilt, the sadness of it all would fade over time. But for now, she prayed for him, and everyone else touched by his death, every Sunday and tried to get on with the business of fulfilling her duties as the future Lady Lyndhurst. Lord Fairbrother was different. Stella regretted being the one to find Lady Philippa's husband and regretted insisting she be there when the widow was told, but Stella had no remorse over the verderer's death. She hadn't even particularly liked the man.

"You never said if you or the others found anything else," she said.

"I also found a cinerary urn. It was quite miraculous. Thousands of years old and completely intact."

"An urn? Where people's ashes are kept?" Miss Cosslett said, the tips of her fingers caressing her lace collar.

When had Daddy given her Stella's dress? Stella knew not to bother asking why. She knew what he'd say. *I bought it. I'll give it to whomever I choose.*

"My, Miss Kendrick, daggers, urns, dead bodies," the reporter added. "You certainly don't shy away from the most unsavory of things, do you?"

Stella regretted ever mentioning the urn, the dagger, or the barrow in front of this woman. She'd only hoped to distract her father from talking about the engagement party. Stella wouldn't make the same mistake again. If it didn't pertain to the wedding, Jane Cosslett didn't need to know.

"Now, now, Jane," Daddy said, unexpectedly coming to Stella's defense. "You're here to get the news out that Elijah Kendrick, the son of a coachman, is marrying his daughter off to the heir of an earldom. Not about the girl's penchant for the macabre."

So much for coming to Stella's defense.

"Oh, Elijah," Miss Cosslett simpered as Tims entered the room holding a silver tray with a folded piece of paper on it. "You know I don't mean anything by it. I'm a journalist, after all. Can't a girl be curious?"

Daddy reached over and patted her cheek. "Of course you can." Stella cringed.

"I have some messages for you, Miss Kendrick," Tims said, coming to Stella's rescue.

Stella plucked up the three notes before her father beat her to it. She glanced at the first one, shielding its contents from the reporter, who was craning her neck around to see. A small giggle of relief escaped Stella's lips. It was from Mr. Gates, the stablemaster at Morrington Hall. Tully was well enough to ride. She relayed the happy news as she unfolded the second note.

Fairbrother stabbed, not drowned, need to speak with you again. Will call around again soon. It was signed, *Inspector Archibald Brown.*

Stella felt a rush of blood to her cheeks as the room lurched suddenly. She took a deep

212

breath, and the room righted itself again as her eyes came to rest on the professor's empty canvas sack. Had she found the weapon that killed Lord Fairbrother? No, it couldn't be. She slipped the notes into the bag, including the third left unread. The correspondence from Lady Atherly would have to wait.

"What did the note say?" Daddy asked.

"Who's it from?" Miss Cosslett said.

Stella, ignoring their questions, reached over and snatched the dagger from Daddy's startled grip, the newspaper teetering on his belly slipping to the floor.

"How dare you!"

Stella wrapped the dagger up again and shoved it out toward the butler. "Would you put this in the safe with the silver, please, Tims."

"Of course, Miss Kendrick." The butler nodded, despite her father's sputtering protests.

Stella didn't believe in what Miss Cosslett called "an astonishing coincidence," but just in case, she wasn't taking any chances. "And no one is to remove it but me."

CHAPTER 16

"Not again," Tom groaned.

With the setting sun seeping around his edges, the bloke in the doorway was a mere silhouette. But Tom Heppenstall knew the shape of that cap anywhere. Tom shifted his weight off his aching ankle as the inspector removed his distinctive hat and sauntered up to the bar. Now what did he want?

Sure, Tom had heard the tragic news. Who hadn't? But it had nothing to do with him.

Tom followed the inspector's gaze to the game of darts on the other side of the room. A farmer in overalls and muddy boots, while drinking from his pint glass, threw the needle-like missile toward the circular board hanging on the wall. The dart missed its target and struck the nearby hand-strewn beam before dropping to the floor. Boisterous laughter followed.

"Pint of Burton, pale," the inspector ordered.

Tom nodded, though the inspector's attention was on the game. Tom slid a glass beneath the tap and allowed the frothy head to just reach the brim. He set the ale down on the bar. The inspector took a tentative sip.

The pub was starting to fill up. Besides the dart players, customers occupied every table, as well as a few seats at the bar. Tom wasn't surprised. As with any decent public house, the Knightwood Oak was rife with men needing to let go of the cares of the day. With the news of Lord Fairbrother's death spreading, speculation had surpassed darts as the pub's most popular sport. Every field hand and shopkeeper's assistant had a theory: suicide by hanging, kicked in the head by his horse, drowning in Hatchet Pond, choked on a grape while eating afternoon tea. And every theory, each more outlandish than the next, brought in more trade. Who was Tom to discourage it?

But when the boy began spreading a particularly scandalous rumor, that he claimed to have overheard the butcher's wife tell the silversmith's daughter what a kitchen maid had said, Tom had had enough. No one wanted to imagine Miss Kendrick catching a dead body with a fishing line. Whoever heard of a noblewoman fishing the Blackwater, anyway? But regardless of how it happened, that Lord Fairbrother was dead was a certainty. And the news of it, debated over chips, pie, and pints, filled Tom's coffers all day. But that didn't mean Tom wanted to talk to any police inspector about it.

"Tuppence," Tom said.

"Inspector Brown," the inspector said, fishing coins from his pocket. Tom remembered the fellow's name. The only policeman Tom had ever seen step foot inside his pub. "I'm looking for Harvey Milkham."

"Haven't seen him." The last time Tom set eyes on the older man was two days before, when he'd almost emptied the pub with a snake.

"Have you heard of anyone else seeing him?"

From the chatter Tom had overheard, Harvey was another keen topic of conversation: his hut burning, threats he'd made at the fete, how he'd saved the American lady's favorite horse. But no one knew what had become of the old snakecatcher.

"Don't think so," Tom said.

Leaving the policeman to his pint, Tom took an order for tonight's special of kidney pie and mash and sent it back to the kitchen. His mouth watered at the smells that wafted through the kitchen door. Had the boy fetched this morning's order of potatoes like Tom had told him to? If not, they might run out of mash before Tom got his supper.

"What about George Parley?" The inspector, half-finished pint in hand, called down the bar. "I know he's a regular here. Have you seen him lately?"

Tom shook his head, scanning the room for any sign of that good for nothing boy. Several tables needed clearing already. Then he slid a pint of Guinness in front of Septimus the caretaker at St. Peter's.

With a hard face and broad, square shoulders, the caretaker looked like he was made of stone. But he wasn't fooling anyone. When his interest was piqued, Septimus was like a sponge cake soaking up brandy. Come tomorrow morning Reverend Paine would be getting an earful of gossip.

"Everyone's certainly heard George lately," Septimus said, before taking a sip and starting back toward the game of darts, foam still clinging to his upper lip.

"What did he mean by that?" the inspector asked. Tom shrugged.

The policeman pinched the bridge of his nose. Then he set his elbow on the bar and leaned in. "I'm here investigating a murder, Mr. Heppenstall. Have you seen George

Parley since yesterday afternoon or not?"

Murder? That would undoubtedly feed the rumor mill.

"You bet George was in last night," Old Joe, perched in his customary place at the end of the bar, declared, his usual broadsheets spread out in front of him taking up valuable bar space. "Don't you remember, Tom? You couldn't get him to shut up."

The policeman regarded Tom with disappointment. Tom shrugged again. "He hasn't been in yet tonight, though."

"What was Mr. Parley going on about, then?" the inspector asked.

"Lord Fairbrother, who else?" Old Joe said. "The fellow is always going on about the official verderer. Ain't that so, Tom?" Tom ignored him.

"Everything is unfair; everything's stacked against George Parley, if you listen to him talk," Old Joe went on. "And whether it was his Cecil Pony Challenge second-place finish or the court's ruling on some enclosure boundary line, he blamed Lord Fairbrother if it didn't go George's way."

"Thank you, Mr. . . . ?" the inspector said.

"Just call me Joe."

"Thank you, Joe." The inspector, his back to the bar, shouted above the din of the pub. "If any one of you happens to see George

Parley or Harvey Milkham, tell them —"

Whoosh! Clank. Wooooooooo!

A deep, reverberating roar resounded across the room, cutting off every half-spoken word in the pub. The whack of a dart as it hit the board, thrown seconds before, pierced the silence it left behind.

Clink. Clank. Wooooooooooo!

Oh, no, not again. Tom sighed.

"What, may I ask, was that?" the inspector said.

"The ghost," the boy uttered quietly, appearing out of nowhere beside the inspector, his cheeks the color of champagne. As if he were the ghost himself. Where had that boy been?

"The what?"

"The ghost, of Old Bertie. It haunts the pub," the boy said, moistening his lips.

Every pub in England had some tall tale of a ghost haunting its rafters; the Knightwood Oak was no exception. In 1748 the pub's landlord, Bertie Roberts, was murdered with an ax by a jealous husband. The tale, as Tom had heard it told, claimed the publican didn't even know the killer's wife. Unjustly cut down in his prime, the ghost was said to haunt the pub, moaning for all eternity about the unpunished wrong. When Tom bought the place, he'd dismissed the occasional grumblings rising from the basement over the years. "The ghost" had been more active than usual the past couple of days, and since the death of Lord Fairbrother, the knocking, the scraping, and the clanging had some renaming the poltergeist from Old Bertie to Lord Fairbrother.

As if the lord would haunt a pub of all places. Outwick House, maybe, but the Knightwood Oak? Never.

But Tom couldn't explain the noises. Yesterday he'd combed every inch of the place, top to bottom, with witnesses, and his only reward was a renewed throbbing in his ankle. He could only hope "the ghost," whatever be his name, wouldn't be bad for business.

"Right." To Tom's relief, the inspector gulped down the last of his beer and set the glass on the bar. "You'll inform me if you see or hear anything, I trust? I've no concern for a ghost, mind," the inspector said, settling his hat on his head. "It's Harvey Milkham and George Parley I'm interested in."

The inspector paused a moment before strolling away. Tom had said nothing. As the policeman navigated a crowd of newcomers arriving through the door, Tom was only too glad to see the back of him.

■ ■ ■ ■

Just a few more feet.

George Parley bent his knees and leaned back. With his arms wrapped on the wooden post, he hauled it slowly toward the new hole he had dug. His muscles ached, and a sinuous vein bulged in his neck as he strained against the formidable weight. Despite the cool breeze blowing off the Solent, his forehead beaded with sweat.

He was too old to be doing this kind of work.

But who could he get to do it? Not Gerald or Edgar; his sons were too lazy. Not any of the farm hands; he couldn't trust the lot of them to keep their mouths shut. No, George would have to do this himself. He yanked harder, feeling a sharp tug in his back as he dragged the fencing the last few inches. He dropped the post into the hole. He stretched his shoulders and rubbed the spot on his back before filling in the empty gaps around the post with dirt and moss. Then he retraced the trail the post had dragged through the soil and smoothed it out with his boot. He stepped back to admire his handiwork.

That'll do all right.

In a day or two, if the posts were any indication, it would look like the fence had always been there, and no one would be the wiser. Especially now that Fairbrother was dead.

George Parley traipsed across the field, his back twinging with random shots of pain, to the old stable, a long, squat, red-brick building with barn doors at both ends. Glass, from the many broken windows, and loosened wooden roof shingles cluttered the ground. Decrepit and neglected, it was the perfect hiding place. George sidestepped a shingle with a protruding nail and pushed back one side of the barn door. Moonlight streamed in through a hole in the roof. The scent of molding hay mingled with that of the freshly milled shipping crates stacked along the aisle. George perched himself on one of the boxes and looked out over his newly expanded paddock. Not a cloud marred the inky black sky and stars twinkled like diamonds. Dawn was a few hours away yet. He slumped over and kneaded the ache in his back with his knuckle.

This was the easy bit. Always had been.

George, retrieving the long-necked glass bottle he'd left by the side of the crate, scared up a mouse that had bedded down in the old hay nearby. It squeaked and skittered away. George took a long, slow swig of the liquor, relishing the burn as it slid down his throat. With the bottle empty, he tossed it into the hay.

Of all the verderers, only Fairbrother ever suspected the crafty bugger. But what was to happen now, with the rest of it? It had already cost him dearly. With Harvey Milkham out of the way, George should reap the benefit of all his hard work. But would he? Who was to say his plans wouldn't all go to pot? George knowingly patted the crate beneath him. It was a chance he would have to take.

CHAPTER 17

"This is a surprise," Stella said, her tone flat and unrevealing. It wasn't like her.

Lyndy hadn't seen Stella since yesterday when she'd accompanied Papa and Professor Gridley to the barrow. After his confrontation with Mother, he'd taken Beau, his Irish hunter, for a ride. Lyndy had resisted visiting the barrow, riding instead down to the cliffs near Barton on Sea, hoping the crisp, salty breeze would cool his anger. But as he looked out over the Solent at the Needles, the jagged tip of the Isle of Wight, a yacht with its white sails billowing drifted into his view and reminded him of Fairbrother, and then of Philippa and Mother's odious plans. He'd abandoned the cliffs and raced Beau toward the barrow, only to change his mind and head for home. When Papa and Professor Gridley returned, Lyndy watched for Stella from the library window, peering from behind the green damask drapes. She wasn't with them.

She'd walked across the heath to Pilley Manor alone, Papa had said. Why? Papa didn't know. Would Lyndy ever understand why that woman did anything? He hoped not.

With his anxiety mounting, Lyndy had abandoned his customary poise and had ridden over to Pilley Manor to see her, disregarding the dinner gong and Mother's disapproving stare, only to be told by the housekeeper that Stella had already retired to her room. Was she ill? Had she worn herself down hiking? Or, as was most under-standable, had the events of the day finally caught up with her? He'd had to wait until morning to find out.

"Is it?" He'd spent a restless night. By the look of her, she had too. Stella followed him outside and down the garden path.

"I wasn't sure I warranted early morning visits anymore." Stella stopped to pluck the pink head off a drooping rose. The sudden sadness in her voice took him unaware.

For as long as the Kendricks had occupied Pilley Manor, Lyndy had made it a daily habit of visiting after breakfast, if not sooner. Often, with Beau and Tully in tow so that they might ride. Sometimes Lyndy brought the carriage and treated her to an early morning picnic; he'd discovered early on Stella adored picnics. But often, as not, they were content to stroll in Pilley Manor's little garden or sit comfortably snug on the short bench beneath the oaks that lined the garden wall. He'd come to anticipate this early morning tête-à-tête. No Mother, no Mr. Kendrick, no chaperone. Just him and her.

For the past two months, they'd spent a great deal of time in each other company. It was the Season, after all. They'd attended the races at Salisbury, twice. They'd accepted invitations to numerous dinner parties, garden parties, card parties, afternoon teas, and balls. As his future bride, Stella was much sought after, and she was a model guest: beautiful, witty, and gracious, even when her hosts were not. Lyndy was proud to show her off and willing to share her with the best of English society. But only because he knew the next morning, and soon for the rest of his life, she would be all his.

"Why would you say that?" Lyndy asked. "I'm only a bit later than usual." Papa and Professor Gridley had made it impossible to escape early. Stifled by Mother from discussing their outing at dinner, they enthusiastically reviewed it over breakfast. Every time Lyndy attempted to leave, they'd pull him back into the wearying conversation. "I came as soon as I could."

Stella said nothing as she settled on the bench, picking off the petals of the rose, one by one, and letting them flutter to the ground where they may. Lyndy began to pace before her, his footfalls crunching on the garden path. Her silence was torturous.

"How was your visit to Furzy Barrow? Papa and Professor Gridley returned quite pleased with how it was all going. I don't know what they were on about, but they were both quite complimentary toward you. Not many women would show such genuine interest."

"It was the distraction I needed," was all she would say.

"You'll be pleased to know that Tully recuperated completely."

"Yes, thank you. Mr. Gates sent a message over yesterday." Such formality in her tone. He didn't know how much of it he could take.

"Will you ride today, then?"

"I may." Again, such formality. He hated it. He preferred her incessant questions over this excruciating reticence. Lyndy yanked on the lapels of his tweed jacket.

"Ah, bloody hell, Stella," Lyndy said, plopping down next to her, the bench being so short their shoulders brushed against one another's. She shifted, so her shoulder no longer met his, but she didn't spring up either. He took that as a good sign. "What is wrong? Why are you so distant?"

She'd said the barrow visit was a good distraction. Was she still troubled by Fair-brother's death? Or was it Philippa and the conversation they'd yet to have? Neither cheered him to think about.

"How can you not know?" Stella, tears welling in her eyes, threw the remains of the rose to the ground.

"Know what?"

"I might as well be frank, right? I have nothing to lose now. Do I?" Tears filled her eyes faster than she could wipe them away with the sleeve of her white linen shirtwaist blouse. The light blue ribbon woven into the bodice matched her eyes.

"Please, speak your mind. You know I prefer it."

And he meant it. Her unabashed outpouring of questions, observations, opinions, and emotions set Stella apart from every other woman he knew. He adored her for it.

"She had one of your handkerchiefs, Lyndy." Ah, it was about Philippa then. Lyndy should've known. "I want to know why."

"Because I gave it to her."

Stella, who had been rubbing a loose rose petal between her thumb and finger, glared up at him. "Who is Lady Philippa to you?"

"She is nothing." He meant it. "Nothing." Lyndy stared at her tearstained cheeks, realizing he'd caused this. If only he'd told her everything yesterday. If only he'd been perfectly honest from the beginning. "She means absolutely nothing to me."

Did she believe him? Why did it matter so much that she did?

Stella sniffled. He longed to offer his handkerchief and wipe away her tears, but it was such a gesture, years ago, that got him in this situation in the first place. Stella slipped a folded piece of stationery from under her skirts. Disappointment, anger, frustration, and misery warred inside him. She'd hidden it from him somehow, and he hated that she had, or felt she needed to.

She held it out to him now. "Then, why is your mother insinuating otherwise?"

He reached for the stationery, like one would a loaded gun. He'd recognized Mother's hand. He didn't read it but shoved it into his pocket. He could imagine what it said.

"Your mother seems to think I am as fickle as the English sun," Stella said, her heartache displaced by anger. "Or maybe it's you she's thinking of." Lyndy inwardly sighed in relief. He could more easily suffer her ill temper than her tears. "Lady Atherly is convinced she can 'extricate us' from our engagement." Stella swiveled to face him. "She says that now that Lord Fairbrother is dead, his widow is free to marry 'the gentleman her heart desired all along.' Lady Atherly's exact words. I'll ask you again, Lyndy. Who is Lady Philippa to you?"

"As I said before, nothing. But . . ." His voice trailed away to silence. He loathed the unpleasant topic.

"I trusted you, Lyndy. I thought you trusted me. But how can we make this work if you don't tell me everything? I may as well give in to your mother and go back to Kentucky with Daddy."

Staying silent, resisting telling Stella everything seemed the surest course. But like a novice boxer, Lyndy had kept his hands up to guard his face only to get punched in the stomach. What had he done?

"But she did mean something to me, once."

"I'm listening," Stella said, folding her arms across her chest and staring at him. He stood up and began to pace again.

It was a long story. Lyndy had hoped to

spare himself the embarrassing details of this youthful romance, but Stella would never understand the extent of his distaste for Philippa if he did. So Lyndy told her the whole story. How he and Philippa had known each other since childhood, he a friend of her brother's at Eton. How Mother had adored Philippa, making no secret of her hope to see the two of them one day wed. How Philippa's beauty, her flirtation, her freely given kisses, her flattery had blinded him. How he'd thought he was in love with her, and how, the moment he'd declared his intentions, Philippa had sought the attention of others. How she'd flaunted others' desire for her in front of him, enjoying his pain. How she'd laughed at him, his earnest declarations of love and jealousy. But always, when he'd sought to break free of her, she would lure him back with promises and kisses. Until he'd had enough, seeing her for what she was. And all the while Mother had pressed for an official announcement of their engagement, not knowing that Philippa had promised herself to Fairbrother, that Papa's expenditures on his fossil expeditions meant seeking an heiress with more money than Philippa had to save Morrington Hall.

When Philippa married Fairbrother,

Lyndy had thought he was free of her.

"And yet here she is, trying to get her fangs into me again." Lyndy sat beside Stella again and took her hand. He felt her resistance, a slight pull away, but he wouldn't release her. "Stella, I want only to marry you."

He put his finger to the side of her chin, her alabaster skin so smooth, so soft, even when streaked with tears, and turned her head toward him. "Do you believe me?" Lyndy had never wanted anything more.

She said nothing. Lyndy waited, his foot tapping of its own accord. What was she waiting for? Why didn't she say anything?

"Do you? Do you believe that I want only you?"

Still, she said nothing. Lyndy leaped to his feet. He couldn't take any more of this. He'd already stooped to begging, what more could he do? But Stella held steady to his hand. Her tug, pulling him back down beside her, surprised him. Then she threw her free arm around his neck and drew him toward her, her lips pressing against his. He'd take that as a yes, then.

"Come on," Stella said. She stood still, holding Lyndy's hand and jerked him up beside her.

"Where are we going?"

"There's something I want to show you."

Stella had been so hurt, so confused when she finally got a chance to read Lady Atherly's note without her father and the nosy reporter being around. How cruel could a woman be, sending such a missive on the day Stella had discovered a dead body? It'd been a horrible repetition of the day Stella arrived in England: a dead man, a betrayal, and a threat to her entire future. She thought she'd never have to live through such a day again. And yet there she was, wrestling with doubts and despair all over again. Learning Lyndy had called after she'd gone to bed early had made her more miserable. She'd barely closed her eyes last night.

Again and again she'd gone back to the same questions. Was it true what Lady Atherly said, that Lyndy was Lady Philippa's "heart's desire"? Lyndy didn't even like Lady Philippa. So why would the lady want to marry him? And why would his mother support such an ill-fated scheme? Unless the newly widowed lady had now inherited a vast amount of money. But if that was the reason, why hadn't Lyndy challenged his mother? Why hadn't he convinced Lady Atherly of his commitment to Stella?

Again and again, Stella had pictured the handkerchief in Lady Philippa's fist. Again and again, she'd come back to the same horrible possibility, that Lyndy had lied to her, that he and Philippa were secretly in love. If her worst fears were right, she faced either a meaningless marriage or having to move back to Kentucky with her father. Both amounted to the same thing, a life without love. Stella could barely face Lyndy, as she'd walked beside him in the garden, as they sat on their private bench, her imagining he might be deceiving her. Stella hated secrets and lies. No matter how much it might pain her, she had to know the truth.

Stella had listened to Lyndy's explanation with dread. But studying his open expression, noting his concerned hesitation, his nervous pacing, the pain and pleading in his eyes, a wave of sheer relief had washed over her; he was telling her the truth and had been all along. She'd never wanted to kiss him so much. So, she did, surprising them both.

"What is it?" Lyndy asked, tightening his grip as she pulled him along.

"It's something I found at the barrow." Stella had thought of him the moment she'd found it, but before she could show it to him, she'd gotten Lady Atherly's note that changed everything. Now she could share it with him like she'd wanted to.

How nice it was to get back to normal again. As normal as her new life was, anyway. Lady Atherly still sought to break the engagement and wed Lyndy to Lady Philippa. Lord Fairbrother was dead, and Harvey was suspected of killing him. At least Tully was better, and Stella knew where she stood with Lyndy.

She led Lyndy back through the garden and into the bright hall of Pilley Manor, sparsely decorated with a few landscape oil paintings and cream-colored floor-to-ceiling wainscoting. Several calling cards, left while she was out yesterday, still lay in the silver tray on the inlay side table. The top one, decorated with a spray of brightly colored flowers, read *Miss Ada R. Snellgrove*. Stella drew Lyndy down the hall to the servants' domain. Reluctant to enter, he released her hand and stood outside the doorway.

Mrs. Downie, a middle-aged woman with reddish-brown hair, kind green eyes, and an enormous backside, was in the kitchen chopping onions. The scent of baking bread filled the room. It smelled amazing.

"Is Tims around, Mrs. Downie?" Stella asked as she approached the long wooden table.

Unlike Mrs. Cole at Morrington Hall, Mrs. Downie had no objections to Stella stepping into her kitchen on the odd occasion. They had all discussed it when Stella moved in, Stella and the servants, that is. Daddy couldn't have cared less what she did. Stella had called a meeting with the members of staff to learn what they were comfortable with and what they were not. As she was technically the mistress of the house, it was her prerogative. With all the rumors floating about the odd Americans, the staff seemed quite relieved to find neither she nor her father nor her aunt was as unreasonable and barbaric as they'd been led to believe. A bit different, yes, but with the rules established from the beginning, and with Ethel, Stella's lady's maid's reassurances, behavior everyone could live with. The household had run quite smoothly and happily, for all, ever since. If only she could do the same when she returned to Morrington Hall.

"No, miss. Mr. Tims is attending to Mr. Kendrick." Of course. Tims, as the only male member of staff, acted as Father's valet, as well.

"Do you know how to open the silver safe?"

"No, but Mrs. Robertson does. She's in

her room if you need her."

"Thank you, Mrs. Downie."

The cook turned to drop the onions in a large black pot. They sizzled as steam rose toward the copper pots and pans lining the wall behind the immense cast iron stove. With her back turned, Mrs. Downie didn't see Lyndy scuttle past when Stella motioned for him to follow her through the kitchen to the small study beyond. The housekeeper, a petite woman in a dark gray and black striped dress, sat at a small secretary desk, her tightly coiffed, graying blond head bent over a ledger. Sun, shining through the only window in the room, struck precisely on the watch the housekeeper wore on a silver chain around her neck. Stella knocked lightly on the door frame. Mrs. Robertson, startled by the interruption, started to complain.

"What on earth . . . ?" She snapped her pen down on the ledger. "Oh, Miss Kendrick, dearie, you startled me. What can I do . . . ?" Having caught sight of Lyndy behind Stella, the housekeeper hastily slid back in her chair and stood up. "My lord." She nodded her head slightly. "Forgive me. I didn't see you there."

"Please be at ease, Mrs. Robertson," Lyndy said. The housekeeper nodded, but her rigid posture didn't change, nor did she sit back down.

"Can you open the silver safe for me, please, Mrs. Robertson?"

The housekeeper had established from the onset that she wasn't above entertaining unusual requests from Stella, but that her rank merited an explanation for it. However, today she didn't hesitate, didn't question Stella, not even with her eyes. She sought the key, among the many dangling from her waist, and led them to the large iron safe embedded in the wall of the butler's pantry. She turned the brass dial back and forth, stopping at each predetermined number, before pulling the heavy iron door open. She unlocked the secondary door inside with the key. She pulled this open as well and then stepped aside.

The wrapped dagger lay on top of a silver serving tray on the middle shelf, like a napkin forgotten among the gleaming tableware, platter, and candlesticks. Stella reached in and pulled out the bundle. When she unwrapped the dagger, a small gasp escaped Mrs. Robertson behind her.

"You found this yesterday?" Lyndy said, lifting the dagger from Stella's palm and carefully inspecting it. He didn't sound happy. Did he too think there was something sinister about it?

"Why, what's wrong?"

"Because unless I am greatly mistaken, you never should have found this in the barrow." He plucked the cloth from Stella's grip and wrapped the dagger again. He placed the dagger back onto the tray in the safe and shut the inner door. It locked again with a click.

"Why not?"

"Because I've seen it before at Outwick House. It is, or was, part of Lord Fairbrother's sword and dagger collection."

"But that means it could be the murder weapon."

Lyndy nodded. Appalled, Stella grabbed the heavy outer door of the safe and swung it shut.

CHAPTER 18

"Didn't take you for the berry-picking type, Mr. Parley." Inspector Brown stepped under the eaves of the abandoned stable just in time to avoid the first sprinkles of the summer morning shower. Set on the edge of large paddocks, interspersed with post and rail fencing, the dilapidated building, smelling of decaying hay and bird droppings, was nearly hidden by the wild-bramble bushes that had grown up around it. It wasn't the sort of place you'd expect to find someone unless they had something to hide.

"What are you doing here?" George Parley, wearing no waistcoat or jacket, slammed closed the lid of a large wooden crate he'd been bent over. There were five of them, as long and as wide as coffins, spread out on the old stable's dirt floor. As Parley rolled down his shirtsleeves, Brown could see the defined curves of the man's thick biceps.

He held up his identification. "I'm Inspector Brown, and this is my constable, DC Waterman."

"What do you want?" Parley's eyes darted from Brown to the crates to the door.

Brown motioned for Constable Waterman to step behind Parley. The landowner was jumpy, and he'd been too difficult to track down to allow him to scurry off like a rabbit before Brown had all the answers he'd come for. Parley warily watched as Waterman crossed by him and stood, at ready, in front of the stable's back door.

"I've been looking for you."

After getting nowhere at the pub last night, Brown had called on Parley at home. "Dad's out on the land," was all the son would tell him. Despite the falling darkness, Brown had peeked through various outbuildings: the stable, a separate tack and feed room, the small carriage house, the pigsty, the chicken coop, and a storage barn. No Parley. When he returned this morning, Brown got the same, "Dad's out on the land." Brown and his constable had combed every inch of the farm until they'd come to the forgotten stable. With telltale signs of recent fence work, Brown had a hunch he'd finally found their man. Brown had been right. But they'd found more than just George Parley.

What were in those crates?

"Why? Why have you been looking for me?"

"I assume you have heard the news of Lord Fairbrother's death," Brown said.

Parley glanced furtively back at Waterman again. "Of course I have. But what does that have to do with me?"

"Would you kindly read Mr. Parley what he was quoted as saying to Lord Fairbrother just hours before the lord's murder, Constable?"

Brown and his constable had been busy. Besides interviewing the residents of Outwick House and making inquiries at the Knightwood Oak pub, they'd questioned a dozen witnesses to George Parley threatening Lord Fairbrother at the Cecil Pony Challenge.

Waterman pulled out his notebook, flipped it open to the right page, and said, "There will be hell to pay."

"What did you mean by that, Mr. Parley?" Inspector Brown said. Despite the cool breeze behind the light rain, George Parley pulled out a handkerchief and wiped his brow.

"I didn't mean anything by it. I was sick and tired of Lord Fairbrother always winning the cup when me ponies should beat the lot."

"You didn't mean that you would kill Lord Fairbrother if he won and you didn't?"

Parley's cheeks darkened to a crimson red. "Of course not. Lord, man. It was a pony competition. I wouldn't kill someone over a pony."

"Lord Fairbrother had a great deal of cash on his person when he died. Would you know anything about that, Mr. Parley?"

The man tightened his lips and glanced back at Waterman. "No, I wouldn't know anything about that."

"Would you burn someone's house down?"

"I don't know what you're talking about."

Was that a hesitation? Parley's eyes darted about as if looking for a way to flee. The man knew something.

"Where were you Monday night, Mr. Parley?"

"Working the land."

"Anyone with you?" Parley shook his head. "And Tuesday night?"

"Working the land. I'm always working the land."

"Except when you're at the Knightwood Oak, isn't that right, Mr. Parley?"

Parley grumbled something incoherent. "A man has a right to relax after a hard day's work."

"Yes. Yes, he does. And where were you yesterday morning?"

"In me bed, alone. Where do you expect?" No alibi for either the arson of the snake-catcher's hut or Lord Fairbrother's murder then.

"What's in the crates, Mr. Parley?"

Parley, taken aback by the abrupt change in subject, stammered, "I . . . they . . . these just arrived."

"May I see their contents?" The crates probably had nothing to do with Brown's investigation, and he probably had no reason to ask, but he did anyway. Parley didn't immediately comply. "Why the hesitation, Mr. Parley? Unless you have something to hide?"

Parley, glaring first at Brown and then at Waterman standing guard at the far end, reluctantly lifted the lid of the crate he'd been inspecting earlier. Packed in straw were rifles, Winchesters, by the look of them, and brand new, by the gloss of the walnut stocks and glint on the barrels. There must have been a dozen in each crate. If Lord Fairbrother had been shot, Brown would've arrested Parley and been done with it. Unfortunately, that wasn't the case.

"Why do you have so many rifles?"

Farmers always had a weapon on hand to scare off predators. Gentlemen had cabinets filled with shotguns used for sport. But Brown had never seen such a massing of weapons in his life. Not even the police station in Winchester, the central station for all of Hampshire, was this heavily armed.

"I'm opening a gentlemen's rifle club, Inspector. These are for that enterprise."

"On the Forest?" Parley nodded. Brown was surprised. He remembered the controversy when the Crown tried to set aside New Forest land for a rifle range. It didn't sit well with many. "And this was approved by the Verderers' Court?"

"It will be," Parley said, less assuredly, glancing back at Waterman again.

"I'm sure you've also heard about Harvey Milkham's house burning down?"

"What does that have to do with me rifles?"

Parley was annoyed. Brown liked him that way. He might say something he would regret. Brown turned his back and took a few steps back outside. The rain had left as fast as it had come, though the gray sky had yet to clear. A few drips trickled off the old stable's steep roof. From his vantage point, Brown had an unobstructed view across the heath to the wood where Harvey Milkham's house had been, several miles away. Brown turned back to Parley, who was wiping his high forehead again.

"You probably even saw the flames, smelled the smoke from here," Brown said.

"I know about the snakecatcher's hut," George Parley snapped. "Had you ever seen the place? It was a mess, a disgrace. Just like the man himself. That hovel was a fire waiting to happen."

"You didn't burn it down, did you?"

"As I said, it was a tinder box. All it needed was a lightning strike, a stray ember from a cigar —"

"Or cigarette?" Parley frowned. "Or ignited gunpowder?"

That got him. Parley's eyes widened in fear. He wet his lips with a few rapid swipes of his tongue. "I didn't burn down the snakecatcher's hut, Inspector. Why would I?"

Brown's question exactly. "And where are you setting this rifle club?"

"Just this side of Norleywood."

"And isn't that Harvey Milkham's land?"

"No, it isn't!" Parley declared. "He should never have built his hut around the old cottage."

"Whose land does it belong to, Mr. Parley? You? Lord Fairbrother?"

At the mention of the dead verderer's name, George Parley crossed his arms against his chest. "If there isn't anything else, Inspector, I have me work to do."

No bother. Brown could easily find out who owned the land; the records were held in Lyndhurst at the King's House, mere steps from his station.

"Don't leave town, Mr. Parley. I may need to speak with you again."

Parley grumbled an incoherent affirmative under his breath. It was all the cooperation Brown was going to get out of the man today. Brown waved for his constable to rejoin him before stepping out into a spot of sun breaking through the clouds.

"Been putting in new posts for your paddock, Mr. Parley?" he called over his shoulder. "I'll see to it that your local agister, Mr. Gerald, stops by to check they've been properly installed."

"What? No. There's no need to . . . Wait, where are you going? You can't just . . . Maybe we can talk about this? There must be some misunderstanding. But this isn't . . . after everything . . ."

Brown, ignoring Parley's sputtering, strolled purposefully back toward Parley's cottage and the waiting horse and police wagon.

"Something's not right here," his constable muttered, falling in step beside Brown.

"I couldn't agree more, Waterman. And if we're right, it's a bit more grievous than a few illegally moved fence posts."

CHAPTER 19

"Are you certain you want to do this?" Lyndy, leaning in toward her, whispered as an eerie hush descended around them.

She and Lyndy stood shoulder to shoulder, gazing at the black crape tied with a white ribbon fluttering on the door. White clouds, like freshly picked cotton, silently floated by in the reflection of the darkened windows. There was no bird trill, no distant snort of a pony, no rustling treetops, only the flutter of the ribbon and the sound of her own exhaling. This was a house in mourning.

Stella tried to swallow away the sour taste in her mouth.

Lady Philippa wouldn't thank them for the intrusion, and if Stella was honest with herself, after everything Lyndy had told her, she dreaded confronting the widow again. But if the dagger she'd found did belong to Lord Fairbrother, it could be the murder weapon and the police would need to know. Stella needed to know.

Unwilling to break the silence, Stella nodded. But before Lyndy raised his fist to knock, Aunt Rachel's hoarse voice jarred the quiet like a silver tray clattering to the floor.

"Oh, my lands, girlie," she shouted.

Lyndy quietly chuckled as Stella cast her eyes back toward the Daimler parked in the shade of the woods encroaching the edge of Outwick House's circular gravel drive. Bundled up in a tan duster coat, goggles, and yards and yards of white veiling, Aunt Rachel, unrecognizable but for her wizened mouth and chin, rested in the backseat of the car. Stella had dutifully brought the old lady along. The old lady had prudently declined to accompany them inside. But that hadn't stayed her tongue.

"Are you fixing to go in or just stand there until you grow roots and crow's nests on your hat?" The older woman shooed Stella toward the door.

"We might as well get this over with," Stella said, and self-consciously tucked a wisp of hair behind her ear. She slipped her arm through Lyndy's (they were in this together, after all, weren't they?) and faced the imposing ten-foot-tall doublesided oak door again. She nodded for Lyndy to knock. He lifted the brass ring, fitted through the teeth of an ornate lion's head, and rapped it once.

Hodgson opened the door. Having spent two months living under the watchful eyes of Fulton and Tims, Stella knew the subtle look of disapproval on the butler's face. Not to mention the skyward pointing of his nose. Visiting a house in mourning was highly irregular, if not wholly inappropriate, and they all knew it. But there were times when overlooking the rules of propriety was warranted. This was one of those times.

"We are so sorry to intrude during Lady Philippa's darkest time," Stella said. "But we need to talk to her. It has to do with the manner of Lord Fairbrother's death."

Stella took a step forward. The butler didn't budge. He filled the doorway, with his broad shoulders and stoic stare, but Stella had made up her mind. She took another step forward, pulling Lyndy along with her, and kept moving. Hodgson maintained his grip on the door but, forced to step back or risk having Stella push him aside, stumbled slightly as he pulled the door wider. Stella stepped past him, across the threshold, holding Lyndy's arm tightly in her grasp.

"My lady is in the morning room."

"Thank you, Hodgson." At one time she might have placed a hand on the butler's arm, to ease the tension between them, but she'd learned not everyone appreciated such outward displays of appreciation and affection.

Stella looked to Lyndy to lead the way. But her acknowledgment of his history with this house and its lady caused him to flinch. Stella gave him an encouraging smile, as much to hide her trepidations as to ease his. His face devoid of expression, he nodded curtly before guiding her across the marble squares of the hall. The sharp *click-clack* of her heels on the floor echoed through the tomblike hush of the house. Hodgson, who accompanied them in contrasting silence, awkwardly dodged around them, determined to reach the closed morning room door first.

"Lord Lyndhurst and Miss Kendrick to see you, my lady," Hodgson announced as Lyndy and Stella strode into a room, furnished in varying shades of gold and overpowered by the scent of gardenias.

Like a blot of ink on a blank piece of yellowed parchment, Lady Philippa sat at her secretary desk, dressed from neck to heel in black. She looked up from slitting open an envelope in her hand. A striking ruby adorned the letter opener while black bordered the stationery. Even with surprise, annoyance, and disdain warring on her face, Lady Philippa was striking. No wonder Lyndy had been dazzled by her. Lady Philippa puckered her red lips in a pout. Lyndy dropped his arm away from Stella and tugged at his collar. Stella, dismayed by his response, felt a grimace on her lips and willed all the muscles in her face to relax. She wouldn't give Lady Philippa the satisfaction of a reaction. But Lady Philippa had noticed, and her pout spread into a smug smile.

Unexpectedly, Cecil Barlow popped his head up from his reclining position on the couch. He combed back his tousled hair with his fingers. By his expression, he was as surprised to see them as they were to see him.

"I say, this is unusual," he said. "Philippa is in mourning. What are you two doing here?"

"We could ask the same of you," Lyndy retorted.

What was the plant hunter still doing here, an unattached gentleman in a young widow's home, especially when that widow should be in social seclusion? Even Stella knew how improper it appeared. Shouldn't Mr. Barlow have moved to the inn in Rose-hurst or returned to London altogether?

Lady Philippa set down her letter opener and her mail and rose from her desk, deliberately smoothing the sides of her black skirt with her hand.

"You obviously haven't learned all you need to know about our English ways, Miss Kendrick. This is most improper," she said, approaching Stella and picking something from Stella's sleeve. A small, shriveled rose petal had clung to the intricate webbing of the inlaid lace. Scornfully rubbing her fingers free of the offending petal, Lady Philippa turned to Lyndy. She cupped his cheek with her palm. "But, Lyndy, I'm surprised at you. You know I am not receiving visitors yet."

"We are not visiting," Lyndy said, gently but firmly removing her hand from his face. "We've come to tell you something relating to Fairbrother's death."

"Very well," she sighed. She sashayed back across the room past several available armchairs, settling herself next to Cecil Barlow on the couch. She didn't ask them to sit. "If you insist, I will make an exception for you, Lyndy. And for your mother's sake, I will overlook Miss Kendrick's lack of

254

decorum." Stella felt the tips of her earlobes burn.

If this wasn't so important . . . Stella pulled the dagger from its bag and unwrapped it.

"Where did you get that?" Philippa shot to her feet, all pretense of patient forbearance abandoned. She crossed the room in a few hurried steps and snatched the dagger from Stella's palm. "This is my lord's." Lyndy had been right. It had belonged to Fairbrother. "I demand to know where you got this."

"At Furzy Barrow, the one Lord Atherly is excavating."

"But how . . . ?" Lady Philippa stared at the dagger, her dark eyebrows furrowed in anger.

"Isn't that near that snakecatcher's hut?" Cecil Barlow offered.

"Yes, but . . ." Stella stammered.

"I knew it. I knew it," Lady Philippa said, carelessly brandishing the dagger. Lyndy put his arm in front of Stella and forced her back. "And that dirty peasant was here, not two days before my poor, dear husband was brutally murdered. He did this. He stole this dagger, and he killed my husband." With each accusation, she violently stabbed the air.

"No. I know Harvey," Stella said. "He

wouldn't hurt anyone."

"Are you defending my husband's killer?"

"No, of course not," Stella said. "I'm saying it wasn't Harvey."

"Out! I want you out!" Lady Philippa slammed the dagger down next to a bouquet of gardenias on the side table, creating waves of water in the vase.

Stella, startled by Philippa's violent reaction, took a step back, as Lady Philippa slumped onto the couch, her hands hiding her face.

"We'll let ourselves out," Lyndy said, his frosty tone contrasting with Cecil Barlow's soothing reassurances as the plant hunter hovered over the distraught widow.

Lyndy turned on his heel and left. Stella hesitated, took a step forward, but thought better of saying anything more. She turned to follow Lyndy but, unable to resist, glanced once over her shoulder. Lady Philippa was staring at her as if she'd been waiting, willing Stella to look back. Without taking her eyes off Stella, Lady Philippa lifted a handkerchief to her cheek, though no tears marred her face. It had a royal blue *L* embroidered on it. As Lady Philippa dabbed her steely eyes, a sly smile slowly spread across her face. Stella's mouth dropped open, as if she was flabbergasted. Lyndy was right; Lady Philippa was wicked.

Raindrops splattered against the windshield as a light shower sprinkled down on the car. Stella, careening down a straightaway, closed her eyes briefly as she lifted her face to the rain. She was so glad she'd given Aunt Rachel her driving bonnet and veil. The cold droplets seemed to sizzle as they met her burning cheeks. But that look. The raindrops did nothing to erase the lasting impression of Lady Philippa's sly, triumphant smile.

Let her smile. Stella had the truth, and Lyndy, on her side. *And a little something extra, besides.* Stella giggled softly to herself.

"Eyes on the road, please." Stella's eyes popped open at Lyndy's gentle reprimand. "I do think it's time I learned to drive this contraption, don't you?"

"And why would that be?" she said, teasingly, steering straight for a deep rut in the road.

The car bounced and jerked as she swerved back and forth, zigzagging across the rut. A flock of black jackdaws, roosting among the high branches of the nearby wood, launched into the sky, cawing and crowing, in protest as the car roared past.

"I wouldn't scare every living creature within a five-mile radius, for one." Stella laughed until a gloved hand clenched her shoulder in a feeble squeeze.

"I'm eighty-years-old, girlie, and I want to die in my bed, not staring down the devil in the back of this thingamajig."

"Sorry, Aunt Rachel," Stella called sheepishly. Loving it so herself, Stella had forgotten how much the old lady abhorred motoring.

"You should listen to your young fella, by the way. He's talking sense. I still don't know what your daddy was thinking, teaching you to drive."

"You agree with Lady Atherly, then, Aunt Rachel?" Aunt Rachel nodded.

If Lady Atherly had her way, Stella would never sit behind the wheel of the car again. Or ride the heath alone or ask another question that didn't pertain to the weather. But like Lady Philippa, the countess was bound for disappointment. Stella wasn't giving up Lyndy, and she wasn't about to relinquish one of the few freedoms left to her.

"Because she's right. For even a busted granddaddy clock is bound to tell the proper time twice a day." Aunt Rachel cackled at her comparison of Lady Atherly to a broken clock and sat back.

"By the way," Stella said to Lyndy, "will you hold something for me?" She slipped something from its hiding spot among the folds of her skirt.

"But?" Lyndy sputtered as he grasped the handle of Lord Fairbrother's dagger. "Philippa took this from you."

"And then left it on the side table."

"You stole this from her table?"

"I did, when she was preoccupied with Cecil Barlow's attentions. It's better for Inspector Brown to see the dagger for himself, don't you think?"

After leaving Outwick House, they had agreed to drive into Lyndhurst and talk with the police. Inspector Brown had requested a second interview with Stella anyway, and he needed to know about the theft of the dagger.

"Besides, I don't trust Lady Philippa," Stella added.

Any woman who would scheme with Lady Atherly to steal Lyndy away, days after being widowed, was capable of anything. Whether she was a woman scorned getting revenge, half crazed by grief, or as manipulative as Lyndy portrayed her, Stella couldn't say, though she had her suspicions. But for whatever reason, Stella wasn't taking any chances that Lady Philippa might lose, hide, or destroy what could be the weapon that killed Lord Fairbrother.

"You could make an exemplary pickpocket," Lyndy said, his expression unreadable.

Was he joking? Or was that a hint of admiration in his tone?

"Don't let your mother hear you say that," Stella said, pressing gently down on the brakes. Nearing the village, they quickly approached more carriage traffic, and Stella didn't want to frighten the horses. "That's all I'd need." Lyndy chuckled.

Stella drove through the streets of Lyndhurst. The town was a mixture of squat merchants' shops with divided windowpanes and red tile roofs, three-story white, plastered buildings with decorative half-timbering and large bay windows, narrow, redbrick Victorian homes with steep, highly embellished gables, and an imposing, redbrick, Gothic church looming from the top of the hill, its steeple jutting well over a hundred feet into the sky. She shared the curving, narrow lanes with a profusion of horses, carriages, buggies, and wagons of all shapes and sizes. At their current speed, a maid walking to market would overtake them.

When her family had first arrived in England, Daddy's Daimler had elicited raised fists or angry shouts as villagers displayed their displeasure at the car. One man, so enraged, banged his fist against the hood as she drove past, risking having his foot run over. But as the weeks passed, more and more residents were drawn to the sparkling, colorful horseless carriage, and more than not, waved as they recognized Stella as she drove past. Today was no different.

Mrs. Bottomley, a portly widow who owned Stella's favorite millinery shop, waved as she placed her newest creation in her shop window. Stella waved back. Mr. Macken, the newsagent sweeping his doorstep, stopped to greet her as well.

"Why are they waving at you?" Lyndy asked as Stella returned Mr. Macken's wave.

"They're just friendly. Not everyone dislikes Americans."

Being in England two months now, Stella felt more at ease. She'd dined or danced with most of New Forest's high society. She'd met almost everyone in Rosehurst from the butcher's daughter to the men who owned the bank and was expanding her patronage to the merchants of Lyndhurst, and on occasion, Lymington as well. Most villagers had ceased staring at her as if she'd grown a horse's mane. Whether she'd won them over with her smile or with her American dollars, she might never know. But being "the American" was no longer the burden it once was.

After parking on the hill near the church, Lyndy and Stella left Aunt Rachel with the car and sought out Inspector Brown. Stella knew right where to go. One night, hoping to free an innocent footman, she had dragged Ethel, her lady's maid, to the police station, with its sweet, musky smell of old paper and burnt coffee and plain, drab, unadorned walls. Would this trip be as successful and prove Harvey innocent of murder? Stella hoped so.

Constable Waterman ushered them into an office off a nondescript hall. The single window, covered with iron bars, looked out across a narrow alley to the crumbling plaster wall of the building next door. Not an inspiring view. But the tiny, tidy office, with its highly polished maple desk, dotted with neat piles of typewritten papers, matching maple shelf, lined with books — *Kelly's Directory of Hampshire 1905, A General View of the Criminal Law of England,* and *New Forest Atlas* — attached to clean yellow walls, reflected the orderly mind of the man who occupied it. The scent of fresh paint still lingered in the air. Lyndy wrinkled his nose in distaste.

"New case, new paint, my lord," the constable explained. "The inspector always likes to get off to a fresh start."

"Right! Out with you, then," Inspector Brown said, shooing the constable out the door.

As there was only the desk chair, Inspector Brown wheeled it around, offering it to Stella. Lyndy stood with his hands resting on the back of the chair while Brown perched on the edge of the desk.

"I'm surprised to see you here. I'd left word that I would call at Pilley Manor."

"This couldn't wait." Stella immediately produced the dagger. "I found this yesterday afternoon, at Furzy Barrow, on George Parley's land."

"George Parley?" Inspector Brown said. "His name keeps popping up."

"Is he a suspect?" Stella asked. She remembered how he'd threatened Lord Fairbrother at the Cecil Pony Challenge, how he'd demanded she give him the dagger. When the inspector didn't answer, Stella added, "Mr. Parley arrived after I found it, and insisted I give it to him, since I'd found it on his land, he'd said. But I wonder since, according to Lady Philippa, the dagger belonged to her husband."

"I have seen it at Outwick House as well," Lyndy said as if Lady Philippa's word wasn't enough. "Someone stole it from Lord Fairbrother's collection."

"Or Lord Fairbrother himself removed it and used it for some reason," Inspector Brown added.

"From my understanding, everything in Fairbrother's collection is expensive, rare, and strictly ornamental," Lyndy said. "I don't see him doing anything but gloating over it."

Inspector Brown nodded. "You would know more than I, my lord," he said.

"Could this have been used to kill Lord Fairbrother?" Stella asked.

"Thank you for bringing this to me," the policeman said. As usual, he didn't answer her question. "I will give this to Dr. Lipscombe, the medical examiner, as soon as he returns from London tomorrow. May I?" Stella placed it in his outstretched hand.

"Be careful. It is still quite sharp. My father cut himself on it when I showed it to him." Stella handed him the bag and linen the dagger came wrapped in. "What was it you wanted to speak to me about, Inspector?"

"I need to know when you last saw Harvey Milkham."

Stella didn't like the tone of the policeman's voice. "Why?"

Inspector Brown held the dagger under the lamp on his desk for a closer inspection. If he was looking for traces of blood, he was wasting his time. She'd already looked. "How many people do you think have handled this since you found it?" He hadn't answered her question.

Stella counted them off in her head. "At least seven."

"I won't bother with that new fingerprinting technique then," he mumbled as he locked the dagger in his desk drawer.

"Why do you want to find Harvey?" she asked again.

"I need to ask him a few questions about the murder if only to eliminate him from our inquiries." Or accuse him of a crime he didn't commit.

"He didn't kill Lord Fairbrother, Inspector."

"How can you be so sure, Miss Kendrick?"

Stella opened her mouth to answer, but the words died in her throat. How could she articulate what was only a hunch? "Call it American optimism or female intuition, whatever you like. I just know."

Inspector Brown pinched the bridge of his nose. "Where and when did you see him last?"

"On the way back from the barrow, yesterday, late in the afternoon. He was picking up the pieces of what was left of his home." She didn't tell him how Harvey wouldn't tell her where he was living, or that he'd snuck away when she wasn't looking. Or that he was drunk.

"And you haven't seen him since?"

"No."

"Harvey's hut wasn't too far from Furzy Barrow, now, was it?"

Stella's stomach clenched. That's what Cecil Barlow had said. "Yes, but —"

Had she made a mistake giving him the dagger? No, the policeman had a right to know. But he wasn't getting anything more from her, and that went for Harvey's snake-catching sack. She'd burn it if she had to.

"Thank you, Miss Kendrick, my lord, for bringing this to my attention. I'll let you know when I have news." As they turned to leave, he added, "And if you see Harvey, you let me know."

"Of course," Lyndy said, but Stella held her tongue. If she saw Harvey Milkham,

Inspector Brown would be the last person she told.

CHAPTER 20

The servants were taking a break for tea when Stella returned from Lyndhurst. Crumbs, of what must've been fruit scones, littered the plain, white china plates in front of them. Stella's mouth watered at the lingering scent of Mrs. Downie's baking, anticipating the scone they'd saved for her. *Unless Daddy ate them all.*

Everyone rose when she entered the kitchen, but she shooed them back into their seats. Although the women sat, Tims, who had left the table to open the door, remained standing. She was heartened to see the steam rising from his cup. At least he wouldn't have to drink his tea cold on her account.

"I am so sorry to interrupt, but we did say we'd meet again to make the final arrangements for the engagement dinner."

"Aye, that we did, dearie," the housekeeper said.

"Would this be a good time? After you've finished, of course."

"We were just finishing up, Miss Stella," Ethel said, reaching over to collect Mrs. Robertson's empty cup. With no kitchen maid and only a day maid who took her meals at home, it fell to Ethel to pick up some of the duties. But she'd told Stella she didn't mind. After all, she had been a housemaid before becoming Stella's lady's maid. Tims frowned as Ethel gathered up the cook, Mrs. Downie's, teacup but said nothing.

"Would you like us to come to the drawing room, then?" Mrs. Robertson asked.

"We can do it right here if it's okay with you." The housekeeper and the cook stole a glance at each other. Stella was all too familiar with that silent conferring between those whom she'd shocked with her "American" ways. Luckily it didn't happen as often as it once had.

"If the miss wouldn't be more comfortable elsewhere, perhaps the library?" Mrs. Robertson offered.

If only they'd judge her less if she told them why she preferred the warmth and comfort of the kitchen to the drawing room where her father sat dictating and criticizing and where Miss Cosslett, who hadn't been this long from Daddy's side in days, could return and ambush her at any moment. But she'd learned speaking so familiarly with servants, even ones willing to make allowances, was by far a bigger faux pas than selecting menus at the kitchen table.

"No, this is fine."

"If you'll excuse me then, miss, I have duties elsewhere," Tims said.

"Of course," Stella said, as Ethel snatched up his partially full cup. The butler's tea had grown cold after all. "And thank you for letting me barge in on your break." The butler nodded stiffly and left.

"He hasn't quite gotten used to me yet, has he?" Stella said, sitting down at the table as Mrs. Robertson went to fetch the ledger containing the dinner party details.

Ethel and Mrs. Downie looked at one another, as the cook placed a cup of tea and a scone in front of Stella, neither wanting to be the one to confirm what Stella already knew. Not everyone was pleased to be serving the Americans. Stella broke off a piece of scone and popped it into her mouth. Slathered with clotted cream and lemon curd, it was as delicious as she'd hoped.

"Don't you have ironing work to do, Ethel?" Mrs. Robertson said when she returned. Ethel leaped up, made her excuses, and left. "She does try, that one. Just needs a bit of reminding."

Stella was glad to hear it. She'd been worried the other servants wouldn't accept Ethel as a lady's maid, having been made so at Stella's request and not because she'd trained for it. But Mrs. Robertson had taken the girl under her wing, and Stella saw the confidence and competence blossom in Ethel since they'd moved into Pilley Manor. Hopefully, it would be enough to sustain her when she and Stella returned to Morrington Hall after the wedding.

"Now, shall we begin with the menus?" Mrs. Robertson said while Cook nodded.

The three women discussed every detail of the upcoming event: which fish to serve; whether to serve sweet jellied aspic or fruit ices; which flowers to place in the centerpieces, being careful not to choose any that might clash with the place settings or dining room decor; whether to borrow china from Morrington Hall or make do with the inferior set of dishes found in the cabinets here. The list went on and on. And if Stella thought the two more experienced women would be forgiving to a newcomer, she was wrong. Mrs. Robertson and Mrs. Downie were no less forgiving in their demands on Stella than Lady Atherly and Lady Philippa would've been. Nor were they any less opinionated being servants, often disagreeing with Stella at every turn. When they came to the seating arrangements, Stella held up her hand in defeat; she had to take a break. She was exhausted.

"I know I'm imposing, Mrs. Downie, but would it be too much to ask for a cup of coffee?"

"Not at all, miss."

When Cook set the cup of steaming, dark liquid in front of her, Stella wrapped her hands around the cup and breathed in the rich scent. Then she pulled the seating chart closer. Lord Fairbrother and Lady Philippa's names had been crossed off, and the names of Miss Cosslett and Professor Gridley had been written in their place.

"Mr. Kendrick requested the modification . . . considering," Mrs. Robertson said, pointing to the recent change. "If you approve, that finishes it."

Stella nodded, knowing her father would have his way regardless and took a sip of her coffee, savoring its sweet heat as it slid down her throat. Mrs. Downie remembered she liked sugar in her coffee. The thoughtfulness soothed her as much as the coffee.

"Do you think it's right to host this party with Lord Fairbrother's death so recent?"

she said.

Cook, stirring something on the stove that smelled of potatoes and cream, and the housekeeper, putting the seating chart in her ledger, stole worried glances at each other again.

"Please," Stella added. "I want your honest opinion."

Stella knew it wasn't the English way, but she had to talk to someone about it, and she didn't care what Lady Atherly might say.

"Well . . ." Mrs. Downie began, tasting the soup she was cooking, "if you want an honest opinion . . ." Mrs. Robertson raised a warning eyebrow, but the cook shrugged and continued stirring. "I wouldn't trouble yourself about it, miss. I doubt anyone is mourning the death of Lord Fairbrother." That wasn't what Stella expected to hear.

"But what about Lady Philippa? Don't you think she grieves for her husband?"

Mrs. Robertson bit her lower lip as she tapped the edge of the ledger on the table, straightening the papers tucked inside. The housekeeper didn't need to say she disagreed. But why? Did she know Lady Philippa had set her sights on Lyndy? No. Stella couldn't imagine Lady Atherly's plans being that widely known. At least not yet.

Stella looked at the cook as Mrs. Downie brushed invisible crumbles from her spotless apron. Neither woman would meet Stella's gaze.

"Was Lord Fairbrother as awful as that?"

Stella had only known the lord a couple of months. He'd seemed cocky and egotistic, not unlike Lyndy when she'd first met him. But Lord Fairbrother had always been civil, even appearing to value her opinion on his horse and pony stock. He seemed a demanding husband but not cruel. At least not in Stella's presence.

"You have no idea, miss," the cook said.

"Now, now, Mrs. Downie," the housekeeper said. "Miss Kendrick doesn't need to be privy to a dead man's faults."

"Yes, yes, I do." If there was something about Lord Fairbrother, something likely to bear on his murder, she wanted to know.

Mrs. Downie shrugged at the housekeeper and gestured toward Stella as if to say, "She's asking, what can I do?" Mrs. Robertson shook her head, raising her eyes entreatingly toward heaven. The cook, taking Mrs. Robertson's silence as permission to speak, turned off the burner, pulled herself out a seat. After settling her expansive backside into the chair and wiping her hands on her apron, she leaned forward across the bare, well-worn oak table.

"What I've heard told," she said, covering the side of her mouth as if to shield what she said from lip-readers, "is that Lord Fairbrother took bribes, as official verderer, I mean." She sat back, crossed her thick arms across her ample bosom, and nodded with satisfaction.

"And where did you hear that, Mrs. Downie?" Mrs. Robertson asked skeptically.

"George Parley's head groom is brother to the greengrocer's delivery boy, Willie. He's a talker, that one, always giving me the gossip when he brings in the produce." She lowered her voice slightly and leaned forward again. "From what Willie's been telling me, George Parley's been moving fences for years, and no one has been the wiser."

"But that doesn't mean George Parley paid Lord Fairbrother to look the other way, does it?" Stella said, despite having heard similar accusations.

"Doesn't it?" The cook stood up, brushed down a fold in her apron, and reached up to fetch a copper pot hanging with others along the wall. "According to Willie's brother, no one's been out to check those fences since you-know-who became official verderer."

"I would have to agree with Miss

Downie," Mrs. Robertson said. "I too have heard such things — about landowners paying Lord Fairbrother for wee favors: extra stallions put out to pasture, harvesting of more wood than they're legally allowed, and the like — and from more respectable sources than the greengrocer's boy." Mrs. Downie, cutting a pad of butter into the pot, snorted at the rebuke.

"Then, you wouldn't be interested to know what Willie told me just yesterday, would you?"

"And that being?" Mrs. Robertson sighed.

"That his brother, the groom, spied an envelope bursting with pounds in George Parley's waistcoat pocket when he handed off his horse. The envelope was gone when his master came back."

"Do the police know?" Stella said.

"Who'd tell them?" Mrs. Downie said, dicing up some onions and adding them to the pot. It smelled heavenly. "And would they listen if we did?"

"But if George Parley and the other landowners benefitted from Lord Fairbrother's intervention on their behalf, even if they had to pay him to do it, wouldn't they mourn his death?" Stella said.

"No."

"But why not? Without him, they no

longer have someone to beg favors from."

"Because he blackmailed them, he did."

"Why, Mrs. Downie," Mrs. Robertson exclaimed, "whoever dared say such a thing?"

"Mrs. Tooker, the cook at Outwick House."

Mrs. Robertson scoffed. "I say, that is most extraordinary. In all my days, I've never heard of such disloyalty." Cook shrugged.

Stella, though not as outraged as the housekeeper, was stunned. Servants inevitably chatted with one another, but to share the secrets of the employers was unnerving, especially with her presumably being the subject of such gossip. Stella wondered if Lyndy, or even Lady Atherly, suspected.

"Whom was he blackmailing?" Stella asked.

Cook continued to stir. "That Mrs. Tooker wouldn't say, but it's true to character, what with his jealousy toward Lady Philippa and their open, heated arguments. I'd be daft not to believe it."

Jealousy? Heated arguments? Because Lady Philippa preferred other men's attention? She certainly enjoyed Cecil Barlow's adoration. She certainly expected Lyndy's.

"What did they argue about?"

"What didn't they?" Cook said, without turning around. "He was known to lash out in anger at any time." She simulated a slap across her cheek, leaving behind a trail of flour she'd just added to the pot.

"What? No!" Stella wouldn't believe it. She had lived her whole life dodging her father's wrath. Lord Fairbrother didn't seem capable of such violence. Could the servants be wrong? Stella doubted it.

"Yes, that is something I heard about as well," Mrs. Robertson admitted. "But one doesn't like to gossip about such things."

How awful. Stella now understood Lady Philippa's desire for Lyndy. Lyndy was as gentle as Lord Fairbrother was cruel. But that didn't mean she forgave Lady Atherly or planned to let Lady Philippa get her way. Stella was going to marry Lyndy. Lady Philippa would have to find herself another husband.

The sudden thought disturbed her, but before she could puzzle out why, Cook banged her spoon on the lip of the pot and said, "No wonder she took a lover."

Stella didn't think Mrs. Downie could've said another thing that shocked her, but there it was. How did Cook know all of this?

"Did Mrs. Tooker tell you that too, Mrs. Downie?" Mrs. Robertson said, sounding as skeptical as Stella felt.

"No, but Nelly did. Did I mention Nelly is me niece?"

"Who?" was all Stella could say.

"Nelly is a chambermaid at Outwick House," Mrs. Robertson explained to Stella before asking of the cook, "and what pray tell did wee Nelly say?"

"She wouldn't say for certain, but when you clean someone's room and make someone's bed every day, you learn things. And she swears Lord Fairbrother wasn't always at home when the linens needed changing, if you get my meaning."

Stella felt the familiar burn at the tips of her ears, but covered her cheeks as they too burned with embarrassment. She understood all too well what Mrs. Downie was implying. Stella's heart pounded at the thought of Lady Philippa welcoming a man to her bed, of Lyndy's denied desire of being that man, of her upcoming wedding night. Anger, fear, passion, and doubt warred within her as she fought to loosen the stifling lace collar around her neck. When had it gotten so warm in here? The stern composure on Mrs. Robertson's face brought Stella instant relief.

"I don't want to hear any more such talk as long as I am in charge of this house,"

Mrs. Robertson said.

Cook shrugged and added a bit of salt and pepper to her dish. "I'm just repeating what I've been told."

"Is there any other gossip I should know about?" Stella couldn't imagine anything, after that unsettling bit of news, but this was the time to ask.

"I think that's quite enough," the housekeeper said, rising from the table. "Mrs. Downie needs to finish preparing lunch."

But Stella didn't agree. Who would've guessed Mrs. Downie would be such a fount of knowledge? Stella had imagined Cook stuck in the kitchen day and night, isolated from the world, only breathing fresh air on her way to church. How wrong she was. Cook probably knew more about life and the lives of those around her than any reporter from London ever could. If Mrs. Downie knew this much about Lady Philippa, maybe she knew about Harvey.

"One more question, if you'll indulge me," she said. Mrs. Robertson pinched her lips but couldn't object. With eager anticipation, Mrs. Downie looked over the spoonful of potato soup she was sampling. "Is there anything I should know about Harvey Milkham?"

"The snakecatcher?" Mrs. Robertson said,

taken aback by the question. She pulled up the chain dangling from her waist and fumbled through the keys. "Well now, once I would've said he kept himself to himself unless someone needed ridding of snakes. But now . . ."

"I heard told he likes to toss potato sacks full of snakes into the pub if it's a busy night." Mrs. Downie chuckled, wiping the corner of her mouth with the edge of her apron.

"Yes, well," Mrs. Robertson continued. "I'm sorry to say, as you are his friend, but whenever there's talk of Lord Fairbrother's murder, Harvey Milkham's name is the first on everyone's lips."

Stella frowned. It wasn't what she wanted to hear. More burdened now than she'd been when she stepped into the kitchen, she thanked the women and rose.

"Don't you worry, dearie." Mistaking the reason for Stella's somber mood, the house-keeper tapped the ledger she held tightly against her chest. "The dinner will be just grand."

"Well, if it is, it's all thanks to you, ladies."

The two servants beamed, pleased by the compliment. Stella forced herself to return the smile but dropped all pretense of gaiety the moment she was away from the kitchen.

*Who cares about a silly dinner when every-
one's branded Harvey the killer?*

CHAPTER 21

Tom Heppenstall had a dilemma. He prided himself on living simply and keeping himself to himself. He knew right from wrong; he knew when someone was cheating him, and when a loyal customer deserved a pint on the house. But this?

Tom paced the length of the bar, rubbing out a smudge with his towel here, wiping up a spill there. Tom limped back down the bar again. His ankle, though better today, still smarted.

But this he wasn't used to.

That day the American lady appeared on his doorstep had put Tom in a similar predicament. What if she'd insisted on entering his pub? Would he have allowed it or denied her? Would he have lost trade by angering his customers? Would he have lost business for angering Lord Atherly? Luckily the lady knew a boundary she shouldn't cross when she saw it, saving Tom from having to make the decision. But here he was again. And Tom couldn't make his mind up.

At the other end of the bar, Old Joe smacked his lips as he set an empty glass next to the broadsheet he was reading. Tom limped down the bar to fetch it.

"What seems to be the problem, Tom?" Old Joe said, without looking up. "Never knew you to pace before."

"No problem," Tom mumbled. Old Joe raised his wispy brows. Tom wasn't a good liar.

Inspector Brown had made himself quite clear. If Tom saw Harvey Milkham or George Parley, he was to contact the policeman immediately. Straightforward enough, especially when it came to the snakecatcher; Harvey hadn't shown a hair of his dirty, gray head since Lord Fairbrother's body was found floating in the river.

But with George, it was different. George and Tom went way back. The two men had gone to primary school together. Tom even stepped out with George's sister before she married that other fellow and moved to Winchester. (Rightfully so. She was too good for Tom or Rosehurst.) And George was as loyal as they came, changing from the Queen's Head in Burley to the Knightwood Oak when Tom took over. But worst of all, Tom knew George would be strolling in any minute. The fellow had grievances, the fellow had dreams, and sometimes a few pints too many were the only remedy when the two coincided.

So, what should he do?

Tom halted halfway down the bar when the door opened and, as Tom feared, George Parley was on the other side of it. Tom flipped the towel onto his shoulder and drew the usual even before George ambled up to the bar.

"We weren't sure whether we'd see you tonight, George," Old Joe said, laying his newly read broadsheet on the stack of newspapers beside him. No one had occupied the seat beside Old Joe in years.

"And why would that be?" George asked, after taking a swig from his beer and licking the foam from his upper lip.

"Because the police have been around looking for you."

"Have they now? Why would that be?"

"Because you were heard threatening Lord Fairbrother not long before somebody killed him. That's why." Old Joe stared at George, expectantly. Tom knew Joe to be a bit of a busybody, but this was more than his usual. George finished his drink and set the glass on the bar. Tom had already put a fresh pint down before him.

"Well, if you must know, Joe, I've already spoken to the police and they —"

"Need to speak with you again," a gruff voice called from across the room.

Tom, George, Old Joe, and every other head in the place shot up to see who had spoken. It was Inspector Brown. A younger, burlier policeman stood beside him. Tom cursed. How could he not have seen the policemen come in? But then again, dilemma resolved.

"Shall we step outside, Mr. Parley? It'll be more private," the inspector said.

George reached for his second pint and gulped half of it down. He wiped his mouth with the back of his hand before answering, "I've got nothing to hide."

"Very well."

The policemen approached the bar, the younger one flipping open a notebook. The inspector produced something wrapped in a clean, thick cut of linen and set it down before them. George recoiled back as when Harvey had dropped an adder on the bar. Old Joe clambered up, and with his knees on the stool, stretched as close across the bar as he could get. Tom, his hand still holding the towel inside a wet glass, scrutinized the bundle from where he stood. The boy, arriving up from the cellar carrying an empty keg, dropped his burden with a thud and gaped over George's shoulder. The inspector flipped off the cloth.

An ornamental dagger? Tom blew out his pent-up breath.

But why the sudden apprehension? What was Tom expecting: a severed finger, a blood-encrusted bullet, or like George, a snake ready to leap out at them? Tom slapped the towel across his shoulder, silently chiding himself on such a flight of fancy. The object was nothing but one of those daggers that you'd see on the king's guards. Tom, in his foolish youth, had once joined a throng lining the streets of Lymington as Her Majesty Queen Victoria passed by on her way to the Isle of Wight. He'd failed to catch a glimpse of Her Majesty in the shadowy recesses of her carriage. But the guards, the coachmen, the horses, all in their rich, colorful ceremonial dress, were enough to humble a simple bloke such as he.

"Where did you get that?" The boy, standing on his tiptoes and craning his neck around George to see better, reached his gangly arm out to touch the thing.

The policeman slid the dagger away, out of the boy's grasping hands. "Have you ever seen this dagger, Mr. Parley?"

George slipped a plain cotton handkerchief from his pocket and wiped his brow before wrapping his fingers around his half-empty beer glass. "Yes, I've seen it."

Old Joe whistled in surprise.

Whoosh! As if mimicking Old Joe, a high-pitched rushing sound of wind echoed through the floorboards. The boy dropped, ear to the ground, to listen.

"It's the ghost again," the boy wailed. Everyone but Tom ignored him. George's honest admission trumped any spectral moaning.

"Get off your knees, lad, and put away that keg." Relation or no, that silly boy had to go.

"Where?" the inspector asked. "Where have you seen it before?" George guzzled down the rest of his beer. The policemen waited.

"I was passing when the American lady found it at Furzy Barrow. Why?"

"It was stolen from Outwick House. You visited Lord Fairbrother there, I believe?"

"On business, mind." George signaled he wanted two more pints, his fingers shaped in a V. Tom obliged. He didn't wonder George needed it, with the accusation like that left hanging, like a noose from the rafters. When George had taken another long drink from his third pint, he said, "What are you accusing me of? Stealing the man's posh dagger?"

"We believe it may be the weapon used to kill Lord Fairbrother." George slammed the glass on the bar, beer sloshing about. Tom was surprised it didn't break.

"I didn't steal anything, and I didn't kill anybody. And good, bloody luck trying to prove I did."

"Right!" Inspector Brown said. "As I said before, don't leave the area, Mr. Parley. We may need to speak to you again. Gentlemen." The inspector tipped his hat, motioned to his constable, who flipped his notebook closed, and the two men left. The place was so quiet Tom could hear the mice scurrying up the walls. George snatched his glass up, tipped his head, and finished what was left in one long gulp.

"Why are you all looking at me like that?" he demanded, again slamming the empty glass on the counter. This time they weren't so lucky. The glass broke, large shards fracturing in George's grip.

"It isn't fair. I'm the one that should've won the Cecil Cup. You saw me mare. A blind codger could see she bested Fairbrother's. And I'm the one whose plans have all been for naught. Do you know how much money I've spent?" He pointed at Tom, and then at Old Joe. "Do you?" Tom had no idea what George was on about.

"Well, I didn't kill the bastard, but after how he's cheated me" — he shoved a finger hard against his chest — "I had every reason to. Give me another round, Tom."

"I think you've had enough." It pained Tom to say it, but George was swaying and could barely keep his seat.

"You've got that right!" George shouted, slipping off his chair and staggering to the door. "I have had enough. More than enough!" He yanked open the door, allowing it to slam against the wall. "And I think it's about time I did something about it." With that, he stumbled into the night.

CHAPTER 22

Stella, a glass of champagne in hand, absent-mindedly nodded at the expected pauses as Baron Branson-Hill cataloged his latest equine acquisitions. Typically, Stella would be happy to talk about horses, but the lanky noble collected horses like Stella collected souvenir spoons; he didn't know the first thing about the animals he bought and sold. But Stella knew better than to say so. As the baron rambled on about purchasing a pair of quarter horses, a couple of Hanoverian horses, and four foals from the Arabian Peninsula, she nodded politely, took a sip of the too dry champagne, and sought out Lyndy. He was speaking with the baroness on the other side of the drawing room. He, too, looked bored.

Why was she even here?

In her letter, Lady Atherly had made it quite clear that she no longer supported the engagement between Stella and Lyndy, but because Lady Atherly had planned the dinner weeks ago, she couldn't uninvite the Kendricks. Stella had wanted to decline, as her father did when Lady Atherly made it clear Jane Cosslett was not welcome, but Lyndy insisted they show a united front. Someone to share in his misery, more likely. Stella took another tepid sip.

"I'm quite looking forward to it," the baron said. Stella nodded distractedly when he paused. "I think your father and I will have a great deal to discuss." Her father? Stella, having let her thoughts wander, had no idea what the baron was talking about.

"When are you seeing my father?"

The baron laughed. "At your engagement dinner party, of course. Isn't that what we've been talking about?" Silently Stella groaned. If this dinner was trying, she couldn't imagine what new torment that evening was going to bring.

"Good evening, Miss Kendrick, Baron." With Lady Alice in tow, Cecil Barlow sidled up next to Stella.

Stella had never seen Mr. Barlow without Lady Philippa. When Lady Atherly revealed earlier this evening that she'd invited him, Stella wondered if he'd show up. But he had, and with bells on. After handing Fulton, Morrington's butler, his Stetson, Mr.

Barlow had heartily shaken hands with Professor Gridley and Lord Atherly, insisting they tell him everything about the expedition to Wyoming. The moment Professor Gridley began his account, though, the plant hunter moved on to the ladies, kissing every hand he could clasp. Lady Alice had blushed crimson from the moment she saw him and giggled, almost uncontrollably, when he'd kissed her hand. She'd followed him around like a puppy ever since.

"Have I told you what happened to me on the drive over?" Mr. Barlow leaned forward heavily on his cane with both hands, the citrusy scent of his fresh orchid wafting around him. Lady Alice, her eyes wide and unblinking, shook her head slowly. "I haven't? Well, you will never believe who Lady Philippa and I —"

"But Lady Philippa is in mourning," the baron admonished. "She shouldn't be 'seeing' anyone."

Despite her feelings for Lady Philippa, being cooped up in her house for months on end was a fate Stella wouldn't wish on anyone. "She confined herself to her carriage, didn't she?" Stella asked. Mr. Barlow nodded. "Then I'm sure Lady Philippa just craved some fresh air. No harm done."

"Well, when you put it that way, Miss

Kendrick," the baron capitulated.

"As I was saying," the plant hunter said, annoyed to have been interrupted, "you'll never guess who we saw."

"We are all a twitter, Mr. Barlow, and could hardly guess," Lady Alice said, batting her eyes as Stella had seen Jane Cosslett do. Why would any woman do that? Did men find it alluring or were they left wondering if the lady had grit in her eyes?

"That snake-catching fellow," Mr. Barlow said, leaning back and taking a glass of champagne from the silver tray held out to him by James, the footman. "The one who killed Lady Philippa's husband."

"Harvey Milkham?" Baron Branson-Hill said.

"That's the one." Mr. Barlow grinned as if the baron caught the meaning of a joke. Stella saw nothing amusing about it.

"I say, Harvey Milkham rid a paddock I had of snakes a few months back. I had no idea the police arrested him for the killing of Lord Fairbrother."

"They haven't," Stella said, seething through her teeth. Her patience and ability to maintain this polite veneer were wearing thin. "And Harvey didn't kill anyone."

"Lady Philippa insists he did," Cecil Barlow said, as if explaining something to a child. He tipped his champagne, so that the long, thin stem of the glass rose above his eyes, and then drained it. "Besides," he said, snatching another as James moved away with the tray, "it's not just Lady Philippa. We all heard him threaten Lord Fairbrother at the Cecil Pony Challenge."

"That's true, he did," the baron said. "I heard him."

Lady Alice nodded. "Where did you see him, Mr. Barlow?" she asked, touching him lightly on the arm.

"Can you believe the chap had the audacity to be along the River Blackwater? It may have even been at the same bend where you discovered Lord Fairbrother, Miss Kendrick."

Stella set her barely touched champagne glass on the nearby side table. She'd heard enough.

"Why would he go there?" Lady Alice asked, hanging on the plant hunter's every word.

"That is an excellent question, my lady." Cecil Barlow beamed at Lady Alice, causing her to drop her gaze and press her fingers to her cheeks. Her face was flush again. "I don't know," he said, lowering his voice to a whisper. "Perhaps he plans to kill again."

Lady Alice gasped as Cecil Barlow flourished his cane above his head as if to strike someone. He lowered it and laughed as Lady Alice sheepishly smiled back. Baron Branson-Hill scowled. It made Stella warm a bit to the horse collector.

"I don't think murder is an appropriate topic for conversation," the baron said.

Let alone as a means for flirting, Stella silently added.

"Dinner is served, my lady," Fulton announced.

"Baron, if you'd be so kind as to escort me into dinner?" Lady Atherly said. As she took the baron's arm, her voice grew sterner. "Alice, Professor Gridley is waiting."

She indicated the professor chatting with Lord Atherly by the fireplace. To Stella's regret, the grate was bare. What wonders a small fire would do for the chill in the air. Lady Alice pouted, but a glare from her mother sent her scurrying, the stiff taffeta of her skirt rustling as she went.

"And, Mr. Barlow, if you'd be so kind as to take Miss Kendrick?"

"Of course, Lady Atherly. I'd be delighted." Cecil Barlow offered his arm as requested, and Stella complied. But as Stella advanced toward the door, hoping to catch up with Lyndy, the plant hunter held her back.

"Mr. Barlow?" Stella said, balking at his restraining hold. Despite his thin build, his forearm was taut and bulky beneath his dinner jacket. Despite his infirmity, he held her firm.

"I wanted to let the others go ahead a bit." He pointed his cane at the door just as the last of the guests disappeared around it. "I've been waiting for a chance to speak to you alone." He hesitated, his eyes roaming down the length of her body. "That dress, by the way, is most becoming." Ethel had chosen a dark purple silk gown with black beadwork around the collar and sleeves. It wasn't one of Stella's favorites.

"You'll crease the silk." Her subtle hint didn't work. He wouldn't loosen his grip. "Let go of me."

He leaned into her close, too close. His breath, with its lingering scent of champagne and something stronger, felt warm against her cheek. She cringed, drawing her face as far away as his grip allowed.

"I didn't want to say this in front of Lady Philippa, or anyone else here. It would be far too upsetting, but . . ."

"Then perhaps I don't want to hear it either, Mr. Barlow," Stella said, tugging her arm again. But he wasn't listening.

"But that snake-catching fellow you're so ready to defend? I saw a knife on him."

Stella eyed him warily. Why was he telling her this? Why not inform the police? "When?"

"At that quaint little competition named after me." Stella didn't remind him that the competition had been called the Cecil New Forest Pony Challenge for several years, long before he'd emerged unscathed from the jungle.

"Where?"

"When he tried to accost Lord Fairbrother in the tea tent. When I was holding the chap back, I saw the glint of it at the bottom of his open pocket. It could've been the one stolen from Lord Fairbrother."

"Or it could've been an open pocketknife."

"I didn't think about it at the time, a funny old chap like that having a knife in his pocket at a pony competition. But obviously, I was too preoccupied to think more about it. But now I see I should've stopped him. I should've taken it from him."

Mr. Barlow drew her even closer, despite her resistance and the blatant repulsion on her face. She tilted her face away, but he was so close the petals of the orchid on his lapel almost brushed her chin. Should she call out for help? What would Mr. Barlow do if she did? She eyed his cane and recalled him feigning to hit Lady Alice with it. Would he dare hit Stella?

"I think the police ought to know what I saw," he said. "What do you think?"

Harvey didn't harm the snakes he gathered; why would he stab a man? But the moment Cecil Barlow repeated his accusations, the police were bound to arrest Harvey. Stella wished she'd never found that terrible weapon. She wished she'd never met this beastly man.

"I think you should let go of me." Stella tested his grip again and tried to pull away. He tightened his hold, his fingers digging through the silk of her sleeve.

"I will go to the station tomorrow." Mr. Barlow indicated toward the dining room with his cane, a broad smile across his face. Unburdening his confession, he seemed quite prepared to enjoy his evening. "Shall we?"

Stella was outraged. She seized the orchid, the petals of the exotic flower like thick satin against her palm, and ripped it from his jacket. With some regret, she dropped it to the floor and crushed it beneath her heel. Having red streaks through its veins, the orchid looked like it was bleeding into the carpet.

"Good Lord! Who does such a thing?" Mr. Barlow gaped at Stella as if her hair had turned blue before bending to retrieve his ruined boutonniere. With his hold loosened, Stella yanked free. She whirled out of his reach, scooped up the train of her dress, and dashed from the room. "Miss Kendrick," Mr. Barlow called, "where are you going?"

Startling a footman carrying a tureen of aromatic beef consommé down the hall, Stella bolted past and threw open the front door. Stella raced across the gravel drive, slipping slightly on the dew-glistened pebbles, but didn't stop running until she felt the burn in her lungs and the cushion of grass beneath her feet.

Holding the chair for Baroness Branson-Hill, a tedious woman who was rambling on about the effects of rain on her silk gown, Lyndy wistfully glanced out the window through the gap where the drapes hadn't been fully drawn. Swaths of pink and orange lit up the horizon. It was a glorious evening. At least the baroness and he could agree on something. Not a raindrop in sight. Mother, noticing his distraction as he seated himself, motioned to Fulton to correct the mistake in the drapery. Lyndy craned his neck, stealing one last glimpse of the sunset, and sighted Stella crossing the lawn. She wasn't wearing her hat. A sure sign she'd left on an impulse. When Mr. Barlow entered the dining room alone, Lyndy threw down his napkin. Without wasting time asking the plant-collecting fellow where'd she gone, Lyndy made a hurried excuse and followed after her, all to the satisfying sound of Mother nearly choking on her first sip of wine.

The fresh, cool breeze, carrying the scent of the sea, hit him the moment he stepped out the door. Once again, his darling American had spurred him to do something uncharacteristic and wonderful. But where was she going? Tugging up her skirt and train in her fist, she stomped across the garden, as if trying to put as much distance between her and the house as possible. Not the stables, surely? Not in that dress. She didn't slow when he jogged out to meet her.

"I say, hold on there," Lyndy teased, when he'd almost caught up. He reached out and grabbed hold of her arm. She jerked away from his touch like a skittish horse. A surge of hot anger radiated through his chest. When had she started shying away from him again? Hadn't they overcome this? Was this because of what he'd told her about Philippa? She'd said she'd believed him, trusted him. So why — ?

She whirled about to face him. She was panting. Her porcelain features were flush, and not just the tips of her ears. Shame, frustration, fury flashed in her eyes. Whatever was wrong had nothing to do with him.

"What happened?" he demanded, more harshly than he intended.

Lyndy's first thought was of Kendrick, Stella's father. He was often the source of her distress. But Kendrick hadn't attended dinner — something about dining with that London reporter instead. Had Mother done something?

"Nothing. It's nothing," Stella said with a strained voice as she tucked a strand of hair self-consciously behind her ear. When Lyndy took a step toward her, she backed away. "I thought I'd check on Tully."

"During dinner?" Her rash behavior wasn't unprecedented. She'd once left in the middle of a party, held in her honor, to take a maid to the police station. But this wasn't about freeing an innocent man from jail. "Did Mother say something? If this is about Philippa —"

"Oh, Lyndy," she said, clenching her fists in frustration. "Why did Lady Philippa have to suggest such awful things?" Lyndy tried to ask what Philippa said this time, but Stella spoke over him, her words tumbling out in a rush. "Harvey couldn't have done this, could he?"

Could all this frustration and anger be about the snakecatcher? For the first time, Lyndy detected a hint of doubt in her declaration. He didn't know what to say. He'd never been certain the snakecatcher wasn't guilty, particularly since he blamed Fairbrother for the destruction of his house. Lyndy could imagine wanting to punish anyone who dared harm Morrington Hall. But Stella didn't wait for his response.

"And to think I just gave it to them." Lyndy approached her cautiously, step by step. She stood her ground, eyeing him warily. But when he lifted his hands and rested them lightly on her tense arms, she softened at his touch. She pointed back toward Morrington Hall. "But that man . . . in there . . . your sister . . ." She wasn't making any sense.

"What are you talking about?" he said, trying to hold her gaze. It was unnerving to hear Stella babble. She was nothing if not straightforward and frank about everything and anything. If she had an opinion or a concern, she expressed it. She didn't babble. "Look at me, Stella." When she complied, he said, "Now tell me what's going on. First things first."

"First, I left my hat in the hall, again." Lyndy laughed. To his delight, she aimed a focused look of consternation at him. There was the woman he adored.

"It's not funny, Lyndy. Your mother —"

"After everything she's done? I don't care one bit about what my mother thinks." He kissed Stella's hair. It smelled of castile soap and rosemary. "Now, what else is bothering you." She attempted a smile, but it faded as quickly as it had come.

"I'm worried about Harvey. I'm worried that there might be something to what Lady Philippa said, after all."

"You've always been so certain of his innocence. What's changed your mind? And how does this concern my sister?"

"I don't like Cecil Barlow."

She startled him, nearly growling the man's name. Lyndy didn't care for the plant-collecting fellow either, but what had he done to deserve such loathing? It must have something to do with the snakecatcher. But what did Alice have to do with any of this? Lyndy insisted she tell him. So she did. She repeated Mr. Barlow's insinuations, about Harvey's proximity to the river, Harvey's possession of a knife.

"If Barlow even did see a knife," he reassured her, "it could've been what Harvey uses to fillet his trout or cut twine or pare apples. Doesn't mean he stabbed anyone with it."

Stella puffed out her cheeks and released a big sigh. "That's what I thought, but . . ."

"There's more, isn't there?"

Stella nodded. "I don't trust that man, especially not with Lady Alice."

Lyndy could feel his jaw tighten. Recalling the look in Stella's eye when he first approached her, his mind swirled with the possibilities. "What did Barlow do?"

She told Lyndy everything. How dare he!

"He shan't get away with this." Lyndy turned on his heel, intent on storming back to the dining room and ferociously pummeling the brute until he'd need two canes to walk. But Stella's hand on his arm restrained him.

"Whatever you're thinking about doing, don't. Lady Alice will hate you for it, and it won't help Harvey or me."

"But it might make me feel better. It has been too long since I've sharpened my pugilist skills on someone's face." Lyndy stared at his raised fist, imagining it connecting with Barlow's cheekbone.

Believing he was jesting, Stella smiled.

Lyndy had spoken in earnest. He'd been quite the fighter at Eton, but her smile was enough to assuage his anger. If she was willing to let the matter drop, so could he, for now.

"But, speaking of hitting someone in the face, I haven't told you what my cook told me earlier." Stella relayed what she'd learned: rumors about Fairbrother's blackmailing schemes, his supposed violence toward Philippa, about Philippa's infidelity. Only the latter seemed believable. But then again, Lyndy never dreamed someone would murder Fairbrother either.

"Do you think I should tell the police?" Stella asked.

"And what, have them suspect Philippa?" It had its appeal. But Lyndy wanted nothing more to do with Philippa, even if it meant keeping her dirty secrets. "No. Who cares about Philippa? Remember, too; it's just servant gossip."

"Servants know more than you give them credit. Besides, once Mr. Barlow tells them about the knife he saw, they'll arrest Harvey." Stella groaned. "Oh, Lyndy, Harvey probably doesn't even know how much trouble he's in."

"Then we'll have to inform him. Fancy a ride?" he said.

Stella's face lit up. He never tired of seeing appreciation and affection in that smile. If only he knew how to get that magical reaction on demand.

"Do you think we can find him?" How immeasurably satisfying it was that she knew what he was suggesting. She couldn't read his thoughts, thank goodness, but to have a woman understand him might be that much better. "Mr. Barlow said he saw him on his way to Morrington Hall. Could Harvey still be by the river?"

"I say we find out."

To his astonishment, Stella enveloped him with her arms and pressed a kiss to his mouth, the taste of salty tears he'd never seen on her lips. But before he could return her embrace, she released him, swiveled on her heels, and bolted toward the stables. He had no choice but to follow.

CHAPTER 23

Lyndy, directing the groom to saddle Beau, paused at the sight of Stella leading Tully toward him. What a transformation. And not just for the horse. Yes, Tully, her eyes bright, her ears twitching, and with a healthy shine to her coat, walked steady and sure down the aisle, but Stella — Stella was beaming. Not a trace of her earlier anger and frustration left on her face. Lyndy couldn't help but smile.

"Doesn't she look wonderful?" Stella asked, gazing adoringly up at the horse as she stroked its neck.

"Yes, she does," he said, reaching out and tracing the curve of Stella's soft, supple cheek with the back of his fingers. He wasn't talking only about the thoroughbred. Stella, enthralled by her horse, didn't even seem to notice. It was just as well. They were on a mission.

Lyndy plucked a strand of straw from

Stella's shoulder and tossed it to the ground. Why could she never enter a horse box without coming away with something clinging to her? What did she do, roll in it? The thought led to an image he hastened to banish from his mind. Oh, how he'd rather roll in the straw with her than search for the snakecatcher. But he'd made a promise. Lyndy tugged down on the cuffs of his dinner jacket.

"We can thank Harvey for your swift recovery, can't we, Tully," Stella said, snuggling into the horse's neck. A melancholy had crept into her voice.

"Shall we, then?" Lyndy said, indicating the horses patiently waiting to ride. Stella nodded enthusiastically.

Lyndy waved off the groom and helped Stella into Tully's saddle, the train of silk dress dangling to one side. Stella tucked it up into her lap, careful not to reveal her stockinged leg. Not their usual riding attire, without question, but Lyndy could care less; he was as eager as she to ride. With her secure, he bounded up onto Beau, took the reins, and then the proffered lantern from the groom, and they were off.

Once past the paddocks and grazing lawns surrounding Morrington Hall, they cantered across the heath, the moonlight enough to easily avoid the dark clusters of gorse, heather, and bracken. What had been a light breeze on Morrington's threshold was a brisk wind, blowing at their uncovered heads. It was exhilarating. Then they passed beneath the overhanging boughs of a woodland. Here a stillness pervaded, broken only by the rhythmic breathing of the horses. The glow of the lantern was all the light that pierced the darkness. They slowed their horses to a walk, Stella staying so close he could hear her stomach grumble.

We should've thought to bring a picnic.

But then, as they cleared the trees, their shadows stretching out far in front of them, he remembered their somber task. But as to their spontaneous departure, he had yet to regret it. As they trotted back out on the open heath again, he drew a deep breath, filling his lungs with fresh, moist, summer air. It more than made up for his empty stomach.

The rippling sound of the river reached them long before they detected its dark, sinuous thread and made their way to the well-trodden spot in the bend. Harvey was nowhere to be seen. They trotted a mile downstream with no success. They retraced their steps back upstream, following close to the bank, Stella nervously glancing down into the rushing water.

"He won't be in there," Lyndy said, re-assuring her.

She nodded and gave him a weak smile as if she agreed she was silly to think so, but Lyndy saw the look in her eyes as she searched the dark, flowing water. She wasn't so confident he was right. The trill of a nightjar rang out, and she snapped her head up.

"What was that?" she uttered suspiciously, pulling back on Tully's reins, forcing the horse to a halt.

"It's just a bird." Stella must be on edge if the birdsong startled her.

She chuckled nervously, before clicking her tongue to her horse to proceed forward again. After continuing upstream for another quarter of a mile, they came across a pockmarked farmer and his teenage son packing up for the night. The water in the tin pail beside their dogcart writhed with trout.

"Successful night?" Lyndy asked. The lad and his father quickly slipped the caps from their heads. If they questioned the formal dinner attire Lyndy and Stella were wearing they didn't let it show on their faces.

"Yes, thank you, milord." The father ad-dressed Lyndy, while the lad stared openly at Stella. It had taken getting used to, men and women gawking at his future bride, but like Stella, Lyndy had learned it was part and parcel with their new life. "On behalf of our family, we'd like to offer our deepest sympathies, miss. We hope your misadventure didn't put you off fishing."

The pair, who couldn't help but recognize him, the earl's heir, so too knew, if only by association, who Stella was. And more of it, they knew what misfortune had befallen her.

"We're rather keen on knowing a lady that likes to fish," the lad blurted. "Even if she's an American." The father jabbed his son in the ribs with his elbow.

"Thank you," Stella said. "Both of you." She smiled at the lad, and his face quickly resembled a beetroot. "I appreciate your concern, but I'm tougher than I look. Besides, now that I've been in that river, nothing could put me off fishing its waters again."

The two men nodded, awkward grins widening on their faces. Like everyone, at least almost everyone, the "American" had won these men over with her straightforward manner and genuine kindness. A sudden flash of irritation swelled up in him. How was it that simple countrymen like these could empathize with Stella, and wish her well, when his mother wouldn't treat her with common courtesy?

"We're looking for the snakecatcher," Lyndy said, his voice taut with frustration. "He was supposedly seen here earlier."

Both men nodded, but it was the father who spoke. "Aye, milord. Harvey was here, all right. Pulled in several beauties, even with carriages rumbling by spooking the fish. I don't know how he does it. He should be called the trout catcher. But he left a while back." He was here and doing nothing remotely nefarious. At least there was that.

"Could you tell which way he went?" Stella asked.

The men shook their heads. "Who can say. He's a bit odd, that one."

"Why do you say that?" Stella asked, sounding a mite defensive. She'd accepted crude comments about herself, but she wouldn't suffer them about Harvey. Lyndy silently chuckled. Leave it to Stella to have a soft spot for horses and hermits.

"Well, seeing how he was reeling them in, Jimmy and me made it to where Harvey was catching 'em," the father explained. "Thought we might try our luck. When we moved to the spot, he was gone all right, but there was all his fish." The fisherman shook his head in disbelief. "Why would a man leave his dinner wriggling on the bank, is what I'd like to know?"

"I can't possibly guess why," Lyndy said as Stella flashed him a worried look. "But the reason can't be good."

"Mr. Heppenstall! Mr. Heppenstall!" The pub door swung open, and the boy stumbled across the threshold.

What was it now? Tom flung the towel from his shoulder and slapped it against the bar. Wasn't it enough the police had to come and disrupt his customers? Couldn't the boy do one simple task without a fuss?

"Why haven't you gone after George Parley? You were to see he got safely on his way."

"I know, Mr. Heppenstall, but . . . but Mr. Parley's pony is still outside and . . ."

"And?"

The boy raised a hand. Smears of something slick and bright red covered his palm. "It's bleeding."

Tom didn't hesitate. He bounded around the end of the bar, hobbling as fast as his ankle would allow. In his wake, chairs scraped against the floorboards as men, pints still in hand, clamored to follow. George Parley's pony, its reins hanging loose on the ground, had joined two free-ranging donkeys in grazing on the green across from the pub. When Old Joe, more youthful than his name implied, got to the pony first and led it gently toward the street-lamp, Tom called out for its owner. A chorus of voices joined him.

"George? George? George Parley! George?"

Men fanned out, some crossing to the green, some heading down Rosehurst's high street. Tom, Old Joe, and the boy stayed with the pony. Alarmed by the commotion, the villagers abandoned their late supper or needlework and turned up lights, drew back curtains, and peered into the street. Tom watched as the men called out in vain.

"George Parley! Where are you, George? George?"

"How is it?" Tom asked Old Joe, turning back toward the pony.

"A bit peckish," Old Joe said, running his hands along the pony's withers as it tried to munch on the nearby flower bed, "but brilliant otherwise." He patted the pony firmly on the shoulder. It whinnied softly and nudged Old Joe, trying to get past him and back to the grass.

"But the blood?" The boy held up his palm again. It had already begun to dry in a darker shade of crimson.

"I've seen but one splotch of blood, on its neck," Old Joe said. "That must be what you touched, lad." The boy nodded. "But there's no cuts to its skin anywhere that I can find."

"Then where did the blood come from?" the boy asked, rubbing his palm against his trousers.

"From George," Tom said. It made sense. He'd broken a pint glass with his bare hand. "He probably patted the pony just as the boy did."

"Makes sense," Old Joe said, releasing his grip on the pony's reins. It ambled over to the back wall of the pub and began happily clipping the weeds. "But why leave his pony behind?"

"You know what George is like in his cups," Tom said. "Can't tell what he'll do." Old Joe nodded knowingly.

"What is it doing?" The lad pointed toward the pony. Pawing the ground, the animal was poking its muzzle into what looked like a hole in the wall. A hole Tom had never noticed before.

"Fetch me a lantern," Tom ordered. The boy raced back inside.

When the boy finally returned (he could've walked to Bournemouth and back in the time it took him) the men from the pub had given up their search and were clustered around Tom and Old Joe. Many sipped at the pints still in their hands or murmured complaints about the chill, but no one spoke of the dread they were all feeling. Where was George Parley? He couldn't have gotten far.

The boy handed over the lantern — leave it to him to fetch the dented tin one Tom had planned to toss — and Tom held it up. Light and shadows sprawled across the base of the back wall. There, on the level with the ground, was a hollowed-out space big enough for a man to crawl through. Where had that come from? With his bad ankle, Tom couldn't kneel to shine the light in the hole, let alone crawl inside. He handed the lantern to Old Joe.

"There's something down there, but I can't tell what it is," Old Joe said, peering into the hole.

"See what it is then, lad," Tom ordered. The boy lay on his belly and took the lantern from Old Joe. He lowered it down the hole. Tom was surprised to see the light disappear completely. The boy slithered in after it up to his waist. Loose gravel trickled down in small streams around him.

"Perhaps a wounded dog dug a hole to

my basement?" Tom speculated out loud. "Or a badger?"

The boy slipped back and poked his head up. "Ah, Mr. Heppenstall. You're not going to fancy what I found."

"Well, what is it?"

"You've got to see for yourself."

Tom sighed as he limped over. Leaning hard against the wall, he slid down its length onto one knee and then the other. Peering into the hollow, he saw nothing but a hard-packed dirt floor. That wasn't his cellar. Could there be a sub-basement he didn't know about? Tom had heard about pubs predating the smuggling days that hid contraband in sub-basements. He just never knew the Knightwood Oak had one.

Straining his back, Tom crouched down further. Pine boughs, covered with potato sacks, lined the opposite side of the floor. Bits and bobs littered the rest of the space: empty glass bottles, some Tom recognized as coming from his wine cellar, empty biscuit tins, a tin mug, a small sack of coffee, a chipped teapot, varying lengths of twine. Evidence of a small fire blackened the corner closest to the hole. The room smelled of smoke, whiskey, and pickles. Someone, and Tom could guess who, had been living down there. The snakecatcher no longer had a roof to call his own, after all.

"Well, lad," Tom said, holding his aching back and sitting back on his heels. "I think we've found your ghost."

Lyndy hadn't been here before. He'd glimpsed the snakecatcher's hut from a distance and never thought it amounted to much, a jumble of salvaged boards, bark, and thatch. Only the stone chimney, a tower of fieldstone once belonging to a previous cottage built two hundred years before, was of any consequence. But that now lay in rubble upon the bed of white ash. Someone didn't merely put a torch to the hut, they methodically destroyed the chimney, and with it, Harvey's claim to the rights of common attached to it.

"What a waste," Lyndy muttered, kicking the scorched remains of a wall hook. The snakecatcher had accused Fairbrother of doing this, but why? Lyndy couldn't imagine what Fairbrother, or anyone, could've gained from such petty violence.

"I don't see any sign of Harvey," Stella said, ducking under a low-hanging branch as she and Tully returned to the clearing. She'd insisted on circling the area for the hermit. "But his pony is still in the paddock. He'll have to come back for her eventually."

"But we have no way of knowing when. I say we call it a night and come back at first light." Stella reluctantly nodded.

Swinging back up into the saddle, Lyndy brushed aside further thoughts of Harvey Milkham's whereabouts, his sights set on procuring a cutlet, some warm bread, and a scotch the moment he got home. A hush descended as they crossed Wosset Moor, the spongy lichen and moss-covered ground absorbing the horses' footfalls. Such a magnificent night. And to think, trapped entertaining Mother's guests back at Morrington Hall, they would've missed it. Lyndy closed his eyes, letting Beau navigate the way, and filled his lungs with the sweet scent of the moor.

"Harvey?" Stella said hesitantly after several minutes of silence. Lyndy, lulled by the quiet and the rhythmic gait of the horse, peeked out through one eye and spotted a figure in the distance staggering through the heather, broom, and gorse. The person was making his or her way toward Furzy Barrow.

"Harvey?" Stella called, loudly this time, spurring Tully to a gallop. Lyndy shot up straight and tapped his heels into Beau's barrel and chased after her.

"I'll show you," the figure yelled, slurring his words and shaking his fist in the air. "I'll show bloody everybody." That didn't sound like the old snakecatcher.

Arriving at the barrow first, the outraged man rummaged through a canvas-covered box left by Papa and Professor Gridley, the tools clanking against one another as he fished about for something. He produced a long-handled shovel and clambered up the undug side of the hill. Stopping at the crest, he thrust the shovel into the earth and frantically began scooping soil into the pit. Moonlight reflected off the figure's nearly bald head.

What was George Parley doing? Did he think he could single-handedly fill in the barrow? It was far too big. Besides, Papa and Professor Gridley weren't done excavating it.

Stella, reaching the barrow before Lyndy, slipped from her saddle, her silk dress shimmering as she flipped the train over her arm. Lyndy leaped off Beau as Stella scaled the slope. But before either of them reached the disgruntled landowner, George Parley began flailing about, flapping his arms in the air as if trying to catch his balance.

"Bollocks!" George Parley yelled as he disappeared, headfirst, into the pit as the land beneath him gave way. The shovel, flung from the man's grip, clattered against the wooden plank on the other side. Puffs of dust, smelled more than seen, announced Parley's contact with the earthen floor below. The man's voice went silent.

"Mr. Parley? Are you okay?" Stella said, reaching the edge first. She peered down, and her hand flew up to cover her eyes. "Oh, God!" She twisted around, turning her back, the train of her dress slipping from her arm and puddling in a swirl around her. Lyndy scrambled to the top of the mound.

"Stella? What is it?" Resting a hand on her shoulder, he cast a glance toward the edge but quickly turned his focus back to her. From the sound of things, Parley was stirring about below.

"Are you all right, or did that fool hurt himself?" Stella shook her head. For the first time, Lyndy noticed the intricate twists and knots tightly woven on the top of her head. She must've sat for hours getting that done. He stepped on the train of her skirt, pressing it into the upturned soil, but as he made to move, she pressed her face into his shoulder. "What's upset you so?"

"Bloody hell!" George Parley's head jutted up over the barrow's edge. Crumbs of soil stuck to the perspiration on his bare scalp.

"I say, Mr. Parley, are you in need of assistance?" Lyndy said.

"You can get me the bloody hell out of here!" Parley dropped from sight again.

"Parley?" Lyndy started to lean over to see what could've happened to the landowner only to see Parley reemerge, on the far side, stumbling and tripping on his feet, and catching himself from slipping more than once with an outstretched hand. Parley furtively glanced back at the barrow, his eyes so wide the whites were visible in the dim light. Clear of the barrow, Parley bolted, like a horse out of the gate.

What the hell just happened?

Lyndy, gently easing Stella back, stepped around her, and peered down into the barrow. He'd seen the inside of it many times before, a well-swept dirt floor with precisely dug shallow holes cordoned off with string, occasionally with trowels and brushes strewn about, maybe bits of broken pottery even. But never had he seen a body in the burial mound, the dark shape lying prone beneath the ledge Lyndy stood on, its limbs splayed out like a flattened spider among the broken strands of twine, its face, chest, and unkempt hair matted with loosened dirt, its glassy, unblinking eyes staring up at him.

Stella joined him as he stood staring down into the pit. Lyndy reached for her hand, and she readily clasped his, her grip firm but her skin cold and soft. "Poor Harvey," she sighed.

"Yes," Lyndy muttered. "What a waste."

CHAPTER 24

"Did he break his neck in the fall?"

Miss Kendrick, a drab, brown, woolen blanket from his police wagon wrapped around her shoulders, waited for Brown to answer. Light from the ring of lanterns Brown had had his constable set out around the barrow cast a shadow across her young, sweet face. To find two bodies in less than a week. Brown felt nothing but pity for her. But he wasn't going to answer her question.

When the groom from Morrington Hall had pounded on the door of the police station, breathless and rambling on about burial mounds and the snakecatcher, Brown had been at his desk, another late night, pouring over statements in the Fairbrother murder. With Parley's spurious denial of the dagger, his hoard of rifles, his blatant threats, Brown suspected Parley had something to do with it. But Lady Philippa insisted Harvey Milkham was the culprit.

Brown had known the old hermit for years — everyone knew the snakecatcher — but without the ability to question Harvey, Brown hadn't been able to rule him out. Now he might never know. Brown kicked the wheel of the police wagon in frustration but couldn't help but admire the smooth brown leather of his new shoes. Matilda lifted her head from grazing and snorted in disapproval.

"Inspector?" Miss Kendrick said, not accepting his silence as an answer.

Brown could've insisted the viscount take the American lady away but knew from experience that she had a will of her own. If Miss Kendrick wanted to be here while Dr. Lipscombe examined the body, there was no telling her otherwise. At least he convinced her and Lord Lyndhurst to wait by the wagon.

"We're ready to bring him out," Dr. Lipscombe called, saving Brown from Miss Kendrick's questions. For now.

A police helmet appeared first as Constable Waterman, holding one end of the stretcher, clambered out of the barrow. Harvey Milkham, covered up to his chin with a white sheet, followed. His body jolted up and down on the canvas as Lord Atherly's groom, holding the other end of the stretcher, shuffled unsteadily across the wooden plank. Brown had recruited the lad to help.

"Oi!" Brown called. "Mind yourself, lad." If the body had been Bronze Age cinerary urns, they'd have broken to pieces.

"Oh, Harvey." Miss Kendrick advanced toward the approaching men, managing to brush a strand of hair from the dead hermit's pale, wrinkled brow before Waterman slid the stretcher onto the wagon and beyond her reach. "Can't we close his eyes?"

"She shouldn't be here," Dr. Lipscombe whispered to Brown. The medical examiner, serendipitously, had been out taking his nightly constitutional when Brown and Waterman drove by and had willingly agreed to accompany them. The doctor had never met the headstrong American before.

"Are you going to be the one to tell her to leave?" Brown whispered back. Dr. Lipscombe creased his brows in disapproval but never mentioned sending Miss Kendrick away again.

"What can you tell us, Doctor?" Lord Lyndhurst said, standing protectively close to his American fiancée without actually touching her.

Brown pinched the bridge of his nose. He admired the two young people and indulged them when he could, but he preferred to be the one asking the questions. Couldn't they respect that, just once?

"I'm sorry, my lord, but . . ." Dr. Lipscombe began. Lord Lyndhurst scowled and crossed his arms against his chest. The doctor hesitated midsentence, startled by the challenge on Lord Lyndhurst's face. "But I don't think . . ." The poor doctor had never encountered the entitled viscount before either.

"Just tell us what you found, Dr. Lipscombe," Brown suggested.

"But . . . but that would be highly irregular, Inspector." Brown waved off the medical examiner's objections. "Very well." Dr. Lipscombe shook his head as he spoke, disagreeing with the decision even as he complied with it. "The victim did not die from a contusion or rupture from blunt force."

"Meaning?" Lord Lyndhurst demanded.

"Meaning he didn't die from a fall. Instead, he bled to death."

"But we didn't see any blood," Lord Lyndhurst insisted.

"Begging your pardon, my lord, but it was dark, and the body and area around it were partially covered in soil from Mr. Parley's endeavors. It would have been difficult for you to tell. Rest assured, we found ample blood to determine that is how the victim died." As if massive blood loss could assure anyone.

"But if he hurt himself so badly, why was he still in the barrow? Did he knock himself out? Otherwise, he would've tried to get up and get help." Dr. Lipscombe glowered at Brown, his eyebrows furrowed as if to say, "This is your fault. I shouldn't be talking to her about this." Brown held up his hands in resignation.

"I apologize, Miss Kendrick," the doctor said. "I didn't explain myself. The victim didn't do this to himself in a fall. He was murdered."

Miss Kendrick stared at the back of the wagon where the body lay, hugged the blanket tighter, and then calmly asked, "Do you think George Parley killed him and was trying to cover him up?"

Excellent question. Brown would have to ask George Parley about that. But first things first.

"How was he killed? Was he shot by a rifle, perchance?" Brown's questions earned him questioning stares from the young couple. They hadn't heard about George Parley's rifles yet.

"No, the victim was stabbed."

"Like Lord Fairbrother," Miss Kendrick said before mumbling, faintly talking something over with herself. Brown caught snippets. "What was he even doing here?" and "I suppose it's possible," and "But why Harvey?"

Did Miss Kendrick know something he didn't? Brown had found the American heiress uncommonly observant and useful in his last murder investigation. He ignored her now at his peril.

"What was that, Miss Kendrick?" Brown asked, as encouragingly as he could.

Lord Lyndhurst, too, was regarding her with anticipation. Miss Kendrick rubbed her hands up and down her arms as if cold but said nothing more. Lord Lyndhurst, throwing convention to the wind, wrapped his arm around her shoulder. Yes, Miss Kendrick knew something. But bullying her now wasn't the way to maintain her trust. Brown would let her recover from the shock of finding her friend first. He turned back to Dr. Lipscombe.

"Can you tell anything about the stab wound? Is there a particular weapon we should be looking for?"

Dr. Lipscombe set his well-worn leather bag into the wagon. Dark shadows surrounded his eyes. He looked exhausted. "It is preliminary, and of course I only had the light of the lanterns to guide me . . ."

"But?"

"But it appears Miss Kendrick is correct in one sense," Dr. Lipscombe said. "I believe this man was stabbed with the same weapon as your other victim. Though the second attack was more sustained than the first."

"Meaning?" Lord Lyndhurst asked.

"Meaning Lord Fairbrother suffered but one stab wound, which punctured his hepatic vein and lung, whereas the killer stabbed this gentleman multiple times to achieve the same effect."

"Would you need skill to do this, Doctor?" Miss Kendrick asked. Another insightful question. What was Miss Kendrick thinking? Whom did she suspect?

Dr. Lipscombe shook his head. "Not necessarily. In fact, from the pattern of the wounds, I would propose the deaths resulted more from luck than skill. Why else would the same person resort to multiple wounds on this victim when only one sufficed on the first?"

Or there were two killers. Brown kept his conjecture to himself.

"Was there a knife in Harvey's pocket?" Miss Kendrick asked. Brown blinked hard.

Now, how could she know that? Brown asked her. "Because tonight Mr. Barlow recalled seeing Harvey with a knife the day he threatened Lord Fairbrother."

"Did he now?" What else had the plant hunter recalled and wasn't telling Brown? Another visit to Outwick House was in order. "Yes. We found a small utility pocket-knife in Mr. Milkham's jacket."

Miss Kendrick and Lord Lyndhurst shared a glance. Lord Lyndhurst had known of this too, then. First the plant hunter, now these two. Who knew what else people weren't telling him?

"And before you ask, yes, it did have blood on it," Dr. Lipscombe chimed in.

Brown wanted to throttle the doctor as Miss Kendrick's eyes widened in horror. She shrugged off Lord Lyndhurst's arm and tossed the blanket from her shoulders, which landed on the ground with a soft thud. She shook her head violently as she hugged her arms around herself. Lord Lyndhurst, not to be put off, rested a reassuring hand on her shoulder.

"No, I don't believe it. Harvey couldn't have . . ."

Startled by Miss Kendrick's reaction — she'd been so composed up until now — the poor doctor held out his clasped hands, imploring her to calm herself. "If you will only let me finish."

"What Dr. Lipscombe is trying to say, Miss Kendrick," Brown interjected, hoping to assuage the young lady's fears, at least as much as he was able, "was that although we found blood on it, the knife was too short, and the blade was single-edged. It couldn't have been the murder weapon. For either death."

Lord Lyndhurst sniffed in disgust.

"But that means . . ." Miss Kendrick began, relief and disbelief in her voice, "with the dagger securely locked up at the police station . . . that we can prove that Harvey is innocent."

"No, Miss Kendrick," Brown insisted, a slow sense of dread creeping up through his chest. "Harvey isn't out of the frame yet. Just because he was killed with the same weapon doesn't mean he wasn't involved."

"But then what does it mean?" Lord Lyndhurst demanded.

Brown pushed out a long exhale. It meant Brown was back where he started.

CHAPTER 25

"Heavens to Betsy, girlie," her great-aunt exclaimed as Stella slammed on her brakes. A trap with two high-stepping horses had turned a corner and crossed right in front of the car. "Why come back to Lyndhurst? This makes two days running."

It was a reasonable question. But Stella was tired of questions.

After returning from the barrow, Stella had lain in bed consumed by questions surrounding Harvey's death, the rhythmic *tick, tick, tick* of the clock on her mantel marking the passing hours. Why would anyone kill him? The only quarrel Harvey had was with Lord Fairbrother. Or at least the only one Stella knew about. Either way, the two men were killed by the same weapon and were undeniably linked. Stella had to learn how. Was the connection through the destruction of Harvey's hut? Had Harvey worked for Lord Fairbrother in the past? Was there a conflict with a third person they both knew? And why at the barrow? Did it have some significance? Did it have something to do with the dagger she found? Or was Harvey just there when the killer happened upon him? Stella speculated and obsessed until raindrops, with growing intensity, splattered against her windowpanes. She climbed out of bed and managed to push one snuggly fitting window up. Fresh, moist air drifted into the room. She'd stuck her face out into the rain allowing the droplets to cool her skin, to dampen her braided hair, to soothe her racing mind. She'd stepped away from the window, climbed back into bed, and fell soundly to sleep with the scent of the rain on her pillow. When Lyndy arrived, as usual, to go riding after breakfast, she convinced him they had to find answers, and that meant going to Lyndhurst again.

"I explained it to you before, Aunt Rachel," Stella said, halting the Daimler next to the King's House, an imposing, rectangular red brick manor with four steeply pointed dormer windows dominating the far end of the high street. "Lyndy and I think there must be a connection between the destruction of Harvey's house and his murder."

The King's House contained both the

Verderers' Court, the governing body charged as guardian of the New Forest, its landscape, and its inhabitants, as well as the New Forest Deputy Surveyor Office, which maintained the New Forest land records. It was as good a place to start as any.

"But shouldn't the police be doing this?" Aunt Rachel said as Lyndy offered her a hand to help her out of the car.

"The police still think Harvey might have been involved," Stella said, unwinding the veil from her hat. She slipped out of the duster coat and tossed it into her seat. Several men, one sporting a polka-dotted waistcoat and a wide-brimmed straw boater hat with a dark green ribbon, eyed her and the automobile as they strolled toward the King's House entrance, disapproval and envy awash on their faces. Stella, used to their reaction by now, ignored them.

"So, you thought you'd look into things on your own?"

Why shouldn't she? Hadn't Inspector Brown said she had a knack for this kind of thing? And didn't she owe Harvey? Hadn't he saved Tully's life? Stella bitterly wished she could've saved Harvey's. Wasn't helping to find his killer the next best thing?

"It's the least I can do."

"And what about you, young fella?" Aunt

336

Rachel said, poking at Lyndy with her cane. "Haven't you figured out how to talk sense into this filly yet?"

Lyndy veered out of the way of the cane before offering Stella his arm and escorting them all toward the massive front doors. "I think your niece is quite sensible."

"What would your mother say if she knew you were encouraging this?"

"If you only knew what Lady Atherly was encouraging him to do," Stella muttered so that only Lyndy could hear.

Lyndy frowned as he pulled on the heavy front door. "Shall we?"

Stella preceded Lyndy in and faced a hallway teeming with men: some rotund, some lean, some finely dressed in tailored suits and shined shoes, others modestly dressed in wool trousers, fraying suspenders, and mud-splayed boots, some sporting highpeaked derby hats, some tugging on broadcloth caps. Whether tapping toes or pacing, all appeared impatient and grumbling.

"Seems court is in session today," Lyndy said, as three more men in sack suits and fedoras entered the building directly behind them. Aunt Rachel had barely room to step out of the way. The ding of a bell reverberated through the hall, prompting the men to converge on a door labeled "Court of Verderers" at the far end.

"There's George Parley."

Stella pointed to the stocky, bald landowner stomping his way through the crowd, hat in hand. Stella stepped forward, ready to join the stream of flowing men, but Lyndy shook his head and pointed to the directory near the stairwell. At the top, printed in capital letters, it read "DEPUTY SURVEYOR."

"You go see about the land records. I'll sit in on the court session." Without waiting for her reply, Lyndy strolled into the assemblage of men heading down the hall. He shadowed Mr. Parley at a slight distance and entered the courtroom not far behind him.

Stella turned against the tide and headed for the Deputy Surveyor's Office. "I think I'll wait for you here," Aunt Rachel said, settling into a bench along the wall.

Stella didn't hesitate. She bounded up the stairs and, finding the well-marked door, pushed it open. Several large desks occupied the bright, whitewashed office, lined with metal filing cabinets and bookshelves of leather-bound ledgers. The *clickety-clack* of typewriters echoed through the room. The clerk at the closest desk, a man in his late twenties with dark, oiled hair, looked up from his work. He twitched his mustache and crinkled his face, trying to prevent his spectacles from sliding down the bridge of his nose.

Bing. The clerk slid back the return.

"Hello," Stella said, approaching his desk, smiling. "I'm looking for some information about a piece of property. Would you be able to help me?"

"Well, I . . . I . . ." His cheeks flushed. "I will certainly try."

"Oh, good," Stella said. "The site in question is that of the old Norley Cottage. The building on the property recently burned down and I —"

The clerk, pressing his index finger into the dimple on his chin, nodded his head vigorously. "You're talking about the old coal-burner's hut, aren't you? Where the snakecatcher used to live."

"Yes, the very same." Stella had wondered if news of the destruction of Harvey's house had reached Lyndhurst. But did they also know about his death?

"What do you want to know?"

"I was wondering if there was any legal reason for someone to want to destroy it."

"Well, it rarely happens, but yes, Miss . . . uh?"

"It's Miss Kendrick." Still peering at her over the rim of his spectacles, the clerk's eyes widened at her name.

"You're the American heiress, aren't you?" Stella nodded. Would she ever be anything but? "May I offer my congratulations on your engagement to Lord Lyndhurst."

"Thank you."

"I hear the wedding is to be later this year."

"Yes." *If Lady Atherly and Lady Philippa don't make a mess of everything, that is.* "You were saying?"

"Of course. Do you know anything about the rights of common, Miss Kendrick?"

"Yes, but only the basics, that commoners have certain rights to use the land of the New Forest, such as let their livestock graze freely, or gather firewood, or let their pigs eat acorns in autumn, or harvest peat for fuel or fodder."

He took off his spectacles and wiped them with a white cotton cloth. "I'm quite impressed, Miss Kendrick, that you know anything at all."

"Thank you?" Stella said, uncertain if he was complimenting her or insulting her intelligence. The clerk blushed again. "But how do rights of common apply in Harvey's case?"

"Well," the clerk said slowly, as if about to explain something to a child, "what you may not know is that rights of common usually belong to the land, not the person. If someone doesn't own the land, he doesn't inherently have any rights. And in the snake-catcher's case, he doesn't own the land. He's merely been squatting on it for some thirty years."

"But Harvey said he'd lost his rights when his hut burned down."

"Yes, he has been allowed the rights of estovers and turbary, or the right to collect firewood and harvest turf, because his hut incorporated the old hearth of the Norley Cottage, to which the rights were attached."

"But that's all forfeit now that the fireplace chimney is destroyed."

"Exactly." He smiled as if pleased with a promising pupil. Stella restrained herself from rolling her eyes.

"If Harvey didn't own the land, then who does?"

"If you'll wait just one minute, I can check." The clerk slid back from behind his desk and ambled over to a row of shelves. After skimming several shelves, he glanced over his shoulder and frowned. He held up a finger. "Just another moment longer, Miss Kendrick."

He approached the desk of another clerk, a similar young man in sleeve garters. The two conferred together in whispers, each sneaking a glance at Stella, as she pretended to admire the paperweight holding down a stack of typewritten forms on the clerk's desk. A scene of summertime at a seaside pier showed through the thick glass dome. The second clerk slipped a thick, brown ledger from a stack of like ledgers on his desk and handed it to the first. As the second clerk blatantly gawked at Stella, ink dripping carelessly from his pen, the first returned, the prize in hand.

"I couldn't find it at first because it has become an active file."

"What does that mean?"

"It means the land was recently sold."

"To whom? By whom?"

The clerk flipped open the ledger and skimmed down page after page with his index finger. "Ah, here it is." He stabbed his finger down. "Oh, dear."

"What is it?"

"Lord Fairbrother owned the parcel and paddock surrounding the old Norley Cottage site."

Lord Fairbrother owned the land Harvey had been illegally occupying for decades? Why would Lord Fairbrother have a sudden change of heart and want Harvey gone? Or perhaps Harvey was wrong. Maybe Fairbrother had nothing to do with the arson. "Poor chap sold it just the day before he died."

"That's the day Harvey's hut burned down," Stella said, under her breath. This was no coincidence.

"I'm so sorry," the clerk stammered, pulling a handkerchief from his vest pocket and handing it out to her. What did she need that for? If she could avoid it, she'd never use another one.

"I didn't mean to mention . . . seeing as you . . ." He fluttered the handkerchief at her.

He thinks that I'll break down in front of him. Harvey's death may not have reached this man's ears yet, but whoever had discovered Lord Fairbrother's dead body certainly had.

"It's all right," she said, waving off the offered handkerchief. The clerk, pouting, stuffed it back into his pocket. "Just tell me who bought the land." With Dr. Lipscombe speculating the two men were murdered with the same weapon, the land's new owner may very well be the killer.

The clerk ran his finger along the length of the page. "It says here, that one Mr. George R. Parley purchased it."

"Oh, no." *Lyndy has just gone into the court with him.*

Stella barely registered the clerk's bewilderment when she thanked him, flung open the door, and hurried away.

Lyndy settled into one of the wooden, spindle-backed armchairs toward the rear of the gallery facing the long, two-tiered, wooden judicial bench, well behind George Parley. Lyndy didn't want the landowner to see him and bolt, as he had last night, before Lyndy found out what Parley was up to. But Lyndy went far from unnoticed. Many men stole a quick glimpse of him over their shoulders, curious as to what brought the son of the Earl of Atherly to the Verderers' Court. Lyndy left others to attend to estate business, so he had no occasion to set foot in the courtroom before.

A clerk stepped in front of the bench, waited for the chatter of those in attendance to fade, and sniffed.

"Please rise," he said, his monotone voice echoing into the centuries-old rafters above.

Chairs scraped, feet shuffled, the floorboards creaked as every man rose to his feet. Someone stifled a cough as the verderers entered the wood-paneled hall. With the heads of deer flanking the royal coat of arms on the wall above them, five men, black crape around their arms, filed into their places along the bench, leaving the middlemost space, the official verderer's seat, vacant.

"This court is hereby called to session," the clerk announced. As the verderers sat, so too did everyone else. The clerk proceeded to read minutes from the last meeting of the court. Lyndy stretched out his feet, crossed his arms against his chest, and yawned. He'd followed George Parley in, to see what the fellow was about, but he wasn't much for these formal proceedings.

"We called this unscheduled session of open court to formally announce the tragic death of our official verderer, the Right Honorable Viscount Fairbrother," said one of the verderers, a man in his late sixties with a long Roman nose and a ring of white hair about his head. "We will dispense with further announcements and suspend presentments until that time His Majesty appoints a new official verderer." A deep mumbling of disgruntlement rumbled through the crowd. George Parley rocketed up from his chair.

"What about me petition? Will I be allowed to open a gentlemen's rifle club besides Norleywood or not?"

How could Parley have petitioned the court to open a rifle club where the snake-catcher's hut was? Unless he knew in advance that the shack wouldn't be there.

"You have no idea how much I've invested in this —"

"Mr. Parley, please be seated," the verderer demanded.

Lyndy glared at the back of George Parley's shiny bald head. The landowner had bathed the dirt of the barrow from his head but traces still stained the thick creases on the back of his neck.

"Not until you tell me the status of me petition," Parley bellowed. "I have me family's future to consider." The long-nosed verderer sighed, seeking the approval of his fellow members. The other four men shrugged.

"Very well. As the court is in the process of drafting its own version of the Crown Lands Bill of 1904 —"

"One rifle club does not pose a menace of debris," George Parley countered, obviously familiar with the bill in question. Lyndy had no idea, and couldn't care less, about the specifics in these laws. Give him the rules of horse-racing any day. The verderer continued as if the landowner hadn't spoken.

"As well as considering the controversy

that arose over the Ranges Act of 1891, and the case brought against it, the court motions to table public comment until the matter can be raised in committee."

"But the Ranges Act involved the preemptive use of the Forest by His Majesty's military," Parley argued. "This is a private enterprise and not without precedent."

"But similar concerns over the threat to the New Forest and the rights of inhabitants apply," the verderer replied. "Do I hear a second?" A second was offered before Parley could object.

"Gah!" Parley threw his arms up in disgust and began shoving his way down the aisle without a by-your-leave, unceremoniously knocking knees, kicking shins, and stepping on toes as he went. Seemingly oblivious to the discontent left in his wake, Parley, his head bent, pounded a fist against his open palm, the smack of each punch reverberating above the din of complaints. A call to order went unnoticed.

"I say."

"Well, I never!"

"I beg your pardon?"

When Parley reached the aisle, his cheeks burned a crimson red and beads of perspiration glistened on his high forehead. When he passed within earshot of Lyndy, Parley was grumbling to himself. Lyndy, though not one to shy from confrontation, was grateful for the barrier of several empty chairs along the row between them. He had no quarrel with the man.

"Damn that Fairbrother," the landowner muttered with each punch of his fist as he headed toward the door. "Damn that rotter to hell."

But Fairbrother was dead. What on earth could Parley mean?

CHAPTER 26

Philippa's hand slipped on the ornately engraved brass knob. Why was she so nervous? Raymond was dead. What was done was done. She had her future to think of now. She smoothed her hair at her temples, let out her pent-up breath, and flung open the door. The stench of cigarettes and scotch assailed her, the lingering scent of the late lord. She left the door slightly ajar and crossed over to the window. Philippa didn't waste her precious time admiring, or rather disparaging, the view of the long gravel drive in all its dismal glory, but quickly lifted the sill. The breeze, heavy with the scent of crushed gravel and newly mowed grass, didn't help improve the foul odor of the room much, but it would have to do.

Squawk! "I said no interruptions." *Squawk!* "Hodgson."

Philippa started. She'd forgotten about

the bird. She'd rarely seen it, but often heard its high-pitched mutterings behind the closed door. Had anyone thought to feed the thing? No matter. She yanked the cover off the gilded wire cage. The small, gray parrot's beady little eyes stared up at her as it cocked its head. It began bobbing and swaying about, mimicking her dead husband's frustrated call of "I said no interruptions." The parrot hopped to its perch and fluttered its dull gray feathers. The bottom of the cage was littered with them. Philippa unlatched the cage door and gloated as the bird leaped from the cage and soared straight out the open window. She slammed the window closed behind it.

Better to forbear the cigarette odor than to allow the bird back in.

She turned and examined the exotic room for the first time, like a child at a zoo. She'd rarely been allowed in here. This was his domain. Her eyes slid across the glass-fronted bookcases to the varying-sized antlers over the fireplace, to the bric-a-brac on the mantel, to the row of silver Cecil Pony Challenge Cups on a shelf, to the unfinished chess game on the mother-of-pearl inlay table, to the birdcage, to the fanned arrangements of daggers, knives, and swords mounted along the opposite wall.

Too much of the dark green wallpaper showed through where the dagger was missing from one of the displays. And it was still missing. Philippa suspected Miss Kendrick of stealing it again, but what did Philippa care? Her husband had so many, and she had no use for them.

Pray, what was she to do with all these things? Philippa mentally shook her head, banishing the thought away, delaying any decisions for another day. Finding the will was task enough for now.

She approached the mahogany desk, cleared of everything but the black and white lacquered writing set, both crystal inkwells adequately filled. Raymond was a great many things, but untidy was not one of them. The desktop was polished to such a sheen she could see her reflection. She brushed the hair at her temple again. So young, so beautiful, and yet already a widow? But that might change very soon. A smile slowly spread across her lips. Lyndy could soon be hers. What a delicious thought.

But only if the will said what she wanted it to. Had Raymond had time to change it? She had to find out.

She chose the top drawer of the desk to start. Tidy piles of blank stationery and envelopes embellished only with the Fairbrother family crest — a cockatrice, the mystical two-legged serpent with a rooster's head — filled the drawer. A sculpted bronze paperweight of a nude woman lying in a vulgar pose held down the paper. Disgusted, Philippa slammed the drawer shut and yanked the next one open.

What on earth?

The chaos that met her was more of a shock than the nude statue in the previous drawer. Letters with bent edges, crumpled envelopes, and paper tablets lying on their spines had all been shoved into the drawer, seemingly at random. Could the will possibly be in among all this? Loath to rifle through the mess, she pulled open the next drawer. It was in the same sorry state. She yanked on the bottom two drawers at the same time. Oddly, the drawer on the left was perfectly tidy, a supply of ink and mucilage lined perfectly alongside tins of paper clips, pencils, erasers, and penholders. The one on the right was like the others, its contents upturned and disheveled as if someone had been searching for something in a hurry. Had Raymond done this before he died? No, he'd never have left his affairs in such a state. Someone else then. But why? Could it have to do with his work as official verderer? Were they looking for the money he'd hidden in his waistcoat? Or was it something else entirely? Unfortunately, she had no idea what her husband had been up to.

Could it have been the will they were after? No, who else would care but her? Even so, it was an affront to have someone in her home, rifling through what were now her things.

"Hodgson," she yelled, not bothering to push the ringer. She knew someone was always within earshot. The butler would be found. And she was right. In a manner of moments, Hodgson stood before her.

"You called, my lady?"

"You're familiar with Lord Fairbrother's habits. Does this look proper to you?" She indicated the desk. As the butler approached, Philippa stepped slightly aside. Hodgson hesitantly rounded the desk, his eyes widening at the sight of the disheveled opened drawers.

"No, my lady. Lord Fairbrother was most particular about his affairs. Quite meticulous, I'd say. I'm astonished to see his desk in such disarray."

"That was my thinking."

She was right. Someone else had been in here. But who? She couldn't fathom anyone she knew doing such a thing. Surely not her friends, her family, or her loyal staff. Not even that meddlesome Miss Kendrick would be so bold. One of Raymond's business associates or a stranger then? That obnoxious reporter, perhaps? Philippa shuddered to think someone like Miss Cosslett had infiltrated the sanctity of Outwick House, and what they might've learned.

"Hodgson, call the police."

Stella fiddled with the flouncy Chantilly lace on her embroidered blouse as Aunt Rachel, her drowsy head nodding on her chest, sat beside her on the bench. The hall, once a hubbub of men, stood vacant and echoing with nothing but the gentle snores of the older woman. Stella didn't know how much longer she could wait. Abruptly the doors to the verderers' courtroom banged open, and George Parley stormed out. Muttering and lost in his thoughts, Mr. Parley stomped down the hall, launched himself against the entrance door, and disappeared. A surge of men soon emerged from the courtroom. Stella leaped to her feet and waved the moment she saw Lyndy among the crowd. He nodded in acknowledgment and weaved his way to her. Stella grabbed his arm and, abandoning Aunt Rachel, pulled him after her into the relatively private space beneath the stairs.

"Why, Miss Kendrick," Lyndy said, smirking. "I wouldn't have thought this the time nor the place, but if you insist." He lifted the brim of her hat, bent down toward her, his handsome face filling her entire view, and placed a quick kiss on her lips. His unexpected touch raised goose bumps on her arms, but she wasn't going to tell him that.

"Lyndy," Stella admonished, swatting his arm playfully. "This is serious."

He leaned back, but she could still feel the heat of his breath on her cheek. "I can't think of anything more serious than kissing the woman who is to be my wife."

He was teasing her; she could hear it in his voice. But there was a sincerity in his gaze that made her pause. If only she could clear the hall of onlookers, many of whom were scowling at her in disapproval. If only she could stop wondering if Lady Atherly was going to ruin everything. If only she could forget what had brought them to the King's House in the first place. She would gladly kiss Lyndy with abandon. But she couldn't, not here, not now. But nothing said she couldn't return his affection in some way. She gave his cheek a peck. He pulled her to him. She whispered in his ear.

"More serious than George Parley having something to do with Harvey's death?" Lyndy frowned, releasing his embrace. She stepped back a bit, self-consciously tucking a strand of hair behind her ear as she glanced around. She caught the eye of a gentleman with a pointed white beard, his face startled at witnessing their public display. She sheepishly smiled. He shook his head in disgust.

"Curious that you should say that," Lyndy said, drawing her attention back.

"Why?"

"Because I just learned that George Parley petitioned the verderers for a rifle club on land that sounded suspiciously near where Harvey's hut once stood, long before the hut burned down."

"And I learned that George Parley owns the exact land where Harvey's hut was."

"But I thought Harvey owned it."

Stella shook her head. "No, he bought it."

"When was this?"

"Tuesday, the day of the Cecil Cup, the day after Harvey's hut burned down."

"But that was after he would've had to file the petition." Lyndy rubbed his chin as if still trying to puzzle it out. "How would he know he'd be able to buy it in the time for his petition to be considered by the court?"

"Because Lord Fairbrother sold it to him," Stella said, pleased with the surprise her pronouncement produced. It was a rare triumph. Lyndy rarely expressed amazement. He was always too busy looking bored.

"And Lord Fairbrother would've known about the petition," Lyndy said. Stella nodded.

Lyndy strolled over to the window and gazed out onto the high street. Stella stepped over behind him. The driver of a passing wagon, laden with newly milled lumber, swatted his pair of piebald geldings with a whip, urging them to pick up the pace. The last of the court attendees, ducking their heads as they held on to their hats, were hurrying away. Dark clouds had rolled in, and splashes of rain sprinkled the glass panes.

"I think George Parley burned down Harvey's house so that he could develop the land," Stella said, in an almost whisper, despite the nearly empty hall. "But I think Lord Fairbrother knew about it, maybe even condoned it. Hence Harvey's accusations toward him."

Lyndy turned his back to the window to face her. "But I asked around a bit. No one knew how Fairbrother was going to vote on the rifle club issue, and his was the deciding vote. Now no one knows what will happen."

"Perhaps George Parley knew, or thought he knew. . . ." Stella remembered the talk of Lord Fairbrother taking bribes. "If George Parley paid Lord Fairbrother to guarantee the petition would be a success, then he had every reason to get rid of Harvey's hut."

"I don't believe it," Lyndy said, starting to pace in front of her. "Parley could've known Fairbrother was going to vote in his favor simply on account of his selling Parley the land. And in which case, Parley would have every reason not to kill him. But then again . . ." He told Stella how he'd overheard Parley curse Fairbrother. "Perhaps Fairbrother decided to vote against Parley, after all?"

"This doesn't help us at all, does it?" Stella said, her shoulders sagging as they strolled, side by side, back to the bench and her slumbering chaperone. "We're not any closer to figuring out who killed Harvey."

"No, but we have information we can pass on to Inspector Brown. Let him deal with it."

"But —" Lyndy caressed her cheek with his fingers when she started to object. Why was he trying to distract her? There was so much more to discuss.

"Don't you have a party to prepare?"

Stella groaned. The engagement party! "You would have to bring that up." She removed his hand from her face, took a step back, and straightened her hat.

"Why not? I'm quite looking forward to seeing how my bride-to-be is as a hostess." Though his expression was unreadable, a glint in his eye gave him away. He was enjoying himself, at her expense.

"I'm afraid, Lord Lyndhurst, you might be disappointed," she countered. "Besides, doesn't it strike you as crass, going ahead with the party considering everything that's happened? And the fact that your mother wants to cancel the wedding altogether?"

"All the more reason to proceed, I say."

"Either way, first we have to tell Inspector Brown what we've learned."

"Why, Miss Kendrick," Lyndy teased, "some would accuse you of being lax in your duties, willing to do anything, even delve into the sordid details of the murder, rather than host a dinner party."

Despite herself, Stella laughed, the sound echoing off the high, wainscoted walls. Aunt Rachel's head bobbed up, and the old lady's eyes fluttered open.

Stella lowered her voice. "And they would be right."

CHAPTER 27

Mr. Hodgson opened Lord Fairbrother's study but blocked Brown's way. Brown's first impression of the room, as much as he could determine from his vantage in the hallway, was of precise order: the desk was clear, the ornately carved ivory chess pieces stood erect on their perspective black and white squares, the books were lined up as if by a ruler. Except for the open, unlatched door of an empty birdcage, there was absolutely nothing to indicate anything was amiss, let alone the chaos Lady Philippa had insisted existed. What was so vital that he drop what he was doing and rush to her aid?

At any other time, Brown might have been more than a bit put out, but the opportunity to search the dead lord's study was worth a bit of bother. Until now, the grieving widow had blocked every request Brown had made to search Outwick House for evidence that might relate to her husband's death. At first, he'd accepted it, out of respect for her grief, but as request after request was denied, he'd begun to suspect Lady Philippa had something to hide. Even now, she was only allowing them access to Lord Fairbrother's study.

"And nothing appears to be missing?" he asked, as his constable, facing the open door, stretched his neck to see past the butler's broad shoulders.

"How would I know?" Lady Philippa snapped.

How indeed? Her response could only mean that this was His Lordship's private sanctum. Brown silently thanked the scamp who ruffled a few of Lord Fairbrother's papers. This might be far more productive than he could've hoped.

"Besides, that's your job, isn't it?" she scoffed. "To discover who's violated my late husband's things, shattering the peace and safety of Outwick House, and why?"

Brown accepted her impatience as part of the job. But then she crossed her arms as if hugging herself, protecting herself. Was that worry or fear in her eyes? Neither was characteristic of the mistress of Outwick House. Yes, she had a right to feel disconcerted, but Brown knew a woman with a secret when he saw one. But did it have anything to do with her husband's death? Uncovering that, he wanted to tell the lady, was also his job.

"We will do our best. I will send for someone from the constabulary in Winchester as well. There is a new fingerprinting technique they can apply to determine —"

"I will not have an army of policemen invading my home," Lady Philippa insisted.

"Right! May we get started, then?" Brown gestured toward the interior of the room, and the lady nodded. "You don't need to remain unless that is your wish?"

She hesitated, as if mulling over her response, then dismissed the idea with a flip of her hand. "No, I have better uses of my time."

She'd meant to appear indifferent, but Brown saw the steeling of her shoulders, the calculation in her eyes. Lady Philippa wanted to be in that room, learn what they discovered, but didn't want him to know. But why?

The butler took a long step aside and watched down the bridge of his nose as they passed. "Hodgson, you will stay to assist the policemen and see that they take nothing with them," she added.

Brown bristled at the implication but bit his tongue. He would take what he needed to take, but he wasn't about to argue the point with Lady Philippa.

"Yes, milady," the butler said, as Lady Philippa sashayed down the hall.

"Right!" Brown said to his constable as they strode into the wood-paneled study.

Brown tried to size up the man who had inhabited this room, but aside from His Lordship's fastidiousness, and the telltale smell of Turkish tobacco, there was little to go on. The deer heads were standard fare in the New Forest. Brown would've been suspicious if there weren't any antlers to speak of. The gilded free-standing globe, the chess set, even the eighteenth-century French vases flanking the mantel, depicting half-clothed female figures, were nothing he wouldn't find in any gentleman's study. Then his eyes were drawn to the elaborate display of armor on the wall, and the conspicuous void. If he'd brought the dagger with him and fitted it in place, he wouldn't have been any less confident that it once hung in that barren spot.

Here was a gentleman who enjoyed his power and displayed it like a peacock. Whoever took the dagger understood this and knew how much the theft would rile the lord. Not a stranger then.

"Be as careful but as thorough as possible," Brown said over his shoulder as Waterman headed for the desk. "Don't overlook anything." Turning to the butler, he asked, "Is there a safe?" The butler hesitated, then shook his head, denying it. Brown didn't believe him. "Let me remind you, Mr. Hodgson. I am not only investigating the trespass of Lord Fairbrother's study but also his murder. There is a safe, isn't there?"

"There is." So why lie? Out of loyalty to his dead master? What did Mr. Hodgson suspect, or know, was inside? Mr. Hodgson remained rooted to the carpet, his expression giving nothing away.

"Can you show me where it is?" Brown said, trying not to lose his patience.

Mr. Hodgson led Brown to a tall, narrow display case blocked initially from view by the open door. Behind the glass was a tableau meant to capture the diverse inhabitants of a tree. Birds, squirrels, butterflies, and the like were frozen in time as they perched, climbed, or were alighting from the mossy trunk. It conveyed motion and life even as nothing moved, all being dead. Brown admired the craftsmanship as the butler pushed against the deceptively light case, revealing a wall safe cleverly hidden behind. "Had Lady Philippa known about the safe?" Brown asked. The butler's only response was to raise a skeptical, high-arching eyebrow. That would be a no, then. If Brown were a betting man, he'd wager a guinea that Lady Philippa suspected its existence. And perhaps its contents as well.

Was that what she'd wanted to see, the safe? But why call the police? Why not order the butler to tell her where it was and open it? Or maybe she had, and Mr. Hodgson had denied its existence as he had with Brown. Brown tried the safe's handle, but it was locked as he'd suspected it would be. As they found only a key to the house on Lord Fairbrother's body, Brown hoped the key to the safe was somewhere handy.

"Do you have the key, Mr. Hodgson?"

"No, but I could attempt to find it." Brown smiled. Butlers didn't "attempt" anything. He knew where the key was all right.

"Then, by all means."

Mr. Hodgson strode about the room as if admiring it for the first time, while occasionally sliding his hand under and over various objects. Brown never took his eyes off him. After a minute or two, the butler returned to Brown and held out a small, black key. How long the butler had shrewdly kept it hidden, Brown had no idea. It could've been in his pocket all along. Brown resisted the urge to ask. He knew the loyal servant would never tell him where the key had been. Stepping aside, Brown allowed Mr. Hodgson to unlock the safe.

The safe was quite full. "Anything appear missing?" Brown asked the butler.

"It appears as my lord left it."

Good. But that didn't mean Brown couldn't have a peek. Brown had Mr. Hodgson pull over a narrow table that had been set beneath the window and methodically emptied the safe. Brown called Waterman over to help him catalog everything, item by item.

"A copy of Lord Fairbrother's will," Brown said. Waterman wrote it down. Brown skimmed its contents. As expected, Lord Fairbrother's heir inherited his title and his properties in London and Kent, but Lady Philippa stood to gain a great deal, including possession of Outwick House. Brown put the will in the safe and reached for the next item on the table.

"A green velvet box with . . . a pearl necklace inside," Brown said, as Waterman recorded that too.

Piece by piece, paper by paper, Brown

examined the entire contents of the safe. It included a great deal more pieces of jewelry: tiaras, necklaces, bracelets, earrings, brooches, all bejeweled with gems the colors of the rainbow, sapphires, emeralds, rubies, and diamonds. Brown had no doubt they were all worth a great deal of money. Would Lady Philippa inherit these as well, or did they already belong to her? Brown would have to find out. It might make a difference.

There were receipts and provenance for paintings. There were correspondences with local landowners, members of Parliament, and other members of the Verderers' Court, none of which appeared to have any bearing on the murder. There were deeds for land, including a bill of sale for a piece of property near Norleywood dated the day before Lord Fairbrother's death. The name on the bill was George Parley. An item of importance then. When the butler turned his head to itch the end of his nose politely, Brown slipped the bill of sale into his jacket pocket. Then Brown came to a stack of envelopes, tied together with a green ribbon.

Love letters, perhaps?

"Find me a letter opener," Brown said.

Constable Waterman retrieved a pearl-handled one from the top drawer of the desk. Mr. Hodgson pursed his lips but said nothing as Brown slit open several of the envelopes. Each contained, not a letter but cash in differing amounts of ten-pound notes. Like the one found on the dead man's body. What were they for? A wagering scheme? To minimize his losses to an envelope amount and no more? Brown didn't think so. He'd no indication Lord Fairbrother was a gambling man. He won competitions; he didn't bet on them. Was this a kind of payment system then? Surely it wasn't for the servants' salaries. Each envelope contained more than Mr. Hodgson, the highest paid member of staff, earned in a year. And why was he carrying one on the night he died?

"Do you know what these envelopes are for, Mr. Hodgson?"

The butler shook his head. "I have never seen these before, Inspector." By the unease on the butler's otherwise stoic face, Brown tended to believe him. Perhaps Lady Philippa or Fairbrother's estate agent or valet would know. Brown would have to keep asking.

When all the contents of the safe were recorded in Waterman's notebook and securely tucked back into the safe, Brown had Mr. Hodgson lock it again. He pulled the handle to make sure.

"Did you find anything?" he asked Waterman, stepping before the desk. His constable pulled open the drawers one by one to show the disheveled state they were in. He now understood Lady Philippa's concern.

"Just these drawers of disheveled papers, as Lady Philippa described. The papers are all notes concerning Lord Fairbrother's breeding stock, Outwick House estate issues, or Verderers' Court issues."

"Nothing out of the ordinary, then," Brown said.

"Well, unless you include a few recent letters from a solicitor named" — the constable flipped open his notebook — "Sir George Lewis."

The Sir George Lewis? The most sought-after solicitor in England?

"Show me their correspondence," Brown said, holding out his hand. Waterman pulled out the bottom left drawer. It looked completely untouched. The constable slipped his hand under a tray containing ink bottles and produced three open envelopes from where they'd been hidden. Why had Lord Fairbrother hidden them beneath the bottles and not in the safe? For quick access, perhaps?

"Why do you think this drawer was untouched?" Brown held up the unopened letters. "Because the intruder realized he wasn't going to find what he was looking for, that it was probably locked up in the safe, and stopped looking . . ."

"Or he was interrupted," Waterman said.

"Or there wasn't an intruder at all," Brown said. "Besides the servants, Lady Philippa, and her guest, who else would even have access to this room? Perhaps this was simply the work of Lord Fairbrother rifling through his papers before he died." It was the most obvious explanation.

"I think you are mistaken, Inspector," Mr. Hodgson said, setting one of the crystal inkwells to rights. Waterman must've bumped into it during his examination of the drawers. "On further examination, I can say that something was indeed taken." He strolled, not to the weaponry display on the wall, but over to a bookshelf and pointed. "There used to be a framed photograph here."

A photograph? How curious Mr. Hodgson didn't mention the dagger.

Brown joined Mr. Hodgson by the bookshelf, but there was nothing to see but a vacant space on the well-polished, well-dusted, wooden top.

"What was the photograph of?"

"His Lordship served in the Boer War in

South Africa. It was a photograph of his regiment, I believe."

Brown nodded. That would explain the cigarette habit. Brown knew of several men who brought back a taste for Turkish tobacco and cigarettes after the war. But why would anyone want to take the photograph?

"Perhaps Lady Philippa took it?" Brown had already considered the possibility that the lady of the house had removed things from the room, even vital evidence that pertained to the case, before they'd arrived. But when he'd asked the butler, Mr. Hodgson firmly denied it. As if he would know. Perhaps, he did. If Mr. Hodgson was so protective of His Lordship, would a bit of spying on Lady Philippa be above him? It was worth considering.

"As I said before, Lady Philippa had no opportunity to remove anything from the room."

"Well, then, was the frame expensive?" Brown chided his foolish question the minute it left his mouth. As if Lord Fairbrother would have anything slipshod or cheap. But the butler surprised him.

"Not particularly. It was one of those mass-produced articles you find in a shop on the high street. Supposedly it was a gift from one of his men." Brown glanced at the opulence of the room, the priceless weaponry on the wall. Why had they taken a photograph and nothing of any value? Besides the dagger, of course.

"You didn't mention the missing dagger," Brown said.

The butler's expression didn't change. "I didn't think it was pertinent as it went missing before His Lordship's death."

Brown swallowed hard to hide displeasure. Why hadn't the butler told him this before?

"Was Lord Fairbrother aware of the theft?"

The butler nodded. "Most certainly."

"But the photograph was taken since?" The butler nodded again. So again, Brown had to ask, why the photograph? He voiced his question out loud.

"Perhaps one of the servants wanted a souvenir of their late lord?" Constable Waterman offered. Brown thought that an excellent reason and said so, but the butler was shaking his head.

"None of the staff would do such a thing." And why would that be? Because they were too loyal, like Mr. Hodgson, or because they didn't like their lord enough, like the scullery maid? Before Brown could ask, the butler added, "The night Lord Fairbrother was killed, I noticed the conservatory door was open. I believed it was one of the maids feeding a stray cat. She has been reprimanded before for doing so. But when I asked Mrs. White, she insisted Nelly was innocent. Perhaps the intruder could've gotten in that way?"

"Was the door jammed or the window broken?" Brown said, tightening the grip on his hat. Why was this the first time he was hearing of this?

"No, it was unlocked and slightly askew. The door requires a firm push for the latch to catch. But for the new footman, who was attending a funeral in Burley and was off the estate all night, members of staff know of its peculiarity. An outsider would not."

But an outsider wouldn't have been able to unlock it in the first place.

"What time was this?"

"About half past eleven." If his broken watch was any indication, Lord Fairbrother would've been dead by then.

"Right! I'll need to look at the conservatory door, and then I want to talk to this kitchen maid who's been feeding the cat. Waterman, you can go to Burley and confirm the footman's story," Brown said, opening the first of the letters from Sir George Lewis.

He scanned its contents and allowed

himself a slight, satisfied grin. Now they were getting somewhere. He folded the letter and tucked it, and the others, into his jacket pocket. The butler opened his mouth to protest, but Brown cut him off.

"But first, let's see what Lady Philippa has to say."

CHAPTER 28

"What took you so long?" Stella's father yelled from somewhere down the hall.

After they left the King's House, Stella and Lyndy had walked down the high street to the police station only to learn that Inspector Brown had been called out to Outwick House. With neither of them having any desire to see Lady Philippa again so soon, they opted to track the policeman down later. Facing the need to finalize the engagement party plans, Stella had driven Lyndy back to Morrington Hall, declining his invitation to luncheon. Daddy must've been listening for her and Aunt Rachel's return.

"Jane never got her invitation," he added, his shout like a trumpet in a tearoom. He was going to give everyone in the house a headache.

Because I never sent her one, Stella silently replied as she handed Tims her duster coat.

Stella dreaded the evening enough. She certainly didn't want a reporter watching and recording her every move.

"I'm as tired as wings on a hummingbird," Aunt Rachel said, handing off her hat and coat. She wagged a finger at Stella. "Don't even think about going out this afternoon, girlie." Then, with Tims's back to them as he hung up the coats, Aunt Rachel winked. Stella could've hugged the old woman.

Stella was supposed to spend the afternoon preparing and dressing for tonight's engagement dinner. What if she snuck out for a short ride first?

The rush of excitement at the prospect evaporated the instant Stella envisioned where her rides usually took her — to visit Harvey. Stella swallowed hard, warding off tears bubbling up as Aunt Rachel, unaware of the war of emotions her generosity had created, hobbled up the stairs. But Tims's patient posture, maintaining a stoic stare slightly over her shoulder, as he waited for her to unpin her hat, helped her settle herself again. She rewarded him with a smile, but unlike the female servants of Pilley Manor, Tims refused to bend protocol and engage Stella in a friendly manner. He accepted the wide-brimmed straw from her without expression and attempted to corral the long, pink motoring veil. Stella never realized how much the veil looked like the fairy floss she'd seen at the World's Fair last year. And here Tims was suddenly battling with it and losing. The ridiculousness of it lightened her heart. Stella, stifling a giggle with the back of her hand, offered to help, but the butler scowled, insisting that she leave him to it. Stella shrugged and headed down the hall toward the kitchen. She'd check in on the preparations one more time.

"Did you hear me?"

Stella paused when she reached the open doorway of the drawing room. Daddy, alone for once, was sitting on the end of the plush red couch, his feet up on the seat of an armchair. A silver tray with coffeepot and teacup lay beside him. He had the latest edition of *The American Stud Book* propped up on his bulging belly.

"I heard you," she said, as Tims, having wrangled the hat and veil, slipped by her and disappeared behind the servants' door. Daddy had hired a village lad to help with the additional preparations, but Stella could imagine how much Mrs. Robertson and Mrs. Downie were relying on Tims to help.

"I sent Jane another one," Daddy said. "Imagine the woman reporting on the wedding not attending the engagement party?"

Stella could easily envision such a thing. "No need to thank me."

Wonderful. That's all she needed.

"Jane says you still owe her an exclusive interview," he added. "Says she's been trying to track you down, been to Morrington Hall and everything, yet you refuse to talk to her about the flowers, the church, the dress. She needs to know this stuff. For the society pages."

Stella couldn't care less about the society pages, but she didn't bother to tell him that. He couldn't care less what Stella thought.

"I've been preoccupied." Stella studied the wallpaper border lining the wainscoting, large cream-colored oak leaves tumbling and twisting among a background of green branches and rose-colored petals, like a wavy garden beckoning her to move along with it.

"What's more important than doing what your father tells you to?"

Helping keep a promise to a murdered friend, perhaps? Trying to protect my future against Lady Atherly's plans, maybe? Ensuring I'm free of you.

"Where are you going?" he shouted after her as Stella, more propelled by her exasperation toward her father than an eagerness to prepare for the engagement dinner, obeyed the siren call of the wallpaper garden and scooted down the hall toward the stairs.

"To get ready for the party, Daddy," she called. "Where else?" For once, she was glad for the excuse.

Brown followed Mr. Hodgson up the steep, dimly lit servant stairs, his breath growing shorter with every step. Brown was getting too old for this.

He'd inspected the conservatory door. It'd showed no sign of being tampered with. If what the butler said was true, it must've been left unlocked. Whether inadvertently or on purpose, Brown had no way of knowing. He'd questioned the maid, who insisted she hadn't stepped foot in the conservatory for weeks. After a reprimand, she'd resorted to feeding the cat outside the scullery. She'd showed him the empty dish in the gravel just beyond the door. Brown tended to believe her. Now it was time to ask Lady Philippa a few questions.

Brown was relieved when the butler pushed open the green baize door. A deep-throated laugh rang out as they reached the drawing room. The two exchanged glances. Grieving widow, indeed. Mr. Hodgson's face betrayed none of the revulsion Brown felt as he opened the door before them.

Brown strode in, hat in hand, and stopped midstep.

Lady Philippa and Mr. Barlow, seated shoulder to shoulder on the sofa, heads bent together, were whispering and giggling, oblivious to his presence.

"Inspector Brown to see you again, my lady," the butler announced.

The two looked up. The smile on Lady Philippa's face twisted into a scowl as Mr. Barlow, having some sense of decorum, leaped to his feet. The man wasn't wearing a tie.

"Have you discovered something already, Inspector?" the lady demanded, smoothing her skirt over her lap. She had dressed from head to toe in black, making her flushed cheeks all the more apparent.

"Someone has stolen a photograph of Lord Fairbrother's army regiment," Brown said, watching her reaction. She puckered her lips and wrinkled her nose as if she'd just bitten into a lemon. She was as surprised as he was.

"Photograph?" she sneered. "Who would take such a trifle?"

"We would like permission to ask the servants if they might've taken it, as a remembrance of His Lordship."

"I've already told the inspector, milady,

that no member of staff would have done such a thing."

"Just so, Hodgson," Lady Philippa said, nodding her approval. "Permission is denied. You've already badgered the loyal servants of this household enough, Inspector. You may leave us, Hodgson."

Brown sighed. He was beginning to wonder if she wanted him to find her husband's killer. At least his breathing had returned to normal after the arduous climb.

"Very good, my lady." The butler nodded and backed out of the room. From the expression on her face, Lady Philippa had already dismissed him from her mind.

"My husband was a very prominent man, Inspector. He had visitors all of the time. It must've been one of them."

Brown had already asked the butler for the names of those meeting with Lord Fairbrother in the days leading up to his death. Brown hadn't been surprised to hear George Parley's name mentioned. He wasn't surprised not to hear Harvey Milkham's.

"Yes, I've considered that."

"Then consider arresting that old snakecatcher as I've insisted you do all along." Her self-righteous tone was grating, but Brown endured. He still had a great deal more to ask.

All along Brown had had difficulty imagining Harvey Milkham getting past the front hall, let alone Lord Fairbrother's private study, to steal the dagger, and now the photograph. He conceded that someone had. But Harvey Milkham? It seemed highly unlikely. But he didn't need to tell Lady Philippa that. Miss Kendrick, who was known to entertain the old hermit at Pilley Manor, aside, everyone knew the chances of Harvey Milkham ever stepping foot in Outwick House.

"Are you not aware that Harvey Milkham is dead, Lady Philippa?"

"Really? How?"

Mr. Barlow put a reassuring hand on Lady Philippa's shoulder. "I hope the snake-catching fellow's death isn't distracting you from finding Lord Fairbrother's killer, Inspector."

"You can be assured we are doing everything in our power to find the culprit."

As they were still in the early days of Harvey's death, Brown had no intention of revealing the possible connection between the two men's murders. Lady Philippa half snorted, half sniffed, as if she hadn't expected anything less.

"Do you know why your husband kept envelopes full of ten-pound notes?" Brown asked, hoping the shift in topic might unsettle her.

Lady Philippa was unfazed. "Why would I? I've never concerned myself with my husband's business affairs."

"Then, I assume you don't know the contents of his will?" She blanched but recovered so quickly Brown wondered if he imagined it.

"I most certainly do. He was my husband, after all." But her indignation was a bit overmuch. Brown suspected she wasn't privy to its contents and was quite put out by it.

"I say, Inspector," Mr. Barlow said. "Why are you questioning Philippa when there's a killer on the loose?"

If only Brown could ask the meddling plant hunter to leave. But doing so would end the interview, and he couldn't have that. Not yet. Brown ignored the question instead.

"Am I right in assuming the jewelry found in the safe belongs to you?"

The lady sighed loudly, showing her displeasure and growing impatience, and smoothed her skirt again. "Yes, every piece belongs to me. They were gifts from my most generous husband."

But then why were they in a safe that she

supposedly had no access to? Why would Lord Fairbrother have them? Was he as controlling as he was generous, perhaps? Brown asked, but the lady rolled her eyes in annoyance.

"And these? Have you ever seen these before?" Brown produced the letters from Sir George Lewis, maintaining a tight pinch on the envelopes. He wasn't taking any chances.

Lady Philippa granted them a glance, and the color drained from her face. This time Brown didn't question her reaction. She was visibly stunned. She opened her mouth, as if to speak, but appeared incapable of uttering even the slightest sound.

"I'll take that as a yes, then."

"What are they?" Mr. Barlow asked, seemingly unaware of Lady Philippa's sudden distress.

As if any of this was the plant hunter's concern. Brown considered the man's continued presence at Outwick House not only a nuisance but unseemly, what with Lady Philippa in mourning. But then again, after reading the contents of Sir George Lewis's letters, Brown knew Lady Philippa to be less upright than he'd assumed. The lady had her secret. And Brown had another suspect.

"They're nothing to concern yourself with, Mr. Barlow," Lady Philippa said curtly, shrugging off the comfort of his hand. She rose from her seat and strode toward the window, the black crape of her skirt swishing as she walked. Mr. Barlow pouted, like a scolded child, watching her.

"Can you tell me again where you were the evening of the murder, Mr. Barlow?"

The plant hunter, recovering from his rebuke, shook his head as if to clear away his confusion. "What? Why, I was here, in the smoking room, and then I retired to bed. But what does any of this have to do with an intruder?"

"And you, Lady Philippa?"

"What are you insinuating, Inspector?"

"I'm not insinuating anything, Mr. Barlow. I'm simply asking a question."

"Are you accusing Lady Philippa of murdering her husband?" Mr. Barlow said. His resentment appeared genuine enough, but Brown cleared his throat and ignored him.

"Lady Philippa?"

"I retired to bed early," she said, as if her attention was on other things. She began stroking the smooth pale green damask drapes that framed the window. Which of her mistakes was she pondering? The impetus behind Lord Fairbrother's desire to engage Sir George Lewis's legal services, or had she more profound regrets? Or was she unrepentant and devising a way out of her predicament?

"According to the servants' accounts, you insisted on not being disturbed."

"I may do what I like in my own home, Inspector." That same wistful tone.

"You didn't go out again, by way of the conservatory, perhaps?"

"Why would she do that?" Mr. Barlow said with a hint of mocking laughter, retrieving his cane leaning against the end of the sofa and sidling up to Lady Philippa. "She just told you she retired early." He laid his hand on the small of her back. She flinched and drew away. He held up his hand in defeat and slumped down into the nearest chair.

"Is that all, Inspector?' Lady Philippa said, her voice cold and tight. The uncharacteristic wistfulness was gone. She'd either determined on a plan or needed rid of him to do so. If he was going to catch this killer, it was time to play his trump card.

"Were you involved in any way with your husband's death, Lady Philippa?"

"I say, why would she — ?"

"Get out," Lady Philippa snarled quietly, cutting off Mr. Barlow's protest. She clutched the drape in her fist as if preparing to tear it down. But Brown waited for an answer.

"Did you need Lord Fairbrother dead to prevent him from disinheriting you, from divorcing you?"

Without warning, Lady Philippa whirled about, snatched up the crystal vase filled with gardenias on the sill, and flung it across the room. Mr. Barlow, seated nearby, threw his arms over his head and cowered into the thick padding of the chair as water, flowers, and vase swept over him. Brown darted backward and ducked, barely managing to avoid the missile before it smashed against the back of the sofa.

Damn. Splotches of dark and light marred his new shoes where water had splashed on them. Brown brushed himself off with a sweep of his hat before surveying the rest of the damage.

For several feet in front of him, embedded shards of glittering glass carpeted the floor, flower stems strewn out among them. A few of the silky, white petals still fluttered slowly to the floor as the scent of gardenia blanketed the room. Brown snatched one from the air. He'd always liked the smell of gardenia. It was one of Mrs. Brown's favorites.

Not anymore, it isn't. He tossed the petal to the floor with the rest.

"I say, Philippa. Was that called for?" Mr. Barlow said, using his handkerchief to dab drops of water that had rained down him as the vase had passed overhead.

Lady Philippa pushed the ringer to summon the butler. Mr. Hodgson arrived almost instantly, making Brown wonder if the butler hadn't gone far. Perhaps Brown was right to suspect the butler of spying. Mr. Hodgson's only response to the broken vase was a raised eyebrow.

"You rang, my lady?" How much did the butler hear and see? If Brown was right, probably everything.

"Please see the inspector out," Lady Philippa said, smoothing the hair at her temples. "And get someone up here to clean up this mess."

"Very good, my lady."

"You didn't answer my question," Brown said, carefully tiptoeing across the field of glass toward the butler, patiently waiting at the door.

"Not another word, Inspector," she said, turning her back on the room once more. She clutched the drapes again in her fist. "The next time, I won't miss."

Was she demanding his silence or declaring her own? Brown couldn't tell. Either way, he didn't care for the threat. If Lady Philippa were involved in her husband's death, he'd find out, flying vases or no.

Chapter 29

Lyndy, reading an article about an American jockey over Alice's shoulder, glanced up as Papa entered the drawing room. Despite the gong, Papa was still wearing his tweeds. Normally Lyndy wouldn't have cared less for Papa's sudden disregard for etiquette, but they might be late for the engagement party at Pilley Manor. Stella might take it the wrong way.

"Papa?" Lyndy said, exchanging a concerned glance with Alice. They'd both noticed Papa's slack jaw and sallow coloring.

"Gone," Papa whispered, his voice hoarse and disbelieving. Alice set aside her magazine, jumped up, and took Papa's arm. She led him toward the sofa. He shuffled and stumbled like a man twice his age. "All gone."

"What is gone, Papa?" Alice asked.

What was he talking about? The money

from the estate? That was old news. Wasn't that why Mother had wanted Lyndy to marry Stella in the first place? And now Mother wanted Lyndy to marry Philippa. When had she become so duplicitous?

I mustn't dwell on that, right now.

"Miss Kendrick should've taken Lady Philippa's advice —" Mother said, as she strode into the room. Her gray silk gown reflected the dour expression of her face. Lyndy cared little for what she was talking about. It was obvious she was praising Philippa at Stella's expense. It had been Mother's way since Lord Fairbrother died, making Philippa a very wealthy widow. Mother, adjusting one of her dangling pearl earrings, took one look at Papa and scowled. "William, why aren't you —"

Papa groaned and clutched his arm. Alice hadn't the strength to keep him upright, and they fumbled against the side table. The Tiffany table lamp, a green and blue mosaic of leaded glass, tottered, and the dragonflies on the shade threatened to take flight. Mother secured the lamp as Lyndy bolted from his seat to do the same for Papa. But Lyndy was too late. Papa crumpled toward the ground.

"William!"

"Papa!"

Lyndy dove headfirst, his knees connecting hard with the ungiving wooden floor beyond the carpet, hoping to cushion Papa's fall. Sliding under his shoulders, Lyndy caught Papa's head inches from the floor. Lyndy eased them both into a more comfortable position and cradled his groaning father in his lap. Perspiration dripped down Papa's face. Red indentations, probably from wearing his magnifying spectacle-mount loupes so much, stretched across the bridge of Papa's nose. Papa and Professor Gridley had been too much in the study staring at bones.

But surely this isn't about a bit of eye strain?

Mother pressed the bell while shouting at the first servant who passed the open door to telephone the doctor. Lyndy loosened Papa's cravat, feeling his father's heart pound as if trying to burst from his chest. Papa's hand shot up and clutched at Lyndy, pulling him by the lapels down to him. His breath smelled of scotch and grew more ragged as he struggled to form words. He sputtered and gasped instead. Lyndy held his ear to his father's mouth, but it was no use.

"Get him up. Get him up," Mother insisted, motioning to Fulton the moment the butler arrived. Fulton rushed over, unceremoniously snatched Papa's hands and pulled while Lyndy heaved his father from behind. Papa did nothing to help them. Fulton dragged as Lyndy pushed and the two managed to hoist Papa onto the sofa. He flopped, like a rag doll, into the corner.

Was Papa delirious? What had happened to reduce him to this pathetic state? Had he lost his mind? Or was he having some sort of seizure?

"Are you in pain, Papa?" Alice asked as she settled in beside him, dabbing his forehead with her handkerchief. Papa groaned, and Lyndy took that as a yes.

"Should I fetch the aspirin powder?" Fulton asked. "Dr. Johnstone prescribed some for one of the staff. I'm quite certain the maid didn't use all of it."

"As fast as you can," Lyndy barked. Fulton hastened off as fast as decorum would allow. *Blast decorum.* Fulton wasn't moving swiftly enough. "Run, man, run."

"Whatever is the matter with him?" Mother said, pacing back and forth in front of the cold fireplace.

The rain earlier had sent a chill through the house, but Mother had refused to order a fire. Until Lyndy was wed and could pay off Papa's debt, she insisted on this bothersome economy. Despite Papa's feverish condition, Lyndy was certain they were all in need of some comforting warmth, including Mother. Although she'd not yet approached Papa, Lyndy had never seen his mother so worried. He could hear her quick, labored breathing as she paced. How often had she scolded him as he paced, insisting he be still? Perhaps they weren't so very different, after all?

Suddenly Mother halted midstep, clenched fists at her sides, and shouted, "Where is Dr. Johnstone?"

"He's on his way, my lady," Fulton answered, scooting across the room, almost comically, and handing Lyndy the aspirin powder dissolved in a glass. If Papa's condition wasn't so serious, Lyndy might've laughed.

Lyndy put the glass to Papa's lips, watching helplessly as some of the precious liquid dribbled down his father's chin. Mother, seeing this, shouldered her way between them.

"Oh, for goodness' sake, must I do everything?"

Lyndy gladly relinquished the glass as she propped Papa's head up. With her lips pinched in concentration, Mother made sure the rest made it past Papa's lips. Lyndy stood back, hoping the medicine would do some good.

Now all they could do was wait.

As Mother nudged Alice aside, settling into the sofa, Lyndy took up the task of pacing, from the southern windows to the eastern windows and back. His mind swirled with concern: for Papa; for Stella, who was having to greet her arriving guests alone and would be fraught with worry; for himself, should Papa not recover. Lyndy didn't want to think about what the death duties and Mother's grief would do to his future, let alone how much he'd miss the infuriating blighter.

"Sit down, Lyndy. You're not a feral cat," Mother chided. "Besides, you're disturbing your father." Lyndy regarded his father. Although his breathing had improved, Papa didn't look like anything would disturb him ever again.

"My God, what happened?" Professor Gridley, dressed for dinner, rushed to Papa's side the moment he stepped in the room. He knelt before him, as Mother tilted her nose in the air, disapproving of the American's emotional display. Or was it Professor Gridley she objected to? Mother had never been fond of the paleontologist, who shamelessly took Papa's money when it was needed to run the estate.

"He collapsed," she said. "We've sent for the doctor. There is no need for you to scuff your trousers, Professor." Professor Gridley, using the end of the sofa, hauled himself up. But he was still shaking his head.

"I was just with him. I've been with him all day. He seemed fine."

"And he will be fine," Mother insisted. "Though his days of fussing over dusty old bones may be over." As if the two weren't mutually exclusive. If Papa recovered, he would do so to study his fossils again. Take that away, and he'd never be the same.

"He mentioned something before he collapsed," Lyndy said. "He insisted something was gone. You were with him. Do you know what he meant?"

Professor Gridley's mouth gaped open. "No," he exclaimed under his breath. "No, it can't be." Without explanation or excuse, he bolted from the room.

"I will never get used to these Americans," Mother snapped, her fear for Father hidden behind her annoyance at the professor's breach in etiquette. "Not even a by-your-leave, he goes racing out of the room. He didn't even answer your question."

Professor Gridley's abrupt departure had reminded Lyndy of Stella's often impulsive behavior, but that didn't bode well. Professor Gridley, if he were anything like Stella, wouldn't be bearing good news when he returned.

"Out of my way, I say," a deep voice barked at the servants clustered outside the door. Word had spread that the earl had collapsed.

"Dr. Johnstone." Fulton announced the physician, a pudgy fellow in his late fifties with a white mustache and round face.

"Good lord, Fulton, what is going on here?" the physician said as if blaming the butler for his master's distress. Fulton, a pained expression wrinkling his brow, merely stepped out of the physician's way.

Dr. Johnstone marched across the room to his patient, pulling a stethoscope from his leather bag as he went. He shooed Mother and Alice away, demanding they give Papa some air. Both women scuttled away without complaint. The physician's brusque manner belied a well-trained mind and a kind heart. He'd been the family physician all Lyndy's life.

After a quick examination, of pulse, eyes, heart, he removed the stethoscope from around his neck and folded it back into his bag.

"His Lordship will recover, but he needs rest." No one smiled, no one cried, no one clapped their hands in joy. Yet the relief in the room was palpable.

Lyndy sighed in quiet gratitude. *If only Stella were here.* She'd be able to express her elation properly, and they would all be better for it.

"I must insist on this, Lady Atherly."

"Of course, Doctor."

"What caused it?" Lyndy asked. Dr. Johnstone grew thoughtful, opened his mouth, and then clamped his lips into a hard frown. Lyndy followed the physician's gaze.

Professor Gridley, taking even Fulton unawares, had lumbered slowly, silently into the room. With his shoulders bent, he stared at his unpolished shoes as he walked, almost bumping into the astonished butler.

"I say, are you ill, man?" Dr. Johnstone asked.

Professor Gridley raised his head, his eyes dull and unseeing when they were usually so lively and bright. It was disconcerting, especially so soon after Papa's narrow escape.

"Bloody hell, Professor, tell us what happened," Lyndy said, recognizing the same grief-stricken look on Papa's face.

"The Fort Union Formation maps, the *Equus spelaeus* tooth, and" — the professor paused — "every last *Miohippus atherli* specimen I brought. I say *Miohippus atherli* because I was going to name it after His Lordship, you see."

"No, we do not see," Mother said. "Speak English, Professor."

"His Lordship's fossils, Lady Atherly, the ones I brought from the expedition in Wyoming," Professor Gridley clarified, unfazed by Mother's deriding tone. "They're all gone. Someone has broken into the study and stolen everything."

Stella was not enjoying herself. How could she be? Aunt Rachel was in bed with a head cold. Daddy had disappeared, reappeared, and disappeared again. Harry Finn, Lyndy's valet who was graciously helping Tims serve at the table, had arrived hours ago. Where was everyone else from Morrington Hall? When the first unfamiliar carriage rolled up, even the stoic, cold Tims bestowed her a look of pity before opening the door. She had dreaded this evening, but she never imagined this. Still, she'd plastered a smile on her face and began greeting her guests, alone.

"How lovely you look in blue, Lady So-and-so. How clever of you to snatch up La Roche's latest foal, Sir Such-and-such.

Wasn't the rain today dreadful, Mrs. Socialite-invited-only-to-please-Lady-Atherly?"

And with each confused, condescending, or curious remark about the conspicuously absent groom and his family, Stella would laugh and say, "I told them to arrive later so I could have you all to myself." Except when she'd greeted Mr. Barlow. To him, when he asked, she simply shrugged before welcoming the next guest. She hoped to avoid the plant hunter as much as possible.

Whether her harmless pleasantry soothed her guests' ruffled feathers, Stella could only guess.

"They're here," a high-pitched voice whispered loudly from behind.

Stella turned to see Ethel's capped head disappear behind the kitchen door. *Dear Ethel.* She understood Stella's distress. They'd spent hours picking out the right dress, a rose-colored silk with lace sleeves, floral metallic thread embroidery, and a flowing train from the House of Worth, picking out the right jewelry, dangling emerald and gold earrings, a matching necklace and hair combs, and commiserating about the importance and strain of the upcoming event. As usual, Ethel had done wonders with Stella's hair, and even Stella had to admit she looked stunning. But beauty only went so far to excuse this debacle.

Stella strained to see around Baroness Branson-Hill, who was blocking her view of the door. She sighed in relief to see Lyndy, Lady Atherly, and Lady Alice arrive. But where was Lord Atherly? Where was Professor Gridley? She excused herself, to the shock and chagrin of the baroness, and shortened the distance between her and Lyndy as fast as the constraints of her formfitting evening gown would allow.

"I am so happy to see you." She wanted to scold them for being late. She wanted to demand what had kept them. She wanted to know what was keeping the other men in their party. But one look into Lyndy's eyes stilled her tongue. "What's wrong?"

"This is neither the time nor the place to discuss the matter," Lady Atherly said, handing Tims her silk wrap without so much as a glance. "Suffice it to say, Lord Atherly is indisposed. He and Professor Gridley shan't be coming."

Not coming? What happened? Stella looked to Lyndy for an explanation. But they were interrupted.

"There he is, Viscount Lyndhurst," Baroness Branson-Hill said. She slipped her flabby arm through his. "You've been a naughty boy, keeping us all waiting. And to think the rain stopped hours ago."

Lyndy, a look of long-suffering on his face, allowed her to lead him to the drawing room. Lady Atherly and Lady Alice followed. When Tims informed her that all the guests, except Daddy and Miss Cosslett, had arrived, Stella, wishing she could disappear, grudgingly trailed after them.

Stella mingled, champagne glass in hand, for what seemed like an hour but was perhaps a quarter of that, waiting for the moment she could talk to Lyndy. Every conversation was the same: Wasn't it sad circumstances that kept Lady Philippa at home? How kind of Stella to invite Mr. Barlow; he was such an entertaining fellow. Where was Mr. Kendrick, their host? Where was Lord Atherly? To the former Stella bit her tongue and kept her opinions of Lady Philippa and Mr. Barlow to herself. To the latter, she begged ignorance. She had no idea where her father had gone off to or what kept Lord Atherly at home. It was trying, smiling and nodding and saying next to nothing at all. But Jane Cosslett wasn't here, thankfully, recording her every word, and so far, no one had pegged Stella with questions about the murders.

"Forgive me, Reverend Paine. May I steal

Lord Lyndhurst from you for a moment?"

She'd sighted Lyndy talking to Lord Montagu and the bishop of Winchester but hadn't interrupted. Lady Atherly had been adamant that a proper hostess didn't intrude on a gentleman's conversation. But when Reverend Paine, the local vicar, started up a conversation with Lyndy, she jumped at her opportunity. The vicar was as trying at a party as he was in the pulpit. Another guest Lady Atherly had insisted on.

"Of course, dear child," Reverend Paine said patronizingly. "He is your fiancé, after all."

"For better or worse," someone uttered. Both Stella and Lyndy turned to see who'd made the remark, but it was too large a gathering. It could've been anyone. Stella turned back to the vicar and forced a smile.

"Though you haven't set a date, have you?" Reverend Paine said as if he hadn't heard. "I'm still waiting."

"Yes. I'll speak to Daddy about it. Thank you. Excuse us."

Stella smiled and nodded her way through the crowd, her arm tucked through Lyndy's. The men smiled back, their most enthusiastic, generous smiles, but the women raised the corners of their pinched lips, their eyes often reflecting emotions other than goodwill. Stella couldn't wait to have a few minutes alone. She led him across the hall to the library and shut the door.

"I need —"

With the words barely out of her mouth, Lyndy's arms were around her. He pulled her toward him, his hand warm on the nape of her neck, and their lips melted together. All thoughts of Lord Atherly's absence, the strain of the evening, even those of Harvey and Lord Fairbrother flew from her mind, leaving only the need for Lyndy and the desire to stay this way forever. But it had to end. When he lifted his head away from hers, a thoughtful expression on his face, she blushed.

"Well, that isn't what I brought you in here for."

"But you weren't explicit in what you needed, either. What kind of gentleman would I be if I denied you this basic need?" His smirk belied the affection in his eyes.

"True." Laughter lit his eyes, and he kissed her again.

He lingered, nibbling the lobe of her ear. Tingles coursed down her whole body. "What is it you do need?"

Stella sighed. She didn't want to spoil the moment, but it was already too late.

Thoughts of murder, missing fathers, and foreboding of the tedious night ahead, banished for a few luscious moments, swirled again in her head.

"What happened to your father and Professor Gridley?"

"Of course. How callous of me not to tell you right away." Stella didn't remind him it was his mother's doing, but patiently waited for him to tell the story. As they pulled apart, he tugged down on the cuffs of his black dress jacket.

"Someone stole all of Papa's fossils."

"Oh, no." Stella's covered her mouth with her fingers.

She knew how precious those bones were to Lord Atherly. She knew what lengths he'd gone to to get them. She knew they were the reason she and Lyndy were engaged in the first place. She could only imagine how devastated he must be.

"And the shock of it all was too much for him to bear." Lyndy described his father's collapse and the subsequent visit from the doctor, who assured them Lord Atherly would recover physically from the trauma. But mentally, Stella wasn't so sure. In the months she'd been in England, Stella had learned much about Lord Atherly's passion for discovering ancient and extinct horse fossils and much about the earl himself. His intellect, his wit, his well-hidden gentleness all reminded her of Lyndy. And this blow might be too much.

"And how is Professor Gridley holding up?"

"He decided to remain with Papa. Perhaps they are already conniving to dig again." Stella hoped so. And she was heartened to think that her inheritance, once she and Lyndy got married, would help fund that next expedition.

"Have you told Inspector Brown about the theft?"

Lyndy shook his head. "Mother thinks there's no need."

"No need? Lord Fairbrother had a priceless dagger stolen and now this. They might not be related to Harvey or Lord Fairbrother's murder, but Inspector Brown should know, just in case."

"You're right. He should know."

Slam! Crash! Stella and Lyndy twisted around toward the commotion in the hall. Was that the front door?

"Is she here?" Stella's father's voice demanded. He was shouting. Stella swung open the library door and hurried out into the hall, Lyndy a step behind her.

Stella had been right. The front door was

wide open. Glass, glistening in the light of the chandelier above, lay shattered on the marble floor beside it. Tims called for someone to clean it up. The door's frosted glass pane, with its pastoral scene of grazing horses etched into it, had cracked and broken. A slight chill of the late summer night air flowed into the hall. Daddy, ignoring the glass, crunched across it, throwing his white dress scarf and hat for Tims to catch. He was furious.

"I say, what is all the commotion?" Lady Atherly sauntered out into the hall. Lady Alice and Cecil Barlow weren't far behind. Lady Alice, barely glancing at the others, obviously left the drawing room in pursuit of the more curious Mr. Barlow. "What happened here?" Lady Atherly scoffed in disbelief, as Ethel, the only maid on hand, dashed in with a broom and dustpan.

"Another reason why we should never have . . ." Lady Atherly left her thought unfinished, but Stella knew what she meant; she was yet again regretting her association with the uncouth Americans. Luckily, Daddy was too upset to notice.

"Where have you been, Daddy?" Stella asked gently, hoping to diffuse her father's anger and cut off any more of Lady Atherly's grumbling.

"I've been to the police station. What a bunch of worthless —"

"Mr. Kendrick, if you will kindly keep your voice down," Lady Atherly said. "We do not want the guests alarmed by your behavior." As if she were in charge. As if they were her guests and not Stella's.

Would Lady Atherly always act this way? Stella could only assume so. Forcing down her growing impatience with her future mother-in-law, Stella returned her attention to her father. Daddy and Lady Atherly. Stella could do without the pair of them.

"Why were you at the police station?" Then Stella remembered the only time her father was concerned enough to call in the police. When they first arrived in England, Orson, their champion thoroughbred stud, had been stolen. Her shoulders tightened in fear. "Has something happened to Tully or the other horses?"

She couldn't bear it if something else had happened to Tully. Then Harvey sprang to mind. A sour taste filled her mouth.

"The horses? Not that I know of." Stella relaxed her shoulders in relief.

"Then, what did happen?" Lyndy demanded, frustratingly pulling on the lapels of his dress coat.

"Jane is missing, damn it! That's what

happened." Daddy pointed a stubby finger at Lyndy as if he had something to do with it. "She's not in her rooms; she's not here. She's not at Morrington Hall. She's not anywhere. Something has happened to her."

"You are overreacting, Mr. Kendrick," Lady Atherly said coolly. "Perhaps the woman simply tired of your company and went back to London."

"Without her case?" Daddy stomped out the door, snatched up a light brown, rectangular suitcase, and dropped it with a thud. It nearly hit poor Ethel as she swept away the last of the broken glass. It had *JAC* monogrammed on the side. "I don't think so. I think she's been the killer's third victim."

CHAPTER 30

Inspector Brown scanned the crowded pub and spotted the bald head he was looking for. If only every murder suspect made his job this easy. Brown had wagered George Parley, being as bullheaded as a wild stallion, wouldn't change his routine to avoid the police. Sure enough, the landowner was firmly established at the bar.

"Thought I might find you here."

"Where else would I be?" George Parley asked, before taking an exaggerated swig from his pint.

"Keeping my head down, if I were you," Brown said, waving the publican over.

"This is keeping me head down, Inspector. I've got nothing to hide from me friends here." George Parley raised his chin as if pointing to Mr. Heppenstall. "Ain't that right, Tom?"

"Yup," the publican agreed.

Brown ordered himself a half-pint. Mr.

Heppenstall grunted in acknowledgment, none too pleased to see Brown again. He was a man of few words, the owner of the Knightwood Oak. And Brown appreciated his taciturnity, except of course when Brown needed answers. But he wasn't here to question Mr. Heppenstall. Tonight, he was here for George Parley.

Despite having two murders to investigate, Brown had spent his evening, first listening to that wealthy American horse breeder bemoan the disappearance of his paramour, a reporter from London, and then, placating the distressed Lord Atherly over the theft of some old bones. After listening to the earl's guest run on about the loss to the scientific community, Brown caught the paleontologist fellow mentioning George Parley's name. Supposedly they'd uncovered some rare fossil in a barrow on the man's land, the same one where they'd found Harvey Milkham's body. A coincidence it might be, but Brown wasn't taking any chances. He'd sent Waterman out looking for the girl, and he'd headed straight for the Knightwood Oak.

The publican placed the half-pint of ale on the bar, and Brown paid him. Having no reason to linger, Mr. Heppenstall reluctantly limped a few paces away. Even as he helped another patron, he kept his eye on Brown. Or was he keeping tabs on George Parley?

Brown wrapped his hand on the glass and leaned in. "No secrets, eh? So, Mr. Heppenstall knows all about your little arrangements with Lord Fairbrother, then, does he?"

George Parley stopped midsip and set his glass down. He licked the foam from his lips. "What do you want from me, Inspector?"

"I want the truth, Mr. Parley."

"I told you the truth."

"The whole truth."

"I've told you the whole truth."

A clattering of glassware beside them startled both men. The lad who worked at the pub suddenly stumbled into sight carrying a pallet of bottles. He rested it on the edge of the bar, panting.

"I heard you found your ghost, lad," Brown said.

The boy shook his head. "No, found that the snakecatcher had been living in a sub-basement no one knew about."

"Seems he might've found it years ago when he was hired to clear the pub of hibernating snakes," the man called Old Joe interjected.

"Just never bothered to tell me about it,"

Mr. Heppenstall grumbled.

"That still doesn't mean there isn't a ghost," the lad insisted.

"Of course," Brown said, chuckling as the publican swiped the side of the boy's head with a snap of his towel. The lad lifted the pallet, nearly losing his grip in his hurry, and disappeared into the back.

"Speaking of the snakecatcher, Mr. Parley . . . Why were you shoveling dirt into the barrow, covering up Harvey Milkham's body?"

George Parley wiped his mouth with the length of his sleeve. His hands were shaking. "I just wanted to reclaim what's mine. That barrow is on me land, and I was done waiting for the likes of Lord Atherly to say when I could fill it in." He reached for his pint as a drowning man might grasp for a rope. "I swear I didn't know the snakecatcher was there." He put the ale to his lips and tilted his head back until the glass was empty.

"So, you have no idea why Harvey Milkham was there, on your land?"

"None. I swear."

"Sorry to hear the verderers voted against your rifle club."

Brown had requested a closed session with the members of the court. Hearing what

Brown had to say, they immediately voted against granting permission to establish the rifle club. George Parley curled his lip and grumbled something incoherent into his glass. Brown's change in subject didn't get him anywhere. Time to change tactics.

"Has anyone seen Miss Jane Cosslett, the journalist in town to report on Lord Lyndhurst's wedding?" Brown called out, raising his voice over the din of the men chatting, throwing darts, and having a laugh. "She's petite, ginger-haired, about twenty-five, give or take a year or so."

George Parley rounded his shoulders as if curling up to the bar would make Brown forget he was there and signaled to Mr. Heppenstall for another drink.

"Why?" the publican asked Brown, pouring another draught for George Parley.

"She's gone missing," Brown said. He took a quick sip of his ale. Too hoppy for his tastes but slipped smoothly down his throat. "It's possible she might've gotten tangled up with the same killer who stabbed Lord Fairbrother and Harvey." Brown didn't believe it. Not now, not when Mr. Kendrick was shouting it at him in his office, but it got the reaction he was hoping for.

A low murmur of disbelief reverberated

through the pub. To a man, the locals were shaking their heads — all except George Parley.

"Do you know where Miss Cosslett is, Mr. Parley?" Brown said, in a voice he'd hoped carried across the room.

"What? Why would I know anything about that girl? I've only seen her once, at the Cecil Pony Challenge."

"Perhaps we should go to the police station and talk about this further." Brown clasped his hand around the man's arm and lifted him from his seat. All eyes were on them.

"I'm telling you I don't know what happened to that girl." George Parley struggled to shrug off Brown's hold. He'd had a few, or Brown wouldn't have been able to detain him. Still Brown had to step lightly. The man was an ox, and there was no saying how much damage he could do. If only Brown had brought Waterman along. His constable would be a suitable match for the belligerent landowner.

Brown leaned in again and whispered, "Then you wouldn't mind telling me everything you know about Lord Fairbrother and the bribes he's been taking from you?"

George Parley's eyes widened. He yanked out of Brown's grip and then wobbled before he regained his balance. The drunken landowner pointed to a vacant table in the corner. "We can talk over there.

"Let me say first that I haven't done anything that a lot of other men haven't done," he began the moment they sat down, his words starting to slur. "There are few commoners in this part of the Forest who didn't know that Fairbrother was willing to 'work' with you, considering you paid him enough."

Brown was skeptical, but he made sure his face didn't show it. He'd accepted the accusations about Lord Fairbrother as possibilities, not pervasive patterns of behavior. But then again, it would explain the envelopes of money found on the dead lord's body and in his private study. But could what George Parley said be true? Could Lord Fairbrother have been that corrupt?

"So, yes," the landowner was saying. "I asked Fairbrother to look the other way when I moved me fences out. And yes, I paid him to ignore the need to investigate the burning of Harvey's hut. As I said before, it was a disgrace anyway. I was doing everyone a favor."

"You admit to burning Harvey's house down?"

George Parley lifted the glass he'd carried

with him, took a long drink, and wiped the beer from his mustache with his fingers before nodding. "It was the only way to get a hold of the land. Only way Fairbrother would sell it to me. I needed it for the rifle club, you see." So Fairbrother was complicit in that too.

"And what about Harvey Milkham?"

"What about him?"

Brown refrained from comment. He had the landowner for arson, if nothing else, so he didn't need to show his contempt, but Brown also wanted to see what more he could learn. "Did you kill him?"

"No!" George slammed his hand on the table, making the beer glass jump and drawing the attention of many fellow drinkers. "I didn't kill Fairbrother, either," he said, much quieter.

"When was the last time you gave him money, to 'look the other way'?"

"The night before the Cecil Cup Competition. He was supposed to vote in me favor at court this morning. Why would I kill him? Without him, I might have done all this for bloody nothing."

Brown sat back in his chair, astounded. Against all his previous conclusions, and despite himself, Brown believed him. But if not George Parley, then who? Could Harvey have killed Lord Fairbrother? And then someone else killed Harvey? It seemed a stretch. But then again, both men were dead, with nary a connection between them but the burnt down hut George Parley admitted to setting light to. Again, he had to ask, if not George Parley, then who?

"And you still say you don't know how Lord Fairbrother's medieval dagger got to be in the barrow?"

George Parley looked sheepishly over the rim of his glass. "I might've taken that one," he mumbled. "As insurance, you see. For his vote." Brown could see how the man's twisted thinking might lead him to do such a thing. "Didn't know the man was going to get himself stabbed, now did I?"

"You did this when you visited Lord Fairbrother at his home?" He nodded. "Did you rummage through his desk, take a photograph?"

"No, why would I do that?" His eyes glazed over in confusion. "His desk, a photograph? What value would be in that? No, that dagger is worth hundreds, if not thousands of pounds. And it was there for the taking. Just slipped it off the wall when Fairbrother's back was turned." There was something in what George Parley said. Could he be telling the truth? Brown tended to think so.

"So how did this precious dagger come to be in the barrow?"

Parley drained his beer. "Dropped it on me way home from here. Had a bit too much, I suspect."

"I suspect you had. Finished?" The man nodded. Brown stood and slapped his hat on his head. "Right! Mr. George Parley, I'm arresting you for arson, theft, obstruction of justice, and interference in the investigation of the murders of Lord Fairbrother and Harvey Milkham. Do you have anything to say?"

The drunken scoundrel, swaying as he sat, nodded. "Do I have time for another?"

"I'm afraid not." Brown hauled him to his feet and shoved him toward the door.

CHAPTER 31

Until the moment Kendrick arrived, spouting claims that the reporter had gone missing and was probably dead, Lyndy had been enjoying himself. It had been a close one with Papa, and Lyndy was glad for the distraction. And what a distraction. A society event without the eyes of Philippa on him, several glasses of excellent champagne, and clandestine kisses in the library.

Although dragged away by the baroness, he'd followed Stella with his eyes as she smiled and chatted while everyone enjoyed their predinner drinks. She'd put everyone at ease. Despite her misgivings about playing hostess, she was a natural. Small talk was never his forte, nor did he much care for it. But after months of teas, balls, and dinner parties, he was yet to tire of watching Stella practice the art of it. Of course, other women exchanged pleasantries with their guests; it was something every fine lady was taught to do. But Stella, curious and engaged, showed genuine interest. And those she spoke to instinctually, if not consciously, felt the difference, endearing her to everyone.

Well, almost everyone.

When the plant hunter had cornered Lyndy earlier, insisting on describing a violent rash he once suffered after tripping over a line of leaf-cutting ants and stumbling into a poisonous vine, Stella had rescued him. Throughout the Season, she'd done it time and time again. She'd done it tonight with that patronizing vicar. Would he ever get used to the eagerness in her eyes as she sought him out? The way her hips swayed as she strolled purposefully across a room? How Stella's unabashed smile and the natural shine on her rosy lips stopped his heart? For all his lusting after Philippa, he'd never felt this way about her. And he'd almost spoiled the lot by not telling Stella about Philippa. Happily, Stella had more patience and perseverance than he did.

And then Stella had ushered him from the drawing room to the library. Mother had scowled while the others had craned their curious necks, twittering and gossiping as they passed. Let everyone wonder where they had stolen off to, he'd mused in gratification. It was their engagement party, was it not? Lyndy had suffered Mother's society friends' judgmental stares his whole life. To see them experience jealousy and regret that they never ached to be alone with their betrothed had filled him with such self-satisfaction, such affection for this lovely woman that had come into his life. When the library doors had closed behind them, he could've as easily stopped the rain from falling as not taken Stella in his arms and smothered her with kisses.

And then Kendrick returned.

"Let that be the end of it, Mr. Kendrick," Mother was scolding, as if Kendrick were a child complaining about not getting a second piece of cake. Lyndy, recollecting the salty taste of Stella's earlobe, the heady scent of her perfume, hadn't heard everything Mother had said.

"I agree," Stella said. "Let the police find Miss Cosslett. I'm sure she'll turn up, safe and sound."

"Silly thing probably realized she wasn't the right sort for such an occasion," Mother said. "You should be thanking your stars she's left and leave it at that."

Lyndy, surprisingly, agreed with his mother. Jane Cosslett's presence would've only added tension to the evening.

"Everyone has been asking after you, Daddy," Stella said.

"Of course, they have, girl," Kendrick said, seeming to come back to himself. "Do you think you're the one they're here to visit?"

As Kendrick took a step toward the drawing room, Mother said, "I'd like to speak with you, Mr. Kendrick, before we are all called to dinner."

Although they hadn't spoken of it again, Lyndy knew Mother's intent. When Kendrick hesitated, he said, "I say, Kendrick, I wouldn't keep your guests waiting."

Mother glowered at Lyndy while putting her hand on Kendrick's arm to hold him back. "The guests can wait for a moment or two longer, Mr. Kendrick. This cannot."

Kendrick stared down at Mother's hand on him. It was so unlike her. She didn't touch anyone. And Kendrick knew it. When the swine looked up grinning like a Cheshire cat, reading more in that touch than Mother intended, she snatched her hand away as if she'd touched a hot stove. But it was too late. A smirk slithered across his face and for a moment, Lyndy felt sorry for his mother. But as usual, she'd brought it on herself. What had Mother been thinking? Would she stop at nothing to break the engagement?

"Get in there, girl," Kendrick barked, "and tell everyone I'll be in shortly. Lady Atherly and I have something to discuss." Stella hesitated, straightening her shoulders and preparing to object.

"Shall I go with you, Miss Kendrick?" Lyndy offered, and Stella rewarded him with a grateful smile. How he loved that smile. But she wouldn't be smiling if she knew of his imminent deception. But needs must. He had to stop this, and he had to do it alone.

"Well, what is it?" Kendrick was saying, as he trailed after Mother heading across the hall to the library.

Once back inside the drawing room, Lyndy and Stella were immediately accosted by Mr. Barlow and Alice. "Do you really think that London journalist has gone missing?" Alice asked.

"Of course not," Lyndy said.

"That reminds me of the story," Mr. Barlow began, "of when I'd run low on water in the deserts of Australia and sent my partner back to Fort McKellar for more. He went missing as well. Shall I tell you the story, Lady Alice?"

"Oh, yes, please." Alice nodded enthusiastically.

"Miss Cosslett hasn't gone missing, Alice," Lyndy insisted. "And I'll ask that you not encourage her, Mr. Barlow."

"Then shall I tell you of my encounter with the giant green anaconda on the Orinoco River?" Mr. Barlow said. Stella's face clouded over. What a rotter! Lyndy clenched and unclenched his fists, recalling what the man had done the last time they'd seen him. But striking the fellow would ruin the evening. Looking at the fop's smug face, Lyndy almost chanced it.

"Mr. Barlow," Alice chided before Lyndy had the chance to, "you know any mention of snakes reminds Miss Kendrick of the old snakecatcher's death."

"Oh, I do apologize, Miss Kendrick. How thoughtless of me."

Bounder. He knew very well what he'd said. And now, Lyndy must leave Stella to this cad.

"If you'll excuse me, I forgot to tell Mother something." Lyndy evaded Stella's confounded, questioning gaze as he left her side. He wasn't one to suffer from guilt, but lying to Stella made him feel wretched. But if he was going to stop Mother's scheme, it had to be now. "I shan't be long."

Lyndy hastened out, stopping short of the library door. He tilted his head to listen, ignoring the wide-eyed stares of the servants as they passed with the first course of watercress soup. It smelled delicious.

"Your husband and I have a contract if you don't remember, Lady Atherly, and I insist he honor it," Kendrick was saying. Lyndy's suspicions were right. Mother was trying to negate the engagement contract. How dare she. "By the way, what kind of coward sends his wife to deliver such an obnoxious proposal?"

Lyndy bristled at the brute's accusation, even though Papa knew nothing of Mother's schemes. Papa didn't know, did he? No, of course not. Papa adored Stella. He'd never countenance Mother's meddling.

"How dare you insult the Earl of Atherly," Mother said. "He is a better man than most, Mr. Kendrick."

How ironic, Mother defending Papa. If Papa hadn't collapsed in front of her, would she be so complimentary? Lyndy doubted it.

"Then why isn't Lord Atherly in here with me, instead of you?" Kendrick asked.

"Because Lord Atherly is completely unacquainted with any of this," Mother said. Lyndy couldn't see Kendrick's reaction, but his silence was telling enough. The American was surprised. "I ask you again, Mr. Kendrick. What would it take for my family to be released from this ill-considered contract?"

"But, silly woman, why would you want to?" Kendrick asked in response. "We both know that you need my money more than ever now. What with the disappearance of those fossils, Lord Atherly will be more eager than a beaver to get at Stella's inheritance. But since I can commiserate with the earl, losing something priceless like that, I'm going to forget you ever mentioned this."

"Priceless, indeed. If it weren't for those godforsaken bones . . ."

"I could draw up charges, you know."

"You wouldn't dare."

If only Lyndy could see Mother's expression. For now, her indignant tone would have to satisfy. But could he trust Kendrick to keep his word and not break the contract? Was the brute in earnest, or was he having fun at Mother's expense? Lyndy didn't know. One thing was certain; those two deserved each other.

"Besides, who could you possibly find more suitable for your impoverished, pompous son than my daughter?" Kendrick mocked.

Pompous? I'll give him pompous. Lyndy yanked on his cuff so hard the gold cuff link popped out. The clink of metal told him about where it had hit the floor. He wasn't about to retrieve it now; he was riveted to the door.

"Lady Philippa, for one," Mother declared.

"The recent widow of Lord Fairbrother? Stands to inherit a great fortune, does she?"

"Indeed, she does. And she is well-known to the family." As if that was a boon.

"My, my," Kendrick said, clicking his tongue. "Talk about ill-considered. I think I'd be more worried about associating with a murder suspect than trying to break our contract, Lady Atherly."

Unexpectedly the door swung open. Kendrick stood framed in the doorway. Catching Lyndy in the hall, Kendrick chuckled as if he'd heard the most amusing joke. Lyndy recoiled when Kendrick slapped him on the back as he passed. "Might want to talk some sense into that mother of yours."

"Lyndy? Is it true?" Mother called, upon seeing him in the hall. Her face as white as Christmas snow, she was clutching the back of an armchair for support. "Is Lady Philippa a suspect?"

Poor Mother. Two shocks in one evening. First Papa's collapse and now Philippa's fall from grace. Lyndy almost felt sorry for her. Almost.

"Lyndy?" What did she expect him to say? What was there to say? "Lyndy!"

Not wishing to leave Stella to fend for herself in the drawing room one moment longer, he ignored his mother's calls to come back and turned on his heel.

"I told you so, Mother," he shouted over his shoulder as he strode across the hall, snatching up his cuff link as he went.

Stella smiled as she looked around the table. The tall white candles in the crystal candelabras lining the middle of the table flickered, illuminating the upturned faces, as her guests listened, captivated by the plant hunter's tale. Everyone seemed softer, gentler in the warm orange glow.

All but one, that is.

The evening was going surprisingly well. Mrs. Downie had outdone herself with the menu. The pink, red, and yellow rose centerpieces added a much-needed splash of color to the silver and white table setting. The conversation, drifting from the upcoming races at the new Newbury racecourse to the merits of London Symphony Orchestra's latest guest conductor to speculation about Stella and Lyndy's wedding trip, had avoided any mention of death or murder. Even her father, soothed by the accolades he received for "making such a fine match for his daughter," had stopped insisting Miss Cosslett was dead. Of course, a glass, or two, of the Kentucky bourbon he'd brought in for the occasion hadn't hurt. When someone remarked upon Lady Philippa's absence, Lady Alice, with her giggles and smiles, had brightened the somber mood by entreating Mr. Barlow to share one of his plant-hunting adventures. His tale recounted his first night in a hut he'd occupied in the Amazon, which was inhabited, unbeknownst to him, by vampire bats. Everyone, even Stella, despite her aversion to the man, was enthralled.

Only Lady Atherly, as dour as ever in her dark gray silk, stared straight ahead while Mr. Barlow spoke, her mouth puckered as if she was eating a plate full of unripe cranberries and not delicious seafood mousse.

"And then what happened?" Lady Alice said, her voice almost trembling in anticipation.

"I woke to find one of those midnight blood-letters sucking on my big toe!" Mr. Barlow declared.

The table erupted in shouts and cries of disbelief. Hands flew, in the air, over mouths, against heaving chests, as the women gasped in horror. The men, no less shocked, flung down their napkins or slapped the edge of the table, rattling the dishes and glassware. Harry, attempting to serve the roast pheasant and sautéed potatoes, stepped back, afraid someone might knock into his tray.

"Oh, dear."

"Good lord!"

"I say, you can't be serious?"

"Well, bless my soul," Aunt Rachel laughed.

"Is this appropriate dinner conversation?" Lady Atherly interjected calmly. No one paid her any heed.

Mr. Barlow nodded in earnest, crossing his hands over his heart, swearing he told the truth. The motion drew Stella's attention to his tie. Had she ever seen him wear one before? For once, he looked the part of an English gentleman. Too bad he didn't act like one.

"And they didn't stop at my toes. No. Sometimes the bats would nibble on my elbows, my fingertips, nose, chin, and even my forehead."

A collective groan of revulsion rose at this. Even Stella felt her stomach churn. She feared Mr. Barlow had yet again gone too far, but the next moment everyone was eagerly exchanging stories, in hopes of surpassing the plant hunter's grotesque suffering, while spearing their asparagus. Stella sampled the potatoes, dripping in rosemary-flavored butter, and kept an eye on Mr. Barlow while Daddy, not to be outdone, added his tale about biting flies, ticks, and the sheer misery of mosquitos to be found during a humid, wet Kentucky summer. When Baroness Branson-Hill elicited knowing nods at the mention of the ills of the English rain, the plant hunter whispered something smilingly into Lady Alice's ear. She giggled and glanced sideways at him, her eyes brimming with adoration. Satisfied with Lady Alice's reaction, he popped a chunk of pheasant into his mouth.

"If you want to talk about rain, Baroness . . ." Mr. Barlow began relating more woeful stories of molding specimens, mud slides, and floods.

Stella had hesitated when Lady Alice all but begged her to seat her next to the plant hunter. To Stella, Mr. Barlow had acted like a brute. But she'd relented, and Mr. Barlow had rewarded her by entertaining her guests so that she didn't have to. But poor Lady Alice was in love with a cad and wouldn't thank her when he reverted to wooing Lady

Philippa in the morning.

"But then why do you do it, Mr. Barlow?" someone asked as the dessert plates and finger bowls were set out. "Why endure such hardships for a flower?" A hush fell on the room. Someone shifted in their chair. Someone set down a fork against their plate with a clink. The butler and footman both glanced up from their tasks to hear Mr. Barlow's answer.

"I can endure anything to get what I want." He knowingly glanced at Lady Alice, who blushed and quickly lowered her eyes to her lap. "And why not plant hunting? What other occupation would allow me to experience the beauty of the world, the music of the babbling brook, the smell of the earth, the mixed scent of a forest's bouquet?"

"Sounds like you should take up gardening," Daddy said. "You'd get all that, and it would be a heck of a lot safer." Bursts of laughter rewarded her father's quip, but Mr. Barlow wasn't pleased. When he set aside his finger bowl, it smacked the table so hard, some of the contents splashed onto the tablecloth. Tims rushed over to dab up the spill.

"What gardener has permanent exhibits under his name in the herbaria of the world?" Mr. Barlow retorted.

"I say, speaking of the music of babbling brooks, Miss Kendrick," Reverend Paine said, trying to defuse the sudden tension. "I heard that you have the voice of an angel." Lady Atherly snickered at the ostentatious compliment. "Would you grace us with a few songs after dinner?"

Stella waited for her father to intervene, to say she wasn't fit to sing for such honored guests. But he was too busy devouring the slice of Charlotte Russe the footman had set before him.

"Thank you for your confidence, Reverend, but whoever told you that was exaggerating."

"It was I who told him," Lyndy said, smirking. As if he would know.

As he dried his fingers with his napkin, Lyndy kept his eyes on his task, avoiding Stella's exasperated glare. What a scoundrel. Lyndy had been trying to get her to sing for him for months. And for months she'd denied him. How could she sing for someone who had attended performances of some of the greatest singers in the world? And now he was forcing her hand, in front of everyone. With the request coming from the vicar, Stella had no choice but to capitulate.

Daddy, wiping his mouth with his napkins, grunted. "Good instincts, there, Reverend. It's one of the few things she does well." Aunt Rachel was bobbing her head enthusiastically. Stella looked askew at her father. Had he just complimented her?

"She's no Jenny Lind, bless her heart," Aunt Rachel added. Stella's great-aunt often bragged how she'd seen the "Swedish Nightingale" perform in Kentucky in 1851. "But no one sings 'My Old Kentucky Home' prettier." Odd praise, but Stella knew the old lady meant well.

"I don't want to get your hopes up, Reverend," Stella said, as the dining room door beyond the baron creaked open. Ethel poked her head in and then quickly back out. "But of course, I'll sing if you'd like me to."

Tims, spying Ethel's entry as well, scuttled abruptly from the room. What could that be about? When the butler returned, his face revealed nothing of what had transpired in the hall. But when he approached Stella's chair and leaned over her shoulder, concern was evident in the tightness of his jaw. Stella closed her eyes, bracing for the news.

"I'm afraid, miss," Tims whispered, "Inspector Brown is here and insists he speak with you." At least she wouldn't have to sing.

"Do you know what he wants to talk to me about?" she asked.

He leaned in so close, Stella felt the tickle of his breath on her neck. Enunciating every word with a grave tone, he said, "It seems they've found Miss Cosslett."

Her eyes flew open in alarm, catching Lyndy staring at her, candlelight flickering across his handsome features. His playful smirk had vanished.

Jane Cosslett stopped, caught her breath, and readjusted the long leather strap that dug into her shoulder. She leaned against a column, crossed her arms, and laughed, not caring who heard her. She'd done it. She'd really done it. Wouldn't Dr. Hale be proud?

Patting her satchel, as if to assure herself everything was still there, she glanced up and down the platform. For an evening train, there were few other passengers about. One young man in a brown fedora stood reading a newspaper. Not the *Daily Mail,* Jane noted with a bit of cheek. Two women, wrapped in matching woolen shawls, occupied the nearest bench — sisters, perhaps even twins, by the look of them. When Jane caught the eye of the one in the purple straw hat, the woman buried her head in her book. Piled beside them were several leather cases on top of a worn, well-traveled trunk. Jane regarded the trunk with envy.

She'd been forced to leave everything she owned behind. Even those new dresses from the House of Worth Kendrick had given her. Jane sighed. How Dr. Hale would've admired her in them. But it couldn't be helped. As it was, that buffoon's coachman had almost seen her.

Jane straightened up, adjusted her gloves, and brushed the dust from her skirt.

She'd had to huddle in the corner of her rented room when Elijah Kendrick's coachman knocked on her door. When the sound of his retreating footsteps diminished toward silence, Jane had pushed back the thin lace curtains flanking the window to see the waiting carriage. Oh, to have ridden in a coach once belonging to Queen Victoria. The rich horse breeder had bought it in London just for tonight — all to impress her. Fool. Jane had watched as the coachman appeared below and alighted onto the carriage. But then he'd looked up. She'd flattened herself against the wall, praying he hadn't caught her spying. He hadn't, but the close encounter had forced her hand.

She'd planned to be packed and awaiting the train before the carriage arrived. Who knew Elijah would send for her so early? After spending days enduring the man's boorish behavior, she should've expected something outlandish like that — expecting a girl to be at his beck and call. He knew nothing of decorum and civility and, as sure as the English rain, when the carriage returned without her, he'd be around to claim her. So, the moment the coach was off, so was she. She'd stuffed her satchel with her prizes and, without a backward glance, had dashed out the inn's back door.

Her trunk and a filthy hem were a small price to pay.

Jane blinked at the screech of the whistle. The sound of safety, of triumph, heralding the arrival of her train. A few others stepped up to the platform in anticipation. As Jane admired the particularly broad-shouldered, solid make of a man approaching, she imagined Professor Gridley's reaction when he discovered the theft: slumped shoulders, gaping mouth, trembling weathered hands. What she would've given to be there. But she couldn't risk being caught. As it happened, she almost was.

Who knew that gaining access to Lord Atherly's study would prove so difficult?

The first time it had been locked. But she'd stolen away from Elijah every chance she got, making as many petty excuses as possible: to view the wedding presents, to visit the church, to examine the wedding carriage, anything to visit Morrington Hall and retrieve the fossils. And Elijah had believed everything. She would've been gratified to see his belligerent denial when the truth came out. What a fool. But then again, that's why she and Dr. Hale had targeted him. Dr. Hale knew something of the American horse breeder and had suggested she gain access to Morrington Hall and the fossils through Elijah Kendrick. The social reporter ruse had been all Jane's idea. She'd followed every salacious detail of Princess Margaret of Connaught's wedding in the paper, after all. And the ruse worked, despite Miss Kendrick's resistance to the idea, despite Lord Fairbrother mentioning he'd seen her, not as a reporter but on Dr. Hale's arm, at the dinosaur exhibit. But Jane never meant to perpetuate the charade for days on end. And when Lord Lyndhurst caught her snooping, she thought it had all been for naught. But Jane shared a common trait with her false persona: persistence. Time after time, Jane snuck into Morrington Hall, through the front door, through the scullery, once even through an open window in the bluest room Jane had ever seen, hoping to find the study unlocked. If a servant saw her, she'd make some excuse. Tonight, her persistence was rewarded, for whether distracted by preparations for the engagement party or lulled into a false sense of security, Lord Atherly had left the fossils out, and his study unlocked.

Jane hadn't paused to admire the earl's extensive collection, his expensive equipment, or other evidence of his undeniable passion for the science; there were too many distracting noises in the hall. Instead, she snatched up every horselike fossil she could conceal down the front of her blouse and snuck out the way she'd come in, the unlocked door to the attached woodshed. When she'd laid out her prizes and examined them, she'd sat on the edge of her bed gaping in awe. Professor Gridley's stolen hoard was more significant than even Dr. Hale had expected. Her years of instructions under Dr. Hale's patient eye cumulated in this moment. Several bones of an undescribed *Miohippus.* Where had they been found? Who had Professor Gridley stolen them from? Would Dr. Hale consider naming it *Miohippus cossletti,* in her honor? Goose bumps rose on the back of Jane's neck. What a blissful thought. And oh, there was a cheek tooth of *Equus spelaeus.* Could it be the first ever found in England? *Astonishing.* To think they'd been rattling between her blouse and corset as she ran.

Jane reached out and caressed the smooth white bones with reverence. Yes, her efforts, her sacrifice, her suffering at the hand of that crass American had all been worth it. And Dr. Hale would think so too.

But oh, to have seen Professor Gridley's face.

Dr. Hale hadn't prepared her to meet the bespectacled Professor Gridley in person. Yes, Dr. Hale had spent the past several years regaling the underhandedness of the American scientist, even spouting hatred for the professor during his and Jane's most intimate moments together. For that alone, she hated Professor Gridley. But then she'd met him at the pony competition. He'd seemed so inconsequential. Curious, yes, intelligent, perhaps, but paleontology's most unscrupulous scientist, stealing, manipulating, discrediting anyone he must to be the first to assemble a complete unnamed *Miohippus* skeleton? It was hard to believe. But Dr. Hale, once the professor's prize pupil, and the first victim of his deceit, thought so, and that was enough for Jane.

With a whoosh of steam and air, the train pulled up alongside the narrow, wooden platform. As Jane advanced toward the carriage steps, a hand seized her arm from behind.

"I say, let go of me!" The handsome, broad-shouldered man she'd admired stood like a rooted tree behind her, his middle thicker, his hands more calloused than she'd assumed. She yanked her arm but couldn't free herself from his firm grip.

"Beg your pardon, Miss Cosslett, but it'll be my job if I do. We've been looking everywhere for you. Say, what have you got in your bag?"

She struggled, slapping him about the head, kicking his shins, yelling for help, but the other passengers did nothing but gawk at her in dismay. What was wrong with them? This man was trying to steal her bag. The offender, stoically taking the beating, tightened his grip, pinching her arm until it hurt, and pried open her satchel with his free hand.

"Lord Atherly's missing fossils!" His deep, baritone voice reminded her of Dr. Hale. "You're the thief? Did you steal the photograph and dagger from Outwick House too?" he said, genuinely surprised. She'd never been to Outwick House. What was he

443

talking about? "Miss Cosslett, my name is Constable Waterman, and I'm placing you under arrest."

Arrested? *Oh, Dr. Hale. Will you ever propose to me now?*

The constable roughly steered her away from the train, past the hovering onlookers, and off the platform, all the while shaking his head in disbelief. "And to think we all thought you were dead."

Knowing how she'd failed Dr. Hale, Jane wished she was.

CHAPTER 32

Daddy grunted something unintelligible from the library doorway. With his hands on his hips, his elbows touched the doorframe. Stella, though no longer seeing the words on the page, kept her eyes on her book.

"Did you hear me, girl?"

Stella kicked off her slippers, tucked her legs up under her skirt, and ignored him. After last night, Daddy could stomp and shout and throw books at her before she'd give him the satisfaction of a reply. How tired she was with putting up with him; he was such a bully. If only Lady Atherly would give up her disruptive plans, Stella could marry Lyndy and be rid of him.

Inspector Brown's courtesy call during dinner last night was a case in point. It should've been but a hiccup in an otherwise successful evening. Considerate of her father's worry, the inspector had stopped by on his way home to say Miss Cosslett had been spotted, alive and well, leaving the White Hart Inn. Afterward, Daddy, instead of being relieved the reporter wasn't dead, fumed and fussed, muttering curses, slamming down his cutlery and barking orders at the staff. The moment the servants cleared the table, Stella, along with the other women, gratefully hurried to the peace of the drawing room.

But Daddy wasn't done. He hadn't sabotaged the evening enough. When Constable Waterman, quick on the heels of arresting Miss Cosslett, arrived and reported the strange turn of events, Daddy's face had turned the color of overripe tomatoes. He then barged into the drawing room, where everyone was lounging and chatting over their coffee, and demanded everyone leave. At once! As the appalled and flabbergasted guests stumbled toward the door, he yanked their shawls and hats from the hall stand and flung them around with wild abandon. Stella mumbled apologies that no one heard. The others, muttering their dismay, were too preoccupied with dashing about trying to catch the hats, loosened feathers, and fallen silk flower embellishments sailing haphazardly around the hall. Lady Atherly's eyes widened in horror to see hers land at the foot of the stairs. Tims, taken unaware, appeared in time to be smacked in the face with the upturned brim of Lady Alice's new hat. Mrs. Robertson, who'd come to see about the commotion, ducked back behind the safety of the kitchen door just as a gentleman's top hat smacked against it.

"How I loathe you Americans," Lady Atherly seethed before marching out the door with nothing on her head. Tims, snatching up Lady Atherly's hat and retrieving her scarf from where it had landed on the corner edge of a picture frame, scurried out after her.

The others hurriedly followed Lady Atherly's lead after Daddy snatched up another gentleman's top hat and flung it out the door after her, yelling, "But not our money, you don't!" The black hat sailed past her and settled on the gravel walk.

Numb with humiliation and fury, Stella urged Lyndy to follow his mother when he'd offered to stay behind. When her father slammed the door behind Lyndy, the last to leave, shouting something about "ungrateful leeches," she'd stepped around Mr. Barlow's Stetson on the floor and positioned herself, hands on her hips, in the middle of the hall.

"Daddy, how dare you!" she'd said. "Miss Cosslett didn't need to make a fool of you.

You're quite capable of doing that all by yourself."

She'd steeled herself for his response, rooting herself to the floor. She wasn't going to back down this time. He had stomped toward her, as she knew he would, like a bull in the ring. He'd reeked of bourbon as he smashed his shoulder into hers. The pain of it had radiated through her back and side.

"Never talk to me that way again," he'd yelled as his feet pounded up the stairs.

Stella was more than happy to concede to his newest demand. She hadn't talked to him that way, or any way, since. And wouldn't until he apologized, which could turn out to be never.

And that would be fine by me. Stella silently turned the page in her book.

Her father stepped into the library. "I said, get rid of this stuff."

He pointed to the pile of newspapers, wedding announcements, and notes still spread out on the far side of the carpet. Until Miss Cosslett had written all her columns for the *Daily Mail,* Daddy had ordered no one touch it. But now, it was evidence of his gullibility. He kicked the pile, spreading the papers haphazardly into a broader mess. But his foot slipped on the slick newsprint and he wobbled backward, frantically waving his arms as he tried to keep his balance. He looked the fool Miss Cosslett proved him to be. He fell back against the wall, and puffing in effort and anger, righted himself again. Stella unconsciously rubbed her shoulder as she pretended to read.

"Just do as you're told," he grunted before storming away. Stella hadn't uttered a word of objection, but he'd sensed that she had no intention of complying.

A swirl of color in the jumble on the ground caught her eye. She put her book down, flopped her feet back on the floor, and padded across the room. There, beneath the black and white newsprint, was one of Lady Alice's glossy magazines. Stella bent over and picked up *McClure's Magazine: For July,* dated 1898. And on the cover was a color portrait of a much younger Cecil Barlow surrounded by illustrated orchids. Lady Alice must've left it by accident when she came to tea last week.

Stella held the fold of the magazine in one hand and flipped through it until she came across a photograph of the plant hunter. He was one of several men, in tall boots, dirt-creased suits, and unshaven whiskers standing beside a wagon laden with wooden crates and saplings with roots bundled in burlap. Two mongrel dogs lay on the ground at his feet. His left hand rested on the wagon wheel while the right clutched his cane. As usual, he'd left his collar unbuttoned, and he wasn't wearing a tie, bandana, or neck scarf. But it didn't capture his likeness. Stella had a photograph of her mother that Aunt Rachel insisted didn't do her justice. But in this case, the camera had created the opposite effect, capturing a man Stella had never met. Intense, pensive, yet benign, almost kind. A man she would like.

When had he changed? Why had he changed?

Stella lifted the magazine closer and studied the photograph, wishing she had Lord Atherly's magnifying glass. And then it struck her. What if it wasn't Cecil Barlow who had changed? What if she'd gotten it wrong all along? Stella curled the magazine under her arm, slid hastily into her slippers, then barged down the hall and into the kitchen. The servants were all still at breakfast.

"Miss Kendrick!" They set down their teacups with a clatter, and Ethel dropped a piece of toast marmalade-side down on her plate as all four rushed to rise to their feet.

Stella slapped the magazine down on the table. "Keep this safe," she pleaded. "The

450

police may need to see it." Before any of them could question her, Stella ran from the kitchen and down the hall.

Stella had to get to Morrington Hall. She couldn't risk waiting until Lyndy finished his breakfast. Her skirt swished along the gravel drive, her slippers little protection from the hard pebbles. In her rush, she'd forgotten to change. No time for that now. She leaped over to the softer lawn, the scent of newly cut grass wafting up beneath her feet, and ran. She reached the iron gate, still closed at this hour, and pushed at one side. With a squeaky creak, it swung open. At the telltale *clip-clop* of an approaching horse, Stella hurried along close to the wall that surrounded the estate, avoiding the traffic in the street. A milk wagon, its cans clinking, rattled by. When she reached the end of the wall, only a few cottages stood between her and the open heath. How she wished she had Tully to ride.

She rounded the corner and collided into the brown tweed vest of Mr. Barlow, the hollow of his neck inches from her nose. She stumbled back and bumped up against the sharp edge of the wall's corner bricks.

"Why, Miss Kendrick, you startled me." The plant hunter's hand reached out to steady her, and she flinched at his touch. She tugged her arm out of his hold, and using the motion to hide her dismay at meeting him, alone, brushed off her skirt. "Isn't it a bit early to be out for a stroll?" he said.

"I could ask you the same thing."

"Having been chased out like a hare from its hole last night, I thought I'd pop over in the quiet of the morning to retrieve my hat." Stella cringed at his knowing smirk. Would she ever escape the shame of her father's diatribe? Would anyone ever attend her parties after last night's debacle? She surprised herself that she cared. But if she was going to be Lady Lyndhurst, it was her duty to care. Wasn't it?

"On the way over the horse threw a shoe. I had to leave it at the livery and walk from there." He pointed to Stella's slippered feet. "What's your excuse?"

Stella bristled at Mr. Barlow's smug, entitled tone. As if he had a right to question her. Just because her father acted like a child didn't make her one. Barlow's attitude reminded her of Lyndy when they'd first met. She hadn't appreciated it then either.

"You've wasted your time. It's already on its way to Outwick House."

Before she'd gone to bed, she'd asked Tims to have all the hats and scarfs left behind returned to their owners. Tims had sent a local boy around first thing this morning. She only wished she could've compelled Daddy to deliver them, along with an apology. But that was too much to hope for.

"Unlike Lady Atherly," he said as if he hadn't heard her, "I adore all things American. I wouldn't want anything to happen to my Stetson." Goose bumps tingled along the length of her arms, reminding her of the need for caution. He wasn't to be trusted.

As they spoke, Stella had slipped slowly along the wall back toward the safety of the house, the rough brick catching now and then on the delicate fabric of her shirtwaist. She reached the iron gate and headed down the long drive. The plant hunter had matched her step for step, the crunch of his footsteps measuring the interminable distance to the front door.

"Besides, the journey wasn't wasted. I encountered you. And what better way to get to know you than to stroll in your lovely garden." He indicated the bench against the far wall, the one that reminded her of Lyndy. She wasn't going to sit there with him. She kept walking.

"Speaking of getting to know each other,

Mr. Barlow, or whatever your real name is —"

When Stella had studied the photograph of Cecil Barlow in Lady Alice's magazine, she'd been struck by the differences in the man in the picture and the one who had entertained everyone at dinner last night. She'd at first chalked it up to his harrowing experiences. Facing death would change anyone. But it wouldn't change which hand gripped a cane. The real Cecil Barlow held his in his right hand, not his left. The man beside her wasn't the real Cecil Barlow.

Whack!

The jolt stopped her in midstride as his cane cracked across her middle. Gasping for breath, she clutched her arms against the burn and doubled over. If not for her corset, he might've broken a rib. He brought it down again, like an unforgiving whip, against her back. A hot sting of pain seared up through her neck to her head, tears instantly flooding her vision.

"Help!" she screamed, stumbling on the gravel, desperate to put any distance between them.

"Shut up, shut up." He shoved her from behind, and she tripped on the hem of her skirt. She flew forward, her arms outstretched to catch her fall, and landed on her hands and knees. With dirty pebbles still embedded in her palms, she scrambled to get up, her feet slipping in the gravel and tangling in her skirt.

"Tell me," he demanded, easily overcoming her. He gripped her shoulder, forcing her back onto her heels and squeezing until her bones hurt. "Tell me!"

Panting from the pain and the shock, Stella glanced up at the house, barely fifty yards away. The red front door looked like a gaping wound on the face of the manor. It stayed motionless and shut. No one heard her screams. No one was coming to her rescue.

Stella looked over at her attacker, staring straight into his eyes. His face, blotched with red, was twisted into a grimace, like Daddy's had been last night. Defiance mingled with anger surged through her. She glanced at the cane, calculating how much more damage it could do. Not enough to make her talk.

"I'm not telling you anything."

"Tell me!" He shook her by the shoulder. She clenched her teeth to the pain. "I burned the photograph. I searched everywhere, but there wasn't anything else to connect us. So how did you know?" With each unanswered question, he lifted his cane higher and higher above her head, until it stretched into the bright blue sky above. Like a sword raised in battle. "Did Fairbrother rat me out after all?"

"Lord Fairbrother?" Stella said, the ground vibrating with the pounding of racing hooves. "You killed Lord Fairbrother? Then you killed Harvey too?" The cane sliced through the air, aimed directly at her head. Stella threw up her hands, hoping to grasp it, if she could, or shield herself better if she couldn't.

"NO!" The scream hadn't come from her.

The wind kicked up by a galloping horse blew bits of dust and gravel into her face as its rider hurtled himself off its back and onto Stella's attacker. As Beau stopped a few yards away, two men collapsed into a heap on the ground. As the cloud of dust settled, Stella saw Lyndy and Cecil Barlow tangled together on the ground, Lyndy punching wildly, Cecil Barlow flailing his cane. After a loud crack of the cane landed on his shoulders, Lyndy slammed the plant hunter's hand into the gravel. The cane clattered from Cecil Barlow's grip and rolled down the slight slope in the drive, well out of anyone's reach. Lyndy, his jaws tight, his cheeks red, and his eyes seething with intensity, squeezed the plant hunter between his knees. Despite the other's attempts to throw him off like a bucking horse, Lyndy pummeled the plant hunter in the chest, neck, and face until Stella had to scream for Lyndy to stop. Lyndy was going to kill him.

"Oh, dearie!" someone cried as the red door gaped open, and the household staff poured out, clustering together on the front steps for safety. Only Daddy was missing. Stella, rattled by the attack, relieved it was over, slid from her heels to her hip, grateful to slump onto the path's soft, grassy edge.

"My God! What's happened?" Tims called. "Shall I telephone the doctor or the police?"

Lyndy rose to his feet, his chest heaving from the exertion, and nodded. "Both."

Tims disappeared back inside. Lyndy's riding trousers were cut and dusty; his knees were scraped and covered in stones. A small scratch zigzagged across his cheek. Catching his breath, hand on his hip, Lyndy stared down at Cecil Barlow lying sprawled out in the gravel unconscious and bleeding from his nose, cheeks, lips, and forehead. Lyndy turned away and dropped to Stella's side. He cradled her back against his chest. Tully, who had whinnied from the gate, slowly approached, but daunted by the smell of blood, kept her distance.

"How badly are you hurt?" Stella asked. Lyndy shook his head dismissively. He swiveled her around in his arms to face him and brushed a hair from her forehead. His knuckles were bloody, and his hair hung in a disheveled mess. The intensity in his eyes was almost frightening.

Lyndy raked his fingers through his hair, then suddenly threw back his head, the force of his slightly unhinged laughter shaking them both. "Shouldn't I be asking you that question?"

"I suppose so." The violent emotions, so unlike him, had taken her aback. But only for a moment. She'd seen a side of him he'd never revealed before. How could she ever have doubted him? The fear, the rage, the panic, the vulnerability, the, dare she say it, love, she saw in his eyes made her ache to see more, know him more. "Lyndy, I . . ." Then he ran a loose strand of Stella's hair through his thumb and forefinger, his face composed and unreadable again.

"Did he hurt you?" he said gently, but the moment was lost.

Stella shook her head. "I'm sore, but I'll heal." Stella shot a glimpse at the sprawling figure on the ground. Lyndy followed her gaze. Stella shivered when a cloud floated in front of the sun and cast everyone in shadow. The man moaned but wasn't going anywhere.

"I'd come, hoping to go for an early ride," Lyndy said, "and then I heard you scream." Someone had heard her after all. She should've known it would be Lyndy. "What happened?"

Stella held out her hands, allowing Lyndy to help her up. "I don't know who that person is, but he's not Cecil Barlow."

Ethel gasped, drawing Stella's attention back toward the house. Daddy stood staring out through the dining room window, his napkin still tucked into his collar. When he caught her watching him, he stepped out of view. He'd soon learn he wasn't the only one to be taken in by an imposter.

Stella faced Lyndy as the cloud rolled past and the sun beamed down on them again. "And I think whoever he is, he killed Lord Fairbrother and Harvey."

CHAPTER 33

If Stella ever saw the inside of Outwick House again, it would be too soon. If she never saw Lady Philippa or heard her name mentioned again, she'd consider herself lucky. Yet, here she stood waiting for Inspector Brown to knock.

Inspector Brown had arrived at Pilley Manor by the time Cecil Barlow, whose real name turned out to be Reggie Baker, had revived from his stupor. As the inspector had handcuffed and arrested him, Reggie Baker scrambled to explain that yes, he'd impersonated the real Cecil Barlow, and yes, he'd stolen the photograph and rifled through Lord Fairbrother's study, and yes, he'd had a dalliance with Lady Philippa, but those were his most heinous crimes; he denied murdering anyone. Through Stella and the inspector's probing questions, Reggie Baker had described how it all happened, how at the Duke of York's Theatre, at the premiere of Barrie's *Peter Pan,* he'd been mistaken for the real Cecil Barlow by none other than the Duchess of Charford. Who was he to contradict His Majesty's cousin, he argued? And with that first lie, his life had instantly changed. For almost a year, he drank the best wine, ate the finest food, was hailed as a hero by the best families in the country. He hadn't wanted for anything. And all he had to do was spout the few facts anyone could read in the newspapers and fill in the gaps with such outlandish tales that no one would question him. And they hadn't, and with neither he nor the real Cecil Barlow having family or close friends, no one gave him away. He'd been immersed in the charade for so long, or so he said, that he'd stopped worrying that the real plant hunter might return — the poor man had probably died in the jungle, after all — or that someone from his past might recognize him. Until, one night at a party in London, he came face to face with Lord Fairbrother, whom he'd fought under in the Boer War.

Lord Fairbrother had threatened to end it all. Reggie Baker couldn't let that happen. So they'd come to an arrangement. In exchange for keeping his secret, Lord Fairbrother supposedly demanded Reggie Baker woo Lady Philippa and get evidence, a letter being best, which the lord could use to divorce his wife. He was supposed to deliver on his promise that night. That's why, Reggie Baker insisted, he snuck in and out of the conservatory, why he met Lord Fairbrother by the river — so Lady Philippa would never know. But when Inspector Brown insisted that he hadn't found any such letter on Lord Fairbrother's body, Reggie Baker admitted that he'd never given the lord one, that he couldn't go through with the arrangement. Reggie Baker had fallen in love with Lady Philippa. He offered Lord Fairbrother all the money he had in the world instead. And when the man died, he'd gone into the study looking for anything that would reveal his secret and found the photograph.

He wasn't a violent man, he'd maintained, blaming his brutality toward Stella on the shock of his discovery. Even as Constable Waterman dragged him toward the police wagon, his heels drawing lines in the gravel, Reggie Baker shouted over and over that he didn't kill anyone. No one had believed the imposter. Why would they? But someone had to inform Lady Philippa of her lover's ultimate betrayal. To no one's surprise but her own, Stella had elected to accompany the inspector and Lyndy wouldn't let her go alone.

"We'll do this and be done with it, and her," Lyndy said, squeezing her hand as she stared at the brass lion's head knocker on the imposing wooden door.

Lyndy was right; it would be a relief to resolve the lingering effect of the murders and Lady Atherly's interference and put it all behind them. But he was wrong too; she hadn't come there for herself, or him, or for the police. Stella was there for Harvey. She had made him a promise. He'd saved Tully, and Stella was going to save him, in the only way she could, from Lady Philippa's false accusations, from anyone disparaging his name again.

She squeezed Lyndy's hand back and nodded. Inspector Brown, scorning the knocker, pounded on the door with his fist. Hodgson showed them in without a word and led them to Lady Philippa's morning room.

"Lord Lyndhurst to see you, my lady," the butler said. "As well as Miss Kendrick and Inspector Brown."

"Lyndy," Lady Philippa said as if he was the only one to enter the room. She held out her hand as if she expected him to kiss it. When he didn't, she pouted, pulling a gardenia from its vase. She lingered over the flower, inhaling its scent, her eyes closed. A smile spread slowly across her face when Lyndy began tapping his toe. She was enjoying his growing impatience.

"This isn't a social call," Lyndy said.

Lady Philippa lifted her eyelids slowly and began plucking the petals from the flower, letting them flutter freely to the carpet. "Pity, though with such riffraff for company, I should think not."

Stella glanced sideways at the inspector, holding his hat in his hand but standing tall and patient. Lady Philippa's derision meant nothing to him.

"This riffraff are better people than you will ever be, Philippa," Lyndy retorted. Stella allowed herself a brief, smug smile.

Inspector Brown cleared his throat. "I'm afraid we have some disturbing news."

"What is it now?"

"We've arrested Mr. Barlow," Inspector Brown said.

Lady Philippa snapped the flower stem in two. "Why?"

"For starters, he attacked Miss Kendrick this morning," Inspector Brown said.

Lady Philippa's head barely moved, but Stella caught her gaze, if only for a moment. Lady Philippa tossed the stems down and crossed over to the partly open southern window, pulling back the drapes. A team of gardeners, weeding, deadheading, pushing wheelbarrows, buzzed around the rose garden like bees. Lady Atherly would be jealous of such industry, such an abundance of staff. Since their financial woes, she'd taken on much of the gardening at Morrington Hall herself.

"What did she do to provoke him?" Lady Philippa taunted. Lyndy took steps toward Lady Philippa's turned back. Stella snagged his sleeve, holding him from getting any farther. Lady Philippa, unaware of Lyndy's anger, released the drape and faced them. "You said for starters, Inspector. What else is Mr. Barlow accused of?"

"Impersonation and entrapment. I'm afraid —"

"You've been made a fool of, Philippa," Lyndy said, finishing the inspector's sentence, though Stella doubted that was what the policeman was going to say. From the glint in his eye, Lyndy was relishing every devastating word. "Your Mr. Barlow was actually a chap called Reggie Baker, who used to serve under Fairbrother in the war. It seems Fairbrother wanted rid of you, so he blackmailed Barker to —"

Lady Philippa paled. But why, Stella

wondered? Because she'd never suspected Cecil Barlow or her husband's duplicity, or because she'd never imagined Lyndy capable of such blunt cruelty? Perhaps both.

"I think she understands your meaning, Lyndy," Stella said. But if Stella expected gratitude for saving Lady Philippa further embarrassment, she should've known better. Lady Philippa's color returned, and she gave an impervious sniff.

"All I understand is that Lyndy is only marrying you for your money. And that now that I'm to inherit, he'll be free to marry me." Lyndy's jaw tightened, and Stella expected him to pace or tug his collar, but instead, he stood as still as she'd ever seen him. Not a finger twitched, not a toe tapped.

"I'll sell Morrington Hall before I ever marry you."

Lady Philippa let out a short, derisive laugh. "Don't be ridiculous. You'd do anything to save Morrington." She pointed at Stella. "Even consider wedding her."

"I'll have you know —" Lyndy began.

"That Mr. Reggie Baker was also arrested for killing your husband, Lady Philippa," Stella said. Stella never thought she'd ever change the subject *to* murder but couldn't take any more of Lyndy and Lady Philippa's sparring. It wasn't flattering, to either one of them.

"Really?" The news immediately transformed Lady Philippa. Her face softened; her voice relaxed. If Stella didn't know of her manipulations, she'd almost think her capable of kindness. "Now, that I can believe."

"And why is that?" Inspector Brown asked. "You'd always suspected Harvey Milkham of killing your husband."

"Yes, but Cecil had fallen in love with me and understandably resented Raymond's demands. Cecil was trying to protect me; I'm sure."

"And what were those demands?" Inspector Brown asked. "That you give him a divorce?"

"You know about that?" Lady Philippa asked the policeman, but kept her hooded eyes pinned on Lyndy. Lyndy's expression, as unreadable as ever, never changed. She dropped her gaze and began rearranging the gardenias in the vase.

"Mr. Barlow, or Reggie Baker, or whatever he's called, mentioned it. We also found the letters exchanged with Sir George Lewis," the inspector continued. "We've since contacted the solicitor. He confirmed that Lord Fairbrother was going to change his will and sue for a divorce in a matter of days, citing neglect, cruelty, and adultery. Quite the motive for murder."

"Yes," Lady Philippa said slowly. "It would've ruined me, all on account of my husband's fits of jealousy. I'm a beautiful woman, Inspector. Is it my fault I attract admirers?" Lyndy snickered in scorn. Lady Philippa frowned. "Cecil couldn't allow Raymond to do that."

"What about Harvey?" Stella said.

"What about him?" Lady Philippa said, plucking another wilting flower from the vase.

"Why would Cecil Barlow kill Harvey?" Stella never understood how anyone could murder such a harmless old man.

"Because the old fool was at the river when Cecil killed my husband, why else?" Lady Philippa dismissed Harvey's death with a wave of her hand.

"How would you know?" Stella snapped angrily.

"He left that disgusting snake bag behind, didn't he? Of course, he was lurking in the nearby woods somewhere."

A rush of light-headedness hit her, and Stella felt the room spin. She steadied herself by focusing her gaze on the long blade of an elaborately etched brass letter opener. The sizable single ruby on its handle gleamed in the ray of sun striking Lady Philippa's secretarial desk. When her head cleared, Stella caught Lady Philippa's eye and stared openly at her. The lady stared back. A crooked smirk, like a scar, marred the lady's beautiful face.

Stella reached down and picked up the letter opener. It looked like the dagger she'd found at the barrow, but for the dark stains in the etched crevices.

"A gift from Lord Fairbrother?" Stella asked as her reflection peered back at her from the blade.

"No, my dear father gave it to me. Raymond prized it, but I refused to give it to him." Lady Philippa held out her hand, wanting it back. "Like Outwick House, it's mine."

"What snake bag?" Inspector Brown said, and probably not for the first time. Stella hadn't been listening. The inspector was glaring from Lady Philippa to Stella and back. He wasn't happy. "I'll not ask again, Miss Kendrick."

"The one Harvey left behind at Blackwater Bend. The one Lady Philippa saw when she killed her husband" — Stella presented the letter opener to Inspector Brown — "with this."

"Oh, God," Lyndy said, in disbelief. "Philippa." He squeezed his eyes shut and slowly shook his head. Stella could only imagine what he was thinking.

"I have no idea what she's talking about, Lyndy," Lady Philippa said, sidling up to him and running her fingers down the length of his jacket lapel. "The girl's mad." Lyndy took a purposefully long step back, far enough to be out of Lady Philippa's reach.

"Right!" Inspector Brown said, taking the letter opener and inspecting it. "Lady Philippa, I'm arresting you for the murder of your husband, Lord Fairbrother."

"Don't be absurd," she scoffed, smoothing her perfectly coiffed, inky black hair. "I just said I didn't kill him, didn't I?"

"Then can you explain the bloodstains on this letter opener?" Inspector Brown said.

What happened next was a blur. Inspector Brown shouted orders to his constable waiting outside the door as Lady Philippa launched herself toward the open French window. The gardeners outside, halting their work, stood gaping as the Marquess of Outershaw's daughter ducked under the raised sash, flung up her skirts, exposing the French silk stockings hugging her bare calves, and threw her leg over the sill. Lyndy, like a released rubber band, sprang after her. He snatched at anything: the delicately weaved lace around her wrist that ripped in his hand, the crook of her jutting elbow, the hard edge of her corset stretched taut beneath the fabric across her back, a fist full of black crape clumped around her hips, the pearl buttons lining her sleeve that popped off or flopped from loosened threads. All the while she squirmed and fought to be free of his grip. Landing a firm hold on her ankle, Lyndy yanked back. Lady Philippa's body, half in and half out, banged against the side of the house, her temple connecting with the open sash. A thin line of blood trickled down the side of her cheek. Stella joined Lyndy, clutching and twisting the hem of the widow's skirt in and around her fists. Lady Philippa wasn't getting out that window.

"Get your hands off me!" The lady kicked and slapped and scratched at them as she fought to gain purchase on the ground beneath the window.

"Ah, Philippa," Lyndy said, irony and sadness mingling in his voice as Constable Waterman appeared, adding his considerable strength to the task. "At first you wanted to marry me, and now you can't stand my touch. History repeats itself, eh, my dear." With Stella as an anchor, the two men hauled Lady Philippa back into the room like a half-empty sack of potatoes and secured her wrists with handcuffs.

"Can you blame me, poor boy?" Lady Philippa said, her chin high, defiance flaring in her eyes once her feet were again flat on the carpeted floor. "You and your feeble attempts at lovemaking."

"Take her away, Constable," Inspector Brown said.

"You were the clumsiest lover I'd ever had," Lady Philippa sneered, as Constable Waterman shoved her roughly past them. Lyndy, his fists clenched at his sides, sputtered curses. "Raymond and I used to laugh at you."

"Neither one of you are laughing now," Inspector Brown said somberly, shaking his head.

Stella touched Lyndy's arm, needing to reaffirm their bond, as the policemen escorted the despicable woman out the door. He patted her hand reassuringly. They were finally free of her. Thank goodness. But at what a terrible price.

CHAPTER 34

Lyndy leaned back in his folding chair, closed his eyes, and relished the warmth of the afternoon sun on his face. Why hadn't he ever done this before? At the high-pitched whistle of the kettle boiling, he opened his eyes again. Stella had been watching him and smiled. He smiled back.

Because it took Stella to suggest it.

The first footman laid the tea service they'd brought from Morrington in the middle of the linen cloth draping the long folding table. Mother reached for the teapot and began to pour.

"Will you please inform Lord Atherly and his guest that tea is ready?" Mother told the footman as he set out several silver, three-tiered stands laden with all the usual delectables: small sandwiches of salmon and mayonnaise or cold beef and butter, wild mushroom tarts, buttermilk scones, jam tartlets, and sponge cake.

Except for the sun sparkling off the silver service and the contented nickering of the horses nearby, they could've been sitting in the drawing room, instead of the grazing lawn beside Moyles Court bowl barrow, the recently dug, unexcavated one near Ibsley.

Although the picnic had been Stella's idea, the spot had been Papa's brilliant suggestion. Set on a slight rise, with a wood at their back, it afforded them a sweeping view of the heath, blanketed with purple, flowering heather as well as the sinuous, sparkling water of the distant River Avon. It was all that the Forest had to offer, yet far from George Parley's land, far from the Blackwater, far from the site of Harvey's burnt hut, far from Outwick House. A fresh, new beginning within the ancient borders of their homeland.

And after the revelations and wretchedness of the past few days, they were all in desperate need of a new beginning.

"Why couldn't we have had tea like civilized people?" Mother said, dropping two lumps of sugar in a teacup and handing it to Stella. "At home, we aren't likely to soil our skirt hems or accidentally swallow an ant."

Despite Mother's grumbling, the act of serving Stella first was a concession, the grudging acceptance that Stella was an honored guest, a soon-to-be member of the family and wasn't going anywhere. It was as close to an apology as any of them were likely to get.

"Consider this lovely day, Frances," Papa said, popping his head over the embankment of the barrow. "I think Miss Kendrick's suggestion was brilliant." Stella rewarded him with a smile. While they'd waited for the footmen to prepare the table, Papa and Professor Gridley had headed straight for the barrow, hoping for better luck in finding another *Equus spelaeus* bone than they had in the last site. Stella's concession to Mother was not to follow them. "At least try to enjoy yourself. What about over here, Professor?" Papa said before disappearing behind the dug-out hill again.

"William, your tea will get cold," Mother called, handing Alice her cup.

Alice took a sip, her hand resting on the cover of the magazine in her lap. It was the *McClure's* Stella had found at Pilley Manor and returned to Alice. Supposedly a maid had mistakenly mixed it in with a stack of newspapers Miss Cosslett and Kendrick were consulting.

Who would've guessed imposters had

infiltrated their circle? First Miss Cosslett, then Cecil Barlow. Alice frowned as she bit into her sandwich as if she'd read Lyndy's mind.

Poor Alice. She'd set her heart on the cad. Even now, she couldn't let go of the magazine. She'd thrown the more recent ones, the ones written about the plant hunter's miraculous reappearance, in the fire. Perhaps she held out hope, that one day, the real Cecil Barlow, the one in the pages of the magazine she held, would reappear.

Stella, sensing his sister's sadness, patted her on the shoulder. It wasn't what any of them would've done — they avoided touching each other when possible — but Stella wasn't like them. Thank goodness. Alice, appreciating the unexpected gesture, returned Stella's smile.

"You're thinking about Mr. Barlow?" Stella asked sympathetically. To her surprise, Alice shook her head.

"No, I was thinking about Lady Philippa. I've known her for years. And yet, I didn't know her at all. None of us did."

Lyndy opened his mouth to disagree. He'd known her to be manipulative, conniving, and shameless. But even he had no idea of what she was truly capable. In that way, Alice was right. Philippa had been yet another imposter. Lyndy counted himself fortunate to have been spurned by her. Lord Fairbrother hadn't been so lucky.

Mother gave an imperious sniff. "Lady Philippa certainly wasn't the right sort, after all, was she? Deceiving us all, as she did. The daughter of a marquess, nonetheless. Who could've possibly known she'd turn out to be . . ."

"Lower than a snake's belly in a wagon rut?" Stella's Aunt Rachel said, leaning her cane against the table and settling into her chair. Lyndy stifled a chuckle. He couldn't have said it better.

"I wonder how Lady Philippa managed it," Alice mused as she reached for a mushroom tart. "I can see Lord Fairbrother. He wouldn't have suspected anything if his wife embraced him, and thus getting close enough to stab him. Though why do it by the river and not in his bed?"

"To throw suspicion on someone else," Stella said. "I wouldn't be surprised if she knew about Lord Fairbrother's midnight meetings at Blackwater Bend. Any one of those men Lord Fairbrother had been blackmailing could be suspect, including Cecil Barlow."

"But what about the poor snakecatcher?" Alice asked, taking a nibble of her tart.

"How did she get close enough to kill him?"

Stella sighed. "I asked Inspector Brown the same thing. As you remember, Mr. Barlow told us Lady Philippa had seen Harvey at the river on their drive over to Morrington Hall. What he failed to say, and Inspector Brown learned, was that Lady Philippa had driven him herself in her phaeton. So, once she delivered Mr. Barlow to his dinner engagement, she must've returned to the river to face Harvey."

"The phaeton the fishermen saw," Lyndy added. Stella nodded.

"And as she'd used one man to make another jealous, Lady Philippa used his affection for me to coax Harvey into her carriage. According to Inspector Brown, she bragged about how easy it was to convince him I needed his help again."

"We do know how much the old fool was fond of Miss Kendrick," Mother said patronizingly.

"Mother!" Lyndy chided. "The snake-catcher's death is not Stella's fault."

"Did I say it was?"

"It would explain why he'd left his trout," Lyndy said.

Stella nodded. "He was in a great hurry to help me. But instead of meeting up with me, Lady Philippa drove him to the barrow and . . ." Stella didn't continue her thought. Lyndy knew she couldn't. The snakecatcher's death had broken her heart. Instead, she squared her shoulders and called toward the barrow. "If it is all right with you, Lord Atherly, I'd like to house Harvey's pony next to Tully in your stables." It had been Lyndy's idea. After all the upsets, he would've suggested painting every room in Morrington Hall bright orange if he'd thought it would bring a smile back to her face. Gratefully, offering to stable Harvey's pony had been enough.

"Pardon?" Papa looked up from brushing the dirt from his trouser leg. He and Professor Gridley had reappeared and were traipsing back to join them. "Yes, of course. That's fine. Speaking of ponies, Professor Gridley has come up with an excellent idea."

"Which is?" Mother said suspiciously, knowing she wasn't going to like what was said next.

Mother offered Papa his tea as he settled into the seat across from her. Mother handed Professor Gridley his tea, which he took and then sipped without sitting down. Mother purposefully filled her plate, avoiding having to acknowledge the American's faux pas. One never stood while drinking tea.

"Please, Professor Gridley, sit here," Stella said, patting the chair beside her. Having more than once made the same mistake, Stella must've recognized the breach in etiquette.

"Well," Professor Gridley said, accepting the chair and filling his plate, "as you have proved to be such an enterprising archaeologist, Miss Stella, we wondered if you and Lord Lyndhurst might consider joining me on my next expedition."

"Consider it an alternative to the grand tour for your honeymoon trip," Papa added enthusiastically, before biting his beef sandwich in half.

Lyndy was speechless. Mother sputtered what sounded an awful lot like "over my dead body."

"Of course, we haven't had a chance to mention this to your father," Professor Gridley said. Mr. Kendrick, still embittered over the fiasco that was Jane Cosslett, had declined their invitation to join them. To everyone's relief.

"By then, Stella will be my wife," Lyndy said. "She won't need to consult her father about anything." Stella smiled at him. It was a happy prospect for them both.

"Quite so," Papa continued. "You're a horse lover, Miss Kendrick. Wouldn't it be a

lovely way to spend your first weeks together, uncovering bones of extinct horses
under the wide-open sky of Montana?"

"It does sound tempting," Stella said.
"And I do miss home, but —"

"Amen to that," the old aunt mumbled
with food in her mouth.

"But why would you, Miss Kendrick,
when you could spend it dancing and dining across the civilized world, Paris, Venice,
Prague, cultivating social ties and friend-
ships that will serve you in good stead for a
lifetime?" Mother said, wiping her fingers
on her napkin, leaving a half-eaten scone on
her plate.

"That too sounds wonderful," Stella said.
"But —"

"Besides, I didn't think there was to be
another expedition," Mother admonished.
"Look at all the trouble this last one
caused."

"But," Stella said, determined to say her
piece, "Lyndy and I haven't talked about it
yet. We first need to finalize the wedding
details. Then we can plan our honeymoon."

"Of course, of course," Papa said, appreciating her not rejecting his plan outright.

"Just keep it in mind," Professor Gridley
said, drinking down the remainder of his

tea in one long gulp, "you are always welcome."

"Thank you." Stella rewarded the professor with a smile.

Lyndy's whole body tingled. He loved that smile. How he fancied to be alone with her and show her how much. Philippa's caustic insults about his qualities as a lover were just that, lies and bitterness spewed by a woman scorned, but they hurt nonetheless, and with all this talk of honeymoons, he couldn't wait to show Stella how wrong they were.

As if reading his mind, Stella rose, laid her napkin on her chair, and said, "If you'll excuse Lyndy and me for a moment." She stayed the old chaperone with a raised palm. "Don't worry, Aunt Rachel. We'll stay in plain view."

Mother pursed her lips. Although she'd grudgingly come to accept that she was stuck with Stella, she might never reconcile with Stella's bold, often rule-breaking behavior. Lyndy loved it. Who else could get away with sneaking off in the middle of tea?

Stella led him past the horses, making sure to pat Tully and offering each animal a peppermint she'd kept in her leather handbag, to the shadows just inside a copse of trees.

She reached for his hand the moment the thick girth of an ancient oak hid them from the others. She was breaking her promise to stay in the chaperone's line of sight, but who was Lyndy to argue? She reached into her handbag again and instead of a peppermint, pulled out a box, tightly wrapped with a bright green silk ribbon. She held it out to him.

"Consider this my engagement present to you. I had them made in Lyndhurst."

What could it be? He accepted the box without taking his eyes from hers.

She fiddled with the engagement ring he'd given her, swirling it around and around her finger as he pulled the ribbon from the box. It fell away easily. He lifted the lid of the box, brushing back the tissue paper, revealing perfectly folded linen squares. In the center, embroidered in the color of new leaves was an *L,* while each corner contained a tiny horseshoe of the same color. "I thought you could use some new handker-chiefs."

Lyndy laughed, snatched the one from his lapel pocket, the one identical to the one he'd given Philippa once, and tossed it away. It floated like a tiny parachute, catching on a bracken frond on the ground. He plucked a new one from the box and stuck it where it belonged, in the pocket over his heart. Then he slipped his arm around her tiny waist and urged her toward him. She yielded willingly, and their lips met, their bodies pressing together in a long, passionate embrace. Somewhere a pony whinnied.

Breathless, Stella tilted her head back, her eyes bright and her cheeks flushed. A sly smile spread across her glossy lips. "I guess you like the gift."

"I do." He wanted to say more. He wanted to say what he truly felt, but he was an English gentleman, after all. Instead, he caressed her flawless cheek and added, "I don't fancy waiting to marry. Let's wed as soon as possible."

So Mother, or anyone, can't get between us again, he thought but hesitated to say.

"Why, Lord Lyndhurst, you read my mind." Stella beamed at him. His heart skipped a beat. She unpinned her hat, whipping it off her head. It landed somewhere in the verdant undergrowth. He dipped his hand into her silky hair. "If I thought your mother wouldn't skin me alive, I'd elope tonight. After the fiasco at the engagement dinner, it would save me from having to attend the wedding breakfast."

Lyndy laughed, her quip so unexpected, so refreshingly Stella.

"But she would, so we can't. But we can ride," she added with a conspiratorial smirk on her face. Stella grabbed his hand and they ran to the horses, leaped into their saddles, and were galloping across the expanse of the Forest before anyone's calls to come back could reach them.

ACKNOWLEDGMENTS

I recently traveled to the New Forest again. By everyone I met, I was welcomed, I was befriended, I was humbly made to feel a part of this incredible community. Thank you. I would be remiss not to mention a few who made my visit one I'll never forget: The Honorable Mary Montagu-Scott, for inviting me to participate in a night of "New Forest Fiction-Past and Present," fellow author and real-life commoner, Sally Marsh, for inspiring me and befriending me, and event organizer, Nancy Fillmore, for her hospitality despite my jetlag. To these women and all of the volunteers, staff and patrons of the New Forest Heritage Centre, I thank you. I can't wait to visit again!

Despite having visited and done research on the New Forest, there are always details I've missed. To find those answers, I've continued to turn to the staff of the Christopher Tower Reference Library. Thank you,

Dr. Kath Walker, for graciously answering all of my inquiring emails and providing me with more historical insight and details than I could have hoped for. A thank you also goes to Zoe Cox, Community Manager of the Forestry Commission, South England Forest District for helping me with details pertaining to the Deputy Surveyor's offices in Lyndhurst. If I embellished anything or got it wrong, it's on me.

On this side of the pond, I'd like to thank Joan Loan for being my first reader and biggest cheerleader, my friend Dorothy Kirkland who proofread for me and is always there with a much needed cuppa, and my fellow Sleuths in Time writers who are quick to encourage, advise and commiserate with me. I'm also grateful to have such a wonderful team at Kensington: John Scognamiglio, my editor, Larissa Ackerman, my publicist, Robin Cook of the production department and an art department who consistently creates covers I love.

AUTHOR'S NOTE

Writing historical fiction, to me, is the best of both worlds. I get to blend historical fact and figures I've discovered in my research with my imagination to create authentic-feeling stories. I try very hard to get my details right. But since the stories are fiction, I allow myself to take liberties on occasion. In this story, the most blatant example pertains to the river in the book's title. Although there is a stream named the Black Water in the New Forest National Park, and a lovely one at that, the river I describe in the book more closely resembles the River Test, a larger chalk stream, known for its trout fishing, found in Hampshire but further to the east. The second relates to *Peter Pan,* the play by James Barrie. Although it did premiere at the Duke of York's Theatre in London in 1904, it did so in late December, months later than indicated in my story.

I also borrowed heavily from the pantheon of colorful historical figures that populated the beginning of the last century in creating several of my characters. Dr. Amos Gridley is based on Dr. James Williams Gidley (1866–1931), who was a renowned American vertebrate paleontologist who discovered the ancient horse species *Equus scotti* in Texas in 1899 and collected the first fossils of the three-toed horse genus *Neohipparion* in Nebraska in 1902. Harvey Milkham is based by the real-life snakecatcher Henry "Brusher" Mills (1840–1905), a beloved character from the New Forest. There's even a pub named for him in Brockenhurst. Cecil Barlow is not based on a single "plant hunter" but an amalgam of people, including Baron von Humboldt, whose real-life adventures and sometimes very words are usurped by my pretender.

Finally, I would like to note that Sir George Lewis, 1st Baronet, Lord Fairbrother's solicitor; Professor Hatcher, the paleontologist; Baron von Humboldt, the naturalist; Princess Margaret of Connaught; Lord Derby, Lord Ellesmere, and Colonel Walker, the racehorse owners; and Lord Montagu, the 2nd Baron of Montagu of Beaulieu, mentioned as a guest at Stella and Lyndy's engagement party, were prominent figures that I did not invent.

ABOUT THE AUTHOR

Clara McKenna has a B.A. in Biology from Wells College and a M.L.I.S in Library and Information Studies from McGill University. She is the founding member of Sleuths in Time, a cooperative group of historical mystery writers who encourage and promote each other's work. She is also a member of Mystery Writers of America and Sisters in Crime.

The employees of Thorndike Press hope you have enjoyed this Large Print book. All our Thorndike, Wheeler, and Kennebec Large Print titles are designed for easy reading, and all our books are made to last. Other Thorndike Press Large Print books are available at your library, through selected bookstores, or directly from us.

For information about titles, please call:
    (800) 223-1244

or visit our website at:
    gale.com/thorndike

To share your comments, please write:
    Publisher
    Thorndike Press
    10 Water St., Suite 310
    Waterville, ME 04901